ALL THE BEAUTIFUL BODIES

CITY OF DARKNESS BOOK 1

DANIELLE PORTER

ALL THE BEAUTIFUL BODIES
City of Darkness Book 1

ISBN-10: 1658211014
ISBN-13: 978-1658211017

Print edition published by Saint Germain Press 2020.

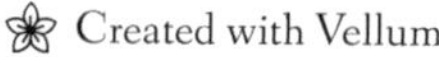

DANIELLE PORTER'S FREE STARTER LIBRARY

Sign up for Danielle's newsletter and receive three of her bestselling Juliette Sobanet books for *free*. Details can be found at *www.juliettesobanet.com*.

For the city of Paris
In all your light, and all your darkness

EVE

The When: Unknown
The Where: Unknown

The slamming of a door slays my dreamless sleep.
The punching of buttons. Six shrill beeps.
A code that kills...
My mind.
My heart.
My soul.

A code I would kill to know.

Alarm: disarmed...and armed again.
No escape tonight, my lovely girl.

Keys, jangling on a hook.
Warning bells that ricochet through my dizzy head.
Bile rushing to my throat.
Don't. Get. Sick.

And then, the footsteps.
I wait for them. So I can count.
Up, up, up, the staircase they go...

One...
Two...
These are—Three.
My final few...seconds...
Four.
Of quiet.
Five. Six. Seven.
Of imagining—Eight. Nine. Ten.
I am somewhere else.
Eleven.
Before it...
Twelve.
Begins.

Thirteen.

Thirteen dirty needles.
Thirteen broken bones.
Twelve drops of crimson.
Plus one more...
For luck.

I am the lucky one.

1

THE MISTRESS OF PARIS: A MEMOIR

BY EVE WINTERS

LE 11 JUILLET 2016
RUE DES BERNARDINS ~ PARIS, FRANCE

MY SISTER PRESSES the lipstick hard against my bottom lip. The soft flesh on her palm is shredded; jagged cuts slice their way all the way down her forearm. Drops of her blood slither off her elbow, splattering onto my white tile floor.

I wonder what kind of knife he used. I wonder if she needs stitches.

Willow, though, she doesn't care. She ignores the bleeding. Even with her fingers shaking, she presses firmer.

"*That's enough, Willow,*" I say.

"No," she argues. "You can't walk in there looking like...*you*."

Fucking bitch.

I don't say it, but she knows I'm thinking it.

When she's finished with me, I turn to face the bathroom mirror.

My lashes are coated in a thick layer of mascara, my eyelids a smoky mirage. My long, midnight-brown hair cascades over my bare shoulders, resting atop my breasts, which are spilling from Willow's inky black dress. My curves fill every inch of its skin-tight fabric, inappropriately so. The scar just beneath my left shoulder, hovering above my left breast, is only partially hidden by the thin dress straps, and I wish it were gone.

I wish it had never happened.

My sister's fake diamonds are dripping from my ears and down my neck; her slutty red thong and push-up bra hugging me beneath the dress. All of this clothing, a useless barrier to the body that is going to be sold to a man I've never met later tonight.

And my lips.

Full, moist, and red.

Blood red.

The color of a prostitute.

I have become her.

"I don't want to do this." My throat constricts. Breath escapes me. "I can't...this isn't me. I don't do things like this."

"Of course you don't. That's why you're going to be me for the night. He's expecting *Willow*." The way she says her own name makes me livid. She knows what a weapon she is; the destruction of her beauty has no end.

Willow takes my clean white bath towel, wipes her bloody palms on it without so much as a wince. She tosses it to the floor in my tiny Parisian bathroom, and my eyes are drawn to the crimson stain. The mark that will forever taint my charming Paris apartment, the home that I have kept hidden from her—from everyone—for the past six months. Tucked away on a tiny street on the Left Bank, a stone's throw from the Seine, this apartment was *all mine*. It was the only thing that has ever really belonged to me.

But now her blood has stained the towels, the tiles. It's smeared on the sink, running down the drain, infecting the pipes, the building, the entire fucking city with its toxicity.

She's toxic. And she's numb. Numb to pain. Numb to life.

And yet, I still want to save hers.

Why?

She saved mine, I remind myself. All those years ago. I can still see her charging over the black-and-white checkered floor, *handling it.*

She handled it, when I was too hysterical, too shocked to do so. There was no hysteria in Willow's eyes when she took in the bloodbath. No shock on her face when she witnessed the dismantling of a family, of an entire life. There was only determination in those brazen green eyes of hers when she finished the job. Almost like she expected that night to come. Like she'd been preparing for it.

While I was blindsided. Bleeding. Lost. A broken little fawn cowering on the floor, screaming for it all to stop.

She was only fifteen, but she grew up that night. *For me.*

Will my debt to her ever be repaid?

Willow takes my shoulders, spins me around to face her. I take in her bruised eyes, the cuts on her cheeks, her swollen lips. I imagine the fist that slammed into them only a few hours ago. Bloody knuckles. Pounding her beautiful face.

I shudder.

My sister. A tired, drained corpse of the girl she used to be. If I do this for her tonight, could things get better for her? For us?

"5,000 euros?" I ask. "You're certain he's going to pay that much?"

"Yes," she says. "Don't let him touch you until you have

the cash in your hands. Go to the bathroom and count it first. Then text me to confirm. And text me when you're done."

Sure, Willow. I'll text you when I'm done letting some stranger fuck me all night. When I'm done taking his money, money that I will give right back to you so you can pay off the thug with the bloody knuckles. So the beating you got tonight doesn't turn into a death sentence tomorrow.

"Okay," I say, although nothing about this situation is okay.

The heels are the last piece of the prostitute puzzle. Four-inch black Louboutin pumps. Worth nearly $1,000. I want to ask Willow why in the fuck she's prancing around in Louboutin pumps when she's in such financial trouble, but I bite my tongue, slip on the shoes, and head to the door.

One last glimpse of my sister and I am sickened that her smooth, voluptuous beauty of a body has now morphed into a bloody, beaten pulp of what it was the last time I saw her over six months ago. When I left her in my adorable Greenwich Village apartment, guzzling wine with Lucas. *My* Lucas. Another thing she has taken from me.

I thought I'd never see her again. I hoped I wouldn't.

But here she is. She always finds her way back to me. After all, she needs someone to scrape her off the floor, save her when she's taken things too far. And this, well this is certainly too far.

I know that what I'm about to do for her is the absolute worst thing she's ever asked from me. But the feeling that nothing I ever do will match up to the way she saved me overpowers all reason, and I know I'm going to do it anyway.

I'm going to spread my legs for money. Hand my body over to a complete stranger. Blow him and bend over for him and tell him he can put it wherever he wants, again, and again, and again. All night long.

Like the high-class prostitute I am, I will do anything he wants me to do.

I am going to *be* Willow.

And I'm going to act like I love it.

Willow reaches into her purse, hands me a thick roll of condoms.

"I'm sorry," she says, for the first time tonight. "I'm so sorry."

I say nothing as I tuck them into my tiny black clutch. I wonder how many of these he will use on me tonight.

"This guy is a respectable American businessman," Willow says. "He's not going to hurt you."

I nod, swallowing the bile, the hatred. "What's his name again?"

"Dex," she says. "Dex Anderson."

And before I close the door, she calls out, "He's married, Eve. The married ones are always the most fun."

I wonder what his wife would have to say about that.

In the cab ride on the way over, the Paris I've grown to love over the past six months is gone. The romance of the city has died. In its place are dark cobblestone alleyways where women are beaten and used, a choppy River Seine where dreams and bodies go to die, and summer air that is so ferociously humid and thick, I have to stop myself from vomiting at every traffic light.

Dex Anderson.

Dex Anderson.

Fuck me, Dex. Fuck me harder, Dex.

What would Willow say?

What would she do?

2

SOPHIA

Ten Months Later

Tuesday the 16th of May, 2017
Park Avenue ~ New York City

His fingers are cold as he runs the zip up the back of my dress. I wonder how they can be so icy when we have just spent the past hour wrapped in a haze of sweaty sheets and steamy breath, but I remind myself that his hands are always cold. Even when they're inside me.

I needed a shock to my system, though. A glass of ice water to the face.

The day his hands warm up is the day I'll have to leave him.

"Lovely dress," he says, eyeing me in the full-length mirror. But he isn't looking at the tight fit of my black cocktail dress—he's looking through it, underneath it. He's seen the scars that lie beneath. He knows the hell this body has been through in the past few years, and he's here anyway.

He knows about everything that lies beneath this perfect Park Avenue wife façade.

Well, not *everything,* but certainly more than Drew knows. More than Drew will ever know.

My mother's sharp English accent slides through my mind, always coming at me without warning.

A husband doesn't need to know the darkest secrets about his wife. That would spoil his perfect image of her.

The perfect old hag was right about a few things, after all.

"Thank you," I tell him before applying my rose-colored lipstick.

He slithers up behind me, reaches a hand around my shoulders, placing it square on my heart. "Why not red? I never see you in red lipstick."

"Not my style," I reply.

He grins at me in the mirror. "I like your style."

"I know you do."

His frigid hand lingers over my beating heart and I wonder if he knows that it only beats this fast for him. That it's never beaten this quickly for anyone, not even in the early days of my romance with Drew.

His hand falls ever so slowly from my chest before he walks over to the nightstand—*Drew's nightstand*—and retrieves his watch. "Where are you going tonight, looking like such a goddess?"

I can't help but grin. "A former student of mine has a book release party tonight. Some memoir she wrote about her affair with a married man."

"How original," he says, catching my eyes in the mirror.

At this, we both have a laugh.

And then, we slide our wedding rings back on.

At the door, he kisses me for longer than he should; he's already late for dinner with his wife.

"You'll tell me when you have news?" he says, not letting go of me. He's worried. I can see it in his eyes.

"Of course," I say before giving him a gentle push out the door. "I'm sure there won't be any news, though."

I've never been *less sure*, but I have to pretend. If not for him, then for myself.

As is our routine, he leaves my place fifteen minutes before I do, which gives me just enough time to lie on the white chaise in the salon and catch my breath. I always lie here after he leaves, gazing out the floor-to-ceiling windows in the Park Avenue penthouse I share with my husband, and I breathe.

Inhaling the view of the Manhattan skyscrapers.

The heavy gray clouds.

The darkness of a city I know so very well.

Exhaling the scent of another man.

Each time I breathe out, I pause to see if there is any guilt in my exhale, but I haven't found any yet. It's been a year and a half, and still, not an ounce of guilt.

Perhaps my heart is as cold as my lover's hands. I've actually convinced myself that I'm just having him over for an afternoon coffee. If Drew ever found out, that's what I would say.

"Darling, don't be silly. It was only a coffee."

But Drew is in Paris, so he wouldn't find out. He *won't* find out.

He spends two weeks out of every month in Paris for work. He's asked me to join him, but I refuse to go because I can't leave my teaching position at New York University. Because I'm writing my next book. Because I have a life here in New York. Because I have galas and book signings and literary events and luncheons to attend. Because I don't like to fly.

I've given him a million bullshit reasons, but there is only one reason I will never again go to Paris. A reason he will never, ever know.

My hand instinctively runs over my stomach. I can feel my heart beating all the way down in my abdomen.

Mocking me with its relentless thumping.

The clouds just on the other side of the glass begin hurling drops of rain over the city. It used to rain like this in London when I was a little girl, and I've always loved it. That powerful sound when the drops hit the glass, the way they wash away the dirt, the lies, the secrets that hide behind the windows.

At least when I was a little girl, I could pretend that it would all be washed away.

I know better now.

I inhale.

I hold my breath.

When my exhale finally explodes, I wonder who my husband is having over for coffee this afternoon. I wonder if she lets him see her scars. I wonder if he keeps fucking her anyway.

3

THE MISTRESS OF PARIS: A MEMOIR

BY EVE WINTERS

LE 11 JUILLET 2016
AVENUE GEORGE V ~ PARIS, FRANCE

IT'S A DARK, ominous ride down Avenue George V tonight. Even with the heat wafting in through the open windows, I'm shivering in the back of the cab. My throat is dry. So dry it's closing.

Better to stop breathing than to throw up, I tell myself.

Dex wouldn't want to fuck a prostitute that tastes like vomit, now would he?

I clench my fists as we pull up to the entrance of The Four Seasons George V Hotel. It's a hotel I've walked past a million times in my nighttime strolls around the city, but I've never been inside. The people who walk through those black and golden doors belong to a world I know nothing of. A world I always imagined to be much happier, safer, and more glamorous than the one I am entering into tonight.

And yet, here I am with my sister's Louboutins carrying me to the door and a fat roll of condoms weighing down my purse.

"*Bonsoir, mademoiselle,*" the doorman says with a polite nod as he lets me in the gate—the gate to what I can only tell myself is going to be absolute hell. I can't seem to believe in anything else right now.

"*Merci, monsieur,*" I manage to say as I walk swiftly past him. I wonder if he knows. I wonder if he sees girls like me strutting in here every night.

Who am I kidding? I'm hardly strutting in these things. My ankles are so wobbly, I'm amazed I haven't bit it yet on this smooth marble floor.

The lobby of the George V is a vision of twinkling chandeliers and tall glass vases filled with the most beautiful peach and pink roses. Their scent makes my stomach curl, and I realize that roses will never again smell sweet to me. They will smell like fear. Trepidation. Horror.

They will smell like the night I sold myself.

To Dex. A man I wish I never had to know.

I keep walking. Over the marble floors. Past the flowers. Beneath the archways. Like I belong here. Like I am actually a guest in this magnificent symbol of luxury. Although I'm certain every well-to-do Parisian and tourist I am walking past knows the truth.

A working girl.

A call girl.

Here to make some wealthy man's wildest sexual fantasies come true.

Little do they know, Dex will be only the third man to ever be inside of me.

Fuck me, Dex. Fuck me harder, Dex.

I hope I'll know what to say. What to do. What if he figures out I'm not her?

I make it to La Galerie Lounge, where Willow instructed me to look for him. A woman in a shimmering black gown runs her long fingers over the keys of a grand piano, but the tune she is playing barely permeates the thumping inside my ears.

I see him.

In a black velvet chair at a table in the corner of the room.

The lights of the chandeliers overhead are dim, but I can still make out the black rose lying across the edge of the table.

That's my sign.

But when his head swivels, when his eyes catch mine, I realize I wouldn't have needed the rose.

The way he's looking at me is enough.

The tips of my breasts. The flesh between my thighs. The soft skin at the small of my back.

It all belongs to him.

Already.

4

SOPHIA

Tuesday the 16th of May, 2017
East 13th Street ~ New York City

The last place I want to go tonight is a French restaurant. The last place I ever want to go is a French restaurant, but when Raoul stops the town car in front of Le Midi, a classic French bistro off of Union Square, I tell myself I just have to make a quick appearance and then I can get the hell out of here.

I'll breathe through my mouth. I won't let the scents of butter and French bread and wine take me back there. *I won't.*

"Thank you, Raoul," I call up to my long-time driver.

"The pleasure is mine, Mrs. Grayson."

"I won't be long," I say as I open the car door.

Raoul shoots me a grin before I go. "Take your time, Mrs. Grayson. Have some fun."

I almost snort back at him, but then I remember that Mrs. Sophia Grayson, the once-acclaimed author, accomplished writing professor, known literary snob, wealthy Park

Avenue wife, and classy socialite wouldn't snort. No. *That woman* would smile, breezily, and maybe give a light laugh before strutting, with the utmost elegance and class, into the book release party of one of her former students.

Even if she couldn't give a sodding fuck about another book release from another student who is going to upstage her.

And so, I give Raoul my breeziest smile, my lightest laugh, and I walk through the doors of hell. Because anything that reminds me of Paris is hell.

Inside the restaurant, the private party is underway. Familiar faces speckle the crowd—mostly those of my former creative writing students, plus a few other NYU faculty members, who, like me, are also authors. The idea of getting sucked into some long conversation about how *scandalous* this girl's book is sounds absolutely dreadful, so I avoid all of them completely and instead head straight for one of the servers dressed in black—or more aptly, for the tray of champagne in his hand. I gladly help myself to a flute, and it goes down quickly...too quickly. I'll need at least two more of these to get through the next hour. I'm not supposed to be drinking, but I need something to wash down the feeling of inadequacy I am inevitably going to feel as I watch my agent Abbey fawning all over some young new author the way she used to do with me back in the days when my books actually sold.

But when I spot Abbey, she is looking anything but celebratory. Panicked is more like it.

"Hi, Abbey," I say, leaning in to give her one of those impersonal hugs that New Yorkers often give.

"You look tired," she says before ignoring me again to scan the crowd.

How sweet.

"Everything okay?" I ask her.

She snaps a flute of champagne off the nearest waiter's tray, throws it back in three gulps, places it back on the tray and gives me her most deadpan stare. "Yeah, fabulous. Except for the fact that the author is late to her own fucking release party and she hasn't been in touch in over twenty-four hours." Abbey rises up on tiptoes and continues scanning the crowded dining room. "I don't even know if she got on the plane in Paris."

"Paris?" I say. "I thought she lived in...actually I don't know where I thought she lived, but I didn't realize she was in Paris."

Abbey turns to me, annoyed. "Sophia, the book is called *The Mistress of Paris*. Did you not read the ARC I gave you?"

A flush creeps up my neck when I think about the advanced reader copy that Abbey gave me last month, which I never had any intention of reading, of course. Come to think of it, I may have already donated it to the library with all of the other books my agent and publisher give me. Abbey had asked me to review the book when it released. That's what I am to her now—*a bloody book reviewer*. Not a star author who is making her loads of money. No, those days are long gone.

"I've been swamped with giving final exams and just... you know, life." And by life, I mean my lover. My fatigue. My very overdue doctor's appointments. I mean keeping my lies straight. I mean a million other things that don't involve reading some book by a former student whom I can barely recall. "I'm sorry I haven't gotten to it yet."

Abbey is too impatient to even finish her eye roll. "Yes, Eve lives in Paris and was supposed to be flying to New York yesterday so that she'd be here for the release." Abbey pulls her cell phone out of her purse, glancing nervously at the time. "The party has officially started, and I haven't even received so much as a text—"

"Abbey, you need to see this."

It's Abbey's intern, Karina. Her normally tanned skin looks a sickly shade of gray. She shoves her phone into Abbey's hands.

As Abbey reads whatever is on the screen, her face goes pale, too. Ghostly. Her bottom lip drops. She blinks. Again...and again.

"Holy fuck," she whispers, not so softly.

A knot forms in the pit of my stomach. "What is it?"

But Abbey doesn't respond. And neither does Karina.

When Abbey finishes reading, she looks to me, blankly. Numbly. She pushes the cell phone into my hands.

There is a headline stretching across the top of the page:

The Mistress of Paris Has Gone Missing

American author Eve Winters, 29, has been reported missing from her apartment in Paris. When police searched Ms. Winters' glamorous apartment situated on the Île de la Cité, overlooking the quaint Place Dauphine, they found clear evidence of a struggle—including blood splattered on the floors and walls—but no sign of Winters. Neighbors reported hearing female screams coming from the apartment Monday evening, but no eyewitnesses have stepped forward. Police have declined to comment further, except to confirm that an aggressive search for the author is underway.

It seems no coincidence that Eve Winters' sexually explicit memoir, The Mistress of Paris*—in which she details her scandalous foray into the world of high-end* *prostitution and her dangerous affair with a married American businessman—released the exact same day she was reported missing.*

The identity of the married man is not yet known.

The identity of the...

The married man.

The married man.

The married man.

I am stuck on this final sentence.

Over and over, the words taunt me. A ferocious cackling.

The identity of the married man...is not yet known.

The restaurant is packed like sardines. It's insanely hot in here. And still, a chill rolls down my spine. I feel frigid inside. I need to get out of here.

Without a word, I shove the phone back into Abbey's hands. I turn and push through the crowd. Before I make it to the door, I spot a table of Eve's books, waiting patiently for their author.

An author who is not arriving to sign them anytime soon...*or perhaps ever*.

Even though something inside me knows I do not want anything to do with this girl's sordid story, I can't stop my shaky hands from grabbing a book.

On the back cover, there she is: *Eve Winters*. My former student.

In the photo, Eve is standing in some beautiful Parisian apartment or suite...or perhaps one of the hotels where she stayed with her married lover. A crystal chandelier overhead casts a golden light over what is otherwise a smoldering photo of the girl. Her dark-brown hair falls in silky waves over her breasts, which are barely covered by the slinky black slip she's wearing.

Although it's not her perfectly messy hair or lack of normal clothing that have rendered me motionless. Speechless.

It's the haunted look in her eyes. I remember her now. I remember those eyes.

Eve was smart. A bright student. A talented writer.

But I always felt a chill when I would look into those eyes.

Something happened to her, I would always think. *Something awful. Something unspeakable.*

Her writing didn't reflect this darkness, however. It was light—unnaturally so. And I always knew there was something much more profound and forbidding lurking beneath.

That darkness is evident in this photo.

But now, she isn't only haunted—*she's gone.*

When I push through the front door of the restaurant, I want so badly for the spring air to take away the feeling of dread that has gripped my insides.

But no.

Instead, all I can think about as I text Raoul to come pick me up is the last line of the news article:

The identity of the married man is not yet known.

5

OFFICER JEAN-MARC DEVEREAUX

MARDI 16 MAI 2017
PLACE DAUPHINE ~ PARIS, FRANCE

OFFICER JEAN-MARC DEVEREAUX asked the rest of his team to leave the girl's apartment.

Well, it wasn't so much a polite request as it was a demand.

He needed time alone amid the wreckage to take it all in. To piece together the scene before him.

The overstuffed suitcase toppled onto its side at the front door.

The glass shards littering the hardwood floors, shimmering in the afternoon sunlight.

The long-stemmed violet roses tossed to the ground, their petals drowning in the very water that once fed them.

Then there was the hair. So much hair. Tufts and tufts of it, mostly long and dark brown.

More importantly, there was the blood. Splattered over hardwood floors, on the gray sofa, the white armchairs, staining the pristine white walls.

Blood everywhere.

But the girl who lived here, a *jolie américaine* by the name of Eve Winters, well that girl was nowhere to be found.

Dressed in his fashionable *combinaison de protection*—the white hooded suit, mask, gloves, and booties that ensured he and his fellow *Brigade Criminelle* officers didn't contaminate the crime scene—Officer Devereaux took purposeful steps around the apartment, making sure not to crush a single rose stem or tuft of hair, dodging the glass and blood entirely. As each ginger step took him farther into the crime scene, he began to imagine, to construct, the story that could have led to the disappearance of the 29-year-old prostitute turned author.

He would have to read her book of course.

After all, it wasn't every day that a victim left an entire three hundred pages of evidence behind.

A copy of Winters' newly released memoir lay on the ground, soaking in the same water with the rose petals. A splash of blood had made its way onto the back cover, staining the forehead of the author in her seductive portrait.

A bullseye right on her lovely face.

She was a target.

And by the looks of her trashed apartment, she'd been hit.

One of Devereaux's team members had tried to give him a copy of the book earlier today before their trip to the crime scene, but he had declined the read—for now anyway. He wanted to see—*to feel*—Mademoiselle Winters' last moments in her apartment before diving into the pages of her memoir.

And what he felt when he took in the roses, the glass, the hair, the blood-stained book cover, was quite clear.

Jealousy.

Passion.

Love gone terribly wrong.

Devereaux knew all about that, but now wasn't the time to think of Mia.

The sight of blood always made him think of her. It was an unfortunate side effect of his profession. Crime scenes usually meant blood, and blood always meant Mia.

Devereaux shook his head, memories be damned, and glanced down at his clipboard. He flipped through the notes his team had briefed him on upon his arrival just an hour ago. Inside the black Coach purse Winters had left behind, they'd discovered a flight itinerary—round-trip, Charles de Gaulle to JFK, leaving Monday night, May 15th and set to return in one week—along with a printed invite to Winters' own book release party in New York which was set to happen later on the evening of the 16th. Winters' passport was also tucked into that same expensive Coach bag, leading the officers to believe she hadn't made it very far. A quick call to Air France by one of Devereaux's colleagues had indeed confirmed that Winters never boarded the flight the night before.

Devereaux lifted his gaze to the black suitcase toppled over by the door.

She was attacked before she could even make it to the elevator.

After the bloodshed, someone must have carried her out of here.

And neglected to clean up the crime scene before they did so.

How very careless, he thought.

The slightest of grins crept over his face.

Officer Devereaux was good at his job. One of the most

gifted and meticulous *procéduriers* who'd ever walked the halls of the famous 36 Quai des Orfèvres.

Paris' Brigade Criminelle was lucky to have him. They knew as much.

But whoever took Eve Winters, well they had no idea who they were dealing with.

6

THE MISTRESS OF PARIS: A MEMOIR

BY EVE WINTERS

LE 11 JUILLET 2016
HÔTEL GEORGE V ~ PARIS, FRANCE

DEX ANDERSON IS...WELL, he's gorgeous. There's no way around it. He has these piercing eyes—blue or green—I can't quite tell from this distance, but the color is irrelevant. It's the power they have over me.

In the first few seconds of meeting his gaze, all sense of control I felt has vanished.

He owns me.

His hair is dusty brown with hints of gold woven in. No gray though, even though he is clearly much older than me. He is wearing a crisp black suit. Black tie. White shirt. Classic and so very Parisian. Like he just stepped out of the pages of *Vogue*.

The corner of his mouth lifts just the slightest bit. He doesn't smile, though. And as I take my first step toward him, I get the feeling that Dex Anderson doesn't smile much. Not at all. Which, strangely, makes me feel a bit more comfortable about taking my next step.

He watches me intently, and as I take step after step through this glitzy lounge, something happens.

The nausea subsides. A strut takes over.

Willow's strut.

I've been watching my sister use her body to slay men our whole lives.

She owns them. And then she destroys them.

And I realize, I know exactly what Willow would do. What she would say.

She is my blood. I've hated that fact for so many years. But by the way my hips sway effortlessly from side to side, my breasts bouncing out of her dress, my tongue running along the corner of my mouth, I know she is inside me. And I am inside her.

We are sisters.

And tonight—as much as I may detest it—we are one.

"Dex?" I say. But it's not my voice. It's a voice that is oozing with sex. Oozing with Willow. It's a voice I despise.

His eyes dance over my body. I can see the color clearly now—they're indigo-blue, like the Pacific Ocean. I find myself wanting to dive into them, swim into their depths. But surely I would drown in such dangerous waters.

He nods to the seat across from him. I sit, obediently. His presence is quiet but powerful, and I know that this is the first thing he will order me to do tonight without even speaking a word.

He slides a glass across the table. It's filled with clear liquid. Vodka, probably.

My hand trembles as I lift the glass to my lips. I take a sip, let the alcohol scald my throat. I'm not a big drinker, and it hurts going down. But it's the good kind of hurt. The kind I want more of. So, I take another sip. And then another.

After the glass is nearly empty, I slide my palm across the table, into Dex's hand.

It's time.

"I'm Willow," I say. "It's lovely to meet you."

He is still silent. Undressing me with his eyes.

I wonder what he sees.

A prostitute?

A liar?

The piano player's voice fills the space between us. Slow and sultry, she's singing a tune I recognize. One I listen to when I'm writing. "Lover Undercover" by Melody Gardot.

How appropriate.

Dex's fingers are strong and thick as they clasp my hand, and I feel a startling pull coming from between my legs as I think about where his hands are going to be in only a short while.

That pull becomes ever stronger, ever more forceful as I realize that I *want* his hands to go there. I want his hands to go *everywhere.*

I tell myself that this unexpected wave of desire I'm feeling *must* be nerves. It has to be. I could never live with myself if I actually wanted to be with this man under such horrifying circumstances. *As his prostitute.*

Finally, he speaks.

"Forgive my silence, Willow, but you've taken my breath away."

And now I am breathless, and he is already standing over me, nodding for me to get up and follow him.

I hope he doesn't notice the way my legs quiver when I stand from my chair. I find him infinitely sexier than any man I've ever laid eyes upon. As we walk, I have to remind myself that this man is *buying me* for the night. That he doesn't actually *like* me.

He chose Willow on a website of high-class escorts; he *did not* choose me.

When we reach the elevator, he leans close to me, runs his hand over the curve of my ass. And in my ear, he whispers, "I hope you won't mind, but I am going to worship your body *all night long.*"

We step into the elevator, and I realize I was wrong.

For tonight anyway, this man *has* chosen me.

7

SOPHIA

Tuesday the 16th of May, 2017
Park Avenue ~ New York City

Eve is calling him "Dex Anderson" in her memoir, which obviously isn't his real name.

Dex Anderson.

Andrew Grayson.

Or *Drew* Grayson, as only I call him.

They are so similar. Would she be that stupid?

Am I crazy to even think this could be possible?

I'm back on the chaise in the salon, voraciously reading this girl's memoir and catching glimpses of the news on my television at the same time. The story of the seductive American author who has gone missing in Paris is plastered all over CNN, and Eve's memoir is no doubt flying off the shelves. The book has nearly broken Amazon's Top 100 Bestseller List, and I'm sure it will be #1 by the morning.

Could Eve's disappearance be a publicity stunt to make her book a bestseller?

Bollocks.

I grab my cell to text Abbey.

You're going to be bloody rich from this book.

But I delete the message before I send it. That's insensitive. Callous. Uncaring. Eve could be dead. Raped. Lying in a ditch somewhere. But I know my agent, and she's already doing the math. She is going to be bloody rich. The longer this girl stays gone, the more money Abbey is going to make.

Abbey. Would *she* know the identity of the married man in the book? Would Eve have told her his name? And if it were Drew, and Abbey has known all along, would she even tell me?

And what about Eve? She had to have known before she signed with her that Abbey is *my* agent. Did the little cow do this on purpose? Stealing my agent *and* my husband?

I want to phone Abbey this instant and bombard her with all of my questions...but then, what if it's not Drew Eve is writing about? What if I make a total and complete arse of myself? I hardly need my agent thinking I've gone totally mad.

No. I won't phone Abbey. Not yet anyway. Must do more of my own investigating before I let anyone in my life know that I suspect my own sodding husband could be the married man in Eve's memoir.

It occurs to me then that Eve has written the dates in her memoir. I turn back to the first page, and my breath catches when I see the date—July 11th, 2016. That was Drew's 45th birthday. I'm almost certain he was in Paris that day. I close my eyes, racking my brain to remember our phone conversation. But when my memory comes up empty, I pull up my calendar on my phone to see what I had going that week.

7/11/16 - 12:00 p.m. – Writing group

Writing group is code for hours spent with my lover. I remember now. I'd tried to phone Drew to wish him a happy birthday before my noon rendezvous, but he hadn't answered. Later that afternoon, while I was buried beneath the sheets, my phone had buzzed on my nightstand. It was Drew. My lover reached over, switched the phone to silent and tossed it in the drawer. Then he continued making love to me all afternoon. By the time I tried to phone Drew back, it would've been late at night in Paris. He never answered.

I'd thought nothing of it at the time. I knew he was sleeping with other women. In fact, I'd given him permission to do so.

"Go, be with other women when you travel for business. Just don't bring it home," I'd said. This was after months of barely letting him touch me. Of hiding in the closet to change my clothes so he wouldn't see me naked. I just couldn't after...after...*no.*

I just could not.

After I'd given him permission to take his sexual desires elsewhere, Drew had nodded silently. Then he'd taken my hand in his and squeezed my fingers so hard I feared my bones might crack.

"I'm never going to leave you, Sophia," he said. "Never."

I could barely look at him. But I nodded all the same.

We've never discussed it since.

I know that Drew assumes I'm not sleeping with anyone else. He thinks that I just do not want to have sex, period. Not with anyone.

He doesn't know that it is only with *him* that I do not want to have sex.

But I love him. Fiercely. So I will never, ever tell him that.

My watery eyes flicker back to my calendar. On the 13th of July, only two days after his birthday, Drew flew home from Paris to surprise me for our 20th wedding anniversary.

I did let him make love to me that night—in the dark, of course. Always and only in the dark. After throwing back two Xanax with a glass of straight vodka. I needed to be numb in order to spread my legs for him. I needed to forget what our love making had created...and what it had destroyed.

On my calendar, I'd noted that Drew flew back to Paris on Friday, July 15th. I had a "writing meeting" later that night.

I push down the nausea that wants to eat at my insides.

So Drew *was* in Paris on July 11th. The day Eve became a prostitute.

I pick the book back up, forcing myself to keep going. Eve has just gotten into the elevator with Dex at the George V Hotel. He's told her he's going to worship her body all night long. Definitely *does not* sound like something my Drew would say...to me at least.

But then, I clearly have not given him the opportunity to worship my body for years.

8

OFFICER JEAN-MARC DEVEREAUX

MARDI 16 MAI 2017
PLACE DAUPHINE ~ PARIS, FRANCE

DEVEREAUX's precious time alone in Winters' apartment was short-lived. He was right in the middle of making the insanely thorough list of notes that would later help him write the insanely thorough description of the crime scene that he, as *le Procédurier,* was responsible for writing, when his *Chef de Groupe*, Julien Breton, stomped in through the front door.

Three years his senior, Breton was Devereaux's boss, as well as an old childhood friend who had grown up in the same middle-class Parisian suburb as Devereaux. In their years with la Brigade Criminelle—Paris' specialized crime squad also known as *la Crim'*—the two men had stood side by side through more atrocious cases than either cared to remember. Given that *la Crim'* was tasked with handling the city's most gruesome homicides, rapes, attacks, and kidnappings, everyday life for Devereaux and Breton was decidedly more morose than their boyhood days spent playing endless soccer matches and chasing endless groups of French *filles*. Now the two men spent their days chasing criminals, and while it wasn't a pretty job, they were damn good at it, even if they rarely agreed on how to approach a case.

Even if lately, they rarely agreed on anything.

Breton squinted and scratched his beard, the way he always did when he first took in a crime scene. Devereaux waited for his boss' typical scolding, letting him know that the crime scene wasn't his to dominate, but it never came.

Instead, Breton let out a nearly inaudible sigh, shook his head and nodded toward the missing girl's book soaking in a puddle on the floor.

"*Putain.* Not even one damn day to have this case to ourselves. It's already all over the news—thanks to her book."

Devereaux nodded. "Figured as much."

"Have you read any of it yet?" Breton asked.

Devereaux shook his head. "Wanted to comb the scene first."

"I had Leroux drive over here so I could skim some of it on the way," Breton said. "Apparently the girl's younger sister—another *prostituée* named Willow—lived here with her. Any sign of her?"

"It's a one-bedroom apartment," Devereaux said. "Fancy. Expensive. But only one bedroom, one bed, one closet, one set of clothes. No photos anywhere. I have more work to do, but as of right now, it appears that only one girl lived here."

Breton nodded. "And Martinez?"

"She's on it. Been out talking to neighbors since we arrived. She should've spoken with the *gardien* by now to confirm who lived here."

"Good," Breton said. "There's a married American businessman in the book—he paid her obscene amounts of money to sleep with him, and *only* him. Looks as though he had no idea she was writing a book about them. Clearly not a coincidence that she disappears the night before the book release. Could be an open-and-shut case once we figure out who this *connard* is."

Devereaux cocked his head at his boss. "Since when do we get the courtesy of an open-and-shut case?" He thought about how absurdly complicated many of their cases were to solve. Some of them took months of following leads that led nowhere until ultimately, they discovered the thread that gave them an answer and a culprit. The complexity of the cases didn't stop him and Breton from solving most of them with success, of course, but still, *open and shut* wasn't the norm in their neck of the woods.

"Since the girl who went missing left us an entire book of evidence," Breton quipped.

"And who says this evidence is true?" By this point, Devereaux was back in the girl's closet, turning all of the shoes over. "All of the shoes in this closet are the same size. Only one girl lived here."

"Maybe her sister wore the same size." Breton walked into the bedroom and leveled a glare at Devereaux. "We need to find out who the married bastard is that hired her. No way he didn't have a hand in making this girl disappear."

Devereaux offered Breton a curt nod, annoyed at his boss' insistence on such a simple theory. There was *always* more to a story like this one, and they both knew it.

"Enough time in here by yourself," Breton snapped. "I'm telling the rest of the team and the *techniciens* to get back in here and do their damn jobs."

Devereaux delighted for a moment in the way his boss' left eye was twitching.

"Late night?" Devereaux asked. He knew he should stop there, but he didn't give a shit anymore. "Baby keep you up?"

Breton's glare hardened at the mention of his girlfriend's baby. The baby who also happened to be Devereaux's niece.

"Coralie wasn't feeling well," Breton said. "She needed me to help feed the baby."

Devereaux knew the drill. His younger sister Coralie hadn't felt well since the day they lost their father eleven years ago. She was only sixteen when they'd lost him, and she was only three when they'd lost their mother. Even though Coralie was a 27-year-old woman now, she still acted like that troubled, lost little girl who'd lost both of her parents too soon. She needed constant help with everything, and most recently, she needed constant help caring for the baby she'd had after a one-night stand with a man she refused to name.

The person she'd always turned to for that help—with both the baby and everything else that had gone wrong in her life—had been her big brother, Jean-Marc. He was ten years older than her and he'd been more like a father to her than a brother. Right after Coralie had given birth to her baby last August, he'd invited them to move in with him. The day Coralie walked into Jean-Marc's apartment and placed sweet Baby Adelaide in his arms was the day Jean-Marc came back to life. He needed that little girl just as much as she needed him...and perhaps even more.

But that all ended when Jean-Marc's boss and former friend Julien Breton decided to start sleeping with his little sister.

That was the day when work became decidedly tenser for the two men.

Devereaux swallowed the stab of jealousy he felt over being replaced. He should've been relieved not to be the one waking up at ungodly hours every night to feed the baby. But he missed being needed. He missed holding his niece every day, every night. She was so sweet. So soft. So innocent.

And with his daily life a constant reminder of all that was evil, harsh, and anything but innocent in this world, he couldn't help but despise Breton for taking that away from him.

He'd had a shot at happiness with Mia, but that was gone now too. *She was gone.*

"Have your report on my desk by 20h00," Breton said. "We have to move fast on this one. Winters might still be alive."

Devereaux turned his back to Breton and walked out into the salon. Nothing about the blood-spattered scene before him said that this girl was still alive, but without a body, he knew Breton was right about one thing.

They had to move fast.

9

THE MISTRESS OF PARIS: A MEMOIR

BY EVE WINTERS

LE 11 JUILLET 2016
HÔTEL GEORGE V ~ PARIS, FRANCE

INSIDE THE DECADENT PENTHOUSE SUITE, Dex has only just closed the door behind us when he presses his body into mine, pushes my back against the wall, and shoves a knee in between my legs. They spread, easily, and I realize that I am totally and completely at his mercy now. He hasn't even kissed me yet, but his hands are already sliding up my thighs, beneath my dress, pulling my thong to the side.

His fingers are warm, and they're more than eager; they're forceful.

He pushes them inside of me before I have time to ask for the envelope with the 5,000 euros. The 5,000 euros Willow specifically instructed me to have in hand *before* I let this man touch me.

But now, one, two, three, *four* of his smoking hot fingers have taken me hostage. Nearly his whole hand.

It's been so long since anyone has touched me...since I've *allowed* anyone to touch me, that even though part of me is terrified, even though it hurts like hell, I am strangely, instantly wet.

He lowers his face to mine, exhales his steamy breath into my mouth, but he doesn't kiss me. His eyes are heavy with lust as he locks them on me. His fingers are pushing so deep inside of me, I have to stop myself from wincing.

But just like the vodka downstairs, *I like the pain.*

I want more.

The thought washes over me before I can stop it. And I hate it. I hate that there is even a small part of me that is getting off on this. It's sick, twisted, disgusting. And if I like it—even a little bit—what does that make me?

Before I get too used to the feeling of his hand inside me, he flips me around, plants my hands on the wall, and lifts my dress up so my bare ass is pressing into his groin. The sound of his belt buckle coming undone makes the hairs on the back of my neck stand up.

Holy shit. He is going to do this, *right now*.

No warmup. No foreplay. No cash exchange.

It only takes seconds before I feel his erection pushing against my skin.

I think of the roll of condoms Willow gave me. They're in the purse that has now dropped to the floor.

"I have to have you *now*," he growls. "I would've spread you open on the table downstairs if I could have."

And that is all the warning I get before I am, officially, Dex's prostitute.

Dex has me bent me over some fancy table in the foyer now. We've knocked over a vase filled with white roses in the process. There is glass everywhere. The sweet scent of roses encompasses our dirty act, but I am surprised to notice that they no longer smell like fear.

They smell of darkness. A darkness I've needed to release for so long. And it is only now, here—bent over for *Dex*—that I am able to release this endless night that has lived within me since I was a teenager.

Dex has been inside of me for less than an hour and no longer am I afraid of him or what he might do to me. I don't give a shit about the money—the penthouse suite we have taken ownership of clearly says he's good for it. And the threat on my sister's life is even too far away for me to worry about right now.

All I care about is making this night last as long as possible. And I am sick with myself for feeling this way. But sex has never felt so intoxicating. So utterly inebriating. So viciously forbidden.

I've never tried heroin. Willow spent years being a total fucking mess on it. She couldn't stop. It's all she could think about. When to get her next hit. How to get the money to score more. More. More. More.

And I never understood it until now.

I spread my legs farther, and I turn around to look at Dex. He has stripped off his black jacket, and the top buttons on his shirt are undone. A shiny silver chain adorns his neck, and at the end of it, a silver cross which glistens beneath the low light of the chandelier with each brutal shove of his hips into mine.

I wouldn't have pegged Dex for a religious man.

I wonder if he'll ask God for forgiveness tomorrow morning, after he pays me and sends me on my way.

Dex reaches forward, cups my chin in his hand and lifts my face up so we are locking eyes. He pushes harder inside of me, the hardest yet, but I don't cry out in pain.

Willow never cries.

I push away the part of me that is still fighting this. The frantic voice that is screaming inside my head, my heart, my soul, telling me what a whore I'm becoming.

Instead, I lick my lips, feel the heat emanating from between my thighs. And I tell him what I want. What Willow wants.

What *we* want.

"Fuck me, Dex. Fuck me harder, Dex."

10

SOPHIA

Tuesday the bloody 16th of May, 2017
Park Avenue ~ New York City

The silver cross.

I gave one to Drew for our tenth wedding anniversary—it's silver with a diamond in the center. He's never taken it off since.

Eve doesn't mention the diamond, though. A million men could be wearing a silver cross. This doesn't mean anything. This doesn't mean that my husband is...

Bloody fucking hell.

I snap the book closed. Can't bear to read another word. I squeeze my eyes shut, wishing it all away. It absolutely cannot be. Surely he wouldn't *pay* for sex...*with her*...

But in my darkness, I see him with Eve. I see *my* husband, *my Drew*, bending my former student over the table, shagging her the way he used to shag me when we were first married. I see the silver cross banging against his sweaty chest. I see him locking eyes with her. Owning her.

And now she is gone.

Could it really be him?

What has he done?

I feel the sick coming up my throat, and I race toward the loo but don't make it. I collapse onto the shiny hardwood floors in my dining room, retching like a child. Crystal and porcelain surround me, but all of our outward symbols of success can't protect me now.

The convulsions send shooting pains through my lower abdomen. And these are the pains that remind me, for the millionth time, of what I have done to him. Of what I have hidden from my husband. Of all the times I've refused his advances, barely letting him touch me.

Perhaps I have driven him to Eve.

Perhaps this is all my fault.

After the retching subsides, I drag myself to my feet and hobble back over to the chaise to find my phone and text Abbey. I don't bloody care if she thinks I've gone mad. I have...haven't I?

Sophia: Did Eve tell you who the married man in her memoir is?

Abbey is a good New Yorker who is glued to her cell phone, so I only have to wait approximately three and a half seconds before the little bubbles pop up on the screen letting me know she is typing her response.

Abbey: Just got off the phone with French police. They wanted to know the same damn thing.

Sophia: And???

Abbey: No. She never told me or her editor. No clue who the bastard is, but I'm sure the police will find him soon enough. I just hope they find Eve...alive.

Bloody hell.

There is only one thing left to do. One place to go.

Even though I'd nearly rather die than be reminded of what happened there so long ago, I realize I have no other choice. If there is even a sliver of doubt in my mind that the man Eve is writing about is my husband, I must go.

I pull up the number for Air France on my phone, and I dial.

When the operator picks up, I clear my throat, trying to sound human. "I'd like a first-class ticket from New York City to Paris, please."

Yes, I may have driven my husband to her.

But I will *die* before I will allow him to ruin us like this.

11

OFFICER JEAN-MARC DEVEREAUX

MARDI 16 MAI 2017
PLACE DAUPHINE ~ PARIS, FRANCE

EVE WINTERS' wrecked Parisian abode had now been entirely taken over by five out of the six members of Devereaux's own Brigade Criminelle team, including their Chef de Groupe, Breton. Three skilled *Identité Judiciaire* technicians were also shuffling around in their white suits, taking photographs, dusting for prints, and shining their Crime Scope over every surface in the apartment, looking for traces of blood and sperm that may have been naked to the invisible eye.

These three particular technicians were Devereaux's favorites to work with on a crime scene because they were relentlessly thorough in their search; they didn't miss a single hair or spot of blood.

But there was one thing almost everyone missed.

Everyone but Devereaux.

It came two hours after his arrival, and it was big.

A crumpled pair of women's underwear stuffed

between two couch cushions.

The silky fabric was black, which made the sticky white substance coating the inside that much easier to spot.

Just as one of the technicians was shining her Crime Scope over a ticking clock mounted on Winters' living room wall—an ever present reminder that they didn't have a second to waste if they wanted to find this girl alive—Devereaux's gloved fingers lifted the panties into the technician's line of sight. "I think you'll want to add these to your collection. Have you found signs of semen elsewhere in the apartment?"

"Yes, stains on the couch and the floor. They appear to be recent."

Devereaux nodded. Rape seemed likely given the state of the apartment, but then again, Eve *was* a prostitute. It could've been her most recent client popping over for one last romp before she headed out of town for the week. Or it could've been a lover.

Or, as Breton had insisted earlier, it could've been the unidentified married man Winters wrote about in her book —who apparently had been both a client *and* a lover.

Devereaux's colleague Martinez hadn't come back yet from interviewing the neighbors, but as soon as she resurfaced, Devereaux would ask her if anyone had noticed Eve's clients frequenting the apartment or if this wealthy call girl turned author kept her work and home lives separate.

Devereaux's hungry eyes combed the apartment floor once more. The one thing that was steering him away from the rape theory was the amount of long dark hair—presumably Eve's—strewn about the apartment.

Rapists didn't usually pull out their victim's hair like that.

Women did.

12

EVE

The When: Unknown
The Where: Unknown

Thirteen.
Eve. Close. Your. Eyes.
Thirteen.
Willow. Open. Your. Veins.
Thirteen.
Wider. Eve. Wider.
More. Willow. More.
Thirteen.
Thirteen.
Thirteen.
It's the only song I know anymore.
A cursed chant echoing through the hollows of my soul.
Through the dazed cavities of my brain.
Until it lulls my shattered bones to sleep early each dawn.
If only I never woke up…
To the slamming of that wretched door.

13

THE MISTRESS OF PARIS: A MEMOIR

BY EVE WINTERS

LE 11 JUILLET 2016
HÔTEL GEORGE V ~ PARIS, FRANCE

WEARING only Willow's crimson bra and panties, I am lounging on the pristine white couch inside Dex's penthouse suite, sipping the glass of champagne he has just poured for me. Everything around me is shimmering in shades of white and gold. The lampshades, chandeliers, vases, flowers—every single object in the suite looks as if it has been touched by an angel.

Except for me.

I am the prostitute in this palace of purity, and I can tell by the devious smirk on Dex's face that he gets off on the contrast.

He walks across the room wearing nothing but a pair of tight black boxer briefs. I try not to stare, but I can't help myself. It is an absolutely divine view, watching the way his sculpted back muscles move each time he takes a step. He grabs his phone and turns on a song I recognize—"Talk Show Host" by Radio Head—then returns his gaze to me.

He nods for me to stand, and so I do.

The seductive beat fills the air between us as Dex's eyes comb the length of my body. And finally, after he watches me for what feels like hours, he smiles. It's the first real smile I've seen on his handsome face all night.

"You're absolutely stunning," he says. "Different from..."

"From what?" I take a bold step toward him.

His gaze rests on my left shoulder and before I realize what he is looking at, I feel his thumb brushing over the jagged line of my scar.

Please don't ask what it's from.

His eyes find mine once more. A slick grin slides over his lips. "From what I was expecting...but fuck, you're beautiful."

My insides flush with warmth. He's looking at me the way men always look at Willow. And while I'm not used to this, not in the least, I can't help but smile back. "Thank you."

He takes a seat in the white armchair, sips the vodka tonic he poured for himself, eyes pinned on me all the while.

"So, you're a dancer?" he says.

"Yes," I say, thankful to be telling the truth about at least one thing tonight. Willow and I were in ballet slippers and tutus as soon as we could walk, and we kept dancing through everything. Through all of the loss. Through every atrocity. Dance is what kept us both alive.

Although, we are treading on some seriously thin ice these days...and I'm not sure ballet can save either of us now.

"Dance for me."

At the sound of Dex's voice, I realize I want nothing more than to please him.

My hips begin to sway to the music, so naturally, like they were waiting to do just this. I place my champagne flute on the coffee table, and I let the music carry my body around the dimly lit room until I arrive in front of this hungry man. With my hands exploring my own curves, my breasts bouncing in front of Dex's lust-filled gaze, my dance moves are clearly nothing like what I learned at the ballet barre. But they are the perfect moves for this night. For this forbidden meeting of bodies and sweat and desire.

My dance continues for several songs, and with each sexy track, I lose myself in a way I haven't for years...or maybe ever. Dex stays planted in his seat as I dance around him and over him, straddling him and bending over for him and doing all sorts of things I've never, ever done in front of a man.

I imagine Willow has been dancing like this for men for years.

And now I understand, just the slightest bit, the power she must've felt each time a man looked at her the way Dex is looking at me now.

It's intoxicating.

I extend a hand to him, and he stands, pressing his warm body against mine. He wraps one hand around my bare ass, and the other finds its natural place between my thighs. Our hips sway in synch to the music as he brushes my hair from my neck and whispers in my ear, "You've put me in a trance, Willow."

I've never been so aroused in my life. I've never wanted anyone the way I want Dex. I've never been so willing to do anything for a man.

And I've never loathed a man more than I do him, right now.

Here I am, prancing around in lingerie, drunk on champagne, high from his sex—and I am here not *only* because I have to be in order to save my sister, but also...*now*...because I want to be.

And I want him to know this.

I slide a hand into his boxer briefs, wrapping my fingers around him.

"Whatever you want...just tell me," I whisper.

I expect him to ask me to do something entirely dirty and out of control, something I've surely never done before.

But instead, he lifts his hands to my face, running a thumb along my flushed cheek, and he kisses me.

His lips are warm and wet and salty. And if the view of his back muscles was divine, his kiss is pure heaven.

My biggest dose of heroin yet.

The music and the alcohol and the feel of his tongue on my lips have put me into a trance, too, and I feel myself coming alive for him.

Not only my body, but my heart. She is pulling, beating, coming back to life.

She's been dead for so long.

Dex doesn't stop kissing me as he picks me up. I wrap my legs around his waist and let him carry me into the bedroom. He lays me down on the smooth white duvet, runs his hands over my every curve, drinking me in. As I become drunk on the feeling of those commanding hands, I forget, for a moment, that I am his prostitute. I forget that he is paying me for this.

And I pretend that he is mine. That he will be mine tomorrow, and the next day. And the day after that.

I reach up, slip off his boxer briefs, and pull him down on top of me.

Our gazes lock in the darkness. A new song has come on—"Into Dust" by Mazzy Star. The softness of the guitar strumming in the background is almost eerie. It's sensual, slow—the most perfect song for this moment.

Under the weight of him, I feel myself finally letting go. Every last bit of restraint I was holding onto has left my body.

"You know what I really want, Willow?" he whispers.

"What, Dex?"

"I want to forget. For one night, I want to forget *everything*."

He is inside of me before I can wonder what it is, exactly, that he would pay 5,000 euros to forget.

He has been fucking me, relentlessly, for hours. We only took a brief break at his suggestion to do yet one more thing I've never done before, but had to pretend I do all the time—cocaine.

He trickled the white powder on the bathroom counter, snorted half of it, and nodded for me to take the other half. And so, like everything else Dex has wanted me to do thus far in this insane night, I did it without so much as a raised eyebrow.

The powder set the insides of my nose on fire, but it didn't take long for me to feel the rush. The high. The exhilaration that turned me into a rabid animal, foaming at the mouth for more of Dex's sex.

And if I'm a rabid animal on cocaine, Dex is the predator.

He is devouring me. Viciously.

I am now lying flat on my stomach while his full weight is bearing down on my back. He has my legs squeezed together while he straddles me from behind. My cheek is smashed into the pillow, his hungry lips hovering over my ear. He lets out a guttural moan and moves even faster, even deeper, pushing me so hard into the mattress that I can barely find my breath.

I can't help but cry out in pain—he is hurting me, and I can feel how much he loves it.

The sick part is that I love it too. This kind of pain is strangely euphoric. I wonder if this feeling—*this drug*—is what has kept Willow screwing everything that walks since we were teenagers.

Just as I'm getting light-headed and my hands are going numb, Dex flips me onto my back and moves up to straddle my face.

My entire body is trembling, but he's clearly not done.

We meet eyes as he towers over me, and for the first time since this forbidden night began, his blue eyes go dark. In the void, I see—*I feel*—that this man isn't just powerful; he's dangerous.

I am glistening with sweat, but still, a shiver runs down my spine.

Dex is possessed with an endless hunger, and I wonder how long it has been since his wife let him fuck her like this.

Years, I imagine.

And for this, I am thankful.

Because tonight, I am his beacon. His release.

His prey.

"Open your mouth," he commands.

The clock reads 4:37 a.m. when I finally feel Dex pulsing inside of me for the last time, forgetting...*everything*.

My insides are throbbing with pain. My body is bruised, desecrated, wrecked. Wrecked in a twisted kind of bliss I've never before known.

My heroin.

Dex stays inside of me as he wraps me up in his arms, squeezing me so tightly to his sweaty body that I am momentarily without breath.

"Good girl, Willow," he whispers into my ear. "*Good girl.*"

As I lie in his arms, unable to sleep, I think that if I had to die, right now, after hours spent in the exquisite pain and pleasure of Dex's sex, *this* would be the perfect death.

14

SOPHIA

Tuesday the 16th of May, 2017
Somewhere over the Atlantic

I READ Eve's words as I am sitting in my comfy first-class seat, catapulting over the Atlantic Ocean to what feels like my own very imperfect death.

I close the book. I close my eyes. And I shudder.

The perfect death.

This is the writing prompt I give to my seniors each year for their final creative writing exam at NYU. They are to write at least 2,000 words on the topic in class, on the spot. In fact, I have forty-eight essays on *The Perfect Death* stuffed in my carry-on bag at this very moment, waiting to be graded.

"No topic is off limits," I always tell them. "Nothing is too dark. I've been giving this prompt for years, and trust me, I've read *everything*. There is beauty in death, beauty in the darkness and mystery of it all. I want you to unleash whatever you have lurking inside you. Whatever you've been afraid to say. Now is your moment. Let it out."

I ask my students to do the thing I will not do in my own writing. I haven't yet written about how I've wished for death to come so many times, on so many lonely nights, lying awake next to my husband as he sleeps, so soundly, as if he has no regrets.

I know he has them, of course. Regrets over the loss of his little sister, and years later, his broken-hearted mother. Regrets that he couldn't save either of them—as if a little boy could have had any power over the poverty he was born into or the illnesses that ravaged the only family he ever had.

Still, I know he blames himself, and even with this self-inflicted guilt, my Drew sleeps as soundly as a man who's never experienced an ounce of tragedy in his entire life.

I, on the other hand, lie awake for hours sometimes. Tortured by the past. By my own burning secrets, my own dreadful guilt. I've already felt dead inside for years. But I've never told this to my husband. Nor have I ever written about it in one of my books.

I suppose this is why I so desperately look forward to reading my students' musings on death. They're so young, so unfiltered, so raw. They haven't lived long enough to put up all of their walls the way I have. The way Drew has. The way we all do as life slashes and tears at our insides. Reading my students' essays makes me feel free again, alive, the way I used to be at uni before everything changed. Before I locked up my own soul and threw away the key.

Because no one wants to see what's really in there.

There was one essay over the years, however, that infuriated me. That left me unimpressed and uninspired. That reminded me too much of what I would have written, given the chance.

And it belonged to Eve Winters.

How could I have forgotten about this?

Her essay was beautiful, yes. I remember, at the time, feeling jealous at the effortless way she strung words together, already, at such a young age. It took me years to be that kind of writer, and it seemed that Eve was one of those girls who was just born with it. Gifted.

Which is why I told her what a bullshit essay she'd written.

"It's total rubbish," I said, tossing the essay across my desk.

I still remember the look in her eyes. She didn't appear surprised or hurt, the way I was expecting. Instead she nodded, tucked the paper into her bag, and said, "I know."

"Well, then, write it again. And this time, tell the bloody truth. That's the paper I'll grade."

Her voice came out stronger and more forceful than I'd expected. "I can't."

I took a step toward her, crossing my arms. "Can't what? Write how you really feel?"

"The truth," she said. "I can't write the truth."

A heavy silence settled between us, and there it was again. That haunted, ghostly look in her eyes.

"I won't," she said.

"Then I'm afraid I'll have to grade the paper you turned in, and it's not going to be good. You know I don't inflate grades."

"I know," she said. "Whatever it is, I'll take it."

Eve turned to let herself out of my office. I reached my hand out, grabbed her shoulder.

"Listen to me, Eve. Your writing is eloquent, beautiful, years ahead of your peers. Which is why I'm pushing you. If you don't start telling the truth in your writing now, you'll never make it in this business."

She shrugged me off of her, shot daggers at me with her eyes. "Don't you think that's a little hypocritical?"

"Excuse me?" I said, my voice too shrill for my own liking.

"Professor Grayson," she continued, "I've read every single one of your books. With all due respect, if anyone needs a lecture on telling the truth in her writing, it's you."

That little bitch.

With that, Eve left my office. I gave her a poor grade on her final paper, and we never spoke again.

I knew she was right. I still know she was right. And I hate her for it.

My fingers wrap ever tighter around Eve's memoir, around the brazen words that bear no semblance to the safe, boring, false ones she wrote all those years ago. And I realize that she finally took my advice to heart.

A bestseller and a dead girl in the making.

15

OFFICER JEAN-MARC DEVEREAUX

MARDI 16 MAI 2017
36 QUAI DES ORFÈVRES ~ PARIS, FRANCE

AFTER HOURS SPENT at the crime scene taking notes, Devereaux was back in his office at the infamous 36 Quai des Orfèvres. It was a historic building in the center of Paris that had housed the Brigade Criminelle for over 100 years. It was his workplace, yes, but more than that, it had been his second home for the past twelve years.

And in only a few short months, that home would be taken away from him.

The Brigade Criminelle would be moving to a new state-of-the-art building in Paris' 17th arrondissement. 36 rue du Bastion would be their new address.

As if keeping the 36 would make the place feel like home.

The hallway outside Devereaux's closed door buzzed with the voices of his colleagues, but he paid no attention. Sitting among the piles upon piles of *dossiers* stacked on his desk, the floor, and every other possible surface, he had entered another world.

Eve's world.

He'd just finished the chapter where Dex had bent her over the table in the foyer of their penthouse suite. Where Eve had watched his silver cross necklace banging against his chest. Where Eve had realized that she liked spreading her legs for this man.

And Devereaux could not put the book down.

It all felt so real to him, the way she described her fear over becoming some rich man's prostitute for the night. The way she hated and loved her sister all in the same breath.

The way she enjoyed Dex's total and complete possession of her from the minute he first laid eyes on her, and the way she despised him for wanting him so badly.

It felt so real, in fact, that Devereaux wished he was the one bending her over the table. It had been way too long.

An image of Mia's petite body bent over their kitchen table assaulted him. The way her ass would curve into him, the way her long strawberry hair would cascade down her bare back, the way her little breasts would bounce with each thrust of his hips into hers.

It used to drive him mad.

It still did.

He squeezed his eyes shut just for a moment, and in his darkness, he could still hear her voice. The power that would emanate from those vocal cords when she was gearing up to come. When she would tell him to come inside of her. Always and only inside of her.

It was intoxicating.

But in his memory, when she turned her head around to look at him just as he did what she'd demanded, he didn't see Mia's stunning green eyes or her thin pink lips. He didn't see the innocent freckles on her dainty nose.

Instead, he saw Eve's smoky-blue eyes. Eve's full wet lips.

Eve's smooth olive skin.

Devereaux snapped his eyes open, shook his head. "*Putain.*"

Now wasn't the time to think about sex. Not with the girl he'd lost. And *especially* not with the one he was trying to find.

Eve needed an advocate on her side. A fighter.

Not a predator.

16

THE MISTRESS OF PARIS: A MEMOIR

BY EVE WINTERS

LE 12 JUILLET 2016
HÔTEL GEORGE V ~ PARIS, FRANCE

THE COLD HARD truth of the morning hits me as soon as the first blast of sunlight greets my sleepy eyes. Dex is already in the shower, preparing for his day. Our night of ecstasy is officially over, and all that is left for me to do is collect the money...*and go*.

The idea that I may never see Dex again pulls my stomach into knots.

Who am I kidding? Of course I'm never going to see him again. I am not actually a prostitute, and I certainly couldn't continue pretending to be one just to spend another night—*or perhaps, several*—with him.

I climb out of bed slowly and pace over to the mirror to examine the wreckage. There are a few small bruises on my neck and collar bone; my breasts are raw from Dex's teeth, his rough hands; and when I turn around, I find a large purple blotch spreading across my butt.

The memory of Dex's hand coming down hard on my

ass as he took me from behind startles me, and I have to grab onto the mirror to steady myself.

I remember liking it. *Loving it.*

Was that really me?

My body isn't the only disaster zone—the once-pristine penthouse is now a total mess. Lamps are overturned, pillows are strewn carelessly about, and smears of blood—my blood—stain the angel white sheets. My stomach churns at the sight of crimson. I turn my face away, close my eyes to block it all out, but images of Willow's blood splattered on my bathroom floor assault me.

My blood. Her blood.

Our blood.

In only one night, I have really and truly become her.

Dex walks out of the bathroom just then, towel wrapped around his waist, seeming totally nonplussed with the wreckage surrounding us.

I gesture to the lamps and the pillows. "Should we...?"

He shakes his head. "Not for you to worry about, beautiful; I tip well."

Let's hope so.

I gather my—well, *Willow's*—lacy red thong and bra from the floor and slip them back on. When I turn around, Dex is standing behind me with two large envelopes.

"Speaking of money, I'm sorry I forgot to take care of this when we first got up here last night." He takes a step closer, places a hand on my hip. "After I saw you walk into the lounge...I couldn't wait another second to be inside you."

His words send chills through my entire body. The power he already has over me is astounding.

He hands me the first envelope. It's thick. 5,000 euros thick.

Then he tucks the second one into my bra, leans forward, and kisses the skin on my breast around it.

Even though we had sex for hours and hours last night, even though my body couldn't possibly take more of this insatiable man, I find myself still wanting more of him. But Dex doesn't linger for too long before he walks over to the closet, begins getting dressed for the day. I pull the second envelope out of my bra and realize it is just as thick as the first one. Should I go to the bathroom and count this like Willow instructed me to do?

"Don't worry, it's all in there," Dex says, reading my mind.

I hold up the second envelope. "What's this?"

He grins. Deviously. "Like I said, I tip well."

I haven't followed *any* of the rules Willow gave me:

Collect the money and count it before he touches me.

Text her to let her know I'm okay.

Use condoms.

And I'm sure there are some other unspoken rules, too, like don't kiss on the mouth and don't develop feelings for the man who is paying you for sex, or ever, *ever* expect to see him again.

All of that went up in flames, and so I figure why bother counting the money now?

Tucking both envelopes into my purse, I take a quick trip to the bathroom to freshen up. Then I slip back into Willow's tight black dress, so wishing I had thought to bring clothes for the morning trip home.

There has never been a walk of shame that will be as shameful as this one.

Dex is dressed in a sleek gray suit as he walks me to the door. We stand there for a moment, and I take one last inhale of the man I have allowed to do things to me that no man has ever done. He has seen a side of me that, before last night, I didn't even know existed. I thought only Willow carried around such darkness; clearly, I've been wrong all along.

I must go, though. And if I don't want to become any more like my sister, I must go *now.*

I begin to turn away, but Dex reaches a forceful hand around my waist, pulls me close.

"Willow, I have a proposal for you."

I arch a brow, pretending to act all cool and calm, even though inside I'm already screaming with satisfaction at the thought that he might want to see me again. And screaming at myself for being happy about this.

"Yes?" I say.

"Are you booked this Saturday?"

He's running a hand up the inside of my thigh, making it nearly impossible for me to concentrate.

Yes, I'm booked. This was just one night, Dex.

Say it. Say it. Say it!

But my tongue doesn't obey. "No, I believe I'm free."

His lips brush my ear, his tongue tracing my earlobe before he whispers, "I would like to invite you back for another night...and I'd like to take you somewhere."

"Oh? And where would that be?"

"A club I like to visit from time to time...a very *exclusive* club."

"A swingers club?" The words trickle from my mouth as if I've been to hundreds of them, when in reality of course, I've been to none.

He moves my thong to the side, pushes his fingers inside me. It's raw and painful...but strangely, still amazing.

"God, you are endlessly wet," he breathes.

I run my hand down his chest, wanting to tear this crisp

white shirt right off of him.

He pushes my back up against the door, spreads my legs with his knee.

"So...will you join me?" he whispers.

No. No. No.

When I don't respond, he pulls my hair back, plunges his lips down my neck. His mouth slides farther down, covering the tops of my breasts, before he lifts his face back up to mine.

I lick my lips and tease him a bit with a breathy, "Hmmm...not sure."

With that, he flips me around to face the door, and I hear him unbuckling his pants. Music to my ears.

It takes Dex only seconds to have my dress bunched up around my waist, and to find his way back inside of me. Exactly like it all started last night, when I strutted into this penthouse suite, just a clueless girl pretending to be a prostitute.

My, how things have already changed.

In my ear, Dex's voice booms powerful and clear.

"Just so you know, beautiful, a night at the club with me means double the money and double the tip."

Holy shit.

I think about my blood smeared on the sheets this morning, the bruises splattered on my skin, the way my insides are still throbbing in pain as he takes more of me. More than I ever knew I had to give.

And if I join him at this club? Let other men fuck me the way he is doing now? How much blood will be shed then?

How much blood do you want to shed?

Willow's voice travels through my head. I can barely tell the difference now between her voice and mine.

It's her darkness.

It's mine.

It's ours.

And I know the answer to our question:

I want to shed it all. Every fucking drop.

And so I tell him, "*Yes.*"

"Good girl," he says. "*Good girl.*"

I can still feel Dex inside of me as I take the elevator down to the lobby. I bypass all of the high-class guests as I take a turn down the hallway in search of the restrooms. Inside, I slip into one of the pristine stalls, and I remove the first envelope from my purse. It's time for this phony high-class prostitute to count her bounty.

My hands are shaking, making it difficult to count quickly, but it is all there—5,000 euros worth of one-hundred-euro bills.

I lick my lips. Open the second envelope.

And I count.

Holy shit.

Another 5,000 euros.

I stand in the stall, unable to move. Eyes glued to the cash.

One night. *Ten thousand euros.*

I have been scraping by for months now. Living on what little money I have left in savings. I have been writing and writing and writing to get things moving again. Pitching stories, article ideas, book ideas to every agent and editor I can find, but *nothing* has taken.

I came to Paris to write, to be inspired.

To escape.

Escaping would be a lot more fun with money.

It's something Willow would say. But I have to admit, I agree.

Just a few more nights with Dex would be enough to tide me over for an entire year. And if it were more than just a few nights? If this went on for some time...I could be set for *years*. I could write whatever I want without the pressure of looming unpaid bills. I could buy my own apartment. Travel. Escape whenever and wherever I want. After years of cleaning up Willow's messes, living for her, keeping *her* alive, letting her take, take, take...I would finally have enough—*more than enough*—to live my own life.

I would be tethered to no one.

The price?

My body.

My heart.

No. If I do this, my heart must stay out of it. It's a business transaction. Sex for money. And then, *freedom*.

When I emerge from the stall and gaze in the mirror, I find that I am smiling. Beaming, actually, and I didn't even realize it.

With my head held high, I strut right out of the magnificent George V hotel, not caring if the prissy guests or the stuffy front desk staff or the regal doorman know that in the span of one unexpected night, I've become a whore.

The glorious sum of money in my purse and the promise of more have me not giving a damn.

As I take to the streets of Paris a changed woman, I hear her voice again—it's Willow's voice, my voice, *our* voice. The voice of our darkness.

Strong, devious, and unapologetic, she announces to the world:

And just like that, a prostitute is born.

17

EVE

The When: Unknown
The Where: Unknown

Karma.
You.
Fucking.
Bitch.

No mercy…
Even though I tried.
So hard.
To save her.
And even,
For once…
Myself.

Mother, are you up there?
You're still angry, aren't you mother?
Laughing your crazy sick cackle.

Mother.
It all started with you.

But tonight, no.
It's not you.
Tonight, my lovely...
It all begins with Karma.
Yours.
And Ketamine.
Mine.

You're mine.

18

THE MISTRESS OF PARIS: A MEMOIR

BY EVE WINTERS

LE 16 JUILLET 2016
RUE DES BERNARDINS ~ PARIS, FRANCE

WILLOW HAS MOVED in with me again. This isn't the first time she's seriously screwed up her life and moved back into mine without warning. And this isn't the first time I've opened my arms, my heart, my home to her...and lost myself in the process.

This *is*, however, the first time I've blatantly lied to her.

She is standing in my bathroom wearing a black thong that is tucked so tightly beneath her voluptuous curves, the material is barely visible. Her breasts are spilling out of her black lacy bra, and her gaze is fixed on herself in the mirror as she applies a generous layer of cover-up to the bruises that are still marring her beautiful face.

On the other side of the steamy shower door, I'm shaving my legs. Quickly. I'm running late.

"Going out tonight?" Willow asks.

"Yeah, just meeting some friends out for a drink." By friends I mean Dex. And by a drink, I mean my very first visit to a sex club *and* my second night as a high-end call girl.

"Dex didn't ask to see you again, did he?" Willow asks.

Her question catches me off-guard, but I don't falter. "No."

Through the steamy shower doors, I swear I see her smirk.

"What?" I snap.

"Oh, nothing...I...I'm just happy he paid you."

"Well, I fucked him for you, didn't I?" My hand slips and I slice the skin below my ankle bone. "Shit."

"Yes. You did," she says, immediately humbling her tone. "And you saved my ass, you really did."

I saved your fucking life.

When I don't respond, she turns, looks through the shower door at me. "He hasn't contacted you since that night, has he?"

"He doesn't even have my number," I lie, remembering the moment just before I left the penthouse suite when I gave him my personal cell. I'd told him that the number he'd been using before—*Willow's number*—was only for one-time clients.

And Dex clearly wasn't going to be a one-time client.

"You're not going to try to see him again, are you?" my sister quizzes.

"What is this, Willow? Of course not. I'm a writer; I'm not a goddamned prostitute."

She rips open the shower door so violently I'm surprised it doesn't come unhinged; she certainly has.

She stares me down, her eyes fixating on the blood tricking down my ankle.

"What the hell, Willow?"

Finally, she lifts her gaze. Our eyes meet through the

curtain of steam that is bleeding out into my tiny Parisian bathroom. Who am I kidding? It's not mine anymore. It's hers. Everything she touches, she takes.

"You need to promise me you'll never see him again." Willow's tone is that of a mother bear—and for a moment, it scares me.

"I'm not going to see him again," I assure her.

"*Eve.* I'm serious. This business can be...well, it can be really dangerous. And a man like Dex...well, he's powerful. And I just don't want you—"

"Oh, *now* you warn me about how dangerous it can be? Don't you think it's a little too late for that?" I grab her hands and turn them face-up so the jagged scars slicing her palms are in plain sight. "Selling your body is dangerous enough, but then you go and take the cut you were supposed to be giving to your *Madame* and give it to your cracked-out boyfriend instead, actually believing he would pay you back? Well, you got paid back." I'm so angry I'm shaking her hands now. I can't help myself. If I could, I would cut them myself. "By the sick thug who does your pimp's dirty work for her...and now by me, who has once again, saved you. And I'm finished, Willow. Do you hear me? You can stay here until you get your shit together enough to move out. But I'm never—*never*—cleaning up your messes ever again."

She pulls her wrists from my death grip, and then I see them—the tears she never, ever cries.

Only two, though—one from each of her sad eyes. The tears slide down her cheeks, streaking through the makeup she's just applied to cover up the shame, the guilt, and the horror of everything she has done to land here. On my doorstep, covered in bruises, demanding that I sell my own body to pay her debts. So that she doesn't get hurt again. So that the thug who beat her to a pulp doesn't come back to kill her.

Willow stands in the midst of the steam, in silence, letting the tears roll all the way down to her chin. She doesn't reach up to wipe them away. Instead, she blinks back the others that are threatening to pour, and she speaks. So softly I barely hear her.

"I just don't want you to get hurt, Eve. I don't know what I would have done if something had happened..."

She doesn't finish her sentence. Instead she turns and walks out of my bathroom. A few moments later, I hear the front door to my apartment slam. I hope she never comes back.

Willow's warning hangs in the thick summer air, taunting me for the entire cab ride to the George V. But I ignore her warning. Her two tears. The fear she has lodged into my chest. I have to in order to do what I'm about to do.

When I knock on the regal door of the penthouse suite, the man who is paying me an inordinate sum of money to be his courtesan for another night doesn't even let me walk inside before he bunches up my dress around my waist, pulls down my own barely visible thong, parts my legs, and kneels down in front of me.

I'm backed against the open door, Dex's face between my legs, not caring in the least if someone walks past. I'm in ecstasy. And I never want it to end.

I just don't want you to get hurt, Eve.

My fingers dig into Dex's thick head of hair. My legs spread a little more, and still more.

It's too late, Willow. It's too damn late.

19

EVE

The When: Unknown
The Where: Unknown

Ketamine and karma.
Karma and ketamine.

Willow and Eve.
Kate and Sara.

Two ferocious sisters.
One deranged mother.
An excuse for a father.

A deadly cocktail.
I mixed it in the kitchen.
With the black-and-white tiles.
A blender of crimson.
I drank every last drop.

20

THE MISTRESS OF PARIS: A MEMOIR

BY EVE WINTERS

LE 16 JUILLET 2016
HÔTEL GEORGE V ~ PARIS, FRANCE

CHAMPAGNE AND COCAINE.

Dex has fed me an even stronger cocktail of the two this time for our first trip to the club together.

His hungry mouth on my neck and his forceful hands up my dress keep the windows of the fancy black town car sufficiently steamed up so that I have absolutely no clue what Parisian neighborhood we have arrived in when the car stops.

Before we get out of the car, Dex grabs my chin, looks me intently in the eyes.

"Whatever I need you to do in there tonight, you'll do. Yes?"

I swallow the nerves that are telling me to get out of the car and run the other way, and I force myself to nod. "Of course."

"Good girl."

Minutes later, I have stripped off the thin fabric of my

dress and have handed it over to a woman wearing four-inch heels and nothing else. Her gaze flashes back and forth between the package that protrudes from Dex's tight black boxer briefs and my bare breasts before she winks at me.

"*Amusez-vous bien.*" *Have fun,* she says with a crooked smile.

"*Merci,*" Dex tells her as he slides his fingers along the string of my skimpy black thong—the only piece of clothing I am wearing as we cross into this new universe together.

Well, I am wearing heels too—a pair of my sister's shiny black stilettos—and of course more of her fake diamonds around my neck.

Nothing completes the call-girl look like the sparkle of fake diamonds.

Dex leads me past the first main mingling area where women are strolling around mostly naked, a few in lingerie, cocktails in hand, with nearly naked men by their sides, sizing up the other couples they may end up sleeping with later in the night.

"Should we...?" I ask, nodding toward the room.

He shakes his head. "Too tame for us, beautiful. Follow me."

His palm wraps tightly around mine as he leads me down darkened corridors of the *club libertin* as it's called in French, past red-tinted rooms filled with sweaty bodies, spread legs, and the rubbery smell of condoms. I brought that same roll of condoms with me tonight—the roll that I didn't even touch my first night with Dex. I don't expect that Dex will use them on me, of course, but if we invite another man—or other *men*—into the mix, I will want that protection.

The idea of another man inside of me while Dex

watches makes me feel a bit nauseous, but also, strangely, a bit excited.

As if he can read my mind, Dex peers back at me and lifts only the left side of his luscious lips into a devious grin.

"*Ça va, ma belle?*" he whispers. *Everything okay, beautiful?*

I nod, grinning back, trying not to show my nerves. I'm a pro, after all. I am Willow. An experienced call girl who's visited swingers clubs like this one tons of times. A girl who's spread her legs for more men than she can count on any given night, and who's loved every minute.

I lean forward, slice my tongue down his neck and give him a raspy whisper.

"*Oui, ça va.*"

He responds by pressing my back against the wall and kissing me on the mouth. His teeth find my lower lip, and he bites hard. So hard that I immediately taste the salty warmth of my own blood trickling into my mouth.

"Come," he commands after releasing his bite.

I lick the blood from my lip as Dex leads me into a shadowy room at the end of the hallway. Inside, layers of wispy violet curtains frame three large beds covered in silky black sheets and sweaty bodies. On one of the beds, a young girl with long wavy hair the color of black ink lies on her back, tiny breasts taut toward the ceiling as a much older man buries his face between her legs and another lowers himself into her mouth.

Dex's hand cups my ass and squeezes it tight as we weave between the beds, finding similar scenes in each one. An entanglement of legs, hands, lips, and hips swirl through the steamy room, and I wonder which pile Dex will have me jump into.

My gut clenches. My mouth goes dry.

Do I really want to do this?

I don't have much more time to contemplate what I do or do not want to do with my body as Dex pulls me to the back of the room where a hidden door lies just behind the headboard of the bed that is now rocking with a new vigor as the older man between the young girl's legs has risen up and entered her. With each moan she releases, he pushes harder. Soon his movements are borderline violent, but she only cries out in more pleasure as it escalates. I can hardly tear my gaze from them, but Dex pulls on my hand, prodding me through the doorway.

We make our way down an even longer, darker corridor this time, the sounds of ecstasy fading in the background behind us.

At the end of the hallway, another door.

This one requires a key, though. A key that Dex is holding with his other hand.

"I told you this was exclusive," he whispers as he turns the key in the lock. "You didn't think I was going to fuck you in there with all that riff-raff, did you beautiful?"

He doesn't give me a chance to answer.

Instead he pulls me through the door, closes and locks it behind us.

There is an elevator, all shiny glass, right before us. Dex opens the door and nods for me to get in. He doesn't step in with me, though. Instead he pushes the number 6 and begins to close the door.

I reach my hand out. "Why aren't you getting in?"

Dex doesn't smile. He doesn't give me any kind of comforting look. Instead he says, "Remember when I said I would need you to do whatever I asked tonight? Well, I need you to take this elevator up to the sixth floor and not ask another question. Just do what you're told, beautiful. I'll see you soon."

With that he closes the door, and the old, rickety glass elevator carries me up, up, up, all the way to the sixth floor. I'm queasy and sweating the entire way up. What in the hell is this? How could he just leave me?

When I arrive at the sixth floor, I open the door to total darkness. I hesitate, considering pushing the button to go back down to the ground floor, but my hesitation lasts a second too long.

"*Eh, voilà. Mademoiselle Willow.* I have been waiting for you."

It's a voice I've never heard before. A man's voice—deep and strangely soothing, with more than a hint of a French accent laced into his English words.

"Come, take a step forward," he says.

I do as I'm told, albeit on wobbly legs, and just as I have done so, a hand finds the small of my back and prods me forward. I jump, even though the hand is delicate and soft and small. The hand of a woman.

And then her voice in my ear. "*N'aie pas peur ma belle.*" *Don't be afraid, beautiful.*

Now she is behind me, both of her hands on my waist, guiding me forward. I take a deep breath and walk, telling myself I am going to be okay. Telling myself this is *not* the moment where I get kidnapped and sold into some sort of sick sex trafficking ring.

But what in the hell else could this—?

I am stopped by another set of hands. Strong, big—they're his.

"*Eh, voilà,*" he says again, now running those hands over my breasts, his calluses scratching my smooth skin.

Meanwhile the girl is running her hands down over the

curves of my ass, and without giving me a say in the matter, she slips my thong all the way down to the ground.

"*Monsieur Dex* has told me so much about you," the man says, his hands now slithering lower and lower on my abdomen. "I couldn't wait to feel you with my own hands."

"Who are—" I begin. But his fingers find my lips, shushing me.

"We will have all night to get to know each other my dear. But right now, all you need to know is that you are safe and your man Dex will be here soon. He is just opening a few...*presents*...I wanted to give him before he makes his way back to you. And right now, my darling, I need you to open your mouth."

Presents? Is Dex with other women right now?

Of course he is, you idiot. You're in a swingers club.

Why did I ever agree to do this?

"Your mouth," he says again. "*Open*."

My options seem pretty limited at this point, and even though this very well could be a ticket to hell, I take a deep breath in through my nose and do as I'm told. A pill lands on my tongue. Then a glass in my hand.

"Take a drink and swallow," he instructs.

My eyes are only just beginning to adjust to the darkness as I swallow the mystery pill with a gulp of what tastes like straight vodka.

The man's domineering shadow looms over me, his breath hot and eager as he steps forward, sliding a hand behind my neck. The woman is pressed against my back, her hands gripping my hips.

"Have you ever done ecstasy, my love?" he asks, his lips trailing over my collar bone.

I haven't, of course, but now isn't the time to reveal my lack of experience.

I nod my head yes.

"And have you ever been with a man and a woman at the same time?"

I nod yes again.

And again, another lie.

What's one more lie added to the bed of them upon which I'm building my new life?

"And two men, two women?" he asks.

I nod again.

"Three and three?"

I hesitate.

"Ahhh, I see," he says. "Then this is where we must begin. Dex wants to see his new *courtesan* a little bit overwhelmed, you see. In a new situation, something you have not yet experienced. It will make him jealous, angry perhaps, but this jealousy, this anger will make him hungrier for you. And you for him. Are you ready my darling?"

I nod.

The biggest lie of the night.

An hour or so later, the ecstasy has taken over, and I am in love. So much love. With him. With her. With her. With him. With all of them. There are at least six, seven, eight of them. I can't keep track. It's just bodies and lips and hearts rolling around in this massive bed in this elegant bedroom. There is music pumping through my blood and men pumping into me, one after the next after the next. Women kissing me and eating me and mounting me.

I don't know where I end and they begin.

I've never felt so whole.

It is while I am riding the height of this wave that I find a familiar pair of eyes in the shadows. They're watching me, wanting me, adoring me, *loving me*.

It's Dex.

I beam my brightest, sexiest smile in his direction, all the while welcoming a man inside me from behind. I'm on my hands and knees as a woman slides beneath me and circles my nipples with her tongue. I lean down and kiss her, loving how salty and sweet and luscious she tastes. The man behind me pounds harder, and as I moan, I lift my head to find Dex's eyes still on me. There is a woman kneeling in front of him, pleasing him with her mouth. He is gripping her hair, moving her head back and forth.

But his eyes, they only want me.

I nod for him to come my way.

He doesn't hesitate.

In seconds he has removed all obstacles between us, and he is covering me with his body, burying me, kissing me, spreading my legs with his knees, plunging inside of me.

"I've been watching you the whole time," he says, picking up his speed.

"And?"

He flips me over without warning, pushing into me from behind. Even in my ecstasy-filled state, I know this is his way of asserting his control over me.

He presses me hard into the mattress, his face covering mine. "I hated every second, Willow. Every damn second. I want you to be mine. Only mine. Do you understand?"

I nod.

And for the first time of the night, it's not a lie.

I flip over on top of him, coat him in my salty wet kisses. When I make my way back up to his mouth, I tell him, "I'm yours Dex Anderson. Always. Forever. Yours."

We make love into the wee hours of the night, just the two of us. There may be piles of bodies surrounding us or not. I don't really know. I don't care.

All I see, all I know, all I want, is Dex.

He takes me beyond the drugs to a level of ecstasy I didn't know was possible.

There are not one hundred men in the universe who could take me to this place.

Only one.

Only Dex.

Just before the first light of dawn graces our darkened chamber, I am on my hands and knees, legs spread for the only man who is allowed inside me anymore.

When he finishes, I rest my tired body on the sheets. The drugs are wearing off. My eyes are heavy, but my heart is still on fire.

A hint of morning light peeks through a set of angel white curtains.

And I see them.

Three bold drops of crimson staining the pristine white sheets in this glorious, mysterious penthouse suite we have found ourselves in.

One drop for money.

Two drops for freedom.

Three drops for—

Sex?

Ecstasy?

Love?

Dex's hand covers the stains.

A quick glance up, and there, blocking the light, stands my dealer.

The drugs my heart has always needed, served at my bedside in one magnificent package.

He's smiling.

My heart races...almost like I've just taken another hit of cocaine.

It's such a beautiful smile.

I slide my hand beneath his so I can feel...

The blood.

My blood.

Every glorious drop.

Willow's voice arrives with a soft thud in the hollows of my soul...just as Dex climbs back into bed with me.

Be careful what you wish for.

21

SOPHIA

Wednesday the 17th of May, 2017
Charles de Gaulle Airport ~ Paris, France

"One drop for money.
Two drops for freedom.
Three drops for death.
Mine.
Hers.
Ours.
I always knew it was coming.
I just hadn't imagined it knocking on my door so soon."

The final haunting words of Eve's memoir replay in my head as I deboard the plane at Charles de Gaulle. I didn't sleep on the flight. I haven't eaten a single bite since before I got rid of my last meal on the dining room floor.

I have been consumed by her story. By her 275 pages of raw, unadulterated sex, passion, jealousy, and terror.

My own terror over the idea that *my Drew* may actually

be the married man in her book has turned me into a complete madwoman over the course of the six-hour flight.

The sex. The drugs. The money.

The lies. The jealousy. The violence.

The love.

If it's him—if it really is *my husband* she's writing about —I could kill him.

I would kill him.

In a sleep-deprived haze, I ride along on a moving sidewalk that is gliding through some futuristic-looking glass bubble, and I close my eyes, imagining the murder.

Before I do it, I would show him a video of me and my lover screwing like animals, the way he has been screwing Eve. I would show it to him over and over again, make the wanker watch every sordid detail of the dirty things we do to each other in bed, of the way my lover makes me come, endlessly, so that Drew would feel as sick as I'm feeling right now.

And then, with a gun—

No.

A knife.

I would go straight for his heart.

The image of Drew's chest sliced open is soon replaced with a pregnant Eve. My husband's hand on her belly. A baby that looks like Drew. *His* baby.

Their baby.

Eve missed her period, right at the end of the sodding book.

Couldn't even wait another two minutes to finish the damn thing and tell us the results of the pregnancy test.

I grip the railing. Feeling faint. Pain stabbing at my womb.

Or what's left of it.

His heart.

I will go straight for his fucking heart.

Blood-soaked sheets. They're warm. Sticky.

Nauseating.

And I'm alone.

My baby is gone.

Tears fall, but they are meaningless drops in this crimson ocean that has become my bed.

I'm so sorry.

I'm so sorry.

I'm so sorry.

"Madame, madame. Ça va, madame? Madame!"

My eyelids lift. Slow. Heavy. The weight is unbearable.

A blurry face hovering over mine.

The scent of bad breath invading my nostrils.

"Calmez-vous. Je ne vais pas vous faire mal, madame."

Calm down. I'm not going to hurt you.

Only then do I realize I'm crying. Convulsing.

The blood.

The baby.

"I'm sorry," I cry. "I'm so sorry."

"Madame, ça va aller."

And at once, I stop, realizing where I am.

As I lift my head, I find a crowd of concerned travelers circling me.

Bloody hell. I've passed out in the airport. And cried. A hysterical mess on the floor.

My mother's voice pounds through my temples.

Strong start to the trip, Sophia. Well done, love.

I sit up with a start, but I'm too dizzy to get to my feet. And too livid with Eve for writing about the blood on the sheets. As if I needed another reminder when I'm already flying into the city where it all...*no.*

Can't go there.

Mustn't.

"*Lentement, madame. Lentement.*"

The man who is calling me *madame* and telling me to take it slowly better get the hell out of my way. I give him a curt nod, mumble a barely audible *merci,* then leverage my hand on his arm to stand. I'm wobbly and sick.

Really, truly sick.

I haven't received the call from my doctor yet with the results, but I already know.

She'd probably have a fit if she knew I'd flown to Paris when I've been feeling as badly as I have been.

But then I imagine *she* probably doesn't suspect that her husband is shagging a pretend-prostitute in Paris, falling in love with her, and possibly impregnating the whore.

No, not at all likely.

Gathering my carry-on and my purse, I push through the bewildered crowd and find my way to the loo to splash some water on my face before I head into the City of Light. The City of Darkness.

The city I wish I could destroy.

Perhaps I will.

22

OFFICER JEAN-MARC DEVEREAUX

MERCREDI 17 MAI 2017
36 QUAI DES ORFÈVRES ~ PARIS, FRANCE

IT WAS another *nuit blanche* for Devereaux, not uncommon the first night after discovering a crime scene. He'd left his report on Breton's desk at 20h00 on the dot and had spent the rest of the night holed up in his office with the door closed, finishing Eve's sordid memoir.

And it was sordid.

The part that was sticking in his mind the most at this hazy moment just before sunrise was Eve and Dex's trip to the sex club. Jean-Marc himself had never visited those types of clubs for leisure. Even if the allure of the whole experience was more than tempting, it simply wasn't in the best interest of an officer of the Brigade to be spotted in those dirty underground bedrooms, swapping partners, losing control.

But for work purposes, he'd combed their grimy floors more times than he'd like to count. Anytime a prostitute went missing—which had been happening quite often in recent years—off to the sex clubs he went.

This time, though, instead of heading straight to the clubs where the owners and the girls who worked for them were as sketchy and tight-lipped as they come, Devereaux went to the one person in his life who knew all about those clubs: his sister, Coralie.

It was 5:37 a.m. when he arrived on rue de Malte in the 11th arrondissement and punched in the door code he knew by heart. He took the stairs two at a time all the way up to the fifth floor, where Coralie now lived with Julien Breton, Jean-Marc's boss.

Jean-Marc's former best friend.

It had only been a month since Coralie had taken the baby and moved out of Jean-Marc's apartment and into Julien's. In that month, Jean-Marc had hardly seen her or the baby. And he'd be the first to admit that his little investigatory spree this morning was just as much to find answers on Eve's case as it was a ploy to hold his sweet niece in his arms. He missed her more than he could bear to think about most days.

Jean-Marc knew his sister was often up this early feeding the baby, and even if she wasn't, he didn't care. He'd wake her up. He'd woken up every night for the first several months of Adelaide's life to feed her and let Coralie rest. Now he needed help, and it was Coralie's turn to wake up for him.

Before he even knocked on the door, he could hear his niece's piercing cry emanating from inside the apartment. The sound was strangely comforting. He missed it—or rather, he missed being the one to hold her in his arms and make that desperate little cry go away.

Jean-Marc knocked once, twice, and a third time before

finally, a flustered Coralie answered the door. In the dim light emanating from inside the apartment, Jean-Marc noticed that his sister's short blond hair was stuck to her cheeks, and the dark circles which had lined her big blue eyes for years now seemed even more pronounced than before.

"Mais qu'est-ce que tu fous là ?" What the hell are you doing here? Coralie hissed at her brother.

"It's wonderful to see you too," Jean-Marc said in French, pushing past her into his boss' apartment, stopping when he noticed the piles of dirty baby laundry on the couch. He'd spent many a night on that same black couch, popping open another beer, talking out the latest case with his boss and closest friend. Now that couch served a new purpose. Devereaux didn't know if he'd ever get used to it.

"Is Julien with the baby?" he asked his sister.

"No, he's asleep," she snapped. "I was just going to go get her."

Why the fuck is he asleep? Jean-Marc wanted to ask but he bit his tongue. Instead, he offered to help. "I'll go get her."

Coralie placed a firm hand on her brother's chest. "*Non.* I'll do it. Stay here. I'll bring her to you."

"Okay..." Jean-Marc said, already quite satisfied to see that things didn't seem to be running all that smoothly in lovers' paradise, after all.

A few moments later, Coralie emerged with a red-faced Adelaide and practically tossed the baby into her brother's arms. He gratefully accepted the package, walking his little niece to the window and humming a lullaby in her ear. She always loved it when he sang to her, and this morning, it seemed, was no different. He had her calmed down in minutes.

Coralie, however, was anything but calm. She proceeded to circle the apartment in what appeared to be an attempt to tidy up, but in reality, she was only making the place more of a mess than it already was.

Jean-Marc shook his head while holding his niece tightly to his chest.

"You never should've moved out," he whispered.

She tossed a baby towel to the floor and flipped her angry gaze up to her brother. "Oh, what? I was supposed to live there with you forever and never have my own life? I fell in love, Jean-Marc. Don't you want that for me?"

Love seemed like a strong word for what he'd witnessed between his sister and his boss. More like *lust*.

"I want you to be happy. But this..." he trailed off, his eyes combing the dirty baby bottles on the kitchen counter, the piles of unwashed laundry, the toys littering the floor. "Did you ever think that maybe Julien wasn't ready for all of this?"

"Maybe *you* weren't ready for me to have my own life." Coralie snatched the towel up from the floor and tossed it onto the armchair. "What are you doing here so early?"

Jean-Marc continued bouncing Baby Adelaide in his arms, wishing he could just be alone with the baby and not have to deal with his sleep-deprived, emotionally exhausting sister. But he had questions to ask her. Work to do.

And now that she and the baby lived with Julien, and Mia was gone, all he had left was his work. So he'd better get to it.

"I need to ask you a few questions," he said. "About those clubs you used to go to."

"What clubs?"

Jean-Marc leveled a glare at his little sister. "You know what I'm talking about."

Coralie crossed her arms over her chest. He realized then that she was actually wearing clothes—a long-sleeved black sweater, black pajama pants, and socks. Normally, his promiscuous little sister was barely clothed; she couldn't be bothered to get dressed most days when she'd lived with him. Coralie was curvy and voluptuous the way their mother had been, which wasn't all that common for a French woman, and drew way too much unnecessary male attention to her, in Jean-Marc's brotherly opinion. He was actually happy to see she was wearing real clothing in Julien's apartment. At least she looked more like a mother this way, even if she still wasn't totally acting like one.

"Fine," she said. "What do you want to know, and why is it so urgent that you're knocking on my door before it's even six in the morning? *Putain.*"

Jean-Marc held the baby in his left arm so he could reach into his back pocket with his other hand. He pulled out a photograph of Eve Winters and presented it to his sister.

"Did you ever see this girl at the clubs?"

Coralie took the photo in her hand and stared blankly at Eve's face. She shook her head and handed the photo back to Jean-Marc. "Never."

"You're sure? You barely looked at it."

He shoved the photo back into her line of sight. She took one more quick glance before replying, "I'm sure."

"Ever hear the name Eve Winters?"

She shook her head again and went back to moving dirty laundry from one location to another. Her version of cleaning. "No, doesn't ring a bell."

Jean-Marc wasn't sure how many names or faces *would*

ring a bell in his sister's dazed head given the amount of heavy drugs she was on when she used to frequent those clubs, but still, he thought it was worth trying.

Or maybe he'd just really needed to hold Adelaide.

He tucked the photo back into his pocket and continued bouncing his chubby little niece as she drifted off to sleep in his arms.

"Do you know of a club with a glass elevator?" he whispered so as not to wake the baby. "Apparently this elevator takes you to a more exclusive part of the club."

She let out a forced laugh. "You and I both know I wasn't visiting the *exclusive* parts of those clubs, Jean-Marc."

He cringed internally, hating to think of his sister in those environments. Doing drugs, sleeping with God knows how many men...*and* women. Accepting money for sexual favors. It was a fucking disaster. He'd often seen Coralie's pregnancy with Adelaide as the thing that had saved her from herself. But watching her now, an angry young mother standing in a pile of her baby's dirty laundry, shooting daggers at him with her crazed eyes, he wasn't so sure she could ever be saved from herself. If becoming a mother and living with two different Brigade Criminelle officers—one after the other—didn't make her straighten up, what in the hell would?

"You're sure you've never heard the name Eve Winters?" he pressed.

She gave a firm nod. "Positive. Why are you asking? Who is this girl and what happened to her?"

"An American writer. Well, prostitute turned writer. Released a book this week about her prostitution escapades, then went missing on release day."

"That all sounds terribly sad, but if you'll excuse me, I

need to put my baby down and try to sleep before she wakes up in two hours and needs to eat again. I'm fucking exhausted, Jean-Marc."

Coralie reached for Adelaide, but Jean-Marc held onto her for a few extra seconds, savoring the feel of her soft head of hair brushing up against his chin as she slept. Finally, he kissed his little niece on the forehead and gave her back to his sister.

Coralie promptly turned her back on her brother, but Jean-Marc reached for her arm. Coralie had been through a lot—they both had. He could at least try to be kinder to her.

She flinched, yanking her arm away from him.

"Coralie, listen. I...I'm sorry I haven't been so supportive of this...situation. It's just that I miss Adelaide and..."

She shot an accusing glare in his direction. "I bet you don't miss me, though, do you?"

She didn't give her brother a chance to respond. Instead she took off down the hallway and left him alone in the living room.

Jean-Marc walked to the door to let himself out, but before he did, a white-hot rage shot through his chest and he answered her anyway.

"No, I don't fucking miss you at all."

23

THE MISTRESS OF PARIS: A MEMOIR

BY EVE WINTERS

LE 21 JUILLET 2016
HÔTEL GEORGE V ~ PARIS, FRANCE

"BEAUTIFUL, I forgot to mention earlier, I leave tomorrow for the States. I'll be home for three weeks."

Dex announces this in the darkness while one of his hands is still inside of me. I don't hear the words, "I'll be home for three weeks," though. What I hear is: "I'll be having sex with my wife for the next three weeks." And the fact that he's addressed me as *Beautiful* while telling me this feels like an insult.

Turning away from him, I adjust my legs so that his hand slides out of me. I don't want any part of him inside of me right now; I just want to collect my money and go.

But his erection at my back clearly doesn't care.

He wraps his arms around me, trails kisses up my back.

"Don't worry," he says, "we never have sex."

"I didn't even say anything."

"You didn't have to," he replies. "Listen, Willow, my wife decided a long time ago that the sex part of our marriage was finished. Which is why I..." he trails off as he flips me around to face him.

I reach a hand up to trace the rugged contours of his face, which I can barely make out in the darkness.

"Why you fuck prostitutes," I finish for him.

Instead of answering me, he cups my face in his hands and brushes his lips over mine, softly at first. Then harder, and harder still, until he is back on top of me and back inside of me, making me remember why I keep coming back for more.

He stops for a moment, breathes heavily over my lips.

"No, that's why I'm fucking *you*."

He picks up the pace again, dominating me with his insane strength. And I love it. I love that it's just me and him. And I love that he just told me his wife never wants to have sex with him.

"I was serious when I said I don't want you to be with anyone else, Willow." Dex's voice is hard, raspy, demanding. He pins my wrists over my head, pushes my legs even farther apart, and growls, "When I watched you last week at the club with all those men, I wanted to kill them."

The way he says this leaves barely a trace of doubt in my mind that if the perfect storm of jealousy and lust and sex were to brew, Dex may actually do what he's saying he wanted to do.

He could kill.

But would he?

The sick part of me that is so taken with this man—especially with his darkness—loves that he wanted to kill other men simply because they'd been inside of me, too.

He shoves into me harder. I'm getting used to his force, to his size. To the pain he causes me when he fucks me like this.

And just like the first night, *I want more.*

I thrust my hips up toward his, inviting him in deeper. "Why did you let it happen then?"

"I've never been such a jealous person before," he says. "And normally I enjoy that sort of...*activity*. It can be exciting watching the woman you're with be pleasured by other men. But with you, I just, I..."

Our eyes lock, and I get it. I know what he wants to say but isn't saying. Because I feel it too.

"I don't want you to be with anyone but me," he says. "You won't spread your legs for anyone but me. *Ever.* I will be your only client from now on. Do you understand?"

I nearly tell him that I'm not with anyone else, that I haven't been with anyone else—well, with the exception of the wild ecstasy night at the club of course—and that I don't plan to be.

But he thinks I'm Willow, the high-end call girl who sleeps with a different millionaire every week—or possibly every night—and so that answer wouldn't really hold up.

Dex buries me beneath his body weight. I tighten my legs around his waist, squeeze him to me before answering.

"I understand."

"Good." Dex flips me onto my stomach, gets started on me from behind. His lips brush over my ear. "I'll pay you ten times more than what you would make if you had a different client inside of you every night for the next three weeks. And you won't let another man touch you during that time. Do you understand? *You will wait for me.*"

"I'll wait for you," I confirm in an exhale of breath.

Dex comes inside of me for the third time tonight, and I am amazed that he has anything left to give. But when he takes my hand and leads me into the bathroom, where he lays out a line of coke on the counter and nods for me to get started, I realize that while I don't know everything about him yet, I know this one thing:

With Dex Anderson, there will always be more.

Much more.

In the morning, my purse will barely close due to all of the cash I have stuffed inside. Thousands and thousands...and *thousands*...of euros. He must have already planned to pay me off for the three weeks he knew he'd be gone in order to have had all of this cash ready to go.

Dex Anderson, always prepared to fuck, I think.

As the crass words enter my mind, I shudder. I've already become so much like Willow; I barely know where she ends and I begin.

As such, I've learned a thing or two in my week and a half as a prostitute—I've brought a change of clothes for the morning so I don't have to strut out of the George V in my four-inch heels and skin-tight prostitute dress with no underwear beneath. As Dex walks me to the door of the suite in the morning, I'm wearing jeans (still with no underwear, because at this point they're totally useless), a white tank top, and a pair of sandals.

Before I leave, though, Dex wraps his arm around my waist, his lips brushing over my ear. "Just you and me from now on," he whispers.

You, me, and your wife.

I can't help but think this. He's going home to her for three goddamn weeks. *It's not just you and me,* I want to tell him. But I keep my mouth shut, like the good little escort I've become.

"Before you go, there's one more thing I wanted to mention," Dex says, pulling back so that our eyes are locked.

"What is it?"

"About my wife," he says.

Just like I said: you, me, and your frigid wife who won't let you touch her.

"You need to know that I'm never going to leave her, Willow. Ever."

My stomach tightens at the finality of his words. But even more so at the pained expression on his face as he says this. We've only known each other for a week and a half, but already, this man has demanded my exclusivity. He has paid me more money than I've made in the past three years combined, and he has been inside of me more times than I ever thought possible in the span of three nights together.

Three dangerously intoxicating nights.

As he grabs my face to kiss me one last time, I wonder what exactly is tying him so tightly to his wife.

When our lips part, I stay close. "I know you're never leaving her," I say. "I would never expect that of you, Dex. That's not what *this* is."

It's what Willow would say—I know this for sure. But it's not how I feel. Not even close.

Dex nods, but his eyes still look so undeniably haunted and lost that I can hardly stand to look at him. So I kiss him once more before I go, and then I leave him alone in the doorway, so he can prepare to fly home to a wife who will never give him what I can.

The stab of pain I feel in my heart as the distance between us grows makes me wonder what exactly *this* is, what it will become, what *I* will become...and if I will even survive.

With a bag full of cash and a knife carving through my heart, I weave my way through the humid streets of Paris, alone and forlorn, wondering what on Earth I will do with myself for the next three weeks. I stop on the Pont Neuf and stare out at the choppy waters of the Seine, remembering my mother.

Her voice floats through my coked-up head, unwelcome and sick.

Love always hurts, my lovely girl. Always.

She was crazy, but she was right.

My face turns to the sky, and as if in response, the rain starts to fall.

It can't clean the soot off my heart, though, nor can it clear the guilt from my conscience, or the disgust I feel over what I've become.

A liar.

A prostitute.

An addict for Dex's sex. His body. His drugs.

His love.

How fucked up am I that I could ever mistake what is going on here for love?

What do you think of me now, mother?

The rain pours harder. And still, I'm dirty.

I will never be clean.

But then again, maybe I don't want to be.

For the next three weeks, I wonder incessantly if Dex was lying to me about his wife never wanting to have sex with him. What woman *wouldn't* want this gorgeous man to make love to her? To bury her beneath the sheets night after night, to make her his? And since this thought is driving me so insane that I can barely breathe at night, I stay up in this state, my heart a shallow, lost beat.

Willow is gone every night. Says she's out with friends, but I know better.

She's still out screwing for money and lying to me about it. But what can I say now that I've been doing the exact same thing?

I can say nothing.

And so I write.

I write it all down—every forbidden touch, every wicked thing I've done with Dex, and every dirty thing I did on our night at the club.

I write down how I've loved every second with Dex. And how I loved every minute with all those anonymous men and women at the club.

And I write down how I secretly want Dex's wife to die.

Nothing painful or horrible. Just a quick unexplained death in her sleep would do the trick.

So that Dex and I could be together. Because if she were gone, *I know* he would want to be with me. I know this for sure.

I also know that I'm becoming crazy. I'm becoming my sister.

But ever since the night when my blood mixed with my mother's on the checkered kitchen floor, and Willow and I were the only ones left standing in a family that never should have been, I have been this crazy. This dark. This much like my sister.

It only took a few nights with Dex to bring it out in me.

And since I can never go back, I write it all down.

The truth of my existence.

My darkness.

My madness.

24

EVE

The When: Unknown
The Where: Unknown

Kate. Kate. Kate.

I actually thought she would listen.
I actually believed I could save her.
But she didn't want my—

Pop.
Needle in my Neck.
Drugs oozing...
Through thick, murky blood.
Oh yes, I remember this.
And I forget.
All.
Else.

This will hurt.
Love always hurts, my lovely girl.

25

SOPHIA

Wednesday the 17th of May, 2017
Arc de Triomphe ~ Paris

My entire body is revolting against my arrival in Paris. As soon as we cross into the city limits, I have to ask the driver to stop so that I can vomit on the side of the road. With the Arc de Triomphe towering majestically only a few blocks away, here I am in one of the *least* triumphant moments of my life, on hands and knees, retching on the sidewalk like a *chienne malade*.

I don't glance up to see the way the Parisians are looking at me, for I'm sure I would find only disdain in their eyes. Or worse—*pity*.

And let me die on this boulevard before I accept anyone's pity for the life I have chosen.

I wipe my mouth and climb back into the cab.

"*Ça va, madame?*" the driver asks.

I catch his dark eyes in the rearview mirror and nod.

"*Allez, s'il vous plaît.*"

"*Bien sûr, madame.*"

He's certainly the most polite cab driver I've ever encountered in Paris, but I'm sure he can see that I'm not someone he'd want to cross at the moment. It wouldn't end well for him.

Now that every last bit of bile is out of my system, hopefully I can get on with what I came here to do: spy on my husband.

The driver buzzes us down the Champs-Élysées. The skies are a vapid shade of gray, and drizzles of rain fall lazily to the sidewalks. We pass by a haze of umbrellas and cigarettes and designer shops before I spot it—the elegant awning of the Cartier shop to my left. I squeeze my eyes closed, not wanting to remember.

But I can't stop the assault.

It wasn't this Cartier shop. It was the one on rue de la Paix. I can still see him taking my hand, leading me up the grand red-velvet staircase.

Dressed in an innocent white sundress, I was young enough to be his daughter, but the saleswomen knew better.

The diamond heart necklace.

It was radiant. The most beautiful piece of jewelry I'd ever seen. And it was mine. Just like that. He'd bought it for me.

Wrapped it around my neck.

I didn't know then that I was carrying his child.

I still remember watching the diamond heart clatter to the floor. After I'd ripped it from my neck. After I'd ended the life that was only just beginning to grow inside me.

A discarded heart. A discarded baby.

A secret I will never tell.

My discarded heart and I have arrived at Hôtel La Belle Juliette on rue du Cherche Midi in the 6th arrondissement. Close enough to my husband's Left Bank apartment to get a good spy in each day, but far enough away that I won't have to worry about him seeing me in the neighborhood.

I thought about booking a fancy room at the George V, if that is indeed where my husband has been sleeping with Eve for the past year—that is, *if* it is even *my* husband who has been sleeping with Eve for the past year—but thought against it. I do not want him getting even a slight whiff that I may be here. And I don't need to risk running into him with his latest conquest while I'm feeling and looking like absolute hell.

Inside the elegant *Suite Boudoir* that I'm using my secret bank account to pay for, I splash my face with soap and water and glance in the mirror to find that I look worse than absolute hell.

I look like a haggard, ill woman who hasn't slept in over twenty-four hours.

An ill woman who suspects that her life is about to come crashing down because her arse of a husband doesn't know how to keep his secrets under control.

An ill woman who has entered the one city she vowed never to set foot in again...

And yet here I am.

I am that woman.

This is my life.

Bloody hell.

It's 1:00 p.m. Paris time, 7:00 a.m. New York time. At this very moment, I should be back home, slipping on a smart black dress and heels, preparing to attend commencement at NYU. I've sent an email to my department chair to let her know that I'm ill, but that I'll still be sure to read and grade all forty-eight of my students' essays on death *and* turn in final grades by this Friday. That feels totally unreasonable given my recent downward spiral of life events, but whatever. I'll just have to read in between spying odysseys today and tomorrow.

Around 1:00 p.m. Paris time and 7:00 a.m. New York time is also when I usually text Drew to say good morning and see how his day is going. Mustn't break tradition, today of all days.

First a quick peek at the weather in Manhattan—still heaving rain and humid as hell. Commencement would have been dreadful. Can't say I'm sad to be missing it.

Sophia: Hello, love. Just getting ready for graduation. Dreading it a bit with all this rain. How's your day?

He doesn't respond right away, as usual, so I—

My phone dings.

It's Drew.

That was fast...

Drew: Rainy days are the best for writing, *n'est-ce pas*? Perhaps you can squeeze some in tonight after the ceremony.

Drew's random use of French in our correspondence ever since he started this Paris gig a year and a half ago makes me cringe every time.

Sophia: Yes, writing and rain do go quite well together.

Drew: Miss you today.

Bloody wanker.

Sophia: Miss you too, love. Lots.
Drew: How was the book party last night?

The hairs on the back of my neck stand up. Had I even told him I was going to that? I scroll through our most recent texts but don't find any mention of the launch party. Had I told him on the phone? I rack my brain but can't bloody remember. The extreme fatigue I've been experiencing as of late has made my memory fuzzy too. It's maddening.

Sophia: Wasn't much of a party, really.
Drew: Oh?
Sophia: The author never showed.
Drew: To her own launch party? How rude.
Sophia: Haven't you seen the news? The American author who's gone missing in Paris?

I can't believe I'm testing him already, but I can't help myself.

I see the little bubbles that indicate he's typing, but then the bubbles stop. One minute goes by and...nothing. Another minute. Two more. Five more.

Waiting is making me feel ill again. I can't possibly have anything left in me to throw up, but just as I'm feeling a dry heave coming on, Drew's reply comes through.

Drew: Yes, saw something about it on the news this morning. Horrible.

I head to the toilet, toss the phone to the floor. I wait and I wait, but nothing comes. Just an empty retch. Bloody fabulous.

Sophia: Yes, Eve Winters. My former student. The day her memoir released, she went missing from her flat in Paris.

Drew: Assume the book's already a massive bestseller then?

His first conclusion too. I'm not sure if it's comforting or sickening that the first thing we both think of upon hearing the news of Eve's disappearance is all the money she's going to make from her book. That is, if she's even alive to see the money.

But then it hits me—what if Drew is in on it with her? For the money?

It's not like we need it—we have so much we could fill three swimming pools with our stacks of cash and still have some to spare. But even with the extreme level of wealth we've achieved, I've never seen anyone more motivated by money than my husband.

Sophia: Massive.

Drew: How convenient.

Sophia: You're bloody awful. The girl could be dead.

Drew: Don't pretend like you weren't thinking the same thing.

Sophia: *Touché.*

Drew: Have you read the book?

I wait three whole minutes to respond, just to scare the shit out of him.

And also because I'm still collapsed over the toilet, waiting to vomit.

And finally...

Sophia: I have.
Drew: And?
Sophia: Interesting, to say the least.

He doesn't respond to this, and since I need to get the hell out of this hotel and get some food in my stomach so that I can go spy on him, I decide to cut off this maddening text exchange.

Sophia: You should pick up a copy. I think you'd be intrigued. Have to run. Hope your day is lovely. xx
Drew: I'll do that. In all my spare time. Love you, beautiful.

I don't tell him that I love him back. I just can't. Not right now.

I love him too damn much, that's the bloody problem.

26

THE MISTRESS OF PARIS: A MEMOIR

BY EVE WINTERS

LE 11 AOÛT 2016
QUAI DE BOURBON ~ PARIS, FRANCE

I HAVEN'T SMOKED in years. On my second date with Lucas, I whipped out a cigarette and knew immediately by the shocked look in his big brown eyes that it was the wrong move. He told me that he detested the smell, and so just like that, I tossed the cigarette, and with it my filthy habit. I tossed a lot of other things for Lucas, including my entire past.

He didn't need to know the horror stories about my family. He didn't need to know how it all ended, in a bloodbath of epic proportions. He didn't need to know that I'd been hospitalized afterward. Or that I'd tried to overdose three times, only to wake up devastatingly alive, and even sicker than before.

I burned that sordid past along with my last cigarette because I desperately wanted Lucas to love me.

And he did. He loved me more than anyone had ever loved me.

More than I'd ever loved myself, certainly.

I wonder if he still does.

I wonder what he would think if he saw me now—pacing the banks of the Seine before sunrise, chain-smoking the pack of cigarettes I stole from my sister's Louis Vuitton bag. Not caring in the least that I forgot to slip on a pair of pants or a sweater before I left the apartment in my skimpy nighty, because all I can think about is the married man who is paying me to be his whore.

Dex is flying back to Paris today, and as such, I have been up all night tossing and turning in an unending mélange of angst, desire, anticipation, jealousy, and self-loathing.

A typical night for me, really, since he left three weeks ago.

The idea of Dex spending time with his wife has driven me absolutely mad. I've become just like those girls I've always loathed, the ones who obsess over men and allow them to rule every waking moment of their lives.

I've become like Willow.

And Dex still thinks I *am* Willow, of course, so I may as well smoke her entire pack of cigarettes, I reason.

Later tonight, I'm supposed to meet Dex back at the scene of the crime: The George V. I'll have to get my shit together before then. I can't walk in there in a sleep-deprived, smoky haze of jealousy and madness. No, that definitely won't do.

So perhaps just one more cigarette and then I'll make my way home, climb back into bed, and I'll sleep until I have to wake up and primp for tonight.

There is, of course, still a part of me that is screaming:

What in the hell are you doing, Eve???

And really, what in the hell *am* I doing? I've stashed all

of the cash Dex has given me between my mattress and box spring, not having the faintest clue what to do with it. Should I take it with me tonight and give it all back? Tell him I cannot do this anymore, even though I thought I could?

I glance down at my body, only just now beginning to feel the chill of the early morning on my bare arms and legs. I'm hardly clothed, stalking around Paris in the shadows that blanket the city just before dawn. There are bums and strange men trolling around the city at this time of day, and each time I see one, I just take another drag of my cigarette and blow the smoke in their direction.

I don't even care.

Who have I become?

Just as the first hint of dawn is casting its rays along the smooth waters of the Seine, I light the last cigarette. I take drag after drag, walking faster and faster, hoping to shake off this wretched storm of emotions. Hoping that once I get back home, I will know what to do. Hoping that the survival instinct inside of me will be able to find a way out of this. Because even with the promise of so much money, of *freedom*, I know it's not right.

I know it's not me.

This is Willow's life.

It's not mine. It's not me.

It never was.

27

SOPHIA

Wednesday the 17th of May, 2017
La Belle Juliette ~ Paris

The plan is simple. I'll spend my last few afternoon hours getting reacquainted with the city—it's the last bloody thing I want to do, but if I'm going to be spying for the next week, I simply must get used to being here again. First, though, I must get some food into this wrecked body of mine so I can make it through my evening of spying.

Drew phones me most days when he leaves work, which is usually between 6:00 and 7:00 p.m. Paris time. I'll head over to his office building near the Opéra Garnier around 5:30 to be safe, and I'll wait outside and follow him when he exits. If he phones me today when he leaves, I'll just let it go to voicemail, and I'll text him soon after to tell him I'm still tied up with commencement festivities. That should keep a phone call from him at bay for at least another day. I'll follow him wherever he goes tonight, and finally back to his flat on rue de Lille...*if* he even returns to his flat tonight.

If he does go home, I have the access code to his building. He sent it to me when he first bought the Paris flat, in the hope that I would join him here. Of course, I never did join him...*but* like the conscientious wife I am, I did save the code. I also have the key to his flat, which I plan to ransack tomorrow while he's at work, naturally.

Tonight, if Drew retires to his flat, I will let myself into the building and do some listening outside his door. Not getting caught eavesdropping will be the most challenging part of this whole misadventure I reckon, but I'm confident I can pull it off.

The future of our marriage depends on it.

I am sitting inside the windowed terrace at Café de Flore, downing a strong French espresso. I plan to order a second as soon as I finish this one. Maybe even a third.

My first proper meal in over twenty-four hours is on its way, and while I wait, I barely notice the bustling French waiters, the clinking of silverware, or all of the lovely French conversation swirling around my foggy *tête* because I have caught a glimpse of my own reflection in the window, and I've nearly mistaken myself for someone else.

Granted, I did put this disguise on back in the hotel room and I took a nice long gander in the mirror before I left, but I'm so exhausted and starved that I'd nearly forgotten I look like a completely different woman.

And if I do say so myself, I've performed *quite* the transformation.

The new Sophia is wearing—no, can't call her Sophia. She looks *nothing* like me.

Rachel perhaps? No...Natasha? Naomi? Valerie?

No, no, and no.

And then it hits me:

Lucy.

I don't know why, but it just feels right. *This woman* is called Lucy. *Lucy Taylor*.

Lucy Taylor is a slim little thing, dressed all in black, naturally. She's wearing tall black boots, tight black pants, a slick black trench coat, and a black spy-woman hat to match. She has razor-straight black hair that just barely grazes the tops of her shoulders. Her sleek bangs frame her oval face and contrast perfectly with the deep-red lipstick she's wearing.

No one would know that beneath Lucy's head of jet-black hair, *Sophia* has a mop of thick, wavy auburn-blond hair tied up into a tight bun.

The wig was one I had tailor-made when I feared the worst with my illness. Chemo never happened, though—I refused it—so neither did the loss of my hair. The wig stayed hidden from Drew, along with the truth about why I never wanted him to see me without my clothes on.

The scar is small but hideous. Just thinking about it makes me shudder.

I pick up the large glossy-black sunglasses I've brought and add them to the mix so that I am totally and completely transformed into her...into *Lucy*.

Lucy has no scars. Lucy is perfect.

Lucy knows exactly what to do when her husband isn't following the rules.

Nice work, love, I think to myself.

My little hint of self-encouragement is short-lived when I tear my eyes away from Lucy's reflection and find a photograph of Eve staring me in the face. The older gentleman sipping coffee at the table next to me is reading today's *jour-*

nal, and of course, on the front page is none other than an article all about *l'écrivaine américaine disparue.*

I nearly snag the paper straight from his hands, but I stop myself, remembering that the sleek, cool Lucy Taylor would do no such thing. Instead, I wait not so patiently while he finishes up the article he was reading and closes the paper.

"Excusez-moi, monsieur, avez-vous fini?" I ask, nodding toward the newspaper.

His eyes comb the length of my body, and I am immensely relieved that he can't see the real me beneath this façade. He lifts his gaze back to my giant sunglasses and grins.

"Oui, mademoiselle."

I grin right back at him, my first smile since my lover gave me an orgasm yesterday. I love this stranger for giving me the title of *mademoiselle*, rather than the title of *madame,* which is reserved for women *d'un certain âge* or for married women, but I've removed my wedding band since *Lucy* isn't the kind of girl to wear such showy diamonds on her hands.

He hands me the paper, and I can barely get out a *merci* before I am immersed in the front-page article on the missing American writer, who, the day after her disappearance was first reported, still has not turned up.

Miraculously, all the years of French I'd taken as a little girl and all the way through uni have survived, and I can understand nearly everything in the article.

The article states that police are officially calling the disappearance of Eve Winters an *enlèvement.* The word *abduction* in French has the hairs on the back of my neck standing on end. Yes, Eve could have staged this whole dramatic disappearance act to shoot her memoir to the top of the charts, but blood on the flat walls and neighbors hearing screams—would she have taken it that far?

I think back to the Eve I knew as my student. She had an inherent darkness about her, yes. But was she malicious? Cunning? I couldn't know for sure, because how well do we really know anyone? Based on my interactions with her, though, if I had to guess, I would say no.

Eve Winters. Abducted.

I shake the chills off my spine along with the overwhelming fear that my own husband may have played a hand in the crime, and I keep reading.

Authorities are working around the clock to identify both the married man that Eve describes in her memoir, "Dex Anderson," and her ex-boyfriend, "Lucas." Police have given no indication to the press if they have any leads. The police have also been incredibly tight-lipped on any interactions they might have had with Eve's sister, Willow Winters, who is mentioned frequently in Eve's memoir.

The paper also states that after their own extensive search for Ms. Willow Winters in the past twenty-four hours since the story broke, they haven't uncovered a single thing—not a phone number, a Facebook profile, nor any confirmation that she was actually living with Eve in Paris as Eve states in her memoir. In fact, a neighbor of Eve's who has chosen to remain anonymous has stated that she was only aware of one girl living in that flat—and that girl was Eve. The same neighbor also did not believe that Eve Winters was pregnant, but authorities refuse to confirm whether or not they have found this to be true.

She'd better not be bloody pregnant.

I shake my head, force myself to continue reading.

There are rumors that perhaps Willow has been taken into protective custody following her sister's disappearance, as not a single newspaper or news channel has been able to locate her for an interview, but her definitive whereabouts remain unknown.

In addition to the hunt for information on Eve's sister, authorities have also refused to release any information they might have uncovered related to the girls' haunted past, which Eve hints to only briefly in her memoir.

A bloodbath of epic proportions.

That was how Eve had described whatever horrors went down in her family when she was younger.

I stop reading for a moment, and I think of the Eve I knew.

Those haunted eyes.

A bloodbath of epic proportions would explain it.

The article goes on to say that *la Brigade Criminelle* or *la Crim'* for short, which is Paris' specialized crime squad who investigates the city's most heinous crimes, and who is housed at the famous 36 Quai des Orfèvres—conveniently only a stone's throw away from Winters' flat at Place Dauphine—will be handling the case of the missing girl. The particular team within la Crim' who has been assigned to find Eve Winters is headed up by *le Chef de Groupe*, Julien Breton, an officer who has worked for la Brigade Criminelle for over fifteen years, and by *le Procédurier*, Jean-Marc Devereaux, who's been with la Crim' for over twelve. The article describes *le Procédurier* as a senior member of the team who is responsible for writing an exhaustive description of the crime scene, up to the tiniest detail. His observations form the basis of the investigation, and the entire team, made up of five men and one woman, will run with it from there.

Jesus.

What a bloody mess.

My *salade flore* arrives just in time for me to be feeling queasy and utterly uninterested in food.

Could Drew really be behind this?

I take a stab at the lettuce and force it down my throat, thinking about how I would so much rather flee this café, board a plane back to New York City, and pretend that spying on my husband to find out if he has anything to do with my former student's disappearance, *is not* my life.

But as I watch the rain fall in thick sheets beyond the steamy windows of the café, I remember where pretending has gotten me: on the brink of total and utter disaster, where I sit now.

28

OFFICER JEAN-MARC DEVEREAUX

MERCREDI 17 MAI 2017
36 QUAI DES ORFÈVRES ~ PARIS, FRANCE

JEAN-MARC DEVEREAUX SIPPED his hot espresso from a small paper cup, tucked today's newspaper tightly under his arm, and headed up the long winding staircase that was often featured in news articles and television shows on the famous Parisian crime squad and the mythical building they called home: 36 *Quai des Orfèvres*.

And it was just that for Devereaux: *home*.

It was inconceivable to him that in only a few short months, he wouldn't be starting his day this way—taking the stairs two at a time all the way up to the rooftop, where he would breathe in the morning air, drink his *café*, and smoke his first cigarette of the day.

Well, okay, more like his third but who the hell was counting?

The new building would be incredible, sure. State-of-the-art technology, bullet-proof windows, immaculate holding cells for all of their grimy suspects.

But still, nothing would ever compare to this view.

Jean-Marc stood atop his domain and breathed it all in.

The morning sun starting its ascent into the light-blue sky. The long streaks of white clouds that floated overhead, just out of his reach. The magnificent view of *la Tour Eiffel* off in the distance. The River Seine flowing to his left and to his right, converging at the tip of the Île de la Cité, not far from the building he stood atop of, and right next to Place Dauphine, where Eve's abandoned, wrecked apartment was waiting for answers. Waiting for Eve.

Devereaux's team member Martinez had confirmed the day before that the expensive apartment did, in fact, belong to Eve Winters and that no one else lived there. The sister she mentioned in her memoir—*Willow*—had been completely untraceable to his team on Day 1 of their investigation, which told Devereaux one of three things:

Either Willow had been abducted as well.

Or, she'd disappeared of her own volition.

Or, a more interesting theory: *Willow did not exist.*

Jean-Marc finished his coffee and crumpled the paper cup in his fist before flicking open the newspaper to the front-page article all about the missing American author. There, staring back at him, was the same seductive photograph of Eve that graced the back cover of her memoir. Devereaux knew this photograph particularly well. He'd spent most of the night thumbing through the pages of her book and then periodically turning to the back cover and looking straight into her eyes. Studying her. Feeling her.

Wondering if she had just spread her legs for the man who had taken this photo of her, or if she was about to spread them for him.

And late in the night, despite his genuine desire to find the missing girl and to make sure she was safe from whatever men had certainly preyed on her beauty, Devereaux simply couldn't stop himself from imagining—more than a few times—that *he* was the one she was looking at with that sultry gaze.

That *he* was the one who she was about to spread her legs for.

"Devereaux, we've got some interesting news on Winters. Meeting in five."

Jean-Marc snapped out of his reverie and nodded at Martinez, whose characteristically gruff female voice bounced over the rooftops as she spoke.

"I'll be there," he said, tucking the paper back under his arm and then lighting the cigarette that would be his breakfast.

A few puffs of nicotine and this glorious view. That was all he needed to sustain him. Fuck love. Fuck sex. Fuck memories. Fuck it all. He just needed this view, and everything would be okay.

29

THE MISTRESS OF PARIS: A MEMOIR

BY EVE WINTERS

LE 11 AOÛT 2016
HÔTEL GEORGE V ~ PARIS, FRANCE

I FIND my way to Dex later that night after hours of sitting in a deafening silence in my bedroom, staring at the stark-white walls, seeing red.

Everywhere I looked, only red.

It's the color that assaults my vision anytime I'm feeling this distressed.

I wish it were violet, indigo, emerald, yellow—anything but the most wretched color of blood.

When I first came to Paris, I thought I'd be safe from it. I thought that a fresh start in the City of Light would protect me from my past. I hoped naïvely that Paris would erase it all.

That was completely idiotic, of course, seeing as how Paris was where it all began.

And so here I am, back at Dex's door at the George V, trying in vain to see anything other than red.

When I was a teenager, the therapists called it PTSD.

I called it hell.

Dex opens the door to the penthouse suite wearing a grin so wide, I feel immediately horrible knowing I'm going to ruin it.

The grin fades as his beautiful eyes comb my mess of a body. I'm dressed in dark tattered jeans and a loose white T-shirt. My long hair is pulled back into a careless bun because I didn't have it in me today to even step into the shower.

"Willow, what's the matter?" Dex asks, ushering me into the suite.

I don't answer him. I can hardly look at him.

If I do, I'm going to cry.

And Willow—goddamn her—she never cries.

"I'm sorry, I can't..." I trail off, handing him a backpack that contains all of the cash he gave me to stay faithful to him and our arrangement for the three weeks he was away.

"What's this?" he asks. But before he opens it, I see a spark of apprehension in his eyes.

"You're giving me back the money? Were you with someone else while I was away?" he asks.

"No, no, it's not that."

"Then what is it?"

I turn my body away from him and set my gaze on the door.

My rational mind is shouting at me to *leave. Leave. LEAVE!*

But then I feel his hand on my shoulder. Warm, soft, sweet.

"Willow, what's the matter? Whatever it is, you can tell me."

He drops the bag of cash to the floor, and with a gentle pull of his hands, he slowly urges me to turn around.

Those hands, that pull, *this man*—I am powerless against it all.

Dex slides his arms around my waist and draws me closer to him. I still refuse to look into his eyes, so he places a finger beneath my chin and tips my face up just enough so he can see me. Really see me.

"What happened?" he asks again.

The tears that Willow never cries, the tears that a prostitute is *never* supposed to show to her client, they begin to fall down my face, rolling over my cheeks, and I can no longer hide the fact that I am human. That I have a past. That I am damaged.

The perfect girl he thought I was is no longer.

I am sure he will push me out the door and send me back to the hell from which I came.

But he doesn't.

Instead he pulls me tight to his chest, kisses me on the forehead, and lets me cry until I have no tears left.

"What's going on, Willow?" Dex asks as he strokes my hair and pulls me even closer to his warm body.

We are lying in bed now. But there has been no sex. No animalistic ripping off of clothing. No talk of money or of how we are so obviously breaking all the rules of the prostitute-client agreement.

Instead, Dex has let me cuddle up to his chest and listen to the sound of his heartbeat until my breath evened out.

"I...I just had a bad night, that's all."

Dex pauses for a moment, props up on his elbow to look down at me, and tucks a strand of hair behind my ears. "What happened last night?"

Now it's my turn to pause. Do I tell him I couldn't sleep because I've been so torn up over *him*? Over the idea of him with his wife? Over *us*?

"Willow," he says, "I know what we have going on here isn't a *conventional* relationship, so to speak, but whatever is going on, you can tell me."

I wipe at my eyes, being sure to look anywhere but straight into his. The way he looks at me makes me want to tell him everything. I want to tell him the story of how my family fell apart. I want to tell him about the hospitalizations, the overdoses—the downward spiral of *me*. And my saving grace—falling in love with Lucas, moving in with him, thinking I could have a normal life after all.

I want to tell Dex how I ruined that, too. How I left the one man who loved me and never looked back.

I want to tell him that my name isn't really Willow. That I am not really a prostitute. Or, at least, that I *wasn't*... until I met him.

But instead of all of that terrifying truth, I simply say, "I'm pretty sure we're breaking *all* of the rules here."

"Fuck the rules," Dex says. Then he cups my face in his hand and turns my gaze toward his. "I care about you, Willow. A lot."

His words come out so softly, so sincerely, that I can't help but give him one nugget of truth.

"I care about you too, Dex."

He leans in and kisses me, our lips finding one another in this darkened penthouse suite that has already housed so many of our dirty acts. But there is nothing dirty about this kiss. Nothing rough. Nothing forced.

It's sweet. And soft. And everything I could ever want from the man with whom I am most certainly falling in love.

Dex's hand finds the skin on my lower abdomen, just

below my T-shirt. His fingertips brush the sensitive spot back and forth as he kisses me with such tenderness, that for a few moments, I really do forget that there is bag filled with thousands of euros lying next to this bed.

I continue to forget this as Dex unbuttons my jeans and slides his hand down in between my legs. His fingers find their way inside of me, but unlike all of the other times, their movements are soft and intense, not hungry and harsh.

And I am already ready for him. Despite the horrors of the day, I am *still* ready for this man.

He kneels over me, slips off my jeans and T-shirt, happy as always to find that I am wearing neither a bra nor underwear beneath. I reach up and unbutton his pants, and it's not long before we are both naked, and Dex is lying on top of me.

But instead of pushing himself inside of me and screwing me with the fervor of the sex-deprived husband that he is, he pauses for a moment and gazes down at me, giving me a look that is both powerful and endearing.

I can't look away this time. Our eyes lock for what feels like an eternity—a *blissful* eternity—and finally, Dex says what I've been thinking all along.

"I think I'm falling in love with you, Willow."

And then, as he kisses me, he slides inside of me, softly, slowly. I wrap my legs tighter around his waist, pull him in deeper. I feel as if I cannot get close enough to this man. I want every inch of him, every piece of his body, his mind, his heart, his soul. I want it all.

I don't want there to be anything left for his wife.

By the way he makes love to me, over and over again throughout the night, I wonder, now that we have crossed the threshold from a simple prostitute-client arrangement to...*lovers*...where will this take us?

Could we be going somewhere real, somewhere that could actually give me a better life? One with a man whom I love and who loves me in return? With a man who I feel, one day, I could actually show myself to?

Or...like every other close relationship I've had in my life, will it end in the destruction of two lives, two hearts, two souls who have nowhere to go once it's all over?

Dex will have somewhere to go, though. He will have his wife.

Till death do them part.

I, however, will have no one.

I will only have death.

30

SOPHIA

Wednesday the 17th of May, 2017
Quai de Bourbon ~ Paris

So this is *where it all started.*

I am walking along *Quai de Bourbon*, staring at a few shards of broken glass on the concrete, imagining the morning Eve was pacing past this very spot, chain smoking and barely clothed.

This meltdown of hers, in which she saw *only red,* was the meltdown that prompted her to return to "Dex's" arms, lost, forlorn, a wreck. The meltdown that prompted her married lover to hug her, to hold her, the way he never should've done with a prostitute.

The meltdown that led to his first confession of love, and to the first time they made love.

Eve and Dex could have continued on their dangerous prostitute-client path. Eve taking insane amounts of his money while he had all the dirty sex he could ever want. Until he found another prostitute whom he liked better.

But instead, Eve showed her vulnerable side to my husb—.

No.

I'm not even certain it's my husband Eve is writing about. I can't go there until I know for sure.

I shake away my doubts and instead lift my gaze to the everyday life of Paris. A bateau-mouche makes its way down the Seine, the picture-happy tourists packing its seats totally oblivious to the darkness this city holds. The heavy gray clouds threatening to release another downpour aren't stopping them from exploring the city everyone knows as the *City of Light*, the *City of Love.*

I believed in the light and love of this city once, too.

As the boat passes by, I spot a man standing at the railing, taking photos with his iPhone. He lowers it for only a moment and catches my gaze. He smiles at me, bright, boisterous, and flirty. He's a believer in love, that one.

Bloody idiot.

I shake my head back at him, not even close to smiling back.

I don't like being this jaded. I really don't. But given this latest turn of events, how could I be anything else?

Pulling the news article out of my purse, I take another look.

Enlèvement.

Abduction.

Those are the only words I see now.

If I were to go missing, there would be a ton of people who would immediately notice my disappearance. All of my close girlfriends in Manhattan and London. My entire department at NYU. My students who would be waiting in the classroom for a professor who was never going to show.

And, of course, my lover and my husband.

If Eve had not written the book, would her disappearance have made the news? Would it be such a big horrendous deal?

It hits me then, as I take one last look at Eve's seductive look in the newspaper photograph, that for a long time now, I've been wishing I could slip away from my life unnoticed. Wishing I could be lost and forgotten and build an entirely new identity, away from all of the mistakes I have made, the lies I have told, and the husband whom I both loathe and love, in equal parts.

Does Drew love me enough to do whatever it would take to find me, if one day, I simply...*disappeared*?

I glance at the hour on my phone and realize with a start that it's nearly time for Drew to be leaving work.

It's nearly time to find out just how much this man loves me.

31

THE MISTRESS OF PARIS: A MEMOIR

BY EVE WINTERS

LE 13 SEPTEMBRE 2016
PLACE DAUPHINE ~ PARIS, FRANCE

"*VOILÀ*..." I say as I remove my hands from Willow's eager eyes. "Welcome home!"

Willow blinks her eyes as she gazes around the stunning apartment I have just bought right in the center of Paris, on the Île de la Cité.

She spins around, speechless, taking in the polished hardwood floors, the dazzling crystal chandeliers overhead, the chic gray couch, snow-white chairs, and magenta pillows and flowers I have picked out to furnish our new home. She runs a hand over one of the pink pillows and then hugs it to her chest as she walks to the open window and gazes out over the charming tree-lined Place Dauphine.

Slowly Willow turns to me, and with a rare tear in her eye, she smiles. "How, Eve? How did you afford this?"

I am beaming back at her, feeling the most overwhelming joy to be able to give us both this gift. The gift of a home—a *real* home. A gift that wouldn't have been possible if Willow hadn't have showed up at my door two months ago, begging me to spend one night with the insanely wealthy American businessman, Dex Anderson.

Well, that one night turned into two, then three, and now I see him two or three times a week—on the weeks he's in town of course. We are exclusive, and per our arrangement, Dex is paying me upwards of 40,000 euros a month to be with him and only him. He still believes I am a prostitute. He still believes that my name is Willow.

And he is in love with me.

I love him more than I can even admit to myself. It is a love that is so all-consuming, so devastatingly real and beautiful and mind-blowing, that I can hardly see straight on the days I am not with him.

Those are the days when I write, of course. I write about Dex, about our love, about the money, about everything we do together and everything I feel when I am not by his side. The words are pouring out of me in a way they never have before, and I feel that *this* is the story I have always been meant to write. It's as if my entire life has led up to this insane twist of fate where I have become the person I've most loathed—*Willow*—in order to find myself *and* the love of my life.

A love who is still married, though, and a love who says he will never, ever leave his passionless, sexless marriage.

I hate this last part, more than I've ever hated anything in my entire life. More than I hated my sick parents. More than I've hated Willow for all the years she let drugs rule her life, all the years she needed me to clean up her messes.

The irony is that becoming Willow has been the best thing that has ever happened to me. The best, and the worst. Well, if Dex ever *does* leave his wife, it will only be the best. I'm not a total idiot, though, and I am forcing myself to believe that he will not leave her, ever, no matter how much he loves me.

Still, at night, I pray for her to die. Or disappear. Anything to allow Dex's full attention to be on me.

I'm writing every last detail of this beautifully sordid story as a novel, and I've spent the past month pitching the book idea to agents all over the US and UK. After receiving strong interest from three of them—which, given five nonstop years of rejection from the publishing world, is nothing short of a miracle in my book—I've finally signed with one in the US. Her name is Abbey Strumeyer, and she's a total shark of an agent. A tough New Yorker who is a force to be reckoned with in the literary world. Abbey already has interest from editors at several publishing houses, but of course we can't sell the novel until it's finished.

Willow, though, she knows none of this. She believes that I haven't seen Dex since the night I first took her place in his luxurious hotel bed. She knows I've been writing, that I've signed with an agent, and in a few seconds, she's going to believe that I've been offered my very first book deal—which is what afforded us this spectacular apartment.

In reality, of course, it's Dex's money that has given us this gift. It's the intoxicating nights I've spent in his arms, fucking and making love and falling deeper and deeper, and deeper still, into a rabbit hole with this incredible man. I don't know when or where it will end, but I hope it never does.

I smile brightly at my sister, who is still staring at me in disbelief, and I tell the lie.

"I got a book deal for my novel. It was massive...and so I bought us a new home!"

"And you want me...to live with you here?" she asks.

"But I thought you wanted me out once I was making enough money to be on my own again."

I take a step toward my sister, remove the pillow from her arms, and once again in her emerald eyes, I see the look of that 15-year-old, after she'd finished it. After she did what no young girl should ever have to do. And despite all of the years I've despised her actions, her insidious ways, her disregard for anyone but herself, I still see that teenage girl. I still see the sister who saved my life. The sister who ended the madness for us both.

I grab her and pull her to me.

"I love you, Willow," I say, holding her as tightly as I can.

She squeezes me back with an equal urgency, and soon I notice the tears rolling down her cheeks.

"I love you too, Eve. Thank you. Thank you so much."

I run a hand over her long, wavy hair and kiss her on the forehead. We've been through so much. She deserves more. And so do I.

Finally, Willow releases her hold on me, and we turn in unison, gazing out the window. With our arms wrapped around each other's waists and our heads pressed together, we breathe in the late summer air that fills our new magnificent Parisian home.

"It's a new start for us," I say to my sister. "We're never going back to the way it was."

She pauses a beat before replying, "*Never.*"

32

OFFICER JEAN-MARC DEVEREAUX

mercredi 17 mai 2017
36 Quai des Orfèvres ~ Paris, France

Judging by the gathering of dark under eye circles and the massive quantity of coffee being consumed before their morning meeting had even begun, it didn't appear that anyone from Devereaux's team had slept since they first set foot on the crime scene of Eve Winters' apartment yesterday.

Especially their Chef de Groupe, Breton. Devereaux had never seen his boss' eyes looking quite so bloodshot.

Devereaux handed Breton a coffee, wondering if Coralie had mentioned his early morning visit to their apartment. If she had, Breton said nothing about it to Devereaux. He just took the coffee and did his signature clearing of the throat to get the meeting started.

Devereaux took a seat next to Martinez, pulling his pen and notepad from his front shirt pocket. He stifled a yawn. It was going to be a long day.

"Leroux," Breton said. "What have you got so far on

Willow Winters, the sister Eve mentions in her book?"

Leroux, their youngest team member who was no less talented than his older peers, albeit a bit naïve at times, scratched his chin before talking. "No sign of her, Sir. No trace of Willow in Eve's apartment, not a single neighbor Martinez spoke with has ever seen Eve with a sister, and nothing online. Not even a Facebook profile. It's quite possible she doesn't exist."

Devereaux wouldn't be surprised if that were the case. After what he saw in Eve's apartment yesterday, it was obvious only one person had been living there and that person was Eve.

This begged the question: if Eve had lied about having a sister in her memoir, what else had she lied about?

Breton crossed his arms over his chest and shook his head. "It's possible that Eve fabricated her sister's existence, yes. Or it's also possible that whoever took Eve took Willow, too."

"Or that the two girls staged the whole thing to make Eve's book sales skyrocket," Martinez pointed out.

"Quite an elaborate staging with all that blood," Devereaux chimed in. It *was* a theory that was worth considering, he agreed, seeing as how international news was already all over Winters' disappearance, and her book would no doubt be an instant bestseller.

But still. All that broken glass. All that hair. *All that blood.*

"If she does exist," Leroux added, "it's not likely that Willow Winters is her real name, which would explain not being able to find her online."

"Precisely," Breton said. "Keep looking, Leroux."

Leroux nodded, furiously scribbling notes in his notepad.

"I think you're all going to want to hear what I've got on Eve," said Tessier, arguably the least attractive member of the group with his giant nose and receding hairline which Devereaux didn't cease to poke fun of. But damn was that man good at what he did.

Martinez lifted a brow in Devereaux's direction. This must have been the interesting information she'd referred to on the rooftop. Devereaux was all ears.

"The only legal document we have so far on Eve is her passport, which was left in the purse in her apartment," Tessier continued. "Her legal name on the passport is Eve Winters, no middle name. And yet, we can't find much on her at all. No family connections–no mom, dad, sister, aunts, uncles, nothing. And just like her sister, she has no Facebook profile, and absolutely nothing online. No social media. Not even a website for the book. I got ahold of her literary agent, Abbey Strumeyer, and she knows nothing about where Eve is from originally, who her family is, or if she even has a family. She claims she doesn't know the true identity of Eve's ex-boyfriend, whom Eve refers to as 'Lucas' in the book, and she also claims not to know the identity of the married man in the book. She's never even met Eve in person, and also wasn't sure if Eve had ever been pregnant, as the end of her book leads readers to believe."

"Judging by the fact that there wasn't a single item of baby clothing, or anything baby-related in her apartment, I think it's safe to say Eve wasn't pregnant," Devereaux cut in.

"And if she was, she could've lost the baby early on," Martinez added.

"Right," Tessier continued. "Eve's agent did confirm, however, that Eve received a hefty advance for the book from her publisher, so we're working on getting bank transaction records now. If we find any major transfers or withdrawals just prior to her disappearance, or any significant account activity just after, that could give us an idea of whether or not Martinez's theory on Eve staging her own disappearance is correct. And once DNA results from the crime scene come in tomorrow, we'll have a better shot at linking Eve to family in the US or elsewhere. But for now, we have found no clear link from this girl to any family, friends, or lovers...living or dead."

Devereaux flicked his pen between his thumb and forefinger, processing this news. "A girl with no family, no past, no links to anyone," he said aloud. They'd come across girls like this before—prostitutes who'd fled some horrible past, had taken on new names, and were hardly traceable as citizens on this planet. "Maybe she was running from something...or someone. And changed her name. Which is why we can't find anything on her."

"If she wanted to hide, why would she go and write an entire book about her life?" Martinez questioned.

"Good point," Tessier said. "Her agent said that as far as she knew, Eve did attend New York University, so I'm working on confirming that today. If she did, we'll look for her past professors, roommates, anyone who may have known her and could give us a glimpse into her past."

"What about the laptop?" Breton asked Durand, their sixth and final team member.

"Didn't reveal a damn thing," Durand said. "No photos of family, friends, or lovers, and nothing even remotely interesting in her internet search history. Not even so much as a search for a sex toy. Surprising for a supposed prostitute." With his thick black-rimmed glasses and even thicker black mustache, Durand was the nerdiest of the bunch, but also the raunchiest. His dirty imagination had come in handy more than a few times in solving some of the missing prostitute cases that had come up in recent years, and Devereaux appreciated his colleague's comic relief, dark though it was.

"The only document saved on the computer was the word document of her final manuscript for the book," Durand continued. "Even her Gmail account was just emails back and forth between Eve, her agent, and her publisher. Nothing personal whatsoever—no emails from friends or family, and no evidence of the married lover or the ex-boyfriend. It was all business."

"Almost as if she knew we'd be looking," Martinez said. "Maybe she erased it all and then disappeared."

"Definitely a possibility," Breton said. "Any luck on pulling cell phone records?" Breton asked Tessier.

"Her cell phone wasn't located in the apartment yesterday as you know, but I got her phone number from her literary agent. Service provider is Orange, and I should have the records from them by later today, tomorrow at the latest."

"Sooner would be better," Breton said before shooting his bloodshot glare to Martinez. "Besides your theory that Eve staged the whole thing to be the next bestseller, what have you got for us?"

"The neighbors I was able to speak with yesterday said they never noticed Eve bringing a man back to her apartment. She was never with friends, either, they said. Always alone. Kept to herself. Barely said *bonjour* when they crossed her in the hallway. No noise coming from the apartment was ever heard until the screaming the night Eve disappeared. And none of them saw anyone suspicious entering or leaving the building that night."

"What about video footage from the nearest street

cameras?" Devereaux asked.

"I'll be taking a look at that later today," Breton said. "What I think our focus really needs to be on is figuring out who the married man is in her book. Has anyone made a list of wealthy, high-powered American businessmen who spend time in Paris?"

When no one responded, Breton looked to Leroux. "Have a list to me by the end of the day."

Leroux nodded, again furiously scribbling in his notepad.

"Martinez, get moving on checking the more elite swingers clubs in the city and all of the locations mentioned in the book—especially the George V. Check the hotel guests and video footage on the dates Eve writes about in her book. If nothing turns up there, check the Ritz, the Plaza Athénée, anything five-star where a rich businessman would take an escort."

"And if the dates are fabricated?" Martinez said.

"Start with the dates she mentions and if you find nothing, you'll have to search for the entire past year," Breton replied.

"Got it," Martinez said, jotting down a few notes.

Finally, Breton turned to Devereaux. "What have you got for us?"

"I read the entire book last night," Devereaux said.

"And?" Breton prodded.

"As I'm sure you saw in the opening chapter, Eve mentions some sort of traumatic family event involving 'a bloodbath, the dismantling of a family,' and she makes it sound as though her sister Willow—if she even exists—saved her life when they were teenagers. She also mentions something leading me to believe her mother was...wait, let me find it." Devereaux flipped to the page in his notepad where he'd jotted down Eve's exact quote and began reading to his team.

"'Ever since the night when my blood mixed with my mother's on the checkered kitchen floor, and Willow and I were the only ones left standing in a family that never should have been, I have been this crazy. This dark. This much like my sister.'"

"*Putain*," Durand muttered. "This is one twisted *prostituée*."

"Later in the book when she's talking about her ex-boyfriend Lucas," Devereaux continued, "she references 'the horror stories' about her family, writing that it all ended 'in a bloodbath of epic proportions.' She writes that she was hospitalized after the event and tried to overdose three times, unsuccessfully. *If* this part of her story is true, it sounds as though her mother was murdered, and that Eve was nearly killed in the crossfire as well with the sister being her life saver. There is no mention of the father, though."

"Ah, she's got daddy issues. That explains the prostitution," Durand quipped.

Martinez rolled her eyes. "Not every woman has daddy issues."

"Daddy issues or not," Devereaux cut back in, "something awful happened to this girl. Something that would certainly be documented in the US courts and in their medical system, if any of this is true. The murder of her mother and attempted murder of Eve. Overdoses and hospitalizations. It's a past that anyone would want to run from. A past that might make a girl change her name, move to Paris, and become a prostitute to make ends meet." Devereaux paused and looked straight into his boss' tired eyes. "A past that might make a girl cling to the wrong man in the hope that he could save her from her own demons."

33

EVE

The When: Unknown
The Where: Unknown

They're late.
The needle.
The drugs.

I know because I can think.
I can feel.
And the pain is even more blinding
Than the darkness I now live in.

I don't howl into the void, though.
Futile, those cries would be.
A waste of air.
When each breath feels as though...
It could be my last.

Kate, oh my sweet darling, fucked-up Kate.
Where did they take you that night?

Where did you go?
Why didn't I stay with you?

If I had stayed, would you still be here?

My cracked bones.
My oozing blood.
My raspy breath.
It's the only question they know.

You are lodged deep in my marrow, my sweet, sweet Kate.
And it looks as though...
After all these years...
We just may meet the same twisted fate.

34

SOPHIA

WEDNESDAY THE 17TH OF MAY, 2017
BOULEVARD HAUSSMANN ~ PARIS

STILL SUITED UP in full disguise as the sleek and ever-mysterious Lucy, I am standing just across the street from the LCP France headquarters—or *Le Crédit Parisien de France*—which is the bank my husband runs. The beautiful office building where my husband has been working for an entire year and a half, the building which I've never seen in person until today, is situated just behind the regal Opéra Garnier and directly across the street from les Galeries Lafayette, on Boulevard Haussmann. Unfortunately, the boulevard isn't as busy as I would've expected at rush hour, and there aren't any discrete hiding spots near the door for me to spy from, so I'm beneath the Galeries Lafayette awning across the street, leaning against the wall, cell phone out, pretending to text. I have my short black wig, black hat and sunglasses, and so even if Drew did happen to look across the street in passing, there's simply no way he would recognize me.

And still, my hands are shaking.

I pull up our text thread on my phone and send a quick message.

Sophia: Hey love. Still at work?

A few minutes pass before he responds.

Drew: Yes, looks like I may be burning the midnight oil unfortunately. Insane day. I can step out and call you in a few mins though.
Sophia: Actually just got out of commencement. Total chaos here, not a great time to chat. What time do you think you'll leave? Talk then if you're not too tired?
Drew: Not sure, but I'll text when I have a better idea.
Sophia: Of course.
Drew: I miss hearing your voice sweetie.

I bet you do.

God, what happened to innocent until proven guilty? Drew really might be innocent. He may have nothing to do with this mess.

But no matter how hard I try to believe that, here I am dressed as Lucy, about to spy on my own husband. Though it's certainly going to be difficult to stalk him if I don't know what time he's leaving work. I decide to take off down the boulevard in search of a nearby café. I may as well stay close until he texts to say he's heading home.

But just as I've stepped into the crosswalk, I see him.

Drew.

Briefcase in hand, tall and exceptionally handsome in his slick black suit, *like he just stepped out of the pages of*

Vogue—here comes my husband, clearly *not* burning the midnight oil as he just messaged me only seconds ago.

I don't have time to worry about the lie, though, because he's getting closer. At the pace I'm walking, we will run straight into each other.

Fuckety fuck fuck fuck.

I slow down, lowering my face to my phone and pretending to text. I am now totally unsure about my ridiculous Lucy disguise. The man has been married to me for over twenty years for fuck's sake! He'll certainly know it's me.

Christ, I'm a prize idiot.

Lifting my eyes just a tad, I am infinitely relieved to find that Drew is *not* looking at me. I slow down a bit more and feign interest in whatever is on my phone screen, but beneath my massive Lucy sunglasses, I'm watching him.

Drew appears confident as he strides along, not minding the light pouring of rain coming down, wetting the top of his full head of dark-brown hair. There are no "hints of gold" as Eve described in her memoir, but I suspect she changed many of the physical details to protect her lover's identity.

Hell, my lover is saved as *Dahlia* in my phone. He's very careful about when he texts me, but still, if one of his messages were to pop up on my phone when Drew is next to me, he would see *Dahlia* and think it's my best friend from London.

Drew passes by the crosswalk, thankfully not turning his head toward me even once. His eyes are set straight ahead. A few seconds later, he glances at his watch, then begins walking faster.

Where in the bloody hell is he going? Why did he tell me he was staying late at work?

I'm behind him now, and although there are three

people between us, I'm worried he will hear my heart pounding. I feel as though it may burst right through my chest cavity and fall straight at his feet.

I tell my heart to stay the hell out of this. It's business. I just need to find out where my husband is going tonight.

Bloody keep it together, Sophia.

But the voice shooting through my head isn't my own. It's mum's. Always her. When things aren't going right in my life, I hear only the irritating screech of my mother.

I always knew Drew would break your heart.

She's dead, but I know that's what she's thinking. And so I tell her what *I* think.

You don't get a say anymore, mother. You're dead.

Sodding dead.

I shake off the memory of a woman who never truly acted like a mother, and I walk a little faster, despite my body's desire to lie down on the pavement and go immediately to sleep. Drew is really on a mission now, and I must keep up. He weaves his way around the back of the Opéra Garnier, past groups of tourists weighed down with heavy shopping bags from les Galeries Lafayette. There are several businessmen leaving their offices around this part of the city, and even though they're looking quite smart, they don't hold a candle to my husband.

Of course Eve would fall in love with him.

Soon, we reach a crosswalk and the light turns red. Drew stops, pulls his phone from his pocket and starts talking. There are only two people standing between us now. He turns his head just the slightest bit, and even though I am already dangerously close to him, I take another step forward to listen to what he's saying.

"...not a good idea...haven't...talked...fuck...sure...few minutes..."

And it just keeps going like that. Intermittent words sprinkled between the sounds of car horns beeping and drops of rain hitting the sidewalks.

I can't pause the city, unfortunately, so I keep following him for a few more long blocks until we turn up the Boulevard des Capucines. He stops abruptly in front of a set of looming black doors. I stop as well, sliding into the doorframe just beside me, but keeping my head out far enough to continue watching him. He slips his phone back into his pocket, then reaches a hand toward the buzzer. Before he pushes any of the buttons, though, he stops and pulls his phone back out. It looks as though he's sending a text, and within seconds, my phone is vibrating inside my purse. I nearly jump, praying he doesn't turn in my direction. Instead, he presses the top button on the buzzer and quickly disappears inside the building. I pull out my phone to find the text he just sent me.

> Drew: Looks like I'll be at the office really late. Will probably be too wrecked to have a decent conversation tonight. Talk tomorrow? xx

Bloody liar.

I drop my phone back into my purse and with a new fervor, I head toward the building my husband has just disappeared inside.

When I reach the door, I find a few gold plaques lined up on the wall beside the door. The top one reads:

Antoine Danton, Avocat Pénaliste.

My eyes jet to the buzzer. Next to the top button that Drew pushed is the same name, *Antoine Danton*.

In French, *avocat* means lawyer. It also means avocado, and although that fact used to make me giggle when I was a young student learning French, there is no giggling today.

Stepping off to the side, I pull out my phone and search for the exact translation, only to confirm my worst fears.

An *Avocat Pénaliste* is a Criminal Defense Attorney.

My knees nearly buckle. I look at Drew's text again. At his lie.

My husband isn't staying late at work. He's meeting with an attorney.

A criminal defense attorney.

A scene from Eve's book flashes through my mind. It's my least favorite scene involving the married man. I could barely read it on the plane because if it really was—if it really *is*—Drew, doing what he does to her, I don't know how I could ever look him in the eye again.

If it is him, it means I don't know my husband at all.

It would mean he's been lying to me about who he really is for our entire life together.

It would mean that he could truly be a criminal.

The rain is pouring down in sheets now. I don't open my umbrella, though.

Instead, I stare at the gold plaque on the wall. At the clear beads of rain running over his name—*Antoine Danton, Avocat Pénaliste.*

A man who defends criminals.

A man who is going to defend my husband.

My husband, my Drew, a criminal.

35

THE MISTRESS OF PARIS: A MEMOIR

BY EVE WINTERS

LE 21 OCTOBRE 2016
LA CLOSERIE DES LILAS ~ PARIS, FRANCE

IT'S crazy how quickly life can turn around. I learned this, of course, when I was a little girl and things would come crashing down in the worst ways when I least expected it. My disaster of a childhood taught me to see train wrecks coming from miles away.

But those catastrophic years never taught me to anticipate when things might actually get good.

And for the first time in so, so long, things are actually...*good.*

I spend most of my time between my elegant apartment overlooking Place Dauphine and the ridiculously plush penthouse suite at the George V that I share with Dex. The George V really does feel like home now. I don't worry about being the resident call girl. The doormen love me. They smile at me and call me *Mademoiselle Willow*.

It's like in *Pretty Woman* when Julia Roberts' character struts around the Beverly Wilshire Hotel in all of those fancy clothes Richard Gere's character bought her, and the hotel manager adores her.

Dex truly makes me feel like the most beautiful woman in the entire world. We spend on average four nights a week together...well, when he's not home with his wife, of course. Willow is still out most nights, so she hasn't asked any questions about where I am when I'm with Dex, and I haven't asked her what she's doing either.

For the first time since we were little girls doing pliés side by side in ballet class, my sister and I are really, truly getting along, and I don't want to do anything to upset this new peaceful sister relationship we've developed. She loves the new apartment and she seems content. Even if she isn't, I am so blissful on the mornings after I've had Dex inside of me all night that I probably wouldn't notice.

Dex knows that I have a "roommate," which is the reason I've given him that he cannot come to my apartment. To my knowledge, he doesn't know where I live, and I want to keep it that way. He thinks I'm Willow, the prostitute turned high-paid lover, and I don't ever want him to know the truth about who I really am.

I am starting to feel so confident in Dex's love for me that I don't get as crazy with worry anymore when he goes home to his wife. His trips to her are shorter now. A week at most, and sometimes only a few days. He is spending more and more time with me, and I know he would spend all of his time with me if he could; he tells me as much.

Tonight, Dex is on the other side of the Atlantic, and I've just finished having a drink with a friend at La Closerie des Lilas, one of my absolute favorite cafés in Paris. As my friend and I walk out of the café, he gives me the classic French *bises* on each cheek, and we part ways.

I set off down Boulevard du Montparnasse, breathing in

the cool autumn breeze and smiling when I realize how beautiful Paris has become to me again. Tree-lined streets, bustling sidewalk cafés, the elegant sound of the French language swirling through the air—it is simply magnificent.

I have a new apartment, a new man, a new relationship with my sister—a new life.

And I'll never go back.

At this thought, I lift my head to the sky and close my eyes, just for a moment, savoring this feeling.

A strong hand on my arm jerks me from my blissful moment.

Startled, I open my eyes to find Dex standing over me, rage flashing through his gaze.

"Dex, what are you doing here? You're supposed to be home."

"My trip got cancelled," he says as he yanks me down a dark side street.

"What's the matter? Why are you—?"

"Why are *you* out drinking with another man?" Dex pushes my back up against a wall, his commanding hands gripping my shoulders.

"Dex, I'm not out *drinking* with another man. He's just a friend."

"That's not what it looked like to me."

"This is ludicrous! He's only a friend. And what are you even doing here? Were you following me?"

Dex cups my chin in his hand and squeezes so hard I nearly cry out. "I don't care who the fuck he is. I don't want you seeing him ever again. Do you understand?"

He doesn't give me a chance to respond, though. Instead he pulls me toward the street where a black town car waits. He opens the door and nods for me to get inside.

"What is going on, Dex? Why are you acting like this?"

But he doesn't answer. He just pushes me inside the car, climbs in behind me, and slams the door.

"*Chez moi*," he barks up at the driver before reaching forward to close the partition.

We are alone in the back seat, and before I can talk any sense into him, he is leaning over me, shaking my shoulders.

"That man did *not* look like a friend, Willow. I saw the way he was looking at you." His hand slides over to my neck. He pushes down, hard. "Have you been fucking him?"

I try to move my head away, but he has me pinned against the seat and I can't move. "No! Stop it, Dex. You're hurting me."

A wild hurricane of fury is storming in his ocean-blue eyes, and they are dark. Darker than I've ever seen them. As he pushes harder on my neck, I remember that first night I spent with him, when he had me on my back and he was towering over me. I remember thinking that Dex wasn't just a powerful, strikingly handsome businessman.

I remember thinking that he was dangerous.

As I struggle to bring air into my lungs, I know that my instinct was right. He is dangerous.

I dig my fingernails into his hands as hard as I can, breaking the skin. He responds by letting up on my neck and reaching for my pants. Despite my protests, he has them down around my ankles in seconds. He flips me over onto my stomach and presses himself against my back.

With one hand now wrapping around the front of my neck and the other pulling my waist into him, he growls into my ear. "I can't fucking see you with other men, smiling like that. Laughing and flirting like you're a free woman. You are not a free woman. You are mine, Willow. You're fucking mine, and I cannot lose you right now."

"You're not going to lose me, Dex. Please, calm down."

But he's too far gone. I can feel him unbuttoning his pants, pulling them down, getting ready to make me his. Even though I already am. I have been since the minute I first laid eyes on him. He doesn't need to force himself on me to ensure that I will never stray.

I can't say any of this, though, because his hand is wrapping so tightly around my neck that I can barely breathe.

"What would you do if you saw me with another woman?" he spits into my ear. "What would you do if you thought I was fucking my wife the way I fuck you?"

He lets up on my neck just enough to allow me to respond.

"I would want to kill her," I say without hesitation.

"So you do get it."

Dex smashes my body down into the seat, towers behind me, and forces his way inside. The pain is shocking —not because of his size, but more so because of the violence. He's an absolute mad man back there. I'm squirming and trying to get him to stop, but my protests are useless. He wraps a hand around my mouth to quiet me, and his teeth find my earlobe.

He bites so hard, I'm certain he's drawn blood.

"I'm only doing this because I love you, Willow, and I don't want you to ever forget that. Until the day you die, I want you to remember the pain of loving me."

With that, I stop fighting him. I let him take this as far as he needs to so that he knows he has all of me.

It's the most brutal sex we've ever had.

But his point has been made.

I will never, ever forget the exquisite pain of loving Dex Anderson—of this I am sure.

In the morning, I wake up in a bed I've never before seen with Dex's sleeping body wrapped around me.

I blink my eyes and lift my groggy head, confused about where we have ended up.

And then I remember it all. The car ride from hell and Dex bringing me up to his fancy Left Bank apartment for the first time.

I was so upset when we got up here that I ran to the bathroom and washed down two Valium to calm myself down. I don't remember him apologizing for what he did. I don't remember anything, actually, except lying down on this bed and crying myself to sleep.

Dex is still sleeping soundly when I slip out from underneath his strong arms.

I am still fully clothed, and I don't need to check beneath my shirt or jeans to find the bruises; I can already feel them throbbing. I spot my purse on the floor by the bedroom door.

Snatching it up, I head out of his bedroom as quietly and as quickly as I can. Everything in Dex's apartment is white and modern with only a few splashes of black and gray. There is no real color anywhere to be seen.

And only one photo. Of him and his wife. The happy fucking couple.

There is nothing personal anywhere else. His apartment is sterile and hostile all at once. And I have to get out of here.

Because every time a flash of what he did to me in the car assaults my memory, I only see red. My blood. Splashed all over his stark white walls, sprawling over the pristine marble countertops, dripping down the spiral staircase, oozing over the hardwood floors, and speckling the beautiful floor-to-ceiling windows with their extraordinary view of the rooftops of Paris.

Paris—the city I was just beginning to love again.

Now it all looks gray and bleak.

Before I leave Dex alone, still sound asleep as a fucking baby, I write him a note and pin it on the knife rack.

If you ever hurt me like that again, I will disappear from your life forever.

Then I pick up the photo of Dex and his wife, lift it over my head, and smash the glass frame on the corner of the countertop. Shards of glass clatter to my feet. Reaching for the sharpest one, I slice the skin on my palm open. An odd sense of relief washes over me when I see my own blood bubbling over the skin. I smear a bit onto my fingertip, and then I swipe the note with my blood.

I want him to know I'm not fucking kidding.

36

SOPHIA

Wednesday the 17th of May, 2017
Boulevard des Capucines ~ Paris

Two hours have passed. Drew is still inside that sodding attorney's office, and I am still waiting across the street, a drowned rat hovering in a doorway, shivering as my life continues to destruct before my very eyes.

I remember the summer that I spent here, loving the feel of Paris in the rain. Shielding themselves with their black umbrellas, the Parisians would pace down the sidewalks, all brisk and serious. I, however, would leave my umbrella *chez moi,* and gladly take to the rainy streets without one. It felt as if I was the only person who recognized how stunning the city was when raindrops were tapping the awnings of cafés, forming puddles on the skinny sidewalks, and splashing along the River Seine.

I wanted to bathe in the magnificence of this city.

I wanted this too badly, I suppose, which is why I bathed myself in something else that felt magnificent at the time—something forbidden that ultimately would destroy any beauty I ever saw in this city.

Paris is not beautiful to me any longer, in the sunshine *or* in the rain.

In fact, nothing looks beautiful to me anymore.

Except—*strangely*—my husband.

There he is.

Two hours and three minutes after he first pressed the criminal defense attorney's buzzer and disappeared inside, he has emerged. I only get a brief glimpse of his face—a flash of blue eyes, dark hair, a furrowed brow—before he takes off in the other direction.

I pause for a moment, feeling the wind sucked right out of me at the sight of him. He is still so striking, so attractive to me, even after all these years. Even after everything we've been through together. And even with all of the doubts I now have about his character. Up until yesterday, no matter what had happened, I'd always believed with one-hundred percent certainty that this brilliant, gorgeous man was *mine.*

He is mine, I remind myself as I take off after him.

He is still mine.

I jog just a bit to catch up so that I am about three-quarters of a city block behind him. I make sure to always keep at least a few people between us, but not too many that I can't keep my eyes on him.

Just as I used to do during my summer in Paris, Drew doesn't walk with an umbrella in hand either. Instead, he lets the rain soak his full head of hair, the crisp shoulders of his suit, the tops of his shiny black shoes.

Like any good Parisian, I've got my umbrella shielding my face—my *disguised* face—in the event that Drew turns around. I fear that if we make eye contact, I will break.

I will crumble.

My strength is waning with each painstaking step, each unbearable thought that passes through my mind.

If my husband was still mine, I wouldn't have to follow him through the soaked streets of Paris, pretending to be a different woman.

If he was still mine, he wouldn't be lying to me about staying late at work when, in actuality, he was visiting a criminal defense attorney.

If he was still mine, none of this would be happening.

I'm barely keeping it together as we stroll through a puddle-filled *Jardin des Tuileries*. The flowers and trees are all in full bloom, their bright petals spilling over with heavy raindrops. And there goes Drew, walking with a purpose through the flowers and the trees and the umbrellas.

But then, he stops.

He bends down and lowers his nose to the red rose petals.

I slow my pace so that I don't catch up to him, but I get a bit closer just to confirm that he is doing what I think he's doing.

Drew is, quite literally, *stopping to smell the roses.*

It's never something I've seen him do. Not once in over twenty-five years together have I seen this man stop to smell the bloody roses.

He's always in such a rush. Always looking to make more money.

Must be productive. Not a moment to waste.

Work, work, work, and more sodding work.

That is the husband I've always known. The husband I've always loved. I've been busy and productive and money-driven as well, but his drive has always far surpassed mine.

This is how Drew has been since he lost his mother in

college. Since her lack of money and health insurance equaled a serious lack of quality health care when she was diagnosed with lung cancer. This was only compounded by the fact that he'd lost his dear little sister Emmy to leukemia only a few years earlier. Drew always believed that if they hadn't lived in such poverty, if his absent father would have made even the slightest effort to take care of his family, perhaps both his sister and mother wouldn't have suffered so greatly. Perhaps they would've had better care—care that could have saved their lives.

Perhaps Drew wouldn't have had to sit by both of their bedsides, holding their hands, as they took their last breaths.

Of course Drew could never know for sure if money actually would have made the difference between life and death in both the cases of his sister and mother, but he chose to believe that it would have. And because of this, he chose to work insanely hard to amass an obscene amount of wealth so that he would never, *ever* lose the people he loved most because he didn't have the money to save them.

But, as I've tried to remind him over the years—money cannot fix everything.

Case in point—my mother's wealth only exacerbated her drinking habit, which ultimately, led to her death.

Drew ignored my warnings, though—believing wholeheartedly that the higher he climbed, the more exempt he would become from tragedy striking in his life.

But then, tragedy did strike in our Park Avenue penthouse. After years of trying, I couldn't get pregnant, and even when I did, my womb refused to bring a baby to full term.

Our money couldn't fix it. No matter how many dollars we threw at fertility specialists and acupuncturists and healers of all sorts, my body simply said *no*.

Money certainly didn't matter when my third pregnancy resulted in the birth of a sweet baby girl who never even got to take her first breath.

And it didn't help when I was diagnosed with cancer. Ovarian. Which, ironically, could have resulted from all of the hormones and IVF treatments we threw our money at in our efforts to have a baby.

All of that, and the result was still the same: *cancer*.

Just like Drew's mother and sister.

Naturally, I didn't want Drew to know anything about my diagnosis. If I could have the cancer taken care of with a quick surgery to remove an ovary and he'd be off working in Paris and wouldn't know the difference—why the hell not? I didn't need my husband to think for even one second that all of his years of hard work hadn't mattered. That even though we were now one of the wealthiest couples in Manhattan, I was still mortal. I'd still gotten sick.

So, I didn't tell him. I had the ovary removed. I refused the recommended but—in my opinion—unnecessary chemo treatments so that Drew would never find out.

But now, I fear the cancer is back. And I fear that it is grave.

If I'm correct, that could mean that everything Drew has worked so hard to avoid may happen again, anyway.

Drew has lifted his face from the roses and has resumed his walking, while I must tear my heart away from these endless worries and continue onward. I resume my steps far behind his, watching as he reaches the edge of the gardens and stops once more, this time to lift his head to the grizzly gray sky and allow the cool raindrops to wash over him.

And again, I marvel at how in all these years together, I've never seen him do anything like this. I've never seen him do anything that wasn't without a specific purpose—and that purpose usually being to make money. Loads of it.

But today, Drew is stopping to smell the roses. He's breathing in the humid summer air. Feeling raindrops wash down his face.

And I, too, have stopped. My heart is now pounding so violently in my ears, I can barely hear the sound of the rain.

All I can hear is my heart, thudding, beating, *screaming*:

Who are you, Drew?

What are we doing?

How did we get here?

I feel a sudden urge to rush up to my husband, rip off this damn wig and show him, once and for all, who I really am.

Show him my scars.

Ask him to show me his.

And tell him that whatever he has done, I still love him.

Because I do.

Even if he is the married man in Eve's book. Even if he had something to do with Eve's disappearance. Even if he has been lying to me, viciously, for months and months.

This man has still done everything he knew how to do to build a beautiful life for us. He has still loved me just as fiercely as I have loved him—he hasn't left me even though, ever since we lost our little girl, I've refused nearly any and every advance he's made to be intimate. And I've hidden an entire illness from him to protect him. To avoid bringing up all of those old wounds from the past that I never want him to have to feel again.

We've both hidden affairs from each other because our lovemaking created babies that died both in and out of my womb, and the devastation we both experienced over those losses was too much for us to continue on being the couple we once were.

None of that changes the fact that I still love Drew more than I've ever loved anyone or anything in my entire life.

He is the only connection I have to the woman I was before life went dark. The Sophia who has a contagious laugh and makes witty jokes and writes smart books and teaches at a prestigious university. The glamorous Park Avenue wife who has not only beauty, but brains too.

That's the woman Drew has always seen. The woman he's always needed.

But perhaps, he doesn't see her anymore.

Perhaps, he doesn't need her anymore.

Perhaps, he doesn't *want* her anymore.

And can I really blame him?

My husband resumes his walk, but I don't follow him.

I can't.

Instead, I stay in the gardens, alone, until the ashen clouds overhead dissolve into blackness. I can't bear to see where he is going next. I can't bear to think that wherever that may be, it will not include me.

37

THE MISTRESS OF PARIS: A MEMOIR

BY EVE WINTERS

LE 23 OCTOBRE 2016
PLACE DAUPHINE ~ PARIS, FRANCE

DEX HAS BEEN CALLING and texting me obsessively for the past twenty-four hours, and I have yet to respond. Instead, I am transforming the novel I've been working on—the novel that was not so loosely based upon my experience as Dex's prostitute—into *truth*.

I am writing the story as a memoir.

I know that in doing this, I will lose Dex.

And that is exactly why I'm doing it.

I'm changing his name, of course, and some of his identifying details because my purpose is not to destroy his life. It's to tell the truth—the only story I feel I can write these days. And I know that if I release a book about our insane affair, about the lies I've told to be with this man, there will be no future for us.

Our sordid love story will have to end.

After what happened on Friday night, I know that I must do this to save myself. Because on my own, I don't believe I have the power to refuse him. The book, however, will give me that power, and I'm certain it will make *him* want to walk away from *me*...which, judging by the four hundred times he's tried to get in touch in the past twenty-four hours, he is clearly having a hard time doing as well.

I've reworked the book's pitch and the first three chapters, and I'm about to send them off to my agent along with an email that, for once, tells the truth.

Dear Abbey,

I have a new story idea that I believe may be of interest to you. The book I've been working on—*The Mistress of Paris*—has not come purely from my imagination. In fact, it is based upon my own true story working as a high-end call girl in Paris, specifically with one powerful, prominent married businessman. Some of the events that have transpired between us recently have prompted me to rewrite the book as a memoir. I've attached the first three chapters, and I would love to know your thoughts. If you're on board, perhaps we could sell based on a proposal alone?

Looking forward to hearing from you,
Eve

With only a brief moment of hesitation, I hit *Send*. There is no going back now.

38

OFFICER JEAN-MARC DEVEREAUX

JEUDI 18 MAI 2017
36 QUAI DES ORFÈVRES ~ PARIS, FRANCE

AN EXHAUSTIVE SEARCH on murder cases in the US that could resemble what Eve had written about in her memoir had brought Devereaux...*nothing*. He'd discovered a few cases in New York and DC that came close but alas the photos of the girls looked nothing like Eve.

Another coffee and another cigarette and Jean-Marc reached for Eve's book amid the wreckage of his desk. Her beautiful photo on the back cover was certainly a welcome sight among the piles of sordid case files and photos of unsightly crime scenes, dead bodies, severed limbs...the usual.

He turned the book over in his hands. The cover was already a bit worn and folded at the edges—he'd been carrying her story with him wherever he went. Reading her words every chance he got. Getting to know this missing girl more and more with each pass through her haunted story, but wondering if the girl he was getting to know in these pages was actually the true Eve. Or if it was just the version of herself she wanted to present in a book.

He opened up to the first chapter. Might as well take another look while he was impatiently waiting on the DNA results from the crime scene to come in. Once again, he lost himself in her story, in the eroticism of her words, in the tormented affair she carried on with Dex.

And once again, he thought of Mia. Mia had loved him as much as Eve loved Dex. Hadn't she?

It was getting harder to remember. With each passing day, the memory of the woman he had loved more than any other faded just a little bit. Devereaux both hated and loved that fact. He needed to move on, create a new life, hell, maybe even fall in love again. But even just thinking that thought made him ill with guilt.

He'd been planning on proposing to her. He'd wanted Mia to be his wife. He'd even bought the ring.

But she was taken from him just one week before he would have gotten down on one knee and made her his for all of eternity. Or for at least as many days as they both had left on this Earth.

And apparently, for Mia, there weren't many.

Jean-Marc had looked into the eyes of more dead people than he could count. But none had ever haunted him like Mia's.

He shook his head, wiped at the wetness gathering around the corners of his own tired eyes, and refocused on the words in Eve's story.

She saved mine, I remind myself. All those years ago. I can still see her charging over the black-and-white checkered floor, handling it.

Black-and-white checkered floor.

An image flashed through Jean-Marc's mind, an image of just that: *a black-and-white checkered floor.* Splattered with blood. A woman's blood. A mother's blood.

What was that from?

Was his memory playing tricks on him?

No. It was a photograph he'd seen before. He was certain.

Devereaux re-read Eve's words and then closed his eyes until the vision reformed in his mind.

It was a photograph of a crime scene his own father had worked on many years ago when he was a *Chef de Groupe* with la Crim'. It was the last case he'd ever worked on. The case that had driven him mad. The case that had driven him to drink far too much.

The case that ultimately, led to his death.

Devereaux flipped through the pages of Eve's memoir, looking for the other mention of the checkered floor. It didn't take him long to find it.

> *But ever since the night when my blood mixed with my mother's on the checkered kitchen floor, and Willow and I were the only ones left standing in a family that never should have been, I have been this crazy. This dark. This much like my sister.*

And then, it hit him. There was one other line in the book that he hadn't understood. Until now.

> *When I first came to Paris, I thought I'd be safe from it. I thought that a fresh start in the City of Light would protect me from my past. I hoped naïvely that*

Paris would erase it all. That was completely idiotic, of course, seeing as how Paris was where it all began.

"Paris was where it all began," Devereaux read aloud. "*Putain.*" He couldn't believe it hadn't hit him before this moment. "*Les sœurs Marvel.*"

Devereaux tossed the book onto his desk and reached for his laptop. His hands flew over the keyboard as he Googled two names he could never forget:

Sara and Kate Marvel

It took only seconds for pages upon pages of news articles and photos to populate his coffee-stained computer screen. And there they were: the two American sisters whose tragic story had taken the world by storm.

Sara, a 17-year-old studious ballet dancer and her younger sister Kate, 15 years old, also a dancer, but the rebellious one.

Well, not just rebellious—this girl was *promiscuous.*

The girls had traveled to Paris for a one-week summer vacation with their parents. On the last night of the trip, Kate convinced Sara to sneak out to an underground club with some older French men she'd met the night before. It was a night of drinking, drugs, and sex—a night that thoroughly terrified the goody-goody older sister Sara. When she'd had enough, she begged Kate to leave with her, but Kate wouldn't go.

Sara left Kate in the club, snuck back into the Parisian apartment her parents had rented for the week, and went to sleep.

When she woke in the morning, she discovered that Kate had never returned.

Kate didn't come home later that night, or the next morning.

She didn't come home the morning after that, either.

Or ever again, in fact.

Devereaux's father, one of the most experienced and talented officers of la Brigade Criminelle in his time, had led the investigation for the missing girl, and in the process, he got to know the troubled Marvel family all too well. Devereaux remembered his father telling him that the girls' mother suffered from borderline personality disorder, a beast of an illness that manifested itself in unpredictable mood swings, suicide attempts, and constant chaos for everyone around her. The girls' father was an alcoholic, a problem which only worsened when his younger daughter went missing.

Despite being a relatively wealthy family, which enabled them to stay in a swanky Right Bank apartment for the duration of the search for their daughter, their money couldn't save them from the catastrophe which awaited.

Several weeks after Kate first went missing, Devereaux's father's team uncovered a piece of Kate's ripped, bloody T-shirt in an abandoned car, not far from the last club where her sister Sara had left her on that fateful night.

The night after this unfortunate discovery, Sara's mother went off the handle, screaming and tossing knives at her husband. Sara was caught in the crossfire, her mother slashing her with one of the knives before her father came in and ended it all. He'd been drinking for hours that day, and in a violent rage, he met his knife-wielding wife with a severe beating and stabbing, leaving her to die on the kitchen floor.

The black-and-white checkered floor.

And the scar. Eve mentioned it a few times in her book. Just below her left shoulder.

The scar she wished had never happened.

Putain.

Devereaux thought back to the court case that took place in the French court system not long after the murder of Sara's mother. Sara had testified in defense of her father, insisting on her mother's insanity and a plea of self-defense for her alcoholic dad, but despite her heart-rending testimony, the French court had locked Sara's father away in Europe's largest prison, *Fleury-Mérogis,* for life.

Sara Marvel had disappeared completely from the media shortly after, and soon the world moved on to the next tragedy.

Devereaux's father didn't move on, though. He'd continued his search for Kate Marvel to the point of pure and total exhaustion for himself and his team.

Devereaux didn't want to think about those final months with his father. How distracted he'd been. How tired. How *obsessed*.

And what about Sara?

Was it possible she'd returned back to the States, changed her appearance and her name?

Had Sara Marvel become Eve Winters?

Had she then come to Paris only to meet the same fate as her younger sister, Kate?

Was it Kate who'd inspired the character of *Willow* in Eve's memoir?

Was that why Devereaux's team hadn't yet found a single trace of evidence that Willow Winters even existed?

Because Willow was really Kate Marvel, and Kate Marvel has never been found.

Devereaux's heart beat a little faster as he scrolled

through the photos of the 17-year-old survivor, Sara Marvel, and compared them to the photograph of Eve on the back of her book.

Sara had shoulder-length light-brown hair and bangs. Green eyes. A flat ballerina's chest. A somewhat pointy nose. Thin lips.

Eve had long, wavy dark-brown hair, no bangs. Smoky-blue eyes. A voluptuous chest. A rounded, beautiful nose. And full lips.

They didn't look alike at all. But hair dye, contacts, and plastic surgery could easily make those changes.

He pulled up Eve's author photo online so he could compare the two photos side by side directly on his computer screen. So he could zoom in. So he could try to decide if this was, in fact, the same girl.

Both had large oval-shaped eyes. Their cheekbones were similar, too—both of them high and well-defined, like a model. And while the lips differed in thickness, the curves of the lips were similar.

Devereaux dug through the growing case file sitting atop the mountain on his desk. When he found the copy of Eve's passport, he quickly checked the birthdate:

The 23rd of April, 1988.

He would have to go back to the old Marvel sister case files to verify if Eve and Sara had the same birthdate, but this already told him what he needed to know.

If the birthdate listed on Eve's passport wasn't fabricated, Eve was 29 years old when she went missing earlier this week.

The Marvel sister case went down twelve years ago in 2005.

And Sara Marvel was 17 years old when her sister went missing and her mother was killed.

The timeline added up perfectly.

Was it too good to be true?

Devereaux looked at the photos once more.

A twelve-year age difference plus a good plastic surgeon could absolutely produce the differences he'd noted in the two girls' photos.

Devereaux was about to leave his office to pull the old Marvel sister case file to match up more details, but first, one more quick Google search:

Sara and Kate Marvel full names

"*Putain.*" There was his answer.

A loud knock on his door followed by Tessier's shiny head peeking inside tore Devereaux's gaze from the answer to his puzzle.

"The DNA report is in," Tessier said. "You're not going to believe this. We've matched Eve's DNA to—"

"Marvel," Devereaux cut in, swiveling his laptop screen for Tessier to see. "Sara *Eve* Marvel."

39

SOPHIA

Thursday the 18th of May, 2017
La Belle Juliette ~ Paris

A little bit of makeup can go a long way, darling.

It's my mother, of course. Talking at me as I line my tired eyes with a thick black pencil.

For fuck's sake mother, it's been nine years.

Leave. Me. Alone.

But from her place in the sky, or wherever she went after she drank herself to death, my mother will not stop.

I step back from the mirror and take in the view of Lucy Taylor all freshly dressed in black.

Fine, Mother, you were right.

A little makeup *does* go a long way. The atrocity that was my face when I awoke from my broken six-hour slumber this morning has dramatically improved with just a few strokes of under-eye concealer, powder, eyeliner, and mascara.

But just as money and designer bags and an extra olive in her dirty martinis couldn't conceal my mother's nasty drinking habit, neither can a few brushes of powder on my face conceal the illness that is surely lurking beneath.

I was six months overdue for my latest scan, which I finally had right before life promptly blew up in my face. And since I left New York, my doctor has left me not one, but *two voicemails*.

I haven't found the courage to listen to her messages yet, for if the news is bad, I simply cannot deal with it right now.

I'll listen later, I promise myself.

I have more important business to attend to today. Namely: breaking into Drew's flat.

But of course it won't actually be breaking in because I *am* his wife, and I do have both the code *and* the key to let myself in.

With one more nod at Lucy in the mirror, I grab my sunglasses and purse, and I'm off.

A wife in search of the truth.

After she has been burying her own, for *so damn long*.

I'm hiding in a doorway just down the street from my husband's flat, and waiting—not so patiently—for him to leave for work.

Or to go see his criminal defense attorney again.

Who the hell knows at this point?

Lucy doesn't, and I clearly don't either. But we're here all the same, spying, *again*.

Drew didn't text me last night to say goodnight as he usually does. And I didn't text him either.

I wouldn't know what to say to him if I did.

How was your rendezvous with the attorney? Did you

tell him where you've hidden Eve and her sister? Is he going to defend your sorry arse anyway?

P.S. I love you so much that even if you're guilty, I fear I would still take you back. I'd take you back a hundred times over.

No, that certainly wouldn't do. So, I wrote nothing.

But I can't pretend that the lack of a message from him hasn't got me feeling even sicker about the whole debacle than I already was.

Where did he go last night?

I should have followed him.

I am about to check my phone once more just to be sure I haven't missed a message from him, but then, there he is.

Looking too smart for his own good in his dark gray suit, briefcase in hand—a briefcase I gave him for Christmas last year—Drew has just stepped out of his building. He waits for no more than ten seconds before a black town car pulls up to the curb and sweeps him away.

I wonder if his French driver is as nice as our New York driver, Raoul. I wonder so many things about Drew's life in Paris in which I have played no part, and with each question, I feel a stab of guilt for not having made an effort to be here with him.

If I had, perhaps none of this would be happening.

I'm here now, though, and I must do what I came to do.

I wait about ten minutes just to be sure he doesn't come right back for any reason, and then I—or, rather, *Lucy* takes off down the skinny sidewalk and punches in the building code like she lives here.

One look at the endless spiral staircase that leads up to Drew's flat on the fifth floor and my body says a clear and unmistakable, *hell no.* Into the lift I go. I press the button and close my eyes the entire way up. My breath is short and the pain in my abdomen is only increasing with each passing day. Of course this could be due to the stress of tailing my husband, but considering the two voicemails my doctor has left me, I suspect not.

The lift doors open, and there before me looms the door to a world I know nothing of. The world—*the life*—my husband has built in Paris without me.

As I take one cautious step out of the lift, and then another, Eve's description of Drew's flat replays in my head.

White and modern with only a few splashes of black and gray. Marble countertops. Hardwood floors. Floor-to-ceiling windows. Spiral staircase.

Only one photo...of the happy fucking couple.

My feet inch forward another two steps, my hand gripping the key so tightly that my knuckles are turning white. I'm terrified that when I turn this key in the lock, I am going to unlock the door to a place from which I can never return. A flat that looks exactly as Eve has described it—*sterile and hostile all at once.*

This is the moment of truth.

A quick peek down the long spiral staircase to be sure no one is coming, and when I hear no footsteps, no voices, I know it's time.

I thrust the key into the lock...except it won't go all the way in. I turn the key upside down and try again, but still, it won't take. I try again and again, all to no avail.

There is only one lock on this door, and only one key to open it. And it is not the key that Drew has given me.

Has he changed the locks?

But why?

To keep me out? Or someone else?

This is not a good sign, and I'm not sure what else to do at the moment but leave.

The tiny lift sweeps me back down to the ground floor. Panic takes over, and I try to fight it by reminding myself that it's been a year and a half since Drew bought this flat and gave me the key. It's feasible, of course, that something could have happened between now and then that would have prompted him to change the locks. And that something could have nothing to do with me or Eve or whatever the hell he has been doing behind my back.

But as I let myself out of the building and force the humid morning air into my lungs, I know that isn't true.

After his visit to the criminal defense attorney, how could I think otherwise?

My husband is hiding something—*or someone*—inside his flat, and that is why he's changed the locks.

It is precisely for this reason that I must find a way inside.

40

OFFICER JEAN-MARC DEVEREAUX

JEUDI 18 MAI 2017
36 QUAI DES ORFÈVRES ~ PARIS, FRANCE

FOUR OUT OF six of Devereaux's eager team members had piled into Devereaux's stuffy office to discuss the recent DNA findings.

The findings that proved, without a shadow of a doubt, that Eve Winters was really Sara Marvel.

Devereaux's head was still spinning from the discovery. His team members appeared equally as shocked. They couldn't wait for Breton and Martinez to get back from their tasks in the field; they had to discuss this *now*.

"Sara Marvel's DNA was all over that apartment," Tessier said, his eyes skimming over the DNA report. "Most of the prints in the apartment are hers, and the long dark hair belongs to her. The blood does, too. Well, most of it."

"And the rest?" Devereaux asked, reaching for the Marvel family case file which Tessier had promptly pulled upon receiving the news.

"We still have more prints, and hair and blood samples

too, that haven't been matched to anyone yet. Blond hair mixed in with some of Sara's hair, likely confirming the presence of another female on the scene."

It's what Devereaux had thought upon seeing all that hair in Eve's apartment. Girls pull each other's hair out. Men typically take other avenues in their violence.

"And the semen?" Devereaux asked, remembering the black panties stuffed in between the couch cushions.

Tessier shook his head. "No match yet."

Devereaux nodded, opening up the case file. While Tessier gave the rest of the team a quick summary of the Marvel sisters' grim story, Devereaux thumbed through the old photos stuffed in the file.

The photographs spoke louder than Tessier's words. They spoke louder because Devereaux remembered them. He remembered studying this case alongside his father. He remembered the gruesome pictures of Lisa Marvel, the girls' mother, beaten and stabbed, lying on none other than the black-and-white checkered kitchen floor that Eve mentioned twice in her book.

Of course the tiles weren't only black and white; they'd been smeared in crimson as well. The blood of Lisa Marvel, and the blood of her own daughter, Sara.

Devereaux flipped through the disturbing photos until he reached one that was taken of the stab wound Sara's mother had given her when she'd slashed her with the knife. It was below her left shoulder, above her left breast.

Just as Eve had described in her book.

Goosebumps prickled Devereaux's skin. After all these years, how insane was it that they were now searching for *Sara Marvel*? In the same city where she'd lost her sister twelve years ago.

In the same city where her sister had never been found. Where Devereaux's father *couldn't find her*.

Would Devereaux find Sara? Or would this case drive him mad the way Kate's disappearance had driven his own father mad?

Devereaux shook his head, grabbed his coffee, and downed the rest of it in two gulps.

"So the sister who Eve—or *Sara*—mentions in her book, Willow, is likely based upon the memory of Sara's sister Kate?" Leroux asked.

Durand grabbed a piece of paper from the case file and lifted it up to show his team:

"Full names: Sara *Eve* Marvel and Kathryn *Willow* Marvel." Durand paused, pushing his thick glasses up his nose. "I'd say it's more than likely, yes, given that Sara used their middle names in the book."

"So Willow does exist, just not in the way Eve describes in her book," Leroux stated.

"*Existed*," Tessier corrected.

"They never found a body," Devereaux reminded his team.

"True, but the bloody T-shirt, the exhaustive search led by your father," Tessier shot back. "After all that, nothing. I'd say it's likely Kate is dead."

"Dead or not, Kate isn't who we need to be concerned with," Devereaux said. "It's Sara Marvel, and the fact that she has lied in her *supposed* memoir. She's created a character out of her missing sister. Which means the validity of Eve's book, of everything she has written and the leads we are now following based on her book, need to be seriously scrutinized."

"I'd be surprised if the sex scenes weren't real," Durand

piped in with a devious grin. "I read them last night and *putain* are they good."

The rest of the team had a laugh at this. The rest of the team *except* Devereaux.

Was Eve just leading them on a wild goose chase with her book? Could Martinez's theory that Eve was staging her own disappearance to skyrocket her book sales be true?

But all that hair, and all that blood. Leaving her suitcase, her purse, and her passport at the door. Where would she have gone?

"Do we have Eve's bank records yet?" Devereaux asked. "And the phone records?"

"Still working on it," Tessier said. "Breton said they've been held up. Not sure why. Should have them by the morning."

Devereaux thumbed through the case file, looking for Sara's birthday.

There it was: April 23, 1988.

The same as Eve's passport. They really were the same girl. Unbelievable.

"I confirmed that Sara did attend New York University," Tessier continued. "Under the name of Eve Winters, though. We're still looking into contacts she may have had around that time—roommates, other students who knew her, professors. Eve's literary agent Abbey Strumeyer did share a connection with me that could prove to be interesting. Strumeyer has another client—a writer by the name of Sophia Grayson—who was one of Eve's writing professors at NYU. Leroux, will you follow up?"

Leroux nodded, furiously scribbling notes in his bulging notepad.

And Devereaux was furiously connecting more dots in

his caffeine-fueled brain. "You said Sophia Grayson? That name sounds familiar."

"She's written a few books apparently," Tessier added.

Devereaux nodded, making a mental note to Google Sophia Grayson later today, among the four thousand other things he needed to do to find Sara Marvel.

"Does the press know that Eve is Sara Marvel?" Devereaux asked.

Tessier shook his head. "When I spoke with Breton on the phone earlier, he told me to keep it quiet as long as possible."

"Good," Devereaux said. At least he and Breton were on the same page about something.

"Where is he anyway?" Devereaux asked.

"Probably fucking your sister," Durand mumbled under his breath.

Devereaux snatched the piece of paper with Sara's and Kate's full names from Durand's hands. He wanted to punch Durand right through his thick black glasses, but instead he placed the paper on top of the case file, tucked the file under his arm and stood up from his desk.

"What about Martinez?" Devereaux snapped.

"She's watching Breton fuck your sister," Durand said, pushing Devereaux to his limit.

"*Putain*, you're sick," Devereaux said, shaking his head.

The sound of the others snickering made Devereaux's blood boil even more.

When they calmed down, Leroux spoke. "Martinez is pulling video footage from the Ritz. We didn't get anything from the George V, but the Ritz looks promising."

"Good. What about video footage from neighborhood cameras near Eve's apartment?" Devereaux asked.

"Breton said it's coming in later today," Tessier said.

"Good. Keep me updated on all of it," Devereaux said, heading for the door.

"Will do," Leroux said.

Devereaux had more important things to do than lose his temper over Durand's crude sense of humor about his sister's sex life.

He had to find Sara Marvel.

He couldn't allow Sara to meet the same fate as her sister.

It was in his blood to get this done, and nothing would stop him.

41

EVE

The When: Unknown
The Where: Unknown

He gave me more this time.
My veins smiled, cheered, roared.
AHHHHHHHH!

My broken bones, though, will they ever be fixed?
My scars sewn?
My heart held...
By anyone other than this monster with the needle?
Or the monsters of the past?

Father with his fist of liquor...
Knuckles made of blood.
Mother with her tongue of daggers...
Spitting venom at our dreams.

And Kate.

The sister who disappeared.
And left me alone...
With the monsters.

42

OFFICER JEAN-MARC DEVEREAUX

VENDREDI 19 MAI 2017
36 QUAI DES ORFÈVRES ~ PARIS, FRANCE

IT WAS WELL past midnight when Devereaux's eyelids began their unruly descent. A harsh rap on his door saved them from their ultimate plummet.

It was Leroux, looking way less tired than Devereaux felt. Damn that young bastard.

"I've got something," Leroux said in that eager voice that all younger officers have early in their career.

Devereaux straightened himself up and nodded at Leroux to come in. "Let's hear it."

Leroux flipped through his trusty notepad and launched in. "Eve's professor at NYU, the one who has the same agent as Eve, her name is Sophia—"

"Grayson," Devereaux interrupted. *Putain.* He hadn't looked her up yet, but thankfully it appeared Leroux had. "What about her?"

"Her husband, Andrew Grayson, is a banker. He's the CEO of *Le Crédit Parisien de France.* Has a Park Avenue apartment with his wife in New York but he mainly runs the Paris office. The wife teaches at NYU so it wouldn't appear that she can be in Paris with him much. All the photos we've found of them online show this American power couple. They're always together in New York, though. Never in Paris. From what we've found so far, he fits the description of the married man in Eve's book."

"Interesting," Devereaux conceded. "But I'm sure there are tons of other American businessmen like him who split their time between New York and Paris. Have you and Martinez—"

"Yes, we've made a list," Leroux cut in. "And there are other leads we're looking into, but this one is at the top. Martinez confirmed that Andrew Grayson stays at the Ritz often. In a penthouse suite. It's not the George V like Eve mentioned in her book, but—"

"We can't trust everything Eve wrote in that book."

"Exactly," Leroux said. "And hotel staff at the Ritz have confirmed that they've seen a girl who looks like Eve staying there on occasion."

"There are lots of girls who look like Eve in this city," Devereaux said. "We need proof. Has Martinez pulled the video footage from the Ritz to confirm if it was really Eve?"

"She's working on it," Leroux said.

"Does this Andrew Grayson have an apartment in Paris? Surely he doesn't live at the Ritz, no matter how rich the bastard may be."

"Yes, I've got the address." Leroux handed Devereaux a slip of paper.

Devereaux examined the address and nodded up at his young colleague. "Have you called Sophia Grayson yet to ask about her relationship with Eve?"

"We've tried her several times today but no answer."

"How about Grayson himself? Has anyone called to question him yet?"

"Same problem."

"He's not answering?"

"Not once."

"Let me handle Andrew Grayson. You keep trying with the wife."

Leroux nodded, continuing his rapid flip through his notepad. The turning pages were grating on Devereaux's tired nerves, but he was pleased Leroux was here just as late as he was, getting shit done.

"Nice work," Devereaux said to his young colleague.

"Are you heading home soon?" Leroux asked.

Devereaux shook his head and reached for another cigarette. "No, I'll be here."

This was his only real home, after all. Now that he didn't have Mia's warm body waiting for him in their bed, there was no incentive to stop working.

Plus, they couldn't afford to sleep during this case.

Not if they wanted to find Eve alive.

43

SOPHIA

Friday the 19th of May, 2017
rue de Lille ~ Paris

I'm hiding in the back seat of my own hired car this morning as I wait down the street from Drew's flat, watching for him to emerge, so that I can, once again, attempt to break in and search the place. A locksmith will be needed for this part of the plan, and in the event that the locksmith needs to see identification that I am, in fact, one of the inhabitants of the flat, I have left my Lucy Taylor disguise back at the hotel.

Which is why, of course, I'm crouching down inside the back of an Uber like a crazy woman.

And why I feel absolutely, totally naked.

A quick glance in the rearview mirror and my insecurities are confirmed—Lucy looked *so* much better than Sophia.

My Uber driver—a young Frenchman with big brown puppy dog eyes—catches my gaze in the mirror. I quickly look away, not wanting to answer the questions his eyes are certainly asking: *What has got you looking so haggard, lady? Why have we been waiting here for over twenty minutes already? Who are you spying on?*

I'm paying the man to wait here, so he can just *shut up* with his silent judgement.

"Shouldn't be much longer," I call up to him.

He nods, still sizing me up in the rearview mirror.

I keep my gaze glued to Drew's front door, until finally, he walks out. Just like yesterday, my husband is looking as handsome as ever in his smart black suit with briefcase in hand. If he *is* involved in this whole Eve debacle, his face certainly isn't showing signs of distress—well, not from this distance anyway.

Drew's driver doesn't pull up right away as he did yesterday. A few minutes pass, and then a few more. Drew is on his phone the whole time, texting it appears. I take a peek at my phone and confirm, once again, that he is not texting me.

I hovered outside of his office nearly all day yesterday and then followed him home from work last night. Rather than speaking on the phone as we usually do, we shared a brief text exchange once he'd made it back to his flat because he was, apparently, "going to bed early." Although I stood on the sidewalk below his flat for some time after, noticing that the lights streaming from his windows hadn't been turned off.

They stayed on until after midnight, at which point I was so knackered I had no choice but to return to my hotel and pass out. I still had stacks of final papers to grade, but I didn't touch a single one.

I simply cannot be bothered with the deadlines of my teaching job right now.

Drew is still standing on the sidewalk texting, but he's

beginning to look impatient. He takes a step forward and peers to his left and then to his right. That's when he spots my Uber.

His eyes narrow as he inspects the car from a distance. I slink down in my seat a bit more, thinking that he surely cannot see me from this distance through the slightly tinted car windows no less.

But he takes a step in our direction. And then another. And another, until he is walking with a purpose straight toward the car.

I smack my Uber driver in the shoulder. "*Allez!*" I cry before slinking as far down in my seat as I can possibly get. The driver shoots me a confused look, and so I screech again. "*ALLEZ!*"

He takes off down the street, and when we are far enough away, I get the courage to peek up just a bit and I spot Drew standing in the middle of the street, watching us speed away.

Bugger, bugger, bugger.

Did he see me?

No. We were far enough away that even if he saw the outline of a woman in the back seat, surely he wouldn't have known it was me.

Would he have?

I instruct Monsieur Puppy Dog Eyes to drive around a bit while I gather my nerves, and after about thirty minutes of aimless circling, I ask him to return to Drew's flat.

Thankfully, there is no sign of Drew, which I'm hoping to mean that his driver arrived and he is off to work.

Getting out of this sodding vehicle once and for all, I pull out my cell phone and dial the number I'd saved earlier after researching locksmiths in Paris.

My last name—Grayson—is on the buzzer downstairs,

and I *am* Andrew Grayson's wife, so I reckon I won't have a problem convincing the man who is arriving in approximately fifteen minutes to let me into my husband's flat.

I wait *sans* disguise, right outside Drew's building, praying he has actually left for work and that he doesn't catch me here, waiting outside his flat. If he does, I've decided I'll just flash a bright smile and say, "Surprise!"

I'm quite sure at this point it wouldn't be a welcome surprise, but if it comes to that, so be it.

The locksmith takes longer than he said he would; twenty minutes have passed since I phoned.

Thirty.

Forty-five.

I phone again. No answer.

I'm about to call another locksmith when finally, an older man carrying a toolbox and wearing tattered black jeans limps up to me.

"*Madame Grayson?*" he says.

"*Oui, c'est moi.*" I punch in the building code quickly to show how natural it is for me to walk into my own building, and I take the lift with him up to the fifth floor.

It only takes this old man five minutes to open my husband's flat door.

Five minutes, and he doesn't ask for any proof of identity. *Nothing.*

"*Merci, monsieur,*" I tell him with a warm smile and a wad of euros.

"*Je vous en prie, madame.*" His eyes widen when he notices I've paid him much more than he's asked for. But he doesn't ask any questions. He just takes off down the lift and leaves me alone.

Smart man.

Turning around, I find that I am standing inside a flat

that looks like a smaller Parisian version of our modern Park Avenue home back in New York.

A few more steps inside, and I nearly have to steady myself against the wall to keep my balance.

It's *exactly* as Eve described in her memoir. Modern white furniture, a bit of black here, a splash of gray there, but not much actual color. Nothing personal anywhere. No photos on the white walls, just a few pieces of cold modern art that surely cost a fortune.

Floor-to-ceiling windows in the salon. A spiral staircase leading up to a loft. Hardwood floors everywhere.

In the kitchen, marble countertops. And a knife rack—the one Eve pinned her blood-smeared note to.

Bloody hell, Drew.

The knives in the rack call out to me. Perhaps I'll leave my own smears of blood all over his sodding flat.

Make him pay.

But, *no.* I didn't come here to harm myself, or him. I came to search. To spy. To ransack.

To uncover the truth.

Adrenaline pumps through my veins as I pull a pair of white latex gloves from my bag and slip them on. Must avoid staining the place with my fingerprints, certainly.

An impenetrable sadness stabs at my heart each time I think of Eve's description of Drew's flat and look around to find that I am surely in that exact same space.

But I must ignore the sadness, the grief, the desperation that wants to cripple me, for I have work to do.

The salon and kitchen are spotless—unnaturally so, almost as if no one actually lives or eats here, ever. Granted, our home in New York is nearly this immaculate every day, but that is thanks to our house cleaner, Greta, who stops in daily to tidy up. Greta is wonderful. She never asks questions. Not even when she strips the bedsheets and pillowcases which clearly have housed *two* bodies, even when Mr. Grayson is away on business.

I wonder if Drew has a *Greta* here in Paris. Each room is simply too clean and perfect for him not to.

After my search through the kitchen and living room proves fruitless, I head down the hallway, my boots tapping away on the hardwood floors. I pass by three different rooms —two are furnished with beds that look as though they've never been used, and the other contains a sleek black desk that holds a desktop computer screen, a lamp, and a neat stack of papers. I'll come back to this, but first, I want to see Drew's bedroom.

It's the only room that feels lived in, if only because the bed isn't made.

Drew always makes the bed. Always.

Seeing his white comforter and sheets strewn about on the bed is strangely the worst part of this whole thing. It means he truly is someone different here. Someone I don't even recognize.

And of course, it could also mean that he shares this bed with someone, and that *she* doesn't make the bed.

With shaky, gloved hands, I go through each of his dresser drawers, his walk-in closet, his bedside stands, but find nothing of note. Not even a condom. *Nothing.*

Until I discover a shoebox tucked beneath the bed.

I lift the lid and there is the last piece of the puzzle.

A photograph lying in a cracked frame.

Only a few jagged pieces of glass remain to protect the photo that Eve mentioned in her memoir, of *the happy fucking couple.*

This is the frame she shattered. The one with which she sliced her own hand open.

It's a photo that was taken in the days when Drew and I were happy. We were lying on an immaculate white sandy beach in Belize, sipping cocktails, tan legs intertwined as a local took our photograph.

We were beaming.

It was just before we'd started trying for a baby.

Just before the beginning of the end.

And we had no clue what was to come.

As I finally find the courage to pick up the picture, I discover yet one more hidden treasure beneath.

The silver cross necklace with the diamond in the center. The one I gave to Drew for our tenth wedding anniversary. And the same one Eve mentions in her opening sex scene with "Dex."

I can only assume he has hidden it in an attempt to hide all evidence that *he* is the married man in Eve's book.

I am trying not to break down, but here, on my knees in Drew's bedroom, looking at the anniversary gift that I've *never* seen him take off and the photograph of the *we* that we used to be—the *we* that my husband has buried in a box beneath his bed—I simply cannot stop the tears from falling.

And all I can think is that this box is a coffin. That *we* are dead to him.

So dead he can't even keep one sodding photo of us out in his flat.

Sterile and hostile all at once.

Eve was right. It is hostile in here. The most hostile place I've ever been.

And I know there is probably more here that I need to find. More clues which will prove that my husband is the married man featured in Eve's memoir.

But the cross and the photo beneath the bed say everything.

And I must go.

I stash the shoebox back where I found it, but I keep the contents. They don't belong here in this coffin. I don't know where they belong anymore, but I know it's not here.

Back in the salon, I tuck the necklace and the photo into my purse and just before I'm about to leave, I notice the spiral staircase heading up to the loft. I haven't ventured up there yet. And truly, I don't want to.

So don't.

I nearly make it to the front door, my hand reaching for the knob, but I freeze when I hear a male voice in the hallway.

Drew.

No.

The slippery spiral staircase is suddenly looking more appealing. Hurling myself toward it, I take the steps two at a time, praying I don't fall but knowing I have no other choice because his key is already turning in the lock.

I make it up to the loft just as the door opens downstairs. Drew's voice is echoing off the tall ceilings now, and as I scour the small upstairs space for a place to hide, I realize that he is speaking French instead of English.

And that his voice isn't the only one I'm hearing.

There are two more.

A woman's—screeching in ear-piercing French.

And a baby's—cooing and babbling away.

No. No. No.

There is barely anything for me to hide behind in this tiny loft. No bed. No dresser. No desk.

Only one piece of furniture and it is the absolute last thing I'd ever want to see in my husband's Parisian flat.

A crib.

A baby's crib.

44

OFFICER JEAN-MARC DEVEREAUX

VENDREDI 19 MAI 2017
RUE DE LILLE ~ PARIS, FRANCE

When Devereaux arrived at the address Leroux had given him late last night, he looked up toward the top floor of the fancy Left Bank apartment building where American mogul Andrew Grayson supposedly resided while he was running *Le Crédit Parisien de France.* The windows were far too high to allow Devereaux to see anything from his vantage point down on the sidewalk, but soon enough, he'd be face to face with the man who was—at present—the most likely match to the married man in Eve's—or *Sara Marvel's* —book.

Devereaux had called Grayson's office this morning but his secretary said he wasn't in yet, which was why Devereaux decided to show up at the man's front door. He could've called the cell number he'd pulled for Grayson, certainly to give him a head's up that he was about to be questioned by the police, but Devereaux thought surprising the rich bastard would be more fun.

Devereaux buzzed Grayson's name at the front door and waited.

45

SOPHIA

Friday the 19th of May, 2017
Drew's flat ~ Paris

The dots refuse to connect. *Simply fucking refuse.*

Drew is downstairs fighting in French with a woman whose voice I've never heard before.

A baby begins to cry.

I am upstairs in the loft, hiding behind a white crib with light pink bedding.

A woman.

A baby.

A crib.

No.

The pain in my abdomen makes a violent return as I try to make out what they're saying. But they're speaking too quickly, all in French. And the baby is screaming. And there is blood thumping in my ears.

Against my better judgement, I crawl out from behind the crib and keep going until I reach the railing that looks down over the salon. I am nearly flattened on the floor, but I can see them now.

Tears are streaming down the woman's face, and she is quite young. Really just a girl. Twenty-six, twenty-seven perhaps. Petite but still rather curvy, as if she hasn't lost the baby weight. Short blond hair, pouty lips, high cheekbones, and crazy eyes. Drew is standing before her, their arguing making the veins in the side of his head pop out, his cheeks flaming tomato red. He runs his hand through his hair, shakes his head, and takes a step away from the girl as her screams intensify.

I'm making out words here and there but can't seem to string them together into anything coherent.

"...tu savais...pas possible...m'as pas dit...malade..."

...you knew...not possible...didn't tell me...sick...

I give up on trying to understand the words in between, knowing that even if I could understand it all, I wouldn't want to. The scene I'm watching is enough to destroy me and everything I'd ever hoped my life could be.

I don't need this girl's foolish words to do any more damage.

The girl moves a little to the left, and there beside her is a light-blue pushchair. I spot a pair of chubby legs sticking out, kicking. The baby is wearing little white shoes with violet bows on the buckles.

A baby girl.

"*Mais arrête!*" Drew barks at the desperate French girl, which doesn't shut her up, not even for a second. He ignores her cries and instead, bends over the pushchair, emerging with the little girl in his arms. The baby has light-brown curly hair and rosy cheeks, and her violet dress bunches up around her nappy as she kicks and screams nearly as loud as her mother.

Drew bounces her on his hip for a moment, and then he looks down at her little red face, lovingly, so lovingly, and kisses her on the forehead.

"Shhh...my little Adelaide, it's okay, it's okay," Drew says.

My mouth goes dry. My palms are coated in sweat. My vision fades to a blur.

Drew is kissing the baby. A baby who is not ours.

His baby.

His little Adelaide.

Drew kisses the little thing a second and a third time before the mother begins screaming one single phrase. Over and over, and over again.

Wretched and crackling, her shrill voice pierces my ears. My insides. My heart.

By the third time she says it, I understand her.

"Tu veux me tuer? Tu veux me tuer? Tu veux me tuer?"

Do you want to kill me? Do you want to kill me? Do you want to kill me?

Drew kisses the baby one more time, then calmly lays her back down into the pushchair and aims it away from where her screaming mother is standing. Then he walks up to the girl, grabs her shoulders and slams her back against the wall.

"Putain Coralie! Tais-toi!"

Fuck, Coralie! Shut up!

He slams her again. She's crying harder now. Still screaming back at him.

"Tu veux me tuer! Tu veux me tuer! Tu veux me tuer!"

She winds up and smacks him hard across the face.

Drew steps back for a moment, releases his hold on her shoulders, and I think he is going to walk away from her. But no, he doesn't.

Instead, he takes a step forward and slaps her right back.

The cracking sound his hand makes on her face is sickening.

Her screams stop.

Blood begins to trickle from her nostrils.

She crumbles to the floor, sobbing. Wrecked. Curled up in a ball, face buried in her hands.

A loud buzz rings through the apartment. Drew visibly startles. "*Fuck*," he mumbles.

Drew doesn't reach for Coralie. Doesn't help her. Instead he scoops Baby Adelaide back up into his arms, ignores the buzzer which has now buzzed a second time, and begins to sing.

"*Au clair de la lune.*"

It's a French lullaby that my mother used to sing to me when I was a little girl because her mother, who was half-French, sang it to her when she was little too.

Drew's voice is soft and sweet, loving and...*sorry*. I can hear the guilt laced in each note he sings.

But the baby doesn't know guilt. Not yet. She only hears his love.

It is this love and his soothing voice that finally begin to calm her down.

I can't bear to watch for another second. As quietly as I can, I slide back behind the crib, curl up into a ball, and try desperately to catch my breath.

But I can't. I can't seem to find air no matter how hard I try.

All I can see is Drew holding that little girl in his arms, calling her Adelaide, singing to her and bouncing her and kissing her like he loves her.

Kissing her the way a father would kiss his little girl.

Because she *is* his little girl.

Drew's gone and had a baby with another woman.

Because I couldn't have one. I couldn't have a baby who would stay alive in my womb.

They died.

They always died.

Drew has taken both the crazy French girl with the bloody nose and their baby back to his bedroom. They never did let whoever was buzzing downstairs into the building, nor did they climb the stairs up to the nursery where I've been hiding all this time.

I was bracing myself for things to get much, much worse if Drew found me up here.

But he never did.

The screams and cries have stopped.

I suppose they have all laid down for a nap together. How lovely.

Or perhaps Drew is shagging the hysterical girl to calm her down while the baby sleeps. Even lovelier.

It's time for me to go and leave my husband alone...*with his other family.*

I slip my boots off, tuck them beneath my arms, and tiptoe down the spiral staircase as quietly as I can. A soft ribbon of sunlight shines in through the tall windows in the salon, stretching across the floors, lighting up a few drops of Coralie's blood.

I have a strange and sudden urge to lie there, in her blood, and just go to sleep.

Sleep...and never, ever wake up.

As I am pondering this most comforting thought, a flash of Drew's face pops into my mind. Not his face as he looks now, today. But the way he was when we first met as college freshman at Princeton. His skin was pale, and he would blush easily when we talked. His blue eyes were innocent, but there was something fierce in them—something that told me this guy was going to stick around for the long haul.

And he did.

My husband may have stuck around, he may have kept his promise to never, ever leave me, but this man I have loved for so long, this man loves a baby who is not ours.

A loud clatter snaps me from my imagery. *My boots.* Somehow I've let them slip and they've fallen to the floor.

Bugger.

I scoop them up and take off toward the door. It's a loud and clumsy exit, but I make it out of there and begin my race down the stairs.

Down, down, down I go, with only one thought running in loops around my brain.

If Drew sees me, will he hurt me too?

Outside, the spring air is cool and light. The scent of flowers dances around me, and laughter is trickling down the charming little rue from a nearby café. Paris is buzzing, the way it always does, all day, all night. Nothing in this grand city has changed.

As for me, though—I am running, running, running, knowing that *my* world, *my* life, everything I once believed it to be...*is no more.*

46

OFFICER JEAN-MARC DEVEREAUX

VENDREDI 19 MAI 2017
RUE DE LILLE ~ PARIS, FRANCE

AFTER BUZZING a few times with no answer, Devereaux decided to wait outside for someone to let him into the building. It was likely that Grayson had already left for work, but it could be just as likely that he was upstairs not answering the buzzer. And if the latter were the case, Devereaux couldn't wait to find out *why* Grayson wasn't answering.

Devereaux decided to send off a few important text messages while he was waiting. For starters, he needed to know when Eve's cell phone and bank records would be in, as well as when they'd get a look at any video footage taken from street cameras in Eve's neighborhood the night of her disappearance, and why in the hell it was all taking so long. After he sent that question off to Breton, he sent another message off to Martinez asking if she'd secured the video footage from the Ritz. And finally, a message to Coralie to ask how she and Adelaide were doing. Ever since Coralie had moved in with Breton, Devereaux barely heard from his sister. And damn did he miss his little niece. Coralie, not so much, but the baby, desperately.

A swift reply from Breton arrived on Devereaux's phone:

> Breton: Bank and phone records are in. Bank transactions show consistent massive cash deposits beginning in May 2016, suggesting prostitution began 2 months prior to the supposed July meeting with "Dex" as she writes in book. Also, Eve received two massive checks from agent/publisher for book deal—that part was true. There were no questionable withdrawals or transfers to other accounts prior to disappearance. All transactions have stopped since she disappeared—no withdrawals, no transfers, nothing. Phone records show calls to and from agent and publisher. No personal calls—no friends or clients. Eve must have used pre-paid cell to correspond with clients.

If Eve hasn't withdrawn any money since the night she disappeared and wasn't transferring or withdrawing massive sums prior to her book release, it's highly unlikely she staged her own disappearance.

And not using her cell phone for *any* personal calls whatsoever was bizarre. Perhaps she had another cell phone registered under another name? Or as Breton had suggested, a pre-paid phone made sense for her prostitution work. No phone records that way.

Just as Devereaux was about to fire off a response to Breton, the door to Andrew Grayson's apartment building shot open and a woman with long reddish-blond hair flew out looking exasperated. She turned left immediately, not even noticing Devereaux to her right before she took off down the sidewalk, her boots tucked beneath her arms.

Devereaux had caught the door just before it closed, but he was no longer heading into that apartment building to find Andrew Grayson.

Instead, he let the door close and took off down the sidewalk in the direction of the panicked woman racing down the street in her socks.

47

THE MISTRESS OF PARIS: A MEMOIR

BY EVE WINTERS

LE 24 OCTOBRE 2016
HÔTEL GEORGE V ~ PARIS, FRANCE

I'M STANDING at the door of the suite—*our suite*—at the George V, wishing I'd had the courage to stay away. But Dex's messages were becoming desperate, and as much as I hate him right now for how he treated me the other night, the idea of him in such agony—or worse, hurting himself—has simply become too much for me to bear.

I can't believe I've become so pathetic, but here I am, knocking on his door. Barely a second passes before he opens.

Dex is in a state I've never seen him in before.

His hair is a ruffled, greasy mess atop his head. His eyes are bloodshot and drained. His normally clear skin is blotchy and red, and it looks as though he hasn't shaved in days.

I'm simultaneously thrilled and horrified to see him looking such a wreck—which pretty much sums up the overriding sentiment of this entire relationship.

A tragedy of extremes. Thrills and horrors. Ecstasy and pain. Love and grief.

For us, there is no in between.

I take a step toward him, waiting to see what he will say.

He reaches for me. "Willow, I'm so sorry." He wraps his arms around me. "I'm so sorry." Lays his head on my shoulder. "I'm so sorry, Willow. I'm so sorry. I'm so sorry."

And then he cries. Dex Anderson, the powerful, possessive millionaire with whom I have fallen irrevocably in love, sobs on my shoulder like a lost little boy.

I wrap a hand around his head and hold him close to me.

"It's okay, Dex." The words slide past my lips before I can stop them. "I know you are."

He can't stop saying it, though. "I'm sorry. I'm so, so sorry."

I want him to know that I believe him. I want him to know that I'm never going to leave him. How could I have ever thought I would want to get out of this? To never see him again?

I lift his face to mine and look into his cloudy, tear-filled gaze.

"I love you, Dex. I love you so much. All I want is for you to love me back, forever."

Dex scoops me up in his arms, carries me across the threshold and into the bedroom where we will, once again, seal the deal of our love.

He lays me down, kneels over me and kisses my neck, my shoulders, the tops of my breasts. His eyes lock with mine. "I will never hurt you like that again, Willow. I promise. And I will love you forever."

There is nothing to do but believe him.

Which is why, when Dex removes my clothing and

gives me every last bit of himself for hours and hours that night, I decide that I will email my agent first thing in the morning and tell her to disregard the memoir idea. I will write an entirely different book that has nothing to do with me and Dex. Nothing to do with a fake prostitute who falls in love with her married lover. Nothing to do with the man who is going to love me forever.

I decide that I will never, ever allow Dex to know who I really am, because I can never lose him.

I love him more than I love myself, and losing him would mean nothing less than total devastation.

Losing him would mean death. The death of love, of ecstasy, of all that I now treasure in my life.

I would die if I lost him, I know this for sure.

It's the middle of the night and I am wide awake, listening to Dex's heartbeat as he sleeps. With our legs intertwined, our hips glued together, our arms wrapped around each other's waists, and our heads nestled together on one pillow, we form one big body-heart-soul and nothing has ever felt more right.

But in this dark, cozy, blissful little bubble we occupy, I am lying awake because I can't stop thinking about how the man who is wrapped around me right now, who has been professing his undying love for me all night long, is also a man who could be so violent with me, who could hurt me the way he did.

How can those two qualities co-exist in one person?

I know my question is ridiculous, of course, as I grew up with a mother who could love me and hate me in the same breath. One moment, she was showering me and Willow with the most love a mother could ever give, and the next moment, she would take it all away.

But Dex isn't sick the way my mother was.

Is he?

I'm tossing and turning now, unable to stop wondering *who* this man lying next to me really is. Sure, I know that he's a married American businessman who rarely, if ever, has sex with his wife. I know that he's crazy, madly, deeply in love with me, and I with him. I know that we can make love for hours and hours and never tire of pleasing each other. I know that we can lie awake talking and laughing about inconsequential things such as how the French are always going on strike or how the champagne we had earlier was the best champagne we've ever had in our lives or how we both adore the French film *Amélie* but that we absolutely must watch it with subtitles because the dialogue is far too fast for us to pick up on our own.

Beyond what we do in the bedroom and all of those little things we discuss in between our nearly incessant lovemaking sessions, what else do I know about this man? I know nothing of his childhood. Anytime I've asked, all he's given me is that he's not close with his family.

But who made him? Where do they live?

And more importantly, what did they do to him?

Finally, I give my lover a nudge. Softly at first, and then a little harder, and harder still until he begins to stir.

"You okay, love?" Dex whispers as he pulls me closer.

"I can't sleep," I tell him.

He runs a hand through my hair, nuzzles his nose to mine. "Bad dream?"

"No...I need to ask you something, Dex."

He's still buried in the pillow, eyes closed when he says, "What is it?"

"Where do your parents live?"

Dex lifts his head from the pillow but doesn't respond. I can tell I've got his full attention now.

"I'm sorry...I know that's a random question to ask in the middle of the night, but I've just been lying here thinking about how I don't know that much about you. I mean, I know how you are and how you feel about me, but because of our...situation...I guess I just haven't wanted to probe too much into your other life."

"Maybe we should keep it that way."

"Please, Dex. Tell me," I push.

"I don't have parents." Dex's voice comes out chillier than the night.

"They've both passed away?"

"My mother, yes. My father, I'm not sure," Dex responds.

"Oh. How do you not know what happened—"

"I don't want to know," he snaps.

"Don't get cold with me, Dex. I'm just trying to know you more. After what happened the other night, I just..."

"You want to know what happened to me that could turn me into such a monster?"

I'm not sure how to respond to that, so I don't.

We lie in silence for what feels like an eternity until finally, Dex opens up. He tells me a story of abandonment and poverty, of illness and broken hearts, and ultimately, of death. The death of those he loved most, and the death of his youth.

It is a story that is so sad, so utterly heartbreaking, I can hardly keep myself from crying for him.

And it is a story I cannot share here in this book, for if I do, Dex's true identity will be revealed. And the life he's worked so hard to build, after everything that happened to him when he was young, will disintegrate before his very eyes.

As much as I want Dex to leave his wife, as much as I want him to choose me, I still love him more than that, and I will not destroy him.

I will not.

I wrap my arms tighter around his shoulders, push my hips even closer to his. He has no idea how similar we really are—that I, too, lost my innocence so young...*too young*. That I, too, was abandoned by those who should have loved me most.

The difference is that Dex's wife knows about these darkest parts of him. This is partly the reason why he will never leave her, I imagine. She knows all—well, most—of him and loves him anyway.

I, however, could never bring myself to tell Lucas the truth about my past. I wanted so desperately for him only to see the light in me. The idea of Lucas knowing how dark things can get inside me was terrifying. How could he want me if he knew who I really was? Where I'd really been? What I'd seen?

What I'd lost.

When Lucas asked about the ghastly scar that lies just beneath my left shoulder, I told him it was from a horseback riding accident when I was little.

My tumultuous childhood clearly did not lend to horseback riding trips, but Lucas believed me...or at least he acted as if he did.

Dex hasn't ever asked, but if he does, perhaps I'll tell him that I fell while ice skating. Another childhood memory I don't have and yet wish were true.

"I've always felt it was my fault," Dex says into the

silence. "My fault that they're gone. And I just can't lose anyone like that, ever again."

A heavy silence settles between us, and I can feel the pain emanating from Dex's entire body.

"When you saw me with my friend the other night, did you think I was going to leave you?" I ask.

Dex rests his head on my chest, his fingers gripping my sides.

"That's all I could think about. And then in the morning when you left that note, I thought I'd fucked it all up. I thought I'd lost you forever."

I squeeze him tighter to me, realizing that beneath this commanding façade, Dex is just a little boy, terrified of being abandoned.

"You didn't lose me, Dex. I'm right here."

A moment later, I feel a trail of moisture on my skin where Dex's head is lying.

They're tears. His tears.

I don't say anything. I just let him feel what he needs to feel, and I pray that he won't ask about my parents.

His story is grim and devastating, yes.

But mine is...well, it's unthinkable.

Which is why, I suppose, I find my way on top of him before he can ask me where I came from. It's why I roll my lips over his chest and down, down, down, until I feel him throbbing in my mouth.

I know I can't take all of his pain away. Not now, not ever.

But I can certainly make him forget about it for tonight.

In the morning, after Dex has fed me a breakfast of sex

and strawberries, whipped cream and champagne, he heads to the bathroom. I fish my phone out of my purse to compose an email to my agent to call the whole memoir thing off.

Even more after our conversation in the middle of the night, I know that I cannot go through with it. I cannot hurt Dex like that, not after what happened to him when he was young, and I cannot stand to lose him.

But when I open my email, I find a response from my agent to my original pitch.

> Eve,
>
> I read your pages and, excuse my French, but holy shit. Wow. You were clearly meant to write the truth, Eve. This book will be your becoming, and I am honored to represent you in this journey. I don't want you to change a thing in the first three chapters—the writing is exquisite and haunting and everything that makes a memoir powerful and beautiful. We will be able to sell this based on a proposal and the first three chapters alone—of that I have no doubt. I've already sent the pitch to three editors. More to come.
>
> Stay tuned, and get ready, lady. This is going to be big.
>
> Abbey

Chills run down my spine at Abbey's words.

This is going to be big.

Once again, I am simultaneously thrilled and horrified. No one has ever praised my writing like this. And all I've ever wanted for years is to be a writer. A *real* writer.

Dex emerges from the bathroom, naked and grinning like a fool. The fool who I love more than anything.

I slide my phone back into my purse and smile up at

him, wondering if there is a way to do both. Love Dex *and* write this book.

When his lips find mine, I know that this idea is ludicrous. It's one or the other.

My writing career or Dex.

My lifelong dream or the love of my life.

When Dex finds his way inside of me once again, I remind myself that no matter what happened to him when he was younger, no matter how much I don't want to hurt him, and no matter how much I don't want to lose him, *he has a wife who he will never, ever leave.*

That no matter where this love takes us, *it cannot and will not last forever.*

But my words—they *can* last forever.

They *will* last forever.

They will outlive the death of us.

It's an impossible choice that I don't want to think about right now.

And so, instead of making a decision, I let Dex rock me into oblivion all day and into the next night. I let him feed me dose after dose of sex and cocaine and ecstasy and love.

We are riding high, so dangerously high, and I know that the fall will be deadly.

But each time he makes me come, each time he tells me how much he loves me and how he will never, ever stop worshipping my body, I tell death it can *fuck off* for today.

Because for once in my life, I'm alive.

So very alive.

48

SOPHIA

Friday the 19th of May, 2017
La Closerie des Lilas ~ Paris

My hands are still shaking as I gratefully accept a tall glass of red wine from the bartender at the one of the most iconic cafés in Paris—La Closerie des Lilas. This dark cozy bar and greenhouse-like restaurant brimming with live plants, cherry-red chairs, and tipsy Parisians has housed such literary greats as Ernest Hemingway, Gertrude Stein, and F. Scott Fitzgerald. It is also the café featured in Eve's memoir where she meets with a mysterious male "friend" whom she never identifies, and who sparks the vicious sexual encounter she has with Dex afterward.

I am not a literary great. By all accounts, I am a failed writer. Five out of the ten novels I've written have been published, and out of those five, only the first and second novels actually sold well. I reached a mild level of fame in those days, and that fame is what helped me to secure my position as a Creative Writing Professor at NYU. Since then, the other novels have sold...but not well. And in the years that I've been writing and writing and *not* selling many books, a handful of my former students—*students like Eve*—have gone on to write New York Times Bestsellers.

When the Times List comes out next week, I've no doubt Eve's memoir will be perched firmly at the top. The book is already holding down the #1 spot on Amazon's Top 100 Bestseller List. And the longer she stays gone, the longer she'll stay at the top of every sodding list.

I hate her for it. But I hate myself even more for giving her advice that I have never been able to follow.

Until tonight, that is.

I run my hand through my thick head of auburn hair which is in a total knotted mess from my violent jog away from Drew's flat earlier today and my endless, aimless walk all over the city afterward. The young bartender grins as he watches me fix my hair, but I don't smile back. Instead, I nod for him to bring me another glass of wine as I have nearly finished my first.

I proceed to hook myself up to a constant wine drip for the afternoon. The numbing feeling of alcohol pouring down my throat is the only thing keeping me alive at this moment, and it's the only thing keeping my mind off of what I have just seen and heard at Drew's apartment. As the rapid intoxication makes me feel ever more vengeful, I pull my journal from my purse, along with my favorite violet colored pen.

My phone is beeping at the bottom of my bag with a barrage of unread text messages, voicemails, and emails which have been pouring in for the past few days.

I ignore them all.

I imagine there are messages from my department chair

at NYU, checking in to see if I'm feeling better, but more than likely wanting to know why I haven't yet submitted final grades and when exactly I plan on doing so.

There are probably a few more voicemails from my doctor. Perhaps some from my lover, too, and from my best girlfriend, Dahlia, in London.

But I can't deal with any of them right now.

Because for the first time in my bloody, miserable life, I am going to write the truth.

Following another gulp of wine, I take my ink to the paper. It's time to bleed out all of the dirty secrets I've kept from my husband, the despicable lies I've told him. After all, they are the lies that have ultimately led to the sickening scene I witnessed today in his flat.

As devastated as I am, I cannot pretend that I am a victim of this madness.

I am not a victim; *I am the creator.*

And so, I write down all that I have created...and all that I have destroyed.

It was the summer after my third year at Princeton. I'd accepted a prestigious internship at a bank in Paris, back when I thought I wanted to be an investment banker, and only a few years after Drew and I had first gotten together at uni.

I had fallen in love with Drew in those early years together at Princeton, yes, but it was a sort of young, naïve love that I didn't really believe would last much past graduation. It was the having-sex-in-dorm-rooms, drinking-cheap-beer-with-friends, and laughing-until-3:00-a.m. kind of love.

It was fun, sure, and so was the sex, but our connection was missing something. And I wasn't quite clear as to *what* exactly it was missing until my first day interning in Paris when I met the much, much older CEO of the bank—Vincent Rousseau.

With over thirty years on me, Vincent could have been my father, and he wasn't especially good looking either. Hairy with a slightly plump belly—the kind that comes from years of drinking and eating heavy French dinners lathered in butter—this iconic Parisian tycoon wasn't nearly as handsome as my Drew and his boyishly captivating smile. But there was something intriguing about Vincent. He was bigger and burlier than your average Frenchman, and he possessed the power to match. So much power that I, the naïve intern, was completely *powerless* to his advances.

What a sodding cliché I was.

It started my second week on the job. I was working late one night and nearly everyone else had left the office. Everyone except Monsieur Rousseau, *but of course*.

He stopped by my cubicle, passed a quick glance over my work, and then laid a strong hand on my shoulder.

"I, too, enjoy working late, after everyone has left," he said in French. "But it is important to know when to stop... and when to have a drink."

A nervous giggle escaped my lips, but he didn't break a smile.

"Sophia, is it?" he asked.

"Yes," I said.

"Come, Sophia. Join me for a nightcap in my office."

Without saying a word, I stood and followed him through the winding maze of cubes, all the way back to his massive corner office. Vincent passed right by the light switch and instead went straight for the Scotch. A hint of moonlight shining in through the floor-to-ceiling windows was the only light we had as the strong alcohol filled our glasses.

When he handed me mine, I threw it all back in two big gulps.

I was nervous; I knew why he'd brought me back here, and it *wasn't* to talk about my performance on the job.

"Impressive," he said, taking a step closer to me. The moonlight cast an eerie glow over the left side of his face, the wrinkles that lined his eyes, the gray streaks in his dark hair. His eyes combed over my thin frame and finally rested on my chest where the top button of my blouse met my cleavage.

"Perhaps we should...get a bit more comfortable?" As he said this, he stepped even closer, the softness of his belly pressing into my abdomen. I could feel my heart beating all the way down in my stomach.

I knew this was my chance to leave, *if* I was going to take it.

He hadn't yet taken off my clothes.

Nor had he unbuckled his belt and nodded for me to get down on my knees.

He hadn't yet guided his erection straight into my mouth.

Nor had he leaned up against his desk and pulled my head into him, bobbing it back and forth as he moaned and told me what a good little *stagiaire* I was being.

He hadn't yet stood me up, bent me over his desk and shagged me for a solid hour.

No, he hadn't done any of that yet.

And I hadn't yet been unfaithful to Drew.

This was my chance to do the right thing. To be a good girlfriend.

But only the night before, I'd heard from one of my best girlfriends at uni that she'd spotted Drew snogging some slutty freshman at a party during my first weekend away. I hadn't felt as upset as I would've expected, and I'd chosen not to confront him just yet.

When Vincent's warm hands found the top button of my blouse, I decided I wouldn't confront Drew.

And when I slipped my clothes back on over an hour later, I decided that since Drew and I were so young and living across an ocean from each other, summer flings were all a natural part of the deal.

Although my summer fling turned into an almost nightly event.

After everyone would retire home for the evening, I would meet Vincent in his corner office and let him shag me on his desk. He preferred to use the French expression "*faire l'amour*" or *to make love,* whenever he referred to what we were doing on that desk, but I wasn't an idiot. There was no love between us. The man was fucking me.

He never took off his wedding ring those nights, and he never turned over the lovely photo he kept on his desk of him and his wife on their wedding day. Strangely, though, I never felt guilty. I was sure he'd been having flings with young interns like me for years, and so I took solace in the idea that surely I wasn't the first.

Sometimes I even looked straight into his wife's eyes in the photo while he was inside of me, and I noticed him looking at her sometimes too. Our sex was intoxicating and dirty and forbidden. Some nights it lasted hours, and other nights he only had time for me to drop to my knees and take him in my mouth. Our sex was all of the things that make affair sex so bloody amazing...and so bloody dangerous, as Eve Winters has unfortunately found out.

One of the more dangerous decisions we made was to stop the use of condoms. He wouldn't come inside me, though. Always in my mouth, on my breasts, on my back.

Except for that one time.

He was behind me, and I could feel him thickening inside me as he went faster. He asked me something, but I couldn't hear what he said through my own loud breathing. So I said, "yes?"

He held onto me extra tight, and then released inside of me.

It felt so good precisely because it was *so bad*, and so I said nothing later that night when I pulled my panties back on, kissed him on the lips, and let myself out of his office.

He'd asked if I was on the pill.

When I said yes, he thought I was confirming that I was, in fact, on the pill.

And of course, I wasn't.

Looking back, I've no idea why I hadn't gone on the pill that summer, especially when we'd stopped using condoms, but I was young and dumb and something in me liked the risk of it all.

Loved the risk in fact, *until* the day when I realized I'd missed my period.

It was the perfect ending to my cliché summer of shagging my boss on his desk. I'd fallen pregnant, only a few weeks before I was to go back to the States and reunite with Drew.

As a 21-year-old student with a boyfriend waiting for me back at uni and a married baby daddy who ran the bank where I was interning, there was only one solution to this problem, of course.

Terminate the pregnancy.

Just the sound of the word *terminate* nauseated me, though. There was a baby growing inside of me, *a life*, and I was going to end it. Just like that.

Was it right? Was it wrong?

Who would this child become if I let it live? If I gave it life?

I couldn't let myself ponder the likes of it, though. I knew what I had to do.

When I found myself lying on my back inside a sterile white exam room on a rainy Thursday morning, with a French doctor's rubber gloves inside me, I gripped the table, closed my eyes, and prayed I wasn't making a mistake.

The blood that flowed for days afterward scared me half to death, though, and the severe cramps didn't help either. I couldn't tell a soul. Not my mum, not Dahlia, not Vincent, and certainly not Drew. I cried myself to sleep every night that week and told Vincent I was sick with the flu and couldn't come to work.

I stayed locked in my flat for an entire week until my wounds began to heal, although I had a feeling that what I'd destroyed inside of me would never fully heal.

I'd cheated on the boy who loved me, the boy who wanted to marry me, all for the thrill of forbidden sex.

And I'd paid for it.

Instead of going back to my internship the following Monday, I boarded a plane to the US. I called my direct supervisor at the bank and told her I wouldn't be returning, and that I'd realized a career in banking wasn't for me in the end, anyway.

I arrived back in Drew's arms and never looked back.

I was finished with banking, finished with cheating, and finished with Paris.

Paris wasn't the enchanting city of lovers and lights and romance that everyone talked about. It was the city that had opened up the darkest side of me, a side I was determined to bury for good, along with all the blood I'd shed from the abortion.

And here, now, as I write my story for the very first time in the city where it all began, I realize that nothing has changed.

I still have a secret lover.

I am still lying to the man who has loved me and stayed with me for over twenty-five years.

And this city is *still* terrorizing me.

Christ. Have I not learned a goddamned thing? Has this entire sodding life been for nothing?

Why am I even still trying? Drew has an entire other life—an entire other *family*—that I've known nothing about. Yes, I've had a lover for the past year and a half, but Drew has a *child*.

A sweet little baby girl who is not ours.

In my current intoxicated state, I believe that I would actually go back and relive the trauma of the abortion if I could un-know that fact.

Drew has gotten me pregnant three times, but due to the damage the abortion caused my womb—this is my theory, anyway—I couldn't keep any of the babies.

I miscarried relatively early with the first two, but with the third, I carried her nearly full term.

I went into early labor, and when she came out, she wasn't breathing.

She never even got to take one single breath.

And we named her...we named her...

No. Can't bear to think it.

But then I see her little angel face. Her teeny toes. Her

adorable fingers that never even got to feel their mother's lips brush over them. Not once.

Adelaide.

We named our baby *Adelaide.*

The same name Drew called his baby girl in his flat, just this morning.

Now I am the one who can't seem to find my breath. Again. In this godforsaken city.

A hand on my arm snaps me from the terrors of my own mind and into the present moment.

"Ça va, madame?"

He has the darkest eyes I've ever seen. Even more obscure than an inky black sky in winter, they are a sea of gloom and utter oblivion. In them, I see myself. And I know that it is only in a darkness this profound that I will feel safe right now. If this man carried even a hint of light, I couldn't talk to him, couldn't tell him the truth.

"Non," I say to him. *"Ça ne va pas."*

He doesn't move his hand from my arm as he sits down on the stool next to me and orders me a water.

"Drink this," he says in a thick accent.

I guzzle the water, realizing that without the hydration, I was on the verge of passing out.

I'm not supposed to be drinking.

I'm not supposed to be traveling.

I'm not supposed to be watching my entire life crumble.

Or am I?

Monsieur Dark Eyes doesn't give me the time to answer the question, though. Instead he closes my journal and tucks it, along with my violet pen, back into my purse.

"Come," he says, helping me to my feet.

I don't know who this man is, but I'm pissed and tired and sick. And as much as I shouldn't let myself be alone with any Frenchman ever, especially after what happened in this city so long ago, I realize that I don't care.

I'm in a reckless state, and the life I've been living feels meaningless. Pointless. A total sodding sham.

So what do I care if this man harms me tonight?

If he doesn't do it, my own husband might.

I barely make it to the sidewalk outside before I double over and vomit onto the concrete.

It is only after I've retched every last bit of wine from my stomach that I realize this mystery man has been holding my hair back the entire time. "*Merci*," I manage to say as I stumble over to the curb and plop down, unable to stay on my feet for another second.

"Do you need me to take you to the hospital?" he asks as he rubs my back.

"No more hospitals," I slur.

"You're sick, aren't you? Beyond the alcohol...you're ill."

I lift my face to his, and all I see in those dark eyes now is concern. It's a tough kind of love this man gives, I can see that, but there *is* love in those eyes. Immense love. For whom or what, I don't know. But the mixture of darkness and love I find in this stranger's gaze finally gives me the courage to say the thing I have avoided saying to my own husband for the entire year and a half since my reproductive system was first attacked by this horrible disease.

"It was cancer," I say. "Ovarian. And it might be back."

My stranger nods and takes my hand in his. "Come with me, Sophia."

I nod, sliding my head onto his shoulder. I'm so knackered, I can't keep it upright for one more second.

"I'm going to take you to my apartment, and I will call my friend who is a doctor to come over. She will help, and you won't have to go to the hospital. Okay?"

"Okay," I say.

It's not the smartest thing I've ever done, allowing this stranger to load me into a cab and carry me up the stairs to his flat. But as I lie down on his bed, shivering and ill, I realize that I've never made smart decisions.

Why start now?

49

THE MISTRESS OF PARIS: A MEMOIR

BY EVE WINTERS

LE 28 NOVEMBRE 2016
PLACE DAUPHINE ~ PARIS, FRANCE

DEX IS on a private jet back to the States to spend the next three weeks at home with his wife. Meanwhile, I am trying to distract myself from the inevitable feelings of despair I experience each time he leaves me to go back to her.

I am about to pop a double dose of the Xanax Dex gave me before he left because he knew I would fall to pieces the minute he was gone.

He knows me well, that lover of mine.

I've just swallowed the magical calm pills when my phone buzzes with an email from my literary agent.

> Eve,
>
> Not one, not two, not three, but FOUR different houses have now made offers on your memoir, which means we're going to auction. I hope you're smiling. I'll call soon with more details.
>
> Abbey

I stare at the email in total and utter disbelief. My dreams are coming true and going up in smoke, all in one moment. One email.

One late-night decision to turn my novel into a memoir has helped me to produce the best writing of my life, and it is ultimately going to make me lose the love of my life.

I think of Dex arriving in the States, his wife greeting him with a cold peck on the cheek when he walks in the door. I think of him taking her out to dinner, giving her inconsequential details and lies about what he's been up to in Paris all these weeks without her.

I think of how hard he will get at night, lying beside her, thinking of me. Wishing I was there to sit on top of him and take away the loneliness of the marriage he has tied himself to, for better or for worse.

I wonder if in this moment of weakness, he will roll over and make love to her, imagining she is me.

Imagining that he has a wife who actually wants him to touch her.

The idea of him sleeping beside her, of their bodies intertwined, even for a brief, emotionless night of sex, makes me so ill and so full of rage that I could board a plane right now, show up at their front door, and tell her *everything*.

I would never do something that crazy, though...*would I?*

Dex has promised me he will not have sex with his wife during this trip, no matter what.

But he's also promised her that he will never, ever leave her.

And so I must move forward with my life. I cannot be such an idiot to believe that our devastating Romeo and Juliet arrangement is sustainable for a lifetime.

I must take care of myself as Dex is not going to take care of me forever. I must think about what I will do when his massive monthly payments stop arriving at my door.

I'll be able to survive for quite a while on the savings I've amassed just in the last few months of our tryst, but then what?

The email from my agent shines brightly from my iPhone. Going to auction with four different publishers means the book advance from this deal could be massive. It means that four different publishers believe that my story and my writing have the potential to be a huge success.

They could be wrong, of course...but what if they're right?

What if this book is the one that kick-starts the writing career I have dreamed of having since I was a little girl, writing alone in my bedroom to escape the saddest moments of my childhood?

What if this is my moment, and I miss it?

If I say no to this opportunity and Dex's life takes him away from Paris and back to a full-time life at home with his wife at some point, what will be left of me?

I will have given him everything—my heart, my body, my sanity, my soul.

And I will have given everything up for him—my career, my identity, my truth.

He is not giving up everything for me, clearly, and so I cannot—*will not*—do the same for him, no matter how much I love him.

The Xanax is kicking in by the time I hit *Reply* to Abbey's email. I grab a third pill and wash it down with red wine to numb the inevitable feelings of panic that will set in once I send the email I am about to send.

Abbey,

Thank you for being such a kick-ass agent. Bring on the auction. I look forward to your call.

Eve

I lie on the bathroom floor, floating in and out of sleep as I wonder how Dex will look at me when he learns the truth.

I wonder how *I* will look at me once I've finally told it.

The truth of my life is both beautiful and devastating. Extraordinary and haunting.

The eternal pull of opposites, which I can't help but believe, will ultimately, one day, lead to my demise.

50

SOPHIA

Saturday the 20th of May, 2017
Stranger's flat ~ Paris

No matter where I am or what time zone I'm in, I always wake just before dawn. I need those last few moments before the light hits the day to brace myself for what lies ahead. When I was a child, I used those extra morning moments to anticipate what would make mother angry today, and how I could circumvent her drinking and her rage. In more recent years, I wake early so that I can pretend for a few dark moments—brief though they may be—that my life is something else.

Something else entirely.

That perhaps I am one of those women who never wanted children and who is pleased that she couldn't have them with her husband. Or that I am a wildly successful author who doesn't need to teach anymore—who *can't* teach anymore—because I am so busy writing books on deadline. Books for which I am paid millions and millions of dollars. Millions and millions of *my own dollars* that I could use to, perhaps, escape the prison of the life I've built, and become someone new. Someone who doesn't encourage her husband to have affairs...affairs that have the power to ruin everything.

Whatever my early morning daydreams may be, my waking up before sunrise has always been as dependable as the sunrise itself. Which is why, on this particular morning, I am startled to open my eyes and find that the sun has already risen.

I'm even more startled to find myself lying in a bed I don't recognize, in the middle of a small bedroom I've never been in before, drowning inside a man's giant gray T-shirt and sweatpants. I lift up the waist band of the sweatpants to find that I am not wearing any knickers.

Oh bollocks.

I can't worry too much about this, though, because my head is throbbing so fiercely, I simply must rest it back on the pillow.

"Sophia?"

I'm startled back awake in a second. Must have drifted off. I blink a few times before a tall, devastatingly handsome man comes into focus at my bedside.

Have I died and gone to heaven?

As ridiculous as I feel just thinking this thought, I realize this is an actual possibility, considering the recent grim circumstances of my life.

But if I had died, would I have actually made it to heaven with all that I've destroyed in my lifetime?

The bedside god sits down next to me, saving me from the worrisome question of whether I belong in heaven or hell, and he places a soft hand on my arm as if we've known each other for ages.

And it is now that I notice his dark, deeply set eyes. And I remember.

The man at *La Closerie des Lilas.* The one who found me writing in a fury in my journal, drunk on far too much wine, and spilling the entire contents of my stomach on the sidewalk outside while he held my hair back.

"Oh bugger," I say aloud, hands now shielding my eyes. Can't bear to look at him for another second. I'm certain I look like absolute hell and he...well, he looks like the god in the heaven I would imagine...if I believed in God and heaven, of course.

Which, these days, I absolutely do not.

"How are you feeling?" he asks, seemingly unfazed by my display of shame and embarrassment.

"Who are you?" I reply.

He grins, only slightly. Even more devastating.

"*Je m'appelle Jean-Marc.* We met last night at *La Closerie des Lilas.* You were writing and then you got very sick—"

"Oh please don't remind me," I say as I sit up far too quickly.

I lift a hand to my forehead, squeeze my eyes closed. "Should I dare ask why I'm not wearing any knickers?"

"Don't worry...I'm not the one who changed your clothes. It was my friend, Valérie. She is a doctor. She came over to be sure you were going to be okay through the night."

"Oh. Thank you," I say, lifting my gaze to his. I don't remember Valérie the doctor, but then again I don't remember much after getting into a taxi with this man. "I'm so sorry—"

"Please don't worry," he cuts in. Then a pause. Long and thick and heavy. "I have seen worse. Trust me."

By the grave tone of his voice, I get the feeling that whatever this man has seen which is worse than the likes of a 45-year-old woman who spent the night blacked out and vomiting in his flat, is worse on a different kind of scale.

"I have to ask you something," he says.

His hand is still on my arm; I like it there.

"Yes?" I say.

"What you wrote in your notebook last night. It is true?"

"My notebook? What are you...Bloody hell, did you read my journal?" My heart seizes at the thought of someone else reading what I've written.

At the thought of anyone—especially this absolute stranger—knowing the truth.

Sure I had all that wine-fueled courage flowing through me last night to write it all down, but to have this man read it?

"I'm sorry," he says. "I know that was wrong of me, but I was just trying to find out who you were...and what had happened to make you so upset. When I started reading, I... I couldn't stop."

To this, I say nothing.

"It is true?" he asks again.

I am about to jump out of his bed, find my clothes, and get the hell out of here, but then, I do something totally unexpected. Something that is so completely unlike me.

I tell the truth.

"Yes," I say. "That really happened."

He nods, solemnly, then hands me his phone.

"What's—" I begin, but my voice catches when I see what he has pulled up on his phone screen.

It's an obituary. For Vincent Rousseau.

"How did you—"

"You wrote his name down," Jean-Marc says. "I wanted to find him, but it looks as though he's..."

"Dead," I finish. "Vincent is dead."

I am silent as I read the obituary of the man who was my undoing.

He died last year, the 19th of October, 2016, at the age of seventy-six. The article doesn't mention the cause of death, only that he was survived by his wife and two children.

The last time I looked him up was a few years ago when Drew first took the Paris position. I wanted to be sure that Vincent didn't have anything to do with the bank Drew would be working for, and thankfully, he didn't. I couldn't find much information on him at the time, though, other than that he'd retired from the bank he'd been running some years before.

I hadn't looked him up thus far in my spying odyssey because I feared that if he was still alive, I wouldn't be able to board the plane to Paris.

But he is not alive.

"He's dead." I say the words aloud again, if only to convince myself that they're true. "He's dead. He's really dead."

I can't stop them now. Tears of relief, of sadness, of grief —I'm not sure, really.

All I know is that I'm thankful for this perfect stranger's bed. For his warm embrace. For the way he has taken in a broken woman and given her a gift that could, potentially, start to make her whole again.

51

THE MISTRESS OF PARIS: A MEMOIR

BY EVE WINTERS

LE 6 DÉCEMBRE 2016
PLACE DAUPHINE ~ PARIS, FRANCE

MY HANDS ARE SHAKING as I hang up the phone. Only one week after my book went to auction, I have just accepted my very first publishing deal. Four major New York publishing houses made bids to publish my memoir, and my shark of an agent negotiated the book advance up, up, up to a price I am still unable to wrap my mind around.

This ridiculous sum of money in combination with the cash I have stashed away in droves from Dex will be enough money to live on for several years.

I can write, in peace, for many years to come and never again have to worry about money.

Tears are streaking down my face before I realize it.

And although, with this money, I could end my affair with Dex, I've now designed the whole situation so that I truly cannot end it. Not yet, anyway.

Because this book is a true story. And our story isn't finished yet.

As I've learned since my first intoxicating night with Dex Anderson, there is always more.

Much more.

And so, since I am continuing this dangerously addictive affair not only for the purpose of love, but also for the purpose of my art, I have demanded that my agent and publisher release the information about my book sale to the public as the sale of a "novel" rather than as a "memoir," *and* that they do not put the book up for pre-order on Amazon or elsewhere, in order to keep the entire project a secret from Dex and any inquiring minds. The author name will be my own—Eve Winters. Because, of course, Dex still believes I'm Willow. He doesn't know I have a sister, he doesn't know my last name, and he doesn't know I've been writing since I was young.

As for my plan once the book releases, well, I don't know what I will do then. All I know is that by that time, our story—or at least the parts I am writing about in my memoir—will be finished.

Maybe the book will release, and he will never, ever find out about it. Maybe I can continue to love Dex and let him love me, for the rest of our lives.

I know this is a totally unlikely scenario, of course. Only a naïve girl would believe such a farce.

Which is partly why I am crying.

Accepting this deal means that I will, at some point in the next year, have to end my love affair with Dex.

A tragedy, for sure. But it is a tragedy that I hope will ultimately save my life.

52

SOPHIA

Saturday the 20th of May, 2017
Jean-Marc's flat ~ Paris

Jean-Marc hands me my second tiny cup of espresso for the morning while he lights up his second cigarette.

Even if I don't remember everything, it was clearly a long night.

We are sitting on his balcony, the rooftops of Paris just beyond our reach. The clouds blanketing the city are a dismal shade of gray, which only seems fitting. They want to release more rain, I can tell, but I'm sure they're saving it for the moment when I set foot on the streets again.

"How long have you been sick?" Jean-Marc asks.

I vaguely remember the moment the night before when I announced to this perfect stranger that I had—or perhaps, have again—ovarian cancer. Although as I take him in now, he doesn't feel like a stranger at all.

His dark eyes feel familiar and comforting. He isn't scared of me, of what he's seen. And he's only seen the worst parts. He's read all about them in my journal.

Yet he's still here, offering me another café, asking me questions about my life. Which is why I feel that I can answer him. Why I can tell him more about myself than I have told my own husband.

"I was diagnosed a year and a half ago."

"I imagine it's not smart for you to be traveling like this?" Jean-Marc takes a long drag of his cigarette, adding a puff of wispy gray smoke into the darkening skies.

I shake my head. "Nothing I've been doing these days is smart."

"Except drinking this delicious café I have made for you...this is smart, no?"

I can't help but grin, just a little. French men can't stop themselves from being charming. It's in their blood, along with all the tobacco they inhale daily. "Probably the smartest thing I've done all year. It really is delicious. *Merci.*"

He grins back, just a little. "*De rien.*"

Jean-Marc's eyes travel down to the massive diamond on my left ring finger.

"So, your husband...he does not know about...?"

"No, he doesn't know that I had cancer."

His eyes widen. "*Mais, c'est pas possible.* How have you hidden cancer from him?"

I take a sip of my café, thinking about how it's been no small feat. "I was lucky enough to be diagnosed when it was still only Stage 1, which is quite rare for ovarian cancer. My husband had just accepted a job that kept him in Paris for weeks on end, and so I had surgery while he was away, but I said no to the chemo. After that, they just had to monitor me with scans every six months to be sure the cancer hadn't come back or spread anywhere else. I was fine, I thought...but then I missed my last scan. I waited too long, and now..."

"It's back?" he asks.

"I'm not sure yet. I'm waiting on the results." I remember all of the missed calls and messages I spotted on my phone last night, but chose not to pay any mind to.

One of those messages is surely announcing my fate.

I still don't have the courage to listen to it, though. Not yet.

"Why haven't you told him?" Jean-Marc asks. "He's your husband. He should support you through this."

I think back to the day I first found out there was a mass on my left ovary. I'd gone in to see about one last round of IVF. It was some months after we'd lost our little girl. And although Drew was finished trying for a child of our own, I just could not stop. I wanted a baby—*needed* a baby—to mute the grief I still felt over giving birth to the one who didn't survive.

But that day, instead of telling me that yes, all systems were a go for one more round, my doctor told me that there was a large cyst on my ovary that would need to be surgically removed. And biopsied.

I'd walked home in a daze, knowing deep in my gut what the biopsy results would be. No matter how hard I tried to be positive, I could only imagine waking up from surgery to a cancer diagnosis.

I'd wanted to tell Drew. I'd meant to tell him. But when I got home that night, he was sitting at the kitchen table, beaming, with two glasses of champagne in hand.

"What's all this for?" I asked.

"Love, you're not going to believe my news." I hadn't seen Drew look so happy since before our whole IVF, miscarriage, and lost baby misadventures began.

"What is it?"

"You're looking at the new CEO of *Le Crédit Parisien de France.*"

And then he delivered his favorite part of this news, which to me, was the worst.

He told me that instead of having him run their New York offices only, he would be traveling back and forth between Paris and New York regularly, and he wanted me to join him in Paris.

"It could be the start of a new life for us, love." His arms were wrapped around my waist when he said this, his smile absolutely radiant.

I couldn't bear to crush it. We'd been through so much in the years before this, and Drew deserved to have something to be happy about. He deserved to enjoy this moment.

He didn't deserve to think, even for one second, that I may be taken away from him in the same vicious manner that his mother and sister had been.

And besides, maybe I didn't even have cancer. What was the point in mentioning it then anyway?

So, I didn't mention it then. I didn't mention it when we went out and celebrated Drew's new position with his new boss—the older, distinguished French banker Dimitri Dumas, and his beautiful wife Clemence. I didn't mention it when I declined Drew's offer to go to Paris with him the first time, promising I'd go another time. I didn't mention it when he stayed in Paris for two consecutive months while I underwent surgery and discovered that the tumor on my left ovary was, in fact, malignant. I didn't mention it when I had the Lucy wig made in case chemo was on its way. And I didn't mention it when I refused the chemo.

Instead, I told my lover. I told him everything. I let him

take care of me after my surgery—well, as much as he could, in between work and spending time with his wife.

Jean-Marc clears his throat, snaps me from my memories.

"I didn't tell my husband because I was protecting him," I answer finally. "It seemed like the best option at the time, but now..."

Jean-Marc lets the silence between us settle before asking another pointed question. "Your husband does not know about what happened to you in Paris all those years ago, what you wrote about last night in your journal...does he?"

I swallow, hard. "No, he doesn't know about that either."

What I don't tell Jean-Marc is that I attribute my inability to birth a live baby to the secret abortion I had in Paris. I attribute the ovarian cancer to all of the hormones I forced into my body trying to get pregnant.

I trace it all back to my decision to cheat on Drew. This —*all of it*—is my fault.

"What *does* your husband know?" Jean-Marc asks.

"He knows I love him," I say without flinching.

"Are you sure?"

"Yes, of course he does."

"And he loves you?"

I am about to answer *yes* when the sound of Drew's voice singing that French lullaby to his crying baby girl slides into my mind. A most unwelcome visitor.

"He loves me," I say.

"But...?"

"But what?" I snap.

"You don't sound sure, that's all."

My eyes drift over the Parisian rooftops, my feet so

wishing they could dance upon them, flitter away to somewhere far, far away from here. Then a siren blares down below, the siren that is calling me out on all of my lies.

You've been caught, it screeches.

Your life has never been more fucked, it cackles.

I look back to Jean-Marc. He is watching me, patiently waiting for my answer.

"My husband loves me, very much. But if he knew all of me, I'm not sure he would."

A flash of anger sparks in Jean-Marc's eyes for a fleeting second. "Perhaps it is not my place to say so, but your husband is an idiot if he would not love you like this. To me, *this,*" he pauses, taking another inhale of his cigarette, "your vulnerability, your sorrow, your messy hair, tired eyes, your loss of control—*this* is what makes a person beautiful, Sophia. *This* is real life."

I nod toward the cigarette resting in between Jean-Marc's steady fingers.

"May I?" I ask.

He hands it over, and I take a long, slow drag, letting the nicotine fill my lungs.

It stings. It burns.

But like Jean-Marc said, it's real.

He doesn't flinch when I blow the smoke in his direction.

"I like you," he says, lighting another cigarette and letting me keep his. "I like you a lot, Sophia."

53

OFFICER JEAN-MARC DEVEREAUX

SAMEDI 20 MAI 2017
RUE VAVIN ~ PARIS, FRANCE

JEAN-MARC HAD NEVER LET a woman derail him like this.

Well, not since Mia anyway.

No. Sophia Grayson hadn't derailed him; he was simply doing his job...albeit in a most unprofessional manner. He knew that following Sophia to La Closerie des Lilas last night and then taking her back to his apartment when she was intensely ill—not to mention when her husband was currently their Number 1 suspect in the Eve Winters case—was ill-advised and could certainly come back to bite him in the ass, but here they were anyway.

Sitting on his balcony. Drinking coffee and smoking cigarettes together.

When he told her he liked her just now, he meant it. He meant it more than he dared admit to her or to himself.

Jean-Marc took a long drag of his newly lit cigarette, eyeing the way Sophia parted her lips and puffed smoke in his direction. Eyeing the way her long auburn hair flowed in messy waves over her shoulders and over the beautiful breasts he'd covered last night with his large T-shirt. He'd told her it was his doctor friend Valérie who'd come over to take care of her—to change her out of her soiled clothing—but that wasn't true.

He was the one who'd carried her all the way up the stairs to his sixth-floor apartment late last night. He was the one who'd given her anti-nausea medication to stop the vomiting. He was the one who'd changed her out of her clothes and into his, tucked her into bed, and watched her for a good hour to make sure she was going to be okay before he got to work.

Got to work searching her bag and her phone. Her messages, emails, and calls.

The most notable of items he discovered in her bag—beyond her tell-all journal of course—were a photograph of Sophia and her husband, as well as a man's silver cross necklace with a diamond in the center. Devereaux hadn't forgotten the parts in Eve's memoir where she mentioned the silver cross banging against Dex's chest as he took her from behind, or the part where Eve smashed a photograph of Dex and his wife in his apartment.

Considering Sophia had just fled her husband's apartment looking as though she'd seen a ghost, Devereaux concluded that she'd likely discovered these items in his apartment and had also come to her own conclusion that the character of "Dex" was likely her own husband.

The next goldmine Devereaux discovered was of course in Sophia's cell phone.

He'd watched her type in her iPhone password at the café earlier when she'd had no idea he was watching her. And like any good officer of La Crim', he'd memorized the code, no problem.

Once she was asleep, and Jean-Marc typed in that same code to access Sophia's entire personal life, this was when he learned that Sophia's husband had no clue she'd come to Paris—presumably to spy on him.

This was also when Jean-Marc learned that Sophia's husband wasn't the only one with a lover; she had one too. A married lover who also had no idea that Sophia had come to Paris.

In addition to the lover intel, a voicemail Sophia hadn't yet listened to told Jean-Marc that Sophia's cancer had, in fact, come back. Jean-Marc was sorry for her that she would ever have to hear those words out of her doctor's mouth.

And he was sorry that she'd been through so much tragedy in her life. She'd lost a baby girl.

Jean-Marc had too.

The day he lost Mia, he hadn't *only* lost the love of his life. He'd lost his future daughter. She was only seven months along, growing in Mia's beautiful belly.

That night, Jean-Marc had lost everything.

Perhaps this is what had drawn him to Sophia yesterday when he witnessed her mad shoeless dash from her husband's apartment. Perhaps this was why he couldn't take his eyes off of her now.

He felt for her. Deeply.

Or maybe it was the long red hair that reminded him so much of Mia.

Whatever it was, it didn't matter.

He still had a job to do.

"So what brought you to Paris?" Jean-Marc asked his new, unsuspecting female friend.

She breathed out some more smoke, gazed straight into his eyes. "My husband works here occasionally. I came to spend some time with him."

She was a good liar, he thought. Didn't even bat an eye when the lie left her lips. But then, he'd always found women to be more skilled liars than men.

"But it hasn't gone as you'd expected?" he pushed.

Sophia's eyes drifted up toward the cloudy sky overhead and she shifted in her chair. "You could say that."

"What you wrote in your journal last night—that he has another family. A child. That's true too?"

"It's all true," Sophia said, before taking another long drag of her cigarette. This time she coughed when she blew out the smoke. It was a violent cough.

A cough she would understand better once she listened to her doctor's bad-news voicemail, Jean-Marc thought ruefully.

Jean-Marc waited for her to finish coughing before he continued. "Does he know you know?"

She shook her head, wiping at the water that had gathered at the corners of her eyes, presumably from the coughing. "Of course not."

"Are you going to confront him?"

She shrugged. "I haven't decided yet. There's a lot to figure out right now."

Jean-Marc nodded. The woman flew to Paris the day after her former student's book released, the book that details an affair with a married American businessman who fits the profile of her husband perfectly. She comes to Paris and discovers he has another family and a child. And she's hiding cancer from him. Hell yeah, there was a lot to figure out.

"The child he has...how old?" Jean-Marc prodded.

Sophia hesitated, but finally, she gave in. "A baby. She's just a baby." Her voice caught in her throat as she said this. More tears pooled at the corners of her eyes—this time they weren't from coughing, though. She smashed the cigarette into the ashtray and stood abruptly. "Can I take a shower? I need to wash yesterday off of me."

"Of course," Jean-Marc said, standing. "I'm sorry, I didn't mean to—"

"It's fine," she cut him off. "I'm fine."

This time the lie was obvious.

Sophia Grayson was anything but fine.

54

SOPHIA

Saturday the 20th of May, 2017
Jean-Marc's flat ~ Paris

Jean-Marc has given me a cushy white towel and has shown me to his miniscule bathroom to take a shower before I head back to the hotel. I am infinitely relieved when he leaves me alone. He was pushing too much. Asking too many questions.

And his eyes are too dark, his hands too strong, his lips too...he's just too *everything.*

Just before I close the bathroom door, I spy a bedroom across the hall. It's not the one I slept in last night, which seemed to be abnormally empty save for a mattress on the floor and a lamp on a side table. This one looks much more lived in with clothes strewn about and an unmade bed. It must be Jean-Marc's room.

I peek down the hall to see that Jean-Marc has gone into the kitchen and is now completely out of sight. Instead of taking the shower I so desperately need, I find myself drawn to the tall windows in his bedroom and the velvety red curtains framing his rainy view of the city.

Walking through his mess of clothes and over to the window, I run my hands along the drapes and take it all in. The sky is still dismal and gray, and my husband is still out there, being a father to some other woman's child. As for my lover, he is across an ocean, tending to his wife...the one he loves when he is not with me.

And despite all of this, for the first time in so very long, I see—really *see*—the stunning beauty of Paris again.

It's not a perfect city. It's shadowy and flawed and destructive.

Devastating and devastatingly exquisite.

But perhaps *this* is why Paris is so beautiful.

Because *everything* exists here—horror and love. Bleakness and joy. Terror and passion.

This is the eternal pull of opposites that Eve writes about in her memoir, all existing under one mean, grizzly sky in a city that is touted for its love and its lights.

Why isn't Paris praised for its darkness, too, I wonder?

Just as I am envisioning a title for my next book—*City of Light, City of Darkness*—a photo catches my eye. There, squarely on top of Jean-Marc's short black dresser, which sits just next to the window, is a photo of Jean-Marc with a young blond French woman and another man. I take a step closer, hoping my eyes are playing tricks on me, but no, I don't believe they are.

Taking the photo in my hands, I gasp at the sight of her.

How could it be?

Before I can fully process what I'm looking at, I spot the second photo on Jean-Marc's dresser.

It's a photo of a baby. A baby I recognize.

The crazy blond girl. The baby. Drew's baby. *Adelaide.*

A knot forms in the pit of my stomach and I feel faint.

The final punch to the stomach comes when I realize that the two men flanking Coralie in the photo are wearing police uniforms.

Jean-Marc is a sodding police officer.

I drop the photo to the ground and start pulling open dresser drawers like a madwoman. I don't know what I'm searching for, but then, three drawers in, there it is.

A shiny badge.

On it, the words: *Brigade Criminelle. 36 Quai des Orfèvres*.

A police badge. A Brigade Criminelle Badge.

My synapses are firing. Trying to figure this out. Jean-Marc. La Brigade Criminelle. *La Crim'*.

The article I read the other day at Café de Flore.

And then it comes together.

Jean-Marc Devereaux.

A senior member of the highly specialized crime team in Paris in charge of Eve Winters' case. In a photo with Coralie. And he has a picture of my husband's baby on his dresser.

What in the—?

"Are you looking for something, Sophia?"

I slam the drawer shut and flip around, but it's too late. Jean-Marc is standing in the doorway to his bedroom, still smoking one of his goddamn cigarettes, looking from me to his open drawers, and finally, back to me.

55

OFFICER JEAN-MARC DEVEREAUX

SAMEDI 20 MAI 2017
RUE VAVIN ~ PARIS

JEAN-MARC DIDN'T MEAN for this to happen. He didn't think Sophia would venture into his bedroom. He didn't think about it at all, actually.

It wasn't like him to forget such an important detail—closing and locking his bedroom door. Or at the very least, hiding the photo that showed him in full uniform.

Before she'd woken up this morning, he'd put away everything else that made it obvious that he was a police officer. Everything but that damn photo sitting front and center on his dresser.

What an idiot he'd been.

He had absolutely allowed this woman to derail him.

And now he was going to pay for his carelessness.

"You're a police officer," Sophia said to him. Her skin was now an even sicklier shade of gray than it had been last night.

Putain.

He took a step closer to her. "Sophia, please let me explain."

"Devereaux. Jean-Marc Devereaux, that's you," she snapped, taking a step backward, nearly tripping over the mess in his bedroom.

Jean-Marc nodded slowly, careful not to show any emotion. "I'm sorry I didn't tell you before, but you don't need to be afraid, Soph—"

"Don't come any closer to me," she screeched suddenly.

Jean-Marc stopped in his tracks, watching all the trust that had filled Sophia's eyes this morning disappear faster than Eve had from her apartment just a few days ago. Sophia bent over and picked up the photograph that clearly showed Jean-Marc and his boss Julien in their police uniforms. Jean-Marc could've punched the wall for forgetting to hide that fucking photo.

Sophia aimed the incriminating evidence in his direction and practically spat at him. "The blond girl in this photo. How do you know her?"

"Calm down, Sophia. Let's go sit down and I'll explain everything—"

"How do you know this woman?" Sophia yelled, her hands trembling so much she could barely hang on to the photo.

Why was Sophia so fixated on knowing who Coralie was?

"Why are you asking about her? Do you know her?"

"Stop pretending like you don't know what's going on here!"

Jean-Marc reached for the photo in her hands, but she jumped back, looking at it once more. "She's...you look alike. Is...is she your sister? Is she your sodding sister?"

"Yes, Sophia, that's my sister. How do you know her?"

Jean-Marc suddenly had an idea of how Sophia might know her, but he hoped with everything in him that his hunch was incorrect. Because if what he was now suspecting were true, that would mean he'd missed a massive part of the story relating to Andrew Grayson and his wife.

A massive part that had been right underneath his nose all along.

"The baby," Sophia said. "She's your niece. Adelaide is your niece."

Adelaide. Sophia knew his niece's name. And it was the *same name* as the baby she'd lost, the one she'd written about in her journal the night before.

If Adelaide was actually Andrew Grayson's baby, that meant Sophia's husband had named his new baby the same name as the baby they'd lost.

No. This couldn't be true. Andrew Grayson couldn't be the father of Coralie's baby. Coralie had told Jean-Marc it was just a one-night stand. She'd said she didn't even know the father's name. That she'd had no contact with him since the night they'd slept together—the night she'd gotten pregnant with Adelaide. This was the story his sister had been telling him all along.

But since when did he think it was a good idea to trust his emotionally unstable sister?

Putain.

"Sophia, how do you know Coralie and Adelaide?" Jean-Marc's voice raised just the slightest bit this time. He couldn't stay totally calm for her anymore.

Sophia's eyes were frantic. Hands trembling. Skin drained of all color. She was afraid of him now, that much was clear.

"Sophia, I'm not going to hurt you. I just need you to tell me the truth." He grabbed the photo of his adorable baby niece off the dresser and held it up to Sophia's face. "Is this your husband's baby?"

The fear in Sophia's eyes was all the confirmation he needed, but he wanted to hear the words out of her mouth. He wanted to hear her tell him the one thing his sister had always refused to tell him: *the identity of Adelaide's father*.

Sophia's lips trembled as she stared into the baby's eyes. And finally, she gave Jean-Marc the answer he was dreading.

"Yes, that's her. That's his baby. He named her Adelaide! Fucking Adelaide!"

Jean-Marc took a step toward Sophia. "I need you to tell me what you saw yesterday, Sophia. What happened in your husband's apartment?"

"You already know what I saw, you sick arse, because you were following me! You already know because it's your own bloody family I saw in there!"

56

SOPHIA

Saturday the 20th of May, 2017
Jean-Marc's flat ~ Paris

I CHARGE past the son of a bitch who's been lying to me and toward the other bedroom where I've left my things.

If my husband really is the man in Eve's book—and after my hunt through his apartment yesterday, I'm 99% certain he is—and if Jean-Marc is one of the police officers in charge of finding Eve—not to mention the fact that he is the *brother* of the young woman Drew was smacking around in his flat yesterday—then it can be no coincidence that Jean-Marc "found" me last night at *La Closerie des Lilas*, took me back to his place, read my journal, and asked me all those questions this morning about my marriage.

Putain.

It's the French word for *fuck,* and it's the only word that is running frantically through my mind as I strip off Jean-Marc's oversized clothes, squeeze back into my own, and smash my feet into my boots. I gather my purse from the floor, but when I shoot back up to get the hell out of here, there he is again in the doorway, that sneaky wanker of a police officer.

"You don't need to run from me, Sophia," he says. His voice is calm. Too calm. "Just tell me what happened yesterday in your husband's apartment."

"Listen, you didn't even tell me who you really are. I'm not telling you anything." If he has me here, that means he most definitely knows that Drew is the married man in Eve's book. And it likely means that Drew is a main suspect in Eve's disappearance. And this policeman is doing his investigatory work in a most dishonest, despicable way.

"You weren't in a state to answer my questions last night," he replies. "You were extremely ill, Sophia."

"And this morning?"

"You had a rough night. I was going to talk to you after you'd taken a shower."

"Well, that isn't happening; I have to go," I say, pushing past him.

"What do you know about your husband's involvement with Eve Winters?" he calls after me. "She was your student some years ago, no? Do you know who Eve really is, Sophia?"

Putain. Putain. Putain.

When I get to his front door, I stop. Level my gaze on him. "You followed me. You made me trust you. And you didn't tell me who you really are or why you were really helping me. You lied to me."

"I like you, Sophia. That was not a lie. I just want to ask you a few questions."

"You'll have to talk to my lawyer," I say before letting myself out of his apartment and slamming the door behind me.

The endless spiral staircase down to the ground floor has me dizzy and spinning by the time I reach the street. As predicted, the rain has waited for the moment my feet take to the sidewalks to begin its downpour. I don't care, though. I let it soak me, my hair, my clothes, as I walk numbly through the streets, trying to regain my bearings.

When the rain transforms into small pellets of hail, I surrender and step beneath the awning of a little news kiosk on the sidewalk to wait it out.

There is no rest for the wicked, I realize, as the headline of today's paper smacks me straight across my exhausted face.

Surprising Development in Eve Winters Case:
The Mistress of Paris Isn't Who She Says She Is

Jean-Marc's last question rushes into my mind:

Do you know who Eve really is, Sophia?

Apparently not, I think, tossing a few coins onto the counter and tucking the paper into my bag. I don't seem to know who anyone really is anymore, now do I?

I take off through the downpour of hail toward my hotel, wondering if I'm ready for whatever truth is about to be revealed when I open the pages of this newspaper.

Mother's voice slices through my head:

Ready or not, darling, here it comes.

57

THE MISTRESS OF PARIS: A MEMOIR

BY EVE WINTERS

LE 14 FÉVRIER 2017
PLACE DAUPHINE ~ PARIS, FRANCE

THIS WILL BE the last chapter of my memoir because the story must end somewhere.

Because the book is due tomorrow.

Because my life is on the brink of imploding, and I don't have the energy to write about it any longer.

Soon, I must find a way out of this mess.

But for now, I am standing in my pristine bathroom, the one I share with my sister, holding a pregnancy test in my hand. I've been vomiting for days, at random times, with no explanation.

And I have been having unprotected sex with the married businessman whom I love for months now.

I've been playing with fire.

And my house is about to burn down.

Willow is waiting on the other side of the door. She knows everything now. Everything I've been doing all this time. And I know what she's been doing, too. We finally, *finally*, told each other the truth about who we really are.

I love her now more than I've ever loved her before. More than I've ever loved anyone before. We really are one now. One heart, mind, body, spirit, soul.

One woman.

And I will never part from her again. *Ever*.

I am on the toilet now, about to pee on the stick that will determine my fate.

But as I watch, I see only blood falling.

Drop by drop, it taunts me. I count them as they fall...

One drop for money.
Two drops for freedom.
Three drops for death.
Mine.
Hers.
Ours.
I always knew it was coming.
I just hadn't imagined it knocking on my door so soon.

58

OFFICER JEAN-MARC DEVEREAUX

SAMEDI 20 MAI 2017
RUE VAVIN ~ PARIS

THE DOOR SLAMMED in Jean-Marc's face.

Another woman, gone.

Wasn't that just the story of his cursed life these days?

Rather than running after the woman who now reminded him so much of Mia he could hardly see straight, Jean-Marc walked to the window and watched the rain begin its downpour over the city. And then he did something he never, ever let himself do.

He thought back to that day. To the day he'd lost Mia and the baby. To the day that bore such striking resemblances to the day he was now living out that he couldn't stop himself from re-living those final moments with the woman he'd so loved, the woman he'd so tragically lost.

They'd been fighting. Not an uncommon thing for him and Mia. They were a fiery couple—they always had been. She never let him get away with anything, and he was stubborn. Not quick to take the blame or apologize.

But on this particular day, and in this particular fight, Mia had been right.

Of course she had been.

She was seven months pregnant with their little girl. Their second bedroom was about as pink and frilly as it could get, and Mia's belly was growing with each passing day.

Jean-Marc regrettably had not been around for much of it. He was working a lot during this time—hell he always worked a lot. When a girl went missing or when there was a killer on the loose, he certainly couldn't tell his team that he'd rather be home cuddling with his girlfriend.

And if he was being honest with himself, as much as he loved Mia and wanted to be there for her, he also loved his job. It gave him a purpose. Made him feel needed. Important. Intelligent. It fulfilled him in a way that no relationship with a woman ever could.

Probably because he was damn good at his job, and with women, well, he'd never been too skilled.

His career with La Crim' was his reason for being, and it had been this way for so long that when Mia needed to know that *she* and their unborn baby would now be his reason for being, he didn't know how to handle it.

He loved her, desperately.

And he honestly couldn't wait to be a dad.

But it also scared the shit out of him. How would he handle it all? How would he be one-hundred percent present for his intense cases, sometimes working more than twenty-four or forty-eight hours straight with no sleep, and be there for Mia and a newborn at the same time?

He didn't know how he would do it, but he figured it would all work out.

Mia wasn't so sure.

Which was the reason for this particular blowout between the two of them.

He could still hear her frantic voice. The last words she'd ever spoken to him.

"You care more about dead girls than you do about me! You give more time to girls you've never met, girls who've gone missing, than you do to me and your unborn baby! When will this end, Jean-Marc? When will you love me the way I need to be loved?" Mia was yelling and crying and throwing pillows at him. She turned into a little girl when she fought with him, and even though it maddened Jean-Marc to no end, he also loved her so much in those moments.

This particular time, though, after she'd tossed every single bed pillow at him, and the couch pillows too, Jean-Marc didn't know what to say. He didn't offer a single answer to her pressing questions. And so, his fiery little Mia had done exactly what Sophia had just done. She'd raced out of the apartment alone and slammed the door straight in his face.

He hadn't followed her at first. He was angry. Exhausted. Unsure. Unsure of how it would all work out. Unsure if he could ever give Mia and their baby what they needed and continue to give everything to his work the way he'd been doing for years.

But as he'd watched the rain pouring down outside and as he'd thought about his beautiful girlfriend who he was planning to propose to in one short week, and the life she was growing inside of her—*their baby*—he realized he was sure of one thing:

He loved Mia.

He loved everything about her, right down to her hot little temper that had her screaming at him and slamming the door in his face, all so she could spend more time with him.

Because she loved him too.

Putain. What was he doing letting her run out of the apartment like that late at night, in the rain, seven months pregnant? She hadn't even put on a coat.

Jean-Marc grabbed her coat from the rack by the door and took off to find her.

It didn't take long. The car horns a few streets over and the sound of sirens on their way alerted him to the whereabouts of his pregnant girlfriend.

When he turned the corner, through the sheets of pouring rain, he saw her.

A limp, beautiful body lying on the ground between two crashed cars.

Two crashed cars that had undoubtedly crashed straight into the love of his life and their unborn baby.

All because he'd let her run out that fucking door.

The rest of the scene was still a blur in his mind.

Screaming, sirens, blood.

An absolute horror. The worst thing he'd ever seen. The worst thing he'd ever felt.

The worst day of his life.

Mia's eyes had fluttered open briefly one last time before Jean-Marc watched her take her final breath. In that moment, he held her, tighter than he'd ever held anyone or anything in his entire life.

And he told her he loved her. He told her he loved her more than anyone or anything in his entire life. He told her he'd quit his job—he'd do anything, *anything*, if she would just keep breathing.

But the blow to her head when those two cars collided and caught her in the crossfire had been too much.

And so she didn't keep breathing.

Jean-Marc wasn't sure if he would keep breathing after that moment, either.

But he had. Brutal as it was.

Tears streaked down his face now, regret washing over him, making him sick. He couldn't bring her back, though. Nothing he could do would ever bring her back.

Sophia, though, she was still here. Still alive. He thought of her red hair and quick temper that reminded him so much of Mia. Racing out of his apartment into the rain, just like Mia had.

And he knew what he had to do.

59

SOPHIA

Saturday the 20th of May, 2017
La Belle Juliette ~ Paris

Back at the hotel, I'm soaking wet and shivering and frantically skimming the news article about Eve.

My jumbled brain translates the paragraphs in pieces:

Eve's real name is Sara Eve Marvel, of the famous Marvel Sisters Case which took place in 2005.

Her sister, "Willow," is really Kathryn Willow Marvel, or "Kate," who disappeared at the young age of fifteen on a family trip to Paris.

Bloody hell.

Eve is really Sara Marvel? And her sister, Willow, is actually the famous sister, Kate, who went missing in Paris all those years ago?

More violent chills attack my wet body as I continue reading the article, which confirms what I already know and remember about the Marvel sisters and their tragic story. There wasn't a soul on either side of the pond who hadn't heard of the girls and their catastrophic fate.

It is now known that Eve's memoir wasn't entirely true, of course. It is believed that her sister, *Willow Winters,* is a fictional character based upon the memory of her missing sister, Kathryn ("Kate") *Willow* Marvel.

It takes me a minute to wrap my head around this fact —*that there is no Willow*, at least not in the way Eve portrayed her in the book. The real Willow—Kate—has been missing for years, and it's likely the girl isn't even alive.

So my good little writing pupil didn't tell the full truth, after all. But she sure as hell got me—and I'm sure everyone else who read her sordid story—to believe in Willow's existence.

At the end of the article, the reporter postulates that perhaps Sara Eve Marvel has met the same demise as her sister Kate.

That perhaps their disappearances are connected.

I drop the paper to the floor, stare at the white wall ahead of me. All I can see, though, is the haunted look in Eve's eyes back when she was my student.

Back when I knew something horrible must have happened to her, something unthinkable. But I had no clue what hell she'd actually lived through.

She lost her little sister.

She was nearly killed by her own mother.

She watched her father beat and stab her mother to death.

And she testified in defense of her father in her own mother's murder case, only to watch him get locked up for life.

She lost everything.

She was so young.

Years later, she met Drew, *my Drew*, who loved her.

Who loves her.

And now, she's gone.

It doesn't take long for the shock of this realization to take hold in my sick body and land me smack on the bathroom floor. I'm wrapped in a towel, still shivering and totally exhausted, when my phone buzzes.

Drew's name flashes across the screen.

We haven't spoken on the phone this entire time I've been in Paris. The idea of hearing his voice, now, after everything, makes me feel even more ill.

I ignore the call, let the voicemail pick up.

A minute later, I've got a new message.

With a trembling hand, I pick up the phone and listen.

Drew's voice is chipper. Unnaturally so. "Good news, love. I'm taking a flight home today, so I'll be back a week earlier than planned. Plane gets in around 2:00 p.m. Can't wait to see you, sweetie."

And the line goes dead.

I fear my heart may go dead as well.

The news about who Eve really is has just hit the press. The police are onto Drew.

And so, naturally, he's fleeing the city.

I have to beat him home. I have to go.

With the intention of cleaning myself up and boarding the next flight home, I strip off my wet clothes and force my weak body into the shower.

It's not long, though, before the steam envelops me and blackness begins to close in.

It's over, Sophia. It's over.

It's Mother's voice, as always. Spiraling in my head like a tornado.

It's over, darling.

Just. Give. It. Up.

I only have enough time to crawl out onto the bathroom floor, grab my cell, and dial Drew's number.

"Love," he answers. "Did you get my message? I'm about to board—"

"I'm here, Drew. In Paris," I mumble. "I'm sick...I can't—"

The phone tumbles out of my hand as the blackness wins the battle.

60

EVE

The When: Unknown
The Where: Unknown

My name is Sara.
Sara Eve Marvel.
My sister was Kate.
Kathryn Willow Marvel.

It was a smoldering Paris summer
When Kate went missing.
It was no accident then,
that I chose Winters for my new last name.
I detest the heat of summer.

I lost everything in the summertime.
I lost Kate.
I lost my mother.
I lost my father.
And worst of all...
Myself.

Sara could exist no longer,
After what she'd seen.
It was simply too much blood,
For the girl I once was...to survive.

And so, I let her die.
I let everything she had ever been
Burn to ash
In the summer heat
That stole my Kate.

And I became Eve.

No one knew the truth.
Not a single man I've slept with or loved.
Not even Drew.

Drew's wife didn't know either.
But I knew who she was...
The entire time.

Professor Sophia Grayson.
I loved her husband.

I wonder if Sophia knows.
If Drew knows.
The truth
About who I really am.

I wonder
If I'll ever
See any of them
Again.

Or if I'm going to the invisible place
That swallowed up my little sister
And spit out her bloody T-shirt.

A door slams.
My injured body jolts
Atop the sweaty sheets
But can go nowhere.

And so, I count....

One...
Two...
These are—*Three.*
My final few...seconds...
Four.
Of life.
Five. Six. Seven.
Of imagining—*Eight. Nine. Ten.*
I am somewhere else.
Eleven. Twelve.
Before he...
Thirteen.
Arrives.

He's here.

61

OFFICER JEAN-MARC DEVEREAUX

SAMEDI 20 MAI 2017
LA BELLE JULIETTE ~ PARIS

THANKS TO JEAN-MARC'S thorough search through Sophia Grayson's purse the night before, he'd discovered that she was staying at Hôtel La Belle Juliette in the *sixième arrondissement*. He'd also discovered that she'd tucked both of the room keys into her bag, and so he'd taken the liberty of putting one of them in his pocket.

He'd had a feeling he might need it.

When Jean-Marc burst through the door to Sophia's hotel room, he found steam billowing out from the bathroom and heard the ring of a cell phone.

"Sophia," he called out. No answer. "*Sophia*." A little bit louder this time as he approached the bathroom, but still no response.

He opened the bathroom door enough to slip his head in, and there she was.

A naked heap on the bathroom floor. Eyes closed. Blood trickling out of the corner of her mouth.

It was a scene that was all too familiar.

Still, he didn't let the memories of Mia's limp, wet body on the street that day stop him from doing what he needed to do.

It took him mere seconds to confirm that she was still breathing and only another few to call SAMU and have an ambulance on the way. While he worked on bringing Sophia back to consciousness, he noticed her cell still buzzing away on the floor nearby.

The name on the caller ID filled Jean-Marc with a white-hot rage.

Drew Grayson.

That motherfucker.

All along, when Jean-Marc's little sister Coralie had said she had no idea who the father of her baby was—some nameless man she'd met in a nightclub—she *had* known. And all along, it was Andrew Grayson, now the main suspect in Eve's disappearance.

Devereaux reached for the ringing cell phone, and with a swipe of his thumb, there was the bastard's frantic voice on the other line.

"Sophia! Sophia, are you there? Where are you? Are you okay?"

Jean-Marc looked down at Andrew's wife's gray skin and the blood still making its slow decent down her chin. And he decided it was time.

It was time to give this asshole what he deserved.

"Your wife is ill, Mr. Grayson. She has cancer, and she's just passed out in her hotel room in Paris. She'll be on her way to l'Hôpital Hôtel-Dieu in the next ten minutes. I suggest you meet us there."

Jean-Marc let the emergency workers do their job, and he would soon be doing his by meeting Sophia's husband at the hospital, bringing him into the station for questioning, and arresting him for whatever he'd done to make Eve Winters disappear.

But first, there was someone he needed to talk to.

Confirmation had just come in from his colleague Martinez that it was, in fact, Eve who'd been visiting Andrew Grayson at the Ritz. She'd been spotted in the video footage several times entering and exiting the hotel on the same nights as Grayson.

And as Jean-Marc put his car into drive and dialed his sister's phone number, he wondered if she, too, would be found in the video footage at the Ritz.

Had she been selling her body for money?

Was that how she'd met Andrew Grayson?

Was that how she'd gotten pregnant with his baby, and why she'd lied about the identity of the father?

Jean-Marc knew she used to hang out in the kinds of clubs that Eve mentioned in her book. He knew she used to do drugs—heavy drugs—frequently. And he knew she had a thing for men who treated her like shit. But did that mean she'd been a prostitute?

And worse, did her connection to Andrew Grayson mean she'd had something to do with Eve's disappearance?

Devereaux thought about all that hair in Eve's apartment. The brown hair that matched Eve's—or Sara Marvel's—DNA. And the blond hair that they hadn't matched to anyone yet.

If it was his sister all along...

Putain.

Coralie didn't pick up on the first call. She rarely did. So he dialed again.

No answer this time either. Rage seized his chest as he barely came to a stop at a red light. The rain was still pouring down outside, but he couldn't be bothered to notice.

Instead, his fingers flew over his phone screen, typing a text message to his little sister:

I know that Andrew Grayson is Adelaide's father. Pick up the phone. We need to talk.

When he tried her a third time, she answered.

Her characteristic screeching started immediately. "I don't know what you're talking about—"

"Cut the bullshit, Coralie," he cut her off. He didn't have time for her lies. "I need you to tell me the truth about how you know Andrew Grayson and what you were doing the night Eve Winters disappeared." Jean-Marc pressed hard on the gas as soon as the light turned green and didn't stop pushing until he heard his sister's voice on the other line.

"*Putain.*"

"The truth, Coralie. *Now.*"

"Andrew is Adelaide's father, yes."

"How did you meet him?"

"At one of the clubs."

Devereaux had thought as much. "So you've known all along that he was the father?"

"Yes," she said. Her voice was quieter now. "I loved him. And I thought he—" A sob broke through the line.

"You thought he loved you, too," Jean-Marc finished for her. The classic cliché. "Was he paying you, Coralie? For sex?"

Her sobs continued, only worsening, and soon, Jean-

Marc heard his sweet little niece crying in the background, too. *Putain.* He forced himself to take on a more compassionate tone. "Coralie, I know this is hard, but I want to help you. I love you. And I love Adelaide. I just need the truth."

"Okay, yes, fine, he was paying me. You know what a hard time I was having keeping a job and this is when I was doing too many drugs, and I just...I don't know, it got out of control. But we had such a strong connection, and I fell for him...so I went off the pill thinking that maybe if I had a baby, he would leave his wife for me. *For us.*"

Jean-Marc wondered if his sister could hear him shaking his head in disapproval and disgust over the line. He wanted to yell at her for what an idiot she'd been. But he knew that wouldn't help anything. And he needed to know the rest of the story, so he kept his judgment to himself.

"So you went off the pill without telling him?"

"Yes, and it worked. Immediately. But when I told him I was pregnant, he freaked out and wanted nothing to do with me or the baby. He even threatened me—he told me if I ever came near him again he would hurt me."

"*Connard,*" Jean-Marc muttered under his breath. "So this is how you decided to move in with me?"

"You had just lost Mia and the baby, so I thought it would help you, having us there."

"And it did help me. I loved helping with the baby," Jean-Marc said. There couldn't have been anything more true. Having Adelaide to look after had brought him back to life after losing Mia and their unborn baby girl.

Coralie's decision to dupe Andrew Grayson into getting her pregnant had been idiotic, for sure. But if she hadn't have done it, they wouldn't have Adelaide. And after everything he'd lost, a world without his sweet niece was unfathomable.

"You did the right thing, coming to live with me," Jean-Marc reassured her. What he didn't say was that he did not believe she'd done the right thing in moving in with Julien, but again, his disapproval would help nothing right now. "Does Julien know that Andrew Grayson is Adelaide's father?"

Coralie sniffled on the other end of the line and finally answered, "No, he doesn't know."

"You're sure he has no idea you're connected to him?"

"Yes, I'm sure."

"Does Andrew know that your brother and boyfriend are officers of La Crim'? Does he know who we are?"

"No, he's never asked me much about my family, and I've never told him. I knew if I told him my brother worked for la Crim', he wouldn't want anything to do with me, seeing as how he'd been paying me for sex."

Jean-Marc thought their father was probably rolling over in his grave right now. His little girl had become a prostitute. She was an absolute mess. Just the thought of his little sister accepting money from Grayson for sex made Devereaux want to punch that *connard* straight in the nose, or better yet, in the balls. He could only imagine what his father would've done to him if he were still alive.

But at least the *connard* didn't know that the woman he'd scorned was connected to the two badass officers of la Crim' who were going to kick the shit out of him later today.

"Did you ever see Andrew Grayson again after he threatened you?" Devereaux asked his sister.

"Yes, after I had Adelaide, I brought her to him. I wanted him to see how beautiful his daughter was, *our* daughter. And he did see. He loved her, Jean-Marc. Instantly. Just like I was hoping he would. But he was still horrible to me, telling me he couldn't be with me and that he would never leave his wife. But the truth was that the bastard was in love with another woman. Another one of his prostituées."

"Eve Winters."

Coralie's breathing hastened over the phone, and Jean-Marc sensed she was getting ready to lie to him again; she didn't want to be tied to the disappearance of this missing girl. Who would?

"Coralie, we are bringing Andrew Grayson in for questioning later today about the disappearance of Eve Winters. If you were involved in any way, it's going to come out. And if I don't know what the story is, I won't be able to help you. If you can just tell me if you were at Eve's apartment the night she disappeared and tell me what happened there, I can protect you and Adelaide. I *will* protect you."

A long pause followed, and Jean-Marc swerved his car over to the side of the road so he could focus. He wanted to hear this clearly.

Finally, she responded. "Yes, I was there."

Jean-Marc's thumb and forefinger found the bridge of his nose and he squeezed. Hard. He'd been hoping that his instincts were wrong. That the blond hair at the crime scene hadn't been his sister's.

But it *was* her hair. Her blood. Her fingernails. Her fingerprints. She was the other female at the crime scene that they didn't yet have a DNA match for.

Putain.

"Coralie, I need you to tell me what happened that night."

Adelaide was crying even harder now in the background, but Jean-Marc did his best to focus only on the sound of his sister's voice.

"I'd taken Adelaide over to see Drew that day, and

when I got to his apartment, he was crying. He had a book in his hands—her book. She'd left it for him, apparently, before she was supposed to leave to go to the States. He'd never known who she really was until that day. He didn't know she was a writer or that she was writing an entire goddamned book about their affair! He was so devastated by her betrayal, and it was then that I could see how much he loved her. Losing me had never so much as made him shed a tear. But with her...with Eve...he was drowning in it."

"So you went to find Eve?" Jean-Marc prodded, trying to keep her on track.

"I took Adelaide home, asked Julien to watch her, and said I was going out with a girlfriend. Then I went back to Drew's place. Even though I hated that he loved her so much, I wanted to talk to him. Comfort him. Make sure he was okay. I wanted to be the one he went to when he was upset. I thought that maybe if he could see that I'd never lied to him like she had, that I truly loved him, and that he could have a family with me and Adelaide, maybe it would change his mind. But when I got there, I saw him leaving his building. He had the book tucked under his arm. And I just knew. I knew he was going to see her. He didn't spot me, so I followed him. All the way over to Place Dauphine."

"To Eve's apartment."

"Yes."

"And you went inside?"

"Drew was already inside, and I managed to get into the building when someone was leaving. I found her last name on the door. Her *fake* last name—Winters. I had no idea she was really Sara Marvel at the time, *putain*. I don't think Drew knew either because he was still calling her Eve. I listened at the door...I heard them fighting and then...the bastard fucked her. One last fuck before she left him for good. What a goddamned slut. I couldn't let her get away with it, Jean-Marc! What she'd done to him, to me, to Adelaide!" Coralie's voice was completely hysterical now. "If it weren't for her, we could've been a family! She ruined it! She ruined everything. I couldn't let that go unpunished."

Jean-Marc couldn't tell if his sister was on the verge of crying or laughing. She had completely lost her shit.

"Coralie, what did you do?"

"I waited outside in the hallway, listening. After he finished fucking her, he left, and I hid on the next floor up so he wouldn't see me. Once I was sure he'd left, I went to her door and was just about to knock when she opened it up. She was all ready to leave for the airport, but I just...I just lost control. I couldn't see straight, Jean-Marc. I couldn't even see. She was strong. Stronger than she looked, that little bitch. But I got her. I got her in the end."

"The vase," Jean-Marc said, clenching his jaw. His goddamned crazy sister.

"Yes, the vase."

Jean-Marc could still see the glass shards and violet rose petals scattered all over Eve's floor. When he'd stood in the middle of the crime scene that first day and tried to imagine what had gone down, never in a million years would he have imagined that it had been his own little sister who had thrown that vase and cracked it against Eve's head.

"Did you kill her, Coralie?"

"She wasn't expecting that hit. She didn't think I'd actually do it. But I did. She went down so fast." This time, Coralie did laugh. It was a loud, crazy cackle. And it pierced Jean-Marc's ears. He wanted to slap her.

"There was glass everywhere," she continued. "And blood. So much blood. So I left. I just left her there."

"Were you hurt, too?"

"Yes, she'd gotten in a few blows. Like I said, she was stronger than she looked. Hitting me, biting me, scratching me with her long nails."

Jean-Marc suddenly remembered the early morning when he'd gone over to question Coralie about Eve Winters. Coralie had been wearing a sweater, which was so unlike her. She'd thrown it on, no doubt, to cover up the cuts and bruises left from the fight she'd started with Eve the night before. He remembered how on edge she'd been.

It was all making sense now.

"Was Eve breathing when you left?" Jean-Marc asked.

"I don't know. I don't think so, but I don't know."

"And what did you do once you left?"

"I called Drew."

"Did you tell him what you did?"

"Yes, I told him I thought she might be dead. He told me to go home to Adelaide. He told me he would take care of it."

"You're sure that's what he said?"

"Yes. I'm sure."

"And after, did he tell you exactly how he 'took care of it'?"

"No, he said it would be better if I didn't know the truth."

Putain.

Never before in Jean-Marc's long career of investigating gruesome murders and mysterious disappearances did he so loathe the moment where he finally discovered the truth.

His sister was an accomplice in the disappearance of Eve Winters.

An accomplice, and possibly, a murderer.

62

EVE

The When: Unknown
The Where: Unknown

The familiar sound of the plastic top coming off the needle brings a rush of tears to my eyes.

I don't want to cry. I don't want him to see me cry.

But I can't help it.

When will this end?

I have broken bones that haven't mended, wounds that feel raw and infected, and the only reprieve from the pain comes, of course, from the very needle he is about to inject into my skin.

But why?

Why not just kill me?

My tears are making it past the blindfold now, rolling down the sides of my face. They slice through cuts and gashes, the strong sting only bringing more tears to my eyes.

And just as my captor's body heat presses against my side, and I sense the needle coming closer to my neck, it stops.

He stops.

And he sighs.

"*Please*," I say through the gag that has taken permanent residence around my mouth. "*S'il vous plaît.*"

The needle still doesn't come.

And so, I cry harder. I beg harder.

I hate that I am begging. I hate that I am crying like a little girl. But I have to try. I have to try something.

"*S'il vous plaît, s'il vous plaît, s'il vous plaît*," I continue in my muffled speech.

And he continues to hesitate. The needle hasn't yet reached my neck.

Instead, I feel his hands. Coming around the back of my head. Untying the gag.

Untying the gag!

He removes it from my mouth, and I take the biggest, most glorious breath I've taken in days, weeks—I'm not sure how long. And then I cough, a few horrifically deep coughs that make my entire body radiate with pain.

But I can't think about the pain right now. I can talk. *I must talk.*

"*S'il vous plaît*," I say once more, before continuing on in French, "Just take me somewhere and leave me there. I've never seen you. I've never heard your voice. I have no idea who you are or why you want to keep me here, but if you just take me somewhere and leave me there, I will have no way to identify you. You'll never be caught. Please, please just let me go. I don't want to die here like this. Please just let me go."

My captor is silent.

Which means he's considering my proposal.

So I plead more. I cry more. I tell him he'll never be caught.

And finally, another long, tired sigh. And a whisper.

"Putain."

I'm getting to him.

I hear him lay the needle down on a surface near the bed. I hear him scratching something, his head perhaps. Or possibly a beard.

"Please," I beg. "I know nothing about you. You can just let me go and this will all be over. *Please.*"

My hands are tied down to the bed on either side of me, and the fingers on my left hand are brushing up against his body. I reach around with what little movement I have and grab what I think is his wrist. I squeeze as hard as I can.

"S'il vous plaît."

Just as I say this, the door slams downstairs. My body jolts with fear—a reflex I simply cannot control anymore. He stands, abruptly.

But as he does so, my fingers catch something. Whatever has landed in my hand is smooth and small. A cufflink or a button perhaps.

A cufflink or a button that belongs to *him.*

I keep it hidden beneath my fingers on the bed, careful not to move as I hear his feet pounding over the creaky floors, walking away. Away from me, from this bed he has kept me in, from the needle and the drugs he did not give me.

The door opens and closes, and he is gone.

But I have something of his.

And I don't have a gag in my mouth anymore.

I can breathe again.

And while I don't have much, if any, mobility with my wrists and ankles being tied to the bed, I do have teeth.

And I'm not afraid to bite.

A man and woman have been fighting downstairs for some time now.

I'm straining and concentrating harder than I ever have in my life to hear what they're saying. Or at the very least, to recognize their voices.

But I can't.

I can't hear their words.

And their voices are too muffled to even have the slightest idea who they belong to.

I don't remember who brought me here, how I got here, or how my body came to be in such a dismantled, disastrous state. Ketamine injected straight into the neck will do that to you—I know this fact all too well. After I'd lost my entire family, I tried every drug in the book to erase the truth of the past from my broken mind.

And ketamine was my preferred poison. The closer to the brain you injected this powerful drug, the more memory loss it caused. Unfortunately, my past was too etched in stone and in every newspaper all over the world to ever forget.

So, I changed my name. Used the life insurance money from my mother's death to change my appearance. A new nose. Bigger breasts. Injected lips. Hair dye, colored contacts, and voilà, *a new woman.*

A new woman who has, by some horrific twist of fate, landed *here.*

The fighting downstairs continues.

Something in their fucked-up lives must be going terribly awry.

Perhaps it has something to do with the girl they are drugging and holding captive.

Blood is pumping through my ears and pain is seizing me from every angle. I need the drugs. But even more, I need to escape. I need to find a way out.

While the crazies downstairs continue their ranting and raving, I do my best to sit up and bring my teeth toward the binds on my left wrist.

But my injuries are too severe, and my body parts tied down too firmly to make it possible. The reach is just too far.

I try for the right side.

But again, it's too far.

I say fuck it to my injuries—the cuts, gashes, and broken bones—and I begin thrashing my head around on the pillowless bed. I need to get this blindfold off of me.

But it's tied too tightly around my head, and it seems no amount of thrashing will get it to budge.

A cell phone is ringing downstairs. And then the man's voice—low and barely audible. And not long after, the door downstairs—*a slam*.

I wait for a few moments, wondering if I am alone. If they've left me here with no drugs and no mouth gag. If they've gotten sloppy with this whole kidnapping operation.

For a long time, there is no sound. The pain is too great for me to fall asleep or go unconscious, and my mind is spinning like a tornado.

I have to find a way out of here.

I no more than think this thought when I hear the slamming of the door downstairs one more time.

And then, tiny footsteps—not the pounding I usually hear when *he* comes—running up the stairs.

I start to count, but the footsteps are going too fast and before I even reach thirteen, the bedroom door creaks open.

I clench the button or the cufflink or whatever souvenir the man left in my hand, and I wait.

"Eve." It's a female voice.

And then delicate hands, behind my head, untying the blindfold.

She slips it off my face and all of a sudden, there is light.

So much that I'm momentarily blinded. My eyelids are heavy and gooey and all stuck together. I blink as hard and as fast as I can.

I've never wanted to see more in my life.

"Eve," she says again. Her hands cup my face. "Oh, Eve, *je suis vraiment désolée.*"

I'm so sorry.

She's crying now, and even before I can get my vision to return in full force, I know who it is.

It's her. The girl who Drew got pregnant before he met me. The girl I found out about right at the end of our relationship. Just before my book released.

I'd found a photo of her and the baby tucked into Drew's dresser drawer at his apartment.

She's the girl Drew claimed *not* to love.

The girl he'd had a baby with all the same.

And if *she* was sitting here, in the place I'd been held captive, I could only assume that the man who'd been drugging me all this time was the man who'd *claimed* to love me:

Drew.

63

OFFICER JEAN-MARC DEVEREAUX

SAMEDI 20 MAI 2017
L'HÔPITAL HÔTEL-DIEU ~ PARIS, FRANCE

JEAN-MARC'S PALMS were sweaty as he steered his car into the parking lot at l'Hôpital Hôtel-Dieu. After he'd hung up the phone with Coralie, he'd messaged Breton to tell him that he had an important development in the case and that he needed to speak to him immediately.

He'd told Breton to meet him at the hospital—the same hospital where Sophia Grayson had just been taken, and where her husband would surely be arriving soon, if he wasn't already inside.

He'd also told his boss to come alone.

What they were about to discuss couldn't be heard by any of the other team members as it involved a woman they both loved and her involvement in the very case that the two men were trying to solve. Talk about a conflict of interest.

When Breton's knuckles tapped on the window of Devereaux's passenger-side door, Devereaux unlocked the car and let his boss in. The rain was still coming down in sheets outside, and Breton's jacket was soaked. He'd probably walked over from the office, as it was only a couple of blocks away.

"What's going on?" Breton asked, getting right down to business.

"There's something you need to know about my sister," Jean-Marc began. "But first I need to know that you'll keep what I'm about to tell you to yourself until we decide, together, what to do with this information."

Breton nodded. "Understood. Now tell me what the fuck is going on."

Devereaux looked into the eyes of the man he'd known since they were little boys running around the same neighborhood. The man he'd always looked up to in their years together at the Brigade Criminelle. And the man who'd stolen his joy when Coralie had taken Adelaide and moved into his apartment.

Devereaux looked this man square in the eye and broke his heart.

"Coralie is connected to Andrew Grayson."

"What do you mean?" Breton asked. "In what way?"

"He's Adelaide's father."

Devereaux paused, letting the news sink in. There was more, much more, but he would start with the basics.

"Coralie has known all along. She's been lying to me—said she didn't know the identity of the father. That it was a one-night stand."

Breton's eyes darkened. "It's what she's told me, too."

"So you had no idea who the father was?" Jean-Marc confirmed.

"No," Breton said. "I didn't want to know. I wanted her to be mine. *I* wanted to be the baby's father."

Despite Jean-Marc's ill feelings toward Julien's and

Coralie's union, he knew that Julien did love his sister. He'd loved her since she was a teenager, but being thirteen years her senior, Julien had been far too old for her, and Coralie had shown no romantic interest in him whatsoever. He'd tried about a million times, to no avail, to convince her to have a change of heart, until finally, one day, Jean-Marc told his friend to give up. He told Julien it would never have been a good idea for his best friend to be with his little sister, anyway. It was too close for comfort, and if Jean-Marc was being honest, he didn't want his sister's messy life fucking with the solid relationship he'd always had with his friend and boss at la Crim'.

But then somehow, Julien had succeeded. Jean-Marc didn't know the story of how Julien and his sister had finally gotten together, and he didn't want to know. He hated it because it had taken Adelaide away from him, and it had, as he'd always predicted, fucked up both his professional relationship and friendship with Julien.

"Coralie has been lying to us both," Jean-Marc said. "About more than just the father of her baby."

Breton rubbed his forehead, shook his head. "*Putain.* What else?"

"She was involved in Eve Winters' disappearance. The blond hair at the crime scene—it's Coralie's."

Breton's jaw clenched right along with his fists, and for a moment, Jean-Marc thought he might punch the dashboard. "How do you know for sure?"

"I just spoke with her on the phone and she told me everything."

Breton's angry gaze met Devereaux's square on. "The video footage from the neighborhood camera closest to Eve's apartment. It came in yesterday."

"Why didn't you—" Devereaux started, but by the

mixture of rage and fatigue he saw in Breton's eyes, he already knew the answer to the question he was about to ask.

Breton had seen Coralie in the video. That was why he'd been hanging onto it without telling the team.

"She's in the video," Devereaux said.

Breton nodded. "Heading toward Eve's apartment. Just after Grayson. I was hoping it was a coincidence that she was in that damn video. She told me she was going out with a girlfriend that night and had asked me to stay with Adelaide. I didn't question her. Never in a million years would I have thought..." Breton's voice trailed off into the oblivion, his gaze settling on the rain outside.

"I know, me neither," Devereaux said.

"Tell me exactly what Coralie told you happened that night," Breton said.

Devereaux filled his boss in on everything Coralie had just told him over the phone, ending with Grayson's promise to 'take care of it'.

Breton nodded. "It's all adding up. In the video, not too long after Coralie heads toward Eve's apartment, Grayson is seen leaving. But then, he comes back in the direction of her apartment later on."

"What about after that? Do you see him with Eve's body?"

Breton shakes his head. "No, he doesn't show up again in the video. A man like that certainly has a car driving him all over the city and friends in high places. I'm thinking he called for a car to come pick him up, threw Eve in the back seat and paid the driver to keep his mouth shut."

"We don't have any witnesses who saw a car drive up and leave again around that time of night," Devereaux pointed out.

"That doesn't mean it didn't happen. It would've been quick."

"True," Devereaux said.

"It's likely Eve Winters is dead," Breton said.

"More than likely," Devereaux agreed. "Has anyone else seen the video?"

"No. I got it yesterday and watched it alone. I asked Coralie last night what she'd done with her girlfriend on Monday night, where they'd gone. She had an answer all ready to go. So I was hoping I was wrong. I wanted to figure it out before I said anything to you or anyone else on the team."

Devereaux nodded. He understood. Breton was just trying to protect his crazy-ass sister Coralie.

What an absolute mess she'd created.

"I have a guy who can manipulate the video," Breton said. "Edit Coralie out of the footage entirely. That way we can still prosecute Grayson, but keep Coralie out of it."

"Yes, but it will obviously come out that Grayson is the father of Coralie's baby, and when we question him, how are we going to keep him from talking about Coralie's involvement?"

"Do you know if Grayson knows who we are?" Breton asked. "Does he know that you're Coralie's brother and that she's living with me? Will he recognize us?"

"Coralie said he doesn't know us."

"Good. Then you and I will be the only ones to question him. He's going to lie, obviously. And he'll have a good attorney. So we're not going to get much out of him anyway at the start. I doubt he's going to want to admit to the existence of another woman in his life and a child when he's got a wife. If he blamed Eve's disappearance and murder on Coralie, he's smart enough to know that she'd be locked away for life, and then *he'd* be responsible for raising the baby, which I doubt he wants to do. Plus, even with Coralie's attack on Eve, it was Grayson who took care of it in the end. It was Grayson who removed her body from the scene, and whether or not it was really Coralie who killed Eve, we will pin it on Grayson. One DNA sample from him after we bring him in, and he's done."

"And in the end, if he does cave and mentions Coralie's involvement?" Devereaux questioned.

"Then we'll cut him a deal. We'll get him to keep quiet on her involvement for a shorter sentence. We'll do whatever the fuck we have to do. Agreed?"

Jean-Marc hesitated. Manipulating evidence. Hiding the truth of his sister's involvement. This was obstruction of justice. They would both lose their jobs if any of this came out.

But they were in it now. And for as much as Devereaux despised his sister for her madness, for her idiotic actions, he felt he had no choice but to protect her. She was Adelaide's mother after all.

"How quickly can you get the video footage taken care of?" Devereaux asked.

"It will be finished by tonight. We'll bring Grayson into the station and get the questioning started and the DNA samples. Once the video is ready, if he's still not talking, we'll show it to him. Get him to talk, at least about *his* involvement. At the first mention of Coralie, we shut off the cameras. We cut him a deal."

"Got it," Devereaux agreed. None of this was right. None of it felt okay. But just one thought of his sweet niece's face and the idea of ripping her away from her mother, and Devereaux knew he would do whatever it took to protect them.

And once this was all over, he and Breton would work together to find help for Coralie. She was clearly ill and disturbed, and ignoring what she'd just done wouldn't make it go away. Plus, for as much as he wanted Adelaide to grow up with a mother who *wasn't* in prison for murder, he also didn't want Adelaide being in the care of a woman who might actually be a murderer—the same woman who was cackling and totally fucking insane on the phone with him earlier.

"Now tell me what the hell we're doing at the hospital?" Breton asked, cutting into Devereaux's hurricane of concerns.

"There's something I'm going to need your help with," Devereaux said. Since they were seemingly on the same team now, Devereaux didn't feel quite as nervous telling Breton about what had transpired with Sophia Grayson in the past twenty-four hours.

"Grayson's wife, Sophia, has just been admitted to this hospital. She flew to Paris to spy on Andrew a few days ago, and it turns out she's extremely ill. Cancer. I had an encounter with her last night...and this morning."

Breton's brow lifted. "What kind of encounter?"

"It's not what you think."

"Nothing is what I think anymore, is it?" Breton muttered. "What did you do with Grayson's wife, Devereaux?"

Devereaux went on to explain the whole story. If Sophia decided to talk about the fact that Devereaux had followed her and taken her back to his place under false pretenses, he would certainly need Breton's protection in keeping his job.

When Devereaux finished explaining his questionable actions with Sophia Grayson, including the part about how he'd discovered Coralie's connection to Andrew Grayson just this morning, Breton was quiet for a few moments.

"We're on the same team now?" Breton asked. "You and me?"

Devereaux nodded. "Yes."

"Then you have my protection. If Sophia talks—if she's even well enough to talk after what happened to her this morning—we'll figure out a plan. But for now, let's go see what state she's in, and let's get that son of a bitch Grayson."

64

SOPHIA

Saturday the 20th of May, 2017
A hospital room ~ Paris

I WAKE to the sound of a steady but distant beeping. Its rhythm is the only anchor I have to my consciousness at the moment. Each time I hear a beep, I know that I am still alive.

My eyes feel as if they are glued shut. The lids will barely budge, and so I stop trying. I'm so tired.

Soon a low voice interrupts the beeping. Two low voices. A man's and a woman's. Their words flitter in and out of my head.

"Spread...aggressive...long...not sure...scans...cancer..."

Cancer. Cancer. Cancer.

I *am* a cancer.

An aggressive one.

Destroying everything in my path.

Then it hits me. One of those voices is Drew's. I strain harder this time to open my eyes. It works.

Blinking and blinking until the blurry view comes into

focus. Drew is standing in the doorway with his back to me. A woman in a white coat is with him.

Blond hair. Black glasses. Thin lips pursed in a straight line.

A doctor.

Drew knows. He knows.

My eyes are wide open now. And although I'm dizzy and fuzzy and totally out of it, I manage to take a quick glance around the room. I'm in the hospital, of course.

And then it all comes flooding back to me. The blackness that swallowed me up in the hotel bathroom. My panicked phone call to Drew. The call that stopped him from fleeing the country.

Drew must know now that I've been spying on him in Paris.

And he must know that I have hid an entire illness from him. He is probably thinking that perhaps this makes us even.

And perhaps, it does.

But then I remember *her*.

Coralie.

The foolish French girl who was going ballistic in Drew's Paris flat. The foolish French girl who bore his child.

Adelaide.

Perhaps we're not even, after all.

A wave of nausea bubbles up out of nowhere, and before I have time to call for help, I'm grabbing the little tray on the bedside stand and emptying out the contents of my stomach.

The doctor rushes to my side while Drew stands in the doorway looking at me with eyes that know only one thing: *the violence of the truth.*

Bits and pieces of our violent truth are finally coming out, eroding what little trust was left in our marriage. Not just eroding it, but shredding it and spitting it out with my blood, my illness, all over this sterile hospital room.

A nurse rushes in and takes over where the doctor left off. Once she's got me all cleaned up, I rest my head back on the pillow, squeeze my eyes closed and try not to let the tears escape.

I'm so tired of holding them in.

It's the warmth of Drew's hand on mine that finally coaxes the flood gates to open.

When I open my eyes, Drew is wiping my tears, but he's looking down upon me as if I'm a complete stranger. As if I'm someone he's never really known.

Which, of course, is partly true.

"Cancer, Sophia? Ovarian cancer? You had surgery a year and a half ago? How could you not...*fuck*."

He sits down on the side of the bed, rubs his forehead with his hand. His fingers are shaking, just like mine.

"I thought it was going to be okay," I say. "I didn't want to worry you. Not after everything you've been through with your mother and your sister."

He lifts his eyes. They're deadpanned. "But it's not okay. *You* are not okay."

I shake my head. I know.

"It's in your other ovary now," he says slowly, as if each word is physically painful to speak aloud. "And it has spread. To your lungs."

It's the news I was dreading. The news I knew was coming. I didn't know where the cancer was living in my sick body; I just knew it was back. And that it had returned with a vengeance.

"I never wanted you to see me like this." My tears are

coming down in a steady stream now; nothing can stop them. The truth has reared its ugly head and there is no holding back.

Drew slides his hand back over mine. "But you're my wife."

"And you're my husband," I say.

"You could have told me, Sophia. You could have fucking told me."

Drew scoots closer to me and then does something entirely surprising. He rests his chest on top of mine. He squeezes me so tight that I feel suffocated by the weight of him.

But his weight, his pain, his desperation—it feels good. Being suffocated with my husband's love while I lie here, close to death. How close? I couldn't be sure.

But I am sure of one thing.

"I'm sorry I didn't tell you," I say, wondering if he'll apologize for all of the things he hasn't told me.

We hold each other for a long while, all of our lies set aside for this one moment of truth that has finally brought us back together.

It's not long, though, before Drew's phone buzzes atop the sheets.

He pulls away from me, and we both catch the name on the screen—Antoine Danton.

It takes me a moment to register the name, but when Drew's eyes flash with worry, I remember.

Antoine Danton is the name of the criminal defense attorney that Drew visited the first day I followed him around Paris.

"Do you need to answer?" I ask him.

Drew shakes his head, silences the phone. "I'll deal with it later."

"There's no time like the present," I say. "To deal with it all. The other women. Eve. Coralie. And your...your daughter. *Adelaide.*" The excruciating pain of saying her name is nearly enough to kill me. "How could you, Drew? How could you name her *Adelaide*? *How*?" My voice is shrill and scratchy and out of control. The tender moment we have just shared is gone. And now, I'm snapping.

I want to snap his fucking neck.

"How the bloody hell could you, Drew?" I shriek.

Drew lowers his gaze, fixes it on the phone. *Coward.*

"You were there that day. The black car...and in my apartment," he says. His eyes lift to mine for only a brief second, a brief second in which my icy gaze gives him all the confirmation he needs.

"You saw us," he says. "That morning, when I..."

"When you hit her," I finish. "She's so young, Drew. So bloody young."

"I don't love her," he says, as if that makes it all okay.

"You don't love the girl or the baby?" I prod.

"The...the mother. Coralie. I don't love her. I never did."

"But you love the baby, *your baby,* don't you Drew? And Eve—or *Willow* as you knew her—you certainly love her, too. Isn't that right?"

Drew flinches at the mention of Eve's name. His skin is gray now; he looks as though he may topple over.

Maybe he'll crack his head on the floor. Maybe he'll die.

Maybe we'll die together.

The phone screen is still flashing with the attorney's name—it's relentless.

"Answer it," I say, looking away from him. "Just sodding answer it."

He hesitates, and I've had it.

"If you don't want to go to prison for whatever you did to make that girl disappear, answer the sodding phone, Drew! And get out of here. I can't look at you anymore. Please, just go."

He opens his mouth to speak, but then closes it and leaves.

I lie alone in my hospital bed, knowing it is too late for us, for our love. We have taken these lies too far.

I still don't know with absolute certainty if Drew is directly involved in Eve's disappearance...although I know what I believe.

I believe that he is.

I believe that he really could have harmed her.

And yet, as sick as it all is, I do still love him.

Which is, of course, why the pain of this whole ordeal is so brutal.

We are, the two of us, the definition of a fucked-up and dysfunctional marriage.

It seems as if hours pass while Drew is somewhere else, talking on the phone to his criminal defense attorney. It's probably only a matter of minutes really, but time feels skewed in my new reality, and before I know it, I've dozed off.

The feeling of a hand covering mine brings me back.

The hand is cold, though. Not at all like Drew's hands, which are always warm.

Before I open my eyes, I already know who I am going to see.

"*Mon amour*," my lover says. "Why didn't you tell me you'd come to—"

"What are you doing here?" I cut him off.

"I've been calling and messaging you for days and you haven't responded, Sophia," he says. His dark-brown eyes look sick with worry. "I found out your doctor hadn't been able to reach you either, and when I got wind of this mess with Andrew and the book, I knew. I knew you must have come here to find out what was going on...what he had done." There is anger in his voice when he says this last part.

"I arrived this morning to take over for Andrew at the bank and to find you," he continues. "Not long after I arrived, Andrew messaged me and told me you were here in Paris. That you were sick, and he was on his way to you. I got here as fast as I could. I connected the doctors here with your doctors back in New York. And when Andrew arrived, well of course the doctor told him about—"

"The cancer," I finish. "I know. And I know that it's back. In my lungs."

My lover nods, gravely, his eyes not leaving mine for a second.

"Does Drew know about this? About us?" I ask, wondering if the whole truth has exploded today, or only parts of it.

He shakes his head no.

His hands squeeze mine, and for the very first time, the chill of his skin isn't comforting to me. I want warmth. Even though I could not possibly hate anyone more right now, I still want my husband. *I want Drew.*

His name has no more than passed through my mind when he appears in the doorway.

My husband and my lover, now in the same hospital room.

"Dimitri, what are you—" Drew says to his boss. But when he sees the way Dimitri is holding my hands and the startled look that must be in my eyes, Drew takes a step back.

Comprehension sweeps over his beautifully tired face, and in an instant, I know he knows.

Drew knows that Dimitri, his boss, is my lover. And Drew can probably see by the way Dimitri is sitting by my bedside, tenderly holding my hands, that it hasn't only been sex.

A heavy silence breaks through the chorus of machines beeping in the hospital room. It's all coming together for Drew. He's connecting the dots.

His wife was diagnosed with cancer in the fall of 2015 when he first left for Paris. His wife refused to come with him to Paris. Meanwhile, she connected with Dimitri Dumas, his new boss at Le Crédit Parisien, and they began an affair. An affair which has lasted through surgery for ovarian cancer, recovery, and for many months after. An affair which has turned from sex into love into more sex, into an even deeper love.

Drew's eyes find mine. In them, I see the questions he is asking:

Do you let him see your scars?

Do you let him fuck you the way you used to let me fuck you?

Do you love him?

The answer to all of those questions, of course, is yes.

But in regard to love, I still love Drew more, despite everything. And I feel sick with myself, with all of us, for being involved in such a plight.

Dimitri stays firmly planted at my bedside, his freezing hands gripping mine so tightly that I can see he has no intention of letting go, even now.

But I want him to leave.

"Dimitri," I say. The firmness in my voice lets him know.

He leans over, kisses me tenderly on the forehead, and whispers in my ear, not so quietly, "*Je t'aime, mon amour.*"

And then he walks past Drew, shoulders poised in confidence. He's so sure of himself. Sure that *he* is the one I love the most.

Which simply is not true. It never could be.

Drew's fists are clenched at his sides as Dimitri strides past. "How long?" Drew asks me after his boss is gone.

"Not long after you took the Paris position," I answer. There is no use in lying about it now. I may be dying, anyway.

Drew nods quietly, but I can see from the tension in his jaw that he is reeling.

"You didn't realize you'd married yourself, did you?" I snap.

He is quiet for a while, and I know I shouldn't have said that last bit. Didn't need to rub salt in such a fresh wound. Then again, I couldn't really be bothered to care about his sodding wounds right now.

"What did your attorney say?" I ask. "Will you be arrested?"

Drew storms up to my bed in a sudden, ferocious fury. "I didn't take Willow...or Eve, or Sara Marvel! Whatever the hell her name is! I have nothing to do with her disappearance, Sophia. Nothing."

"Well, where in the sodding hell is she, Drew?"

"I don't know," he says. "I don't fucking know."

But what *I* don't know is if my husband is telling the truth. It's one thing to admit to the existence of a daughter after your wife has already seen her in the flesh and blood. It's quite another to admit to involvement in an abduction.

He reaches for my hand, squeezes it hard.

I think of the way he smacked Coralie across the face

with this hand, and I wonder if this is the hand of a man who could make a woman disappear.

My husband gives me the most pained expression I've ever seen on his face.

It's even worse than the way he looked at me when the doctor told us that our baby, our *Adelaide*, was dead.

"Is it too late?" he asks. "For us?"

I don't answer him, though. I can't. Not when he has had a daughter who is not ours, with a woman who is not me. Not when he may have abducted Eve. And not while I am lying ill in a hospital bed.

Dying.

I am dying.

There has never been a greater pain than this.

But I suppose I deserve it.

I've done such horrible things to him.

I'm a whore and a liar and a sick, sick person.

I deserve everything that has happened to me.

Every unimaginable, excruciating event, and more, probably.

Well, as Eve said, *with Andrew Grayson, there is always more.*

Much more.

65

EVE

THE WHEN: UNKNOWN
THE WHERE: UNKNOWN

"It's you," I say, watching her silhouette hovering over me on the bed.

Yes, it's definitely her. The blond-haired, blue-eyed crazy beauty who birthed Drew's baby.

Coralie.

She cups my face tighter in her trembling hands.

"Eve, we have to go," she says in French. "We have to leave now. He'll be back soon. And he's going to kill you, Eve. He's going to kill you if you don't come with me."

"Who? Who is going to kill me?" I cry. I already know the answer, but I have to hear her say it.

"You have to understand, I had no idea he was keeping you here! I thought he'd...oh God, Eve, *come on!* We have to go."

"Who was keeping me here?" I repeat.

"How could you be such an idiot? It was Drew! It's

been Drew all along. And if we don't hurry, he's going to kill us both!"

Coralie tries to hoist me up to a sitting position but I'm in shock and my body is writhing in pain. It was Drew. All along, it's really been him. Walking up those stairs. Sticking a needle in my neck. Making me forget.

Was it him who hurt me like this? Who broke my bones and slashed my skin?

I try to imagine him coming at me with a knife. Cracking my bones in half, but I can't. I don't. I don't want to.

"Is there time to call the police?" I hear the words tumble out of my mouth but am barely aware that it's me talking.

She shakes her head, then grabs onto my shoulders. "You don't understand, Eve. You don't understand!"

"What don't I understand?"

"Eve, *putain*. The police can't help us. I have a car waiting outside to take you straight to the hospital. Come on. We have to get out of here *now*."

"Why can't they help us?"

Coralie squares her frantic eyes in front of mine, her fingernails digging into me.

"The police can't help us, Eve, because Drew is working with them. They've been protecting him all along."

66

SOPHIA

Saturday the 20th of May, 2017
A hospital room ~ Paris

Drew is sitting at my bedside when I open my eyes from my latest slumber. I feel as though I've been sleeping for years, although I imagine it's only been an hour, or even a few minutes...I couldn't be sure.

Or, perhaps I've been sleeping my entire life and I'm just now waking up for the first time.

The truth tends to do that—wake you up, even when you wish you were still sleeping in the comfort of all the lies.

And the truth clearly couldn't give a damn how uncomfortable it's making me.

Drew doesn't yet know I'm awake. I can see by the way he's fidgeting in the stiff hospital chair, checking his phone obsessively, rubbing his head, that his mind is in a million other places.

With his daughter, perhaps.

Or with her mother, Coralie.

Or with Eve, wherever she may be.

Wherever he may have put her.

Or perhaps he's wondering if I'm going to die soon.

I wonder if he wants me to die. If it would be easier for him at this point.

I no sooner think this thought when he lifts his eyes to mine, and I can see that there are tears in them.

He doesn't want me to die.

I know this instantly by the way he's looking at me.

We look at each other for a long while, our eyes saying a million things that our mouths haven't been able to all these years.

Until finally, I have one question that slips through my lips.

"What have you done, Drew?" I whisper.

He stares back at me, blinking, his lips moving, but no sound coming out.

"*What have you done, Drew?*" I repeat.

My words linger in the air, waiting to be heard. Waiting to be met with truth.

And just as I think he is never going to give it to me, the little bit of hardness that was left in his regard cracks and he collapses atop me, crying. I've only seen Drew cry like this once in our lives—when we birthed a lifeless baby girl whom we named Adelaide.

His arms are around my waist, his head buried in my abdomen. He thinks it's safe here, hanging onto this abdomen which is scarred with lies.

And he sobs, because of his own.

"*I'm so sorry. I'm so sorry. I'm so sorry.*"

His apologies bury me, suffocate me, until soon I've taken his tear-streaked face between my hands.

I am not crying, though.

The tears, they just won't come.

Instead I'm wondering what he has done with Eve. If he hit her the way he hit Coralie that morning in his apartment.

If he's done more than hit her.

If he's taken her.

If he's killed her.

Could my husband be a killer?

There was still a tiny part of me hanging on to the hope that perhaps, just maybe, I've been wrong about the whole thing. That Drew isn't the married man in Eve's book. That it is all one big misunderstanding.

But by the way he is crying, and by the anger that is surging through every vein in my body, I know that all hope is lost.

And instead of compassion for the man I pledged to love forever, for better or for worse, I feel something I've never quite felt before for him.

Something I can only describe as hatred.

I hate that he would do this to me, to us.

And even, to Eve.

She's certainly not my friend, but she's been through so much. And he took advantage of her. The older, wealthy, powerful businessman, reeling in the young, poor prostitute with money and sex and drugs and promises of everlasting love.

All while he had a baby with another young woman, and a wife back in New York.

What my husband has done to all of us is vicious.

And I hate him for it.

His weepy puppy dog eyes get no sympathy from me.

Instead, I envision snapping his neck, hard and fast, but

there is one more thing I want to know before he's gone. One more question I must ask.

"How could you name her Adelaide? *How, Drew, how?*"

My body doesn't give him a chance to answer, though.

I am going to be sick. I break away from Drew's grip and reach for the tray on the bedside stand, but I don't make it.

Instead, a pool of crimson gathers atop the white sheets in my lap.

Blood.

My blood, draining from my insides, pouring out of the corners of my mouth, staining everything in its path.

Drew can't stop it.

I can't stop it.

No one can stop the violence of the truth.

Once it has been opened, there is no going back.

The retching is ferocious and evil and taking everything I've got left. Which isn't much.

Drew is yelling down the corridor for the nurses and soon there are a swirl of them around me, sticking me with needles and trying to stop the inevitable downward spiral of cancer.

It takes some time for them to stabilize me, or at least to get the vomiting to stop. My blood is everywhere, though, and I don't think I've ever felt so weak in all my life.

All the while, my husband watches from the doorway, his face as pale as a ghost.

I don't think he could get any whiter until two men holding police badges appear before him.

I can't see their faces—my vision is too blurry and I'm having a hard time keeping my eyes open with the drugs the nurses are pumping into me. But I saw the shiny badges. And I hear the voices.

"Andrew Grayson?" one of the officers says to him.

That voice. *I know that voice.*

I force my eyes open, straining to focus on the one who's talking.

"We need to bring you in for questioning," the officer says in French. "For the disappearance of Eve Winters, or as you may have heard, Sara Marvel."

It's hard to see with the nurses now trying to get the police away from my room, but there he is. Jean-Marc Devereaux.

Of course. That slimy bastard.

While Drew nods and turns a sickly shade of gray, I catch Jean-Marc's gaze turning in my direction.

Summoning all the energy I can muster, I shake my head at him.

Drew says something quietly to the officers before walking up to my bedside.

He grabs my clammy hand with his own and squeezes it. So hard that once again, I think my bones may quite possibly break.

"I'll be back, Sophia. I promise I'll be back."

I can't say anything. I can hardly look at him.

I just want to close my eyes and sleep away this insane nightmare.

It's all too much.

He lowers his face, brushes his lips over my forehead.

"I love you, Sophia. I'll never stop loving you."

I fight the tears that now want to spill over. The tragedy of our love has no end.

And while I still can't bring myself to speak, I blink up at him, letting him know that I've heard him.

With that, my husband leaves in the custody of *la Brigade Criminelle.*

And I am left wondering what kind of a criminal he really is...and if I'll ever see him again.

67

EVE

The When: Unknown
The Where: Unknown

I do *not* trust Coralie, but if she's going to untie me, I will pretend to trust her. Anything to get me unbound and out of this godforsaken room where I've been locked away and fed a diet of ketamine and fear for who knows how long.

Getting me out of the bed and mobile again is no small feat, though, and I'm not sure Little Miss Coralie was prepared for this particular obstacle in her escape plan.

I'm covered in cuts and bruises and I'm certain I have several broken bones. Not the very least of which are my ribs, which are making it insanely painful to breath and move at the same time.

I understand why Drew was drugging me. It was so I wouldn't feel *this*.

Oh how kind of him. The sick bastard.

I must power through, though. *I must get out of here.*

"Allez, allez," Coralie prods as she hoists my arm

around her little shoulders and tries to walk me out of the bedroom.

But my legs are like jelly, their circulation having been severely cut off by the tight ties around my ankles.

I gaze down at my broken body and only now, for the first time, do I realize what I'm wearing. A black T-shirt that doesn't belong to me and a pair of dark gray pajama pants. The clothes fit me well—they must belong to Coralie I reason, or perhaps one of Drew's other conquests.

I am barefoot. The skin on my feet, arms, and hands is slashed and caked with dry blood.

The bastard didn't even bother to bathe me or bandage me up.

"*Attends*," I tell Coralie. *Wait.* I need a second to breathe. And more importantly to make sure I have a good grip on the little present that Drew left me earlier—his button or cufflink or whatever it is in my left hand. I will not leave this gem behind.

Once I feel like I can at least make an attempt at walking, I nod at Coralie and we get started toward the door. A walk to the bedroom door has never been more excruciating, but we get there. Soon we are greeted by a dark hallway, and after a few more steps, there we are at the top of the staircase.

The one with thirteen steps.

Coralie and I take the steps slowly, one by one, and I do my best not to topple over, not to stop breathing.

Every breath feels like a stab to the ribs, but I must keep going.

At the bottom of the staircase, with what little I can see in the dark, it looks as though we are in a scarcely decorated apartment. A lamp here, a chair there, but nothing really resembling a home. Coralie doesn't give me time to fish around the apartment and take the evidence I'd like to take. Instead she leads me to the alarm next to the front door and punches in 6 buttons:

38126*

38126*

38126*

38126*

I will not forget this code.

I force it through my head on repeat as she opens the door and leads me into the hallway of an apartment building. It's dark, and instead of hitting the button that would turn on the light, she leads me straight to the tiny elevator and practically shoves me inside.

I lean my head against the wall and close my eyes for our descent.

Soon, we'll be outside. Soon, I'll be free.

I keep telling myself this to survive the pain.

When the elevator doors open, we're greeted by another dark corridor. And then, finally, a door to the outside.

It's exquisite and exquisitely painful, this first breath, this first step outdoors.

It's dark and hot and raining so hard that it's difficult to see anything. But from what I can see, we're in the interior courtyard of an apartment building and there is a tiny car parked there that Coralie is leading me toward.

I was hoping we'd be walking out onto the city streets, at which point I would scream at the first passerby, "I'm Eve! Eve Winters! I'm alive! Help me!"

But there is no sidewalk. There are no people. Only a dark courtyard and a tiny car and a determined little French woman shoving me into it.

As much as I would love to escape Coralie's grasp—even with her promises of rescuing me—I couldn't run away right now even if I tried. My body simply wouldn't do it.

I follow her lead as she loads me into the front seat—again, no small feat. I'm panting and dizzy and in so much pain I feel as though I may be sick, but I hold it together and get in the car. I squeeze the souvenir from my captor tighter in my left hand.

Just as I do so, a noise coming from the back seat startles me.

It's the cooing of a baby.

I resist the urge to whip my head around quickly, and instead, I grab onto the seat and tilt my head as much as I can toward the sound of the baby until I see her.

Or rather, the top of her head. She's strapped into a car seat and she's just cooing and humming and nearly singing to herself.

Drew's baby.

This is Drew's baby.

I don't have much time to process any of this as Coralie hops into the front seat, starts the car, and hits a little clicker which opens the large door looming ahead of us. She zooms out onto the rainy streets, through traffic lights and past apartment buildings. I know we are in Paris, but she's driving too fast and I'm too dizzy and in too much pain to be able to figure out exactly where we started or where we're going. It's just too damn dark and my focus is concentrated too strongly on trying to breathe to know anything right now.

"You're taking me to the hospital?" I manage to spit out in French.

But she doesn't answer.

"Where are you taking me?" I ask.

She answers by revving up the gas. The car speeds up. The rain pours harder.

"Coralie!" I snap, ignoring the throbbing of my ribs to get one more sentence out. "*Where are we going?*"

Just as I say this, her phone buzzes inside her purse which sits in the center console. She plunges her hand into her bag, swerving as she does so, and when she pulls the phone out, a curse, "*Putain.*"

She tosses the phone onto the center console, and for the first time since I've been taken, I get to see the date and the time.

It's 9:37 p.m. on Saturday, May 20th.

I try to do the math in my head. My book released on a Tuesday...was it May 15th or 16th? I was supposed to fly to New York before that. The day before...I think. It's all so fuzzy. Clearly, though, I never got on that plane. Which means I've been tied up in that room for less than a week.

It feels like an eternity.

Coralie's phone buzzes again. More text messages from someone named *Chéri*.

"Putain!" Coralie cries with a hit to the steering wheel before picking up the phone and tossing it to the floor by my feet.

"Coralie, what's going on?" I ask her. "Is that Drew?"

"Yes, it's him," she snaps. "He's coming for us. We have to go faster."

"Coralie, where are you taking me?" I shriek.

Coralie shakes her head but doesn't respond.

The baby responds though, with a loud cry.

By the scenery changing outside, it is clear that we are getting closer to the outskirts of the city. It is also clear that she isn't taking me to the hospital.

I have no idea where this crazy girl is driving us, but I am quite certain now that she never planned on saving me.

She knows I'm not strong enough to run away from her.

She knows I don't know where we are going.

She knows I have no real way to escape this madness short of opening the car door and rolling my injured body out of a fast-moving car. Which, at this point, may be the only viable escape option I have.

The baby is now wailing from the back seat, and her mom is firmly ignoring her.

I must act now. I eye the door handle, wondering if I have the courage to do it. To open the door. To jump.

Coralie has just pulled onto the *autoroute*. She speeds up. My hand inches toward the handle.

I must get out of this car.

68

OFFICER JEAN-MARC DEVEREAUX

SAMEDI 20 MAI 2017
36 QUAI DES ORFÈVRES ~ PARIS, FRANCE

JEAN-MARC PACED in a slow circle around the table where Andrew Grayson was sitting. Before Devereaux got started on the asshole who'd screwed his sister over and taken Eve Winters, he reveled in this glorious moment. The moment where he let the fear and anticipation of what was about to go down during his 48-hour hold put the distinguished American businessman into a total and complete panic.

Grayson's panic was silent and controlled, of course, but that didn't mean Devereaux couldn't feel it. Taste it. Delight in it.

Devereaux was sure that Breton, who was watching from the other side of the glass, was delighting in it as well.

A few beads of sweat formed at Grayson's temples, and Devereaux waited until they'd begun their descent down Grayson's pale face to begin his questioning.

First things first. Devereaux opened the manila envelope he'd been holding, pulled out a series of photographs, and laid them out on the table for Grayson to see.

"These are screenshots from the security footage in the lobby at the Ritz," Devereaux explained in French. "Here you are, Monsieur Grayson, checking in to the hotel on several different occasions. You'll see the dates and times stamped at the bottom. And here—" Jean-Marc lays out a new set of photos, "are screenshots of the American author Eve Winters—who we now know, of course, is really Sara Marvel—walking into the hotel lobby on exactly the same nights, each time approximately one hour after you arrived. She doesn't check in, but instead bypasses the front desk and heads straight toward the elevator. Every time."

Grayson refused to look down at the photos. Instead, he kept his gaze pinned on Devereaux. "I'm not going to answer any of your questions without my attorney present."

"If you are innocent, Monsieur Grayson, why do you need your attorney here to answer for you?" Devereaux quipped, hovering ever closer to Grayson's sweaty temples. Devereaux noted the dark stains spreading beneath the armpits of Grayson's crisp gray collared shirt, and the circles of wetness blotting all the way down his back.

"Have you read Eve's memoir, Monsieur Grayson? *The Mistress of Paris?*"

Grayson's left leg twitched just the slightest bit before he replied, "I told you, I'm not answering any questions without my attorney present."

"I've already explained to you," Devereaux said, his voice not faltering for a second, "you will have the chance to meet with your attorney *after* our first round of questioning. You are here on a forty-eight-hour hold, and your unwillingness to talk isn't doing you any favors." Devereaux leaned down, his face now barely an inch from

Grayson's. "I will ask you one more time, Monsieur Grayson, and one time only. Have you read Eve Winters' memoir?"

"I'm not answering your questions without my attorney present," Grayson repeated. But this time, his voice wavered. The poor, scared bastard.

Grayson blinked, and Devereaux took this opportunity to hit him across the face with an open palm.

"You're not in the United States anymore," Devereaux said once the first satisfying hit was accomplished. "Your bullshit won't work with us."

And then, another hit, across the other cheek.

It felt good to hit him. Devereaux knew it was a little too early in the questioning to get physical, but he didn't care. And he knew Breton wouldn't care either. He would encourage it.

Devereaux watched as a slow trickle of blood found its way out of Grayson's left nostril, and then he continued. Calm. Steady. "Have you or have you not read the memoir of Eve Winters?"

Drew sniffed up some of the blood, blinked his eyes, and let out a long breath. "Yes, I've read her memoir."

Voilà.

"I see. Then I imagine you remember this moment—" Devereaux pulled one more photo out of the manila envelope and dangled it in Grayson's bloody face. "It's one that Eve describes so vividly in her book—only of course Eve writes that she met you in the lounge at the Hôtel George V, to protect your identity I presume. Here you are, nonetheless, sitting at a table at the bar at the Ritz, drinking with Eve and handing her a black rose. Do you remember this night, Monsieur Grayson?"

Drew nodded, albeit begrudgingly.

"Eve told you her name was Willow that night, correct?" Devereaux pushed.

Drew nodded again, slowly, carefully. "Yes, I thought she was Willow. I *always* thought she was Willow..."

"You're telling me she never told you who she truly was—a writer who was named neither Willow nor Eve, but rather Sara Marvel?"

Grayson clenched his jaw before he spoke. "No. I had no idea."

"Until the book release last week, when you started to get a clearer picture of the woman you'd been paying for sex?"

Grayson didn't respond. Which to Devereaux meant *yes*.

"What were you doing last Monday night, the night before Eve's book released in the States?" Devereaux prodded.

Grayson shifted in his metal chair, still trying to sniff up the blood which was now running down over his lips.

"Eve left me a copy of her book that day, along with a letter. She said she was leaving Paris for a little while. And that she was sorry for lying, and..."

"And?"

"And...that she loved me. That she would always love me." Grayson's pathetic eyes grew watery as he said this.

Serves you right to fall in love with a prostitute when you already have a baby with another woman and a wife across the fucking ocean.

Devereaux didn't say any of that, though; he and Breton were determined to keep Coralie and the baby out of it. Judging by the state Sophia Grayson was in at the hospital when they took Andrew Grayson into custody, they doubted she'd had time or the physical capacity to tell her husband that she'd spent the night at Devereaux's place, or that Devereaux was Coralie's brother.

Granted, Coralie and Jean-Marc did have the same last name of Devereaux, and they did hold a resemblance to one another, but Breton had advised Devereaux simply not to formally introduce himself to Grayson, and the two of them doubted Grayson would put it all together considering the stress he was under.

"Did Eve say where she was going?" Devereaux continued.

Grayson shook his head. "No."

Devereaux pulled a pen from his front pocket, sat down in the chair across from Grayson. "How convenient," he said, tapping the pen in an even, maddening cadence on the metal table. "What happened after you read her letter and her book?"

"Nothing happened," he snapped. "I found out the next day that she was missing. I haven't heard from her since she left the book and the letter at my door."

Flat out lying already. Not Grayson's smartest move, Devereaux thought, but that's what the guilty ones always did at first—they lied to see how far they could take it. To see what evidence was already stacked against them before they started admitting to what they'd done.

"So you mean to say you *did not* go over to her apartment in a rage, fight with her, have sex with her one last time for good measure, and then take her somewhere so that this would all go away." Devereaux phrased it as a statement, not a question.

"If I knew where she was, I would fucking tell you," Grayson growled.

Devereaux was unfazed.

"I highly doubt that, Monsieur Grayson, seeing as how

you already are not telling me the full story. We have street camera surveillance from the night of Ms. Winters' disappearance placing you near Place Dauphine." Devereaux had yet to see the footage as Breton was still having it *edited,* but he trusted that Breton would have the footage soon and he figured there was no harm in using it as leverage to get Grayson to talk.

"I didn't go to her apartment," Grayson said.

Devereaux reached to the end of the table, grabbed a second manila envelope, and removed a plastic bag of evidence. He held it up for Grayson to see and stifled his own grin. "So when we run your DNA, you're saying we *won't* find your semen on the inside of this pair of Eve's underwear?"

Grayson stared at the lacy black panties inside the plastic bag and stayed silent.

Devereaux knew he was getting closer. He stood, circled Drew with rhythmic, purposeful steps. "What were you doing at her apartment that night, Andrew?"

"I'm not answering any more questions until my attorney is present," Grayson said.

Devereaux tucked the plastic bag of racy evidence back into the manila envelope; he didn't want to contaminate it with Grayson's blood.

"You'll talk with him when I fucking say you can." Devereaux walked over to Grayson, pulled him up by his collar and slammed his back against the wall, knocking over his chair in the process. "What did you do to Eve that night, Andrew? What did you do to her?"

Grayson's eyes went dark, but he still refused to fucking respond.

Devereaux's fist thought it was time to make its grand appearance. He took a swing, cracking his knuckles hard against Grayson's jaw. Blood spewed from his lips and nose, but that didn't deter Devereaux. He slammed Grayson's back up against the wall again, harder this time. "Tell me the truth about what you did to Eve that night. This is only going to get worse if you don't talk."

"Fuck! I didn't hurt her," Grayson finally answered, spitting blood from his mouth.

"So you were at her apartment," Devereaux confirmed.

"Yes, I went to her fucking apartment but like I said, I didn't hurt her. I didn't take her. I don't know where the fuck she is!"

Devereaux didn't loosen his grip on Grayson's bloody collar. "What did you do at her apartment?"

"I needed to hear the truth about who she was from her mouth. I needed to hear her say it."

"What happened when you went?"

"She was on her way out. Had her bags packed. I was upset, and she clearly didn't want to see me. She kept asking me to leave, but I didn't want to go. I was afraid if I let her walk out that door, I would never see her again."

Tears had now joined the blood that was pouring down Grayson's face. Devereaux wasn't buying the pity party.

"So instead of doing what she asked, you fucked her?"

"It wasn't like that. It wasn't like that with Willow. I mean Eve, or Sara or whoever the hell she was."

"Whoever the hell she *was*?" Devereaux repeated.

"Who she *is*, I mean. Who she is," Grayson backtracked.

Devereaux loosened his grip on Grayson's collar, guided him back toward the toppled chair and nodded for him to pick it back up and sit down.

"Tell me how it was with her then."

Grayson took a seat, wiping at his nose. "We were close.

We were in love. We did all the things lovers do when they're in love."

"And on this particular night, what did you two lovers do?" Devereaux prodded.

"We had sex. Like always. It was quick, though, because she said she had a flight to catch."

"Was the sex consensual?"

"Of course it was fucking consensual! I'm not a goddamn rapist!"

"That's not entirely true, according to Eve's memoir." Devereaux sat back down, grabbed his pen and continued tapping.

"Her memoir isn't entirely true, as you well know. She's really Sara Marvel for fuck's sake and her sister in the book is Kate Marvel who's been missing and probably dead for years now."

"I'm aware," Devereaux said. "So you had *consensual* sex with Eve and then what happened?"

"That was it. We talked, we had sex, and then she told me she had to go to the airport. So I left."

"Where did you go?"

"I went back to my apartment."

Devereaux nodded, then grabbed the manila envelope with the photos and pulled out a few more, spreading them out on the table in front of Grayson. "This was the state of Eve's apartment when police were called to the scene later that night. Not long after you and Eve had *consensual* sex. And Eve, as you know, was nowhere to be found. Her suitcase and purse, passport included, were left inside her apartment. She never made it to the airport."

Grayson's eyes combed the photos and, once again, they glossed over with tears. Devereaux didn't care if Grayson was sad about what he'd done. He only cared about two things: keeping his sister and niece out of the whole ordeal and getting a confession from Grayson.

"What did you do to Eve that night, Andrew?" Devereaux's voice was calm, level. He didn't need to intimidate Grayson anymore. That part was done. Now he needed his confession.

Grayson shook his head. "This is...this is crazy. I didn't do that. I didn't hurt her. I didn't take her. I had nothing to do with this."

"We have video footage of you in the neighborhood that night, we have your confession on tape that you were at her apartment that night, that the two of you had intercourse, and soon we will have your DNA matched to the DNA found at the crime scene." Devereaux chose the crime scene photo displaying the most blood and held it in Grayson's face. "And you honestly expect a jury to believe that you had nothing to do with *this*?"

"I did not hurt her. I could never...*would never* do that to Eve."

"Was there anyone with you that night to confirm your whereabouts after you supposedly *left* Eve's apartment and went home?"

"No," Grayson said. "I was alone."

Good. He wasn't going to bring Coralie into this, not yet anyway.

Devereaux nodded. "I see." He stood, scooped the photos off the table, and headed for the door. "Another officer will be in to question you shortly. Don't get too comfortable. There's a cement cell that has your name on it as soon as our DNA reports come back."

Devereaux closed the door and slipped into the room next door where he found Breton. He expected Breton's eyes to be glued to Grayson through the glass, but instead,

Breton's brow was furrowed as he typed quickly into his phone.

"What's up?" Devereaux asked.

"It's Coralie," Breton said. "She's not responding."

"What's new?" Devereaux quipped. "She never responds. Well, not to me anyway."

Breton lifted his gaze and Devereaux could see at once that it was more than that.

"I've been worried about her lately," Breton said. "She's been acting strange, which all makes sense now that we know what we know. So I went on her phone recently and shared her location with my phone."

"What's she doing?" Devereaux asked.

"I'm not sure what the hell she's doing," Breton said, looking back down at his phone. "Looks like she's driving outside the city. I have to go get her." He nodded toward Grayson, who was still sweating bullets and wiping at his bloody face on the other side of the glass. "I trust you can handle this. I have to go make sure your sister and the baby are okay."

Devereaux didn't fight with Breton this time. Instead he nodded at his boss, his best friend, and decided to trust him with the safety of his sister and his niece from this day forward.

"Call me if you need me," Devereaux said as Breton let himself out.

Devereaux lit a cigarette and watched Grayson squirm on the other side of the glass. When he finished his cigarette, he lit up another one and watched him squirm some more.

69

EVE

The When: Saturday May 20th, 2017
The Where: Somewhere outside of Paris

"Coralie, I'm going to be sick," I say to her in French. I grip my stomach and reach for the button to roll down the window. "*Arrête la voiture*!" I cry.

I cap my mouth with my hand for full effect while she looks at me in a panic and swerves to the side of the road. Coralie took us off the main highway about ten minutes before and it now appears that we are on some back-country road. As soon as the car is stopped, I open the door and hurl myself out onto the wet ground. I fall to my knees and make the retching sound.

"*Oh putain,*" she mutters from the driver's seat.

I continue the retching. It hurts like hell, but I don't care. I keep it up until I hear her getting out of the car and opening the back door on the driver's side to soothe the baby.

"*Adelaide, mon cœur, shhhhh, ça va aller mon cœur.*"

This is it.

I crawl into the field as quickly as I can, and as soon as I'm far enough away from the car, I stumble to my feet and try my best to run.

It's a pathetic attempt but my adrenaline is flowing and pushing me as far as this broken body will allow.

Until I hear a cry behind me. And feel a smack to my right shoulder.

"*Salope!*" Coralie cries.

I'm on my knees after that first hit, this time actually thinking I may really vomit. It wasn't her hand she hit me with. It was something hard. Something metal.

No.

I swivel around and defend myself from her punches. She's on top of me, thrashing, hitting, screaming, and in the madness, I realize this is an all too familiar scene.

The ketamine had made me forget, but it's all coming back to me now.

It was Coralie who attacked me that night at my apartment. Just as I was trying to leave for the airport.

And now, we're at it again.

Except this time we are in a field in the middle of nowhere, with no lights in sight, fighting beneath sheets of relentless cold rain.

And Coralie has a gun in her hands.

My cries are useless. She's totally lost it. She wants me dead.

I use any and all strength I have left to get her off of me. Finally, with the rain on my side, she slips off and I take this moment to rise up and tackle her. We are on our sides now, and I'm doing everything in my limited power to pry the gun out of her hands.

Just as I think I may be getting closer to loosening her death grip, a shot fires.

It takes a moment to register, but not long.

She's shot me in the thigh.

I resist the urge to howl into the blackness and instead I look at her. I look straight into her crazy eyes and even in the darkness, I find that they are just as shocked as I feel.

I reach over and grab the gun right out of her hands.

I push it straight into her stomach, and I don't think. I don't say a word.

I just shoot.

The shot rings through the night just as the rain finally stops its pouring.

Coralie grips her stomach and opens her mouth, but no sound comes out.

I hover over her with the gun, pinning her to the ground.

"It was you, that night at my apartment," I say to her through labored breaths. "You did this to me, and then asked Drew to come clean up your mess. Is that what happened?"

Coralie's mouth is still hanging open, but no words are coming out.

"Coralie!" I shriek. "Tell me what happened that night!"

"Drew would never hurt you," she mumbles. "Only me. He only hurts me."

What in the hell is she talking about?

I shove the gun harder into her wound, making her gasp. "Tell me the truth," I growl.

Through the moonlight peeking down at us from behind the clouds, I see blood trickling from the corner of her mouth.

"I'm sorry, Sara," she says. "I'm so sorry."

Sara?

"You know who I am?" I say.

She rolls onto her back and mumbles toward the sky, "*Marvel. Sara. Kate and Sara. The sisters. Kate, she's so beautiful. Still so beautiful.*"

"You knew Kate?" I ask, gripping her T-shirt.

Her eyes roll in my direction. The moonlight catches her haunting glare and I feel as though I'm looking into the eyes of a ghost.

She's fading. She's nearly gone.

"Did you know Kate?" I ask, frantic to get an answer out of her before she takes her last breath.

More blood trickles from her mouth before she blinks at me. "I *know* Kate."

"What do you...what are you saying? You know her? Is she still alive? Is Kate still alive?"

"*The diamond girl. She's...his...diamond girl.*"

I get nothing more from the lips of Coralie. No more words. No more breath. *Only blood.*

One last sputtering of crimson before her eyes roll to the sky and rest on the moon shining overhead.

It's over. She's gone.

And in the distance, there is the crying of a baby.

Her baby. Drew's baby.

A baby who will no longer have a mother.

But I am alive, asking the stars if my sister still is, too.

70

OFFICER JEAN-MARC DEVEREAUX

SAMEDI 20 MAI 2017
36 QUAI DES ORFÈVRES ~ PARIS, FRANCE

IT HAD BEEN over an hour since Breton had left the station to go find Coralie and Adelaide, and Devereaux was doing his best to concentrate on the task at hand: grill the shit out of Andrew Grayson to get a confession.

While he'd gotten Grayson to at least admit to being the married man in Eve's book and even to being at her apartment the night of her disappearance, he *still* couldn't get a full confession out of the bastard.

By now, the blood on Grayson's upper lip and just beneath his nose was dry and the circles beneath his eyes had taken on a new shade of desperation. The more Devereaux pushed and prodded, the more exasperated Grayson became. Devereaux was tempted to re-open the scars that were already beginning to form on Grayson's face in an attempt to get what he wanted, but at this point, he didn't think more violence would be the answer with this guy.

This was the point in the questioning when Devereaux would've sent Breton in. A new officer, a new angle—sometimes that's all that was needed to get a beaten-down, exhausted suspect to give in and tell the fucking truth.

But Breton was still gone, and Devereaux and Breton had agreed they wouldn't bring any of the other officers on the team in on this initial round of questioning with Grayson because of the possibility that Grayson may still open up about Coralie and her involvement.

So, Devereaux had no choice but to keep interrogating Grayson.

And since nothing else had worked up until this point, it was time to go for the jugular.

"Monsieur Grayson, are you aware that your wife had flown to Paris to spy on you as soon as Eve's book released in the US?"

Grayson nodded. "I'm aware."

"Are you also aware that your wife has been having an affair as well?"

Grayson bit the inside of his cheek and avoided Devereaux's penetrating gaze.

"Monsieur Gray—"

"Yes, I'm fucking aware."

"When did you first find out that your wife has been having an affair with Monsieur Dimitri Dumas, your boss at *Le Crédit Parisien*?"

"What in the hell does this have to do with anything?"

"Answer the question, Monsieur Grayson."

"I just found out today, at the hospital."

"I see. And before Eve's book released, was your wife aware that you were having an affair...or more specifically, that you were paying for prostitutes?"

"We had an agreement," Grayson said.

"What kind of agreement?"

"That I could see other women while I was away from home, but that I would never leave the marriage."

"Why did Madame Grayson agree to this?"

"I still don't see how this has anything to do with Eve's disappearance."

"That is why you run a bank, not a police force," Devereaux quipped. "Now please, answer the question."

"My wife was the one who'd suggested it. She wasn't feeling especially...*sexual*...after we'd had some difficulty having a baby."

Devereaux didn't want to dive too deep into the baby topic with Grayson because anything on that front could lead to his confession that Grayson had a baby with another woman in Paris—Coralie. He needed to take a different angle.

"And did this arrangement extend to your wife as well—what I mean is, was she permitted to see other men while you were away?"

"No, that wasn't the initial agreement."

"So you could go have your fun—and by the chapters in Eve's memoir, it appears you certainly did—but your wife wasn't allowed to do the same?"

"No, it wasn't that she wasn't *allowed*...it was just that we never discussed *her* doing it too. She was the one who never wanted to have sex, so I thought she just didn't want to have sex. Period. I never thought that she just didn't want to..."

"Have sex with you," Devereaux finished for his sad suspect.

Grayson nodded, once again biting the inside of his cheek. This was a sore spot. A good one. Devereaux would have to dig deeper.

"Did your wife give you permission to pay for sex? Or to fall in love with another woman?"

"Of course not."

"And yet, here we are."

Grayson lifted his tired face. "Yes, here we are. And no matter how you try to come at this, I'm going to give you the *same fucking answer*: I didn't hurt Eve. I didn't take Eve. I didn't kill Eve. I fucking loved her, okay! I love her! I would never have hurt her like that."

"What about the scene in Eve's memoir where you saw her talking with a male friend at La Closerie des Lilas and then raped her in the back of the car? You don't think that hurt her?"

"I didn't rape her," Grayson snapped. "I never raped her."

"You're saying she was willing? Because the way she wrote that scene did not at all sound like she consented."

"She didn't...I mean our sex was like that sometimes. Rough. She liked it that way. She liked when I dominated her."

"She liked it when you raped her?"

"I didn't fucking rape her!"

"Just like you didn't fucking hurt her or take her or kill her, right Monsieur Grayson?"

Monsieur Fucking Grayson didn't have time to answer because of the harsh knock on the door.

"*Putain*," Devereaux muttered under his breath. He stood up and headed for the door.

Tessier and Leroux stood on the other side, grave expressions on their faces.

Devereaux closed the door behind him. "What is it?"

His colleagues shared an uneasy glance before Tessier squeezed Devereaux's shoulder. "You should sit down."

71

EVE

The When: Saturday May 20th, 2017
The Where: A field outside of Paris

Cold rain. Wet clothes sticking to my skin. Pain bursting through my thigh. Radiating through my entire body.

I'm alive. I'm still alive.

My eyelids pop open with this realization. I gasp for breath, but with the massive raindrops pouring into my mouth and the extreme tightness in my chest, I can hardly find air. I roll to my side, painfully so, but I manage. And when I do, *there she is.*

Coralie.

The moonlight is still shining down on her limp body, lighting up the hole in her stomach, the blood seeping out.

I put that hole there.

But as I stare at the blood pooling around the wound that I inflicted, I notice something.

Her stomach is still moving.

Up, up, up, ever so slightly. And then, back down.

Am I imagining this?

I lift my gaze to her lips and place as much of my concentration on them as I can.

It takes a few moments, but then, there it is.

There is breath.

Coralie is breathing.

She's passed out and she's bleeding, but she is most definitely breathing.

And so am I.

The sound of the baby screaming pierces the darkness. I have to get to the baby. To the car. To Coralie's phone.

I twist my neck toward the car and find that we didn't come too terribly far into the field. But still, in my state, the trek back could take a while.

Go. Sara. Go.

It's Kate's voice, in my head.

Go, Sara, go!

I try my best at crawling even though my left thigh is dragging behind me like a dead tree trunk. The ground is muddy and slippery and the rain will not stop its relentless pouring.

Go, Sara. GO.

Kate's voice spurs me forward. Inch by inch. Breath by excruciating breath.

I want to quit. I want to close my eyes and pass back out so I don't have to feel this pain. This fear.

What if I don't make it?

What if we die here?

What will happen to the baby?

No.

I keep going. Grasping at pieces of muddy earth to pull me forward.

Forward. Forward. Forward.

Keeping going, Sara.

Until finally, I reach the car.

The passenger's side door is still open. The baby is still screaming.

I grip onto the bottom of the car, hoist myself up with my arms, putting all my weight into my right leg, and I gain just enough leverage to see inside the car, where Coralie tossed the phone at my feet earlier.

A guttural cry escapes my lips as I pull myself up even farther to reach the phone. Once I have it in my hands, I rest the top of my body on the floor of the passenger's side and push the button to light up the phone screen. There are a series of text messages that have come in. Several missed calls too. All from the same person.

Chéri.

Even though my eyelashes are dripping with rain and my vision is blurry, I can make out that they're all in French. My translation skills kick in automatically.

Where are you?

Coralie?? Where are you going?

Coralie! Answer me!

And I remember that they are, of course, all from *Drew*. The man who was holding me captive.

The baby is crying so hard now, it sounds as if she may get sick. My body is crashing, giving out. I need to figure out how to get into this phone to call for help.

I'm pressing buttons and using every piece of energy still within me to keep the top half of my body in the car and out of the rain, but the pain in my leg is so strong, so powerful, so unending, that I feel as if I may pass out. Breath is escaping me. And I can't get into her fucking phone.

My hands are shaking so badly that soon the phone tumbles right out of my fingers, as I feared it would. Blood is pounding through my ears. Blackness is coming. Closing in.

My body is sinking, falling out of the car.

But it doesn't land on the cold wet ground, as I'd anticipated.

Instead a pair of strong hands catches me, scoops me up.

I am in someone's arms. A man's arms.

A silhouette is above me. The moonlight is shining down on the back of his head.

I can't see his face. His eyes.

Who are you? I want to ask.

But no words will come out.

All I hear before I pass out in this stranger's arms are the words:

"Ça va aller. Ça va aller."

It's going to be okay. It's all going to be okay.

72

OFFICER JEAN-MARC DEVEREAUX

DIMANCHE 21 MAI 2017
SCÈNE DE CRIME

OFFICER JEAN-MARC DEVEREAUX had never before dreaded his arrival on a crime scene as much as he did at this moment.

He rode in the passenger's seat of Tessier's car, both of them dead silent. The rain was still pouring down. Streams of headlights zipped past them on the *autoroute*, but Jean-Marc saw none of it.

He could only see red. Blood. Mia's blood.

And now his little—*No*.

It was all he could do not to punch through the dash of Tessier's car and yell at the sky or God or whoever the hell might be listening.

Although, after the news his colleagues had just delivered to him, he was quite certain that no one was listening.

And so he stayed silent for the entire drive.

The red and blue flashing lights up ahead were his sign that they'd arrived.

It was the last place he ever wanted to be.

Tessier parked the car behind the other police and emergency vehicles, and the two men stepped out into the darkness. Tessier placed a hand on Devereaux's shoulder as they walked along the wet gravel, but Devereaux barely felt it.

Devereaux didn't feel the cold rain pouring down on his skin, either. He didn't hear the ground crunching beneath his feet. He didn't hear the voices of the other officers he knew so well or the emergency workers who'd arrived on the scene.

Instead, he walked. A numb corpse making his way through the muddy field until he reached his partner, his colleague, his best friend, his boss, Julien Breton.

Julien was on his knees, kneeling over her. The red and blue flashing lights lit up his face, which was streaked with tears and rain and sorrow.

Julien lifted his eyes to Jean-Marc. He didn't need to say anything. Jean-Marc already knew. But he said it anyway.

"I'm sorry," Julien mouthed. "I'm so sorry."

Jean-Marc couldn't respond.

Julien stood and left Jean-Marc alone with the body of his baby sister.

Lifeless, caked in blood and mud and rain. He wanted to wrap her in a blanket and tell her everything would be okay.

Instead he fell to his knees beside her, cradled her beautiful face in his hands and told her that he, too, was sorry. Because he was.

He was sorry that she had suffered so much after the loss of their mother when they were only kids.

He was sorry that she had suffered again, greatly, at the loss of their father eleven years ago.

He was sorry that he could never fix her, no matter how hard he'd tried. He was sorry that she'd never been truly happy. That she'd turned to drugs and alcohol and sex and toxic men to feel better.

He was sorry that he'd been so busy with work that he hadn't done more.

He was sorry that her sweet baby girl would grow up without her mother.

Because for as messed up as his sister had been, Jean-Marc knew that Coralie had loved that baby. In fact, the only times he'd seen Coralie's eyes light up this entire past year was when she would hold Adelaide.

But now, the light was gone.

A baby's cry rang through the darkness.

Perhaps little Adelaide sensed that she'd lost her mother. Perhaps she knew she'd lost her father, too. For Andrew Grayson would certainly be locked up once they got a statement from Eve confirming that he was the one who'd kidnapped her.

After Coralie had attacked her, of course.

The truth about his little sister's madness would certainly come out.

But what did it matter now that she was gone?

Jean-Marc pressed his body against his little sister's. She was cold. So cold. "I'm sorry, Coralie, I'm so sorry. I'm so sorry. I'm so sorry."

No matter how many times he whispered his apologies into her hair, he knew it wouldn't fix her. He knew it wouldn't change the past.

And he knew it would never, ever bring her back.

73

SOPHIA

Sunday the 21st of May, 2017
L'Hôpital Hôtel-Dieu ~ Paris

Eve has been found.

Alive.

It's on the news in my hospital room.

My heartrate speeds up as I glue my eyes to the television screen.

The reporter is standing in a field somewhere outside of Paris. There are police milling around behind him. He continues his report.

Eve was barely conscious when an officer of the Brigade Criminelle found her late last night, lying in a field in the rain, not far from Paris. She'd been shot in the thigh. She'd suffered many other serious wounds as well—broken bones and lacerations.

She was rushed to L'Hôpital Hôtel-Dieu for care late last night.

Bloody hell. She's in the same hospital as me.

I don't have too long to contemplate the fact that Eve

and I are sharing the same roof because the reporter goes on to say that Eve was not alone in the field last night.

A body was found.

The body of a young woman called *Coralie Devereaux*.

A photo of Coralie flashes across the screen. Wild eyes. Short blond hair. High cheekbones.

She's a vixen.

And she's dead.

Shot in the stomach and the chest.

Shot by Eve, in what is speculated to be an act of self-defense.

Goosebumps prickle my arms as Coralie's face disappears from the screen and the reporter continues. A baby girl was also found—Coralie's baby girl. The baby is alive and unharmed. She was crying in her car seat in Coralie's nearby parked car when the officer arrived on the scene.

Drew's baby.

Drew's baby doesn't have a mother.

I don't know why, but this news—all of it—brings a stream of tears rolling down my face.

Eve is alive, breathing somewhere in this very hospital.

Coralie, the mother of my husband's baby, is dead.

Eve killed her.

And the baby, Adelaide, what will happen to her?

I can still see her chubby little legs kicking in the stroller. The way she calmed down when Drew sang to her.

At least she still has her dad.

Or does she?

As far as I know, Drew is still in a 48-hour hold at 36 Quai des Orfèvres, the home of the Brigade Criminelle. Dimitri, my lover, has been gone, tending to the mess this is creating for the bank. A media storm of epic proportions.

When Drew's face flashes across the TV screen, and

the reporter begins to speculate on the connections between the dead girl, the author, and the married American businessman, I simply cannot listen to another word.

I flick the TV off. I dry my tears.

And I gaze out the window at the steely Parisian skies, wondering if I'll ever see the sun again.

74

EVE

The When: Sunday May 21st, 2017
The Where: A Hospital Room

The minute my eyes open, I just know.

Coralie has died.

Did I kill her?

The jarring memory of gunshots popping through the darkness confirms my worst fear.

It takes me a moment to comprehend the rest.

I'm not in that horrible room by myself anymore. I am no longer blindfolded. Tied down. An animal in a cage. There are no more shots to the neck of ketamine, making me forget everything. Taking away the pain of my broken bones and the slices to my skin. For a time period anyway, until it would wear off and he would come back and give me more.

No, the drugs I'm receiving now are coming through tubes and machines, going straight into my veins through the hospital IVs.

I am no longer being held hostage.

I am safe.
I am alive.
And Drew cannot hurt me anymore.

75

SOPHIA

Sunday the 21st of May, 2017
L'Hôpital Hôtel-Dieu ~ Paris

How strange that it has all come to this.

I am standing at the bedside of my husband's prostitute. My husband's lover. My former student. A now famous author.

Sara Marvel.

Eve Winters.

Watching her sleep.

I'm dragging an IV by my side. I'm not supposed to be on this floor. But I'm heading into surgery later tonight. And who knows if I'll come out alive.

I had to see her before I go under. I had to look into those wounded, tragic eyes of hers once more.

If only she would open them.

I take a step closer, watching her chest rise and fall. Listening to the machines beeping at her bedside. Marveling at where all of our loves and lies have landed us.

In the same hospital in Paris.

A catastrophic masterpiece for sure.

I wonder which one of us will live to write about it.

Eve, surely. For my fate seems to be sealed. Or at least, on a very limited timeline.

I rest a hand on her arm, on one of the only spots that isn't covered with a bandage. She is a mess of bruises, bandages, casts, and tubes.

But she's still here.

My gaze drifts down to her abdomen. I watch it rise and fall ever so slightly with each breath in. Each breath out. And I wonder if she was ever actually pregnant. If the test at the end of her book was positive or negative. Or if that part was even true at all.

"I'm not."

The sound of Eve's raspy whisper startles me so much that I rip my hand from her arm and jump backward.

"I'm not pregnant," she says, louder this time.

And we meet eyes. She already knew what I was thinking.

"Were you?" I ask. "Ever?"

"If I was, it's gone," she says.

Eve's eyes are daring and harsh as she stares me down. They're not scared or apologetic like I imagined they might be.

"Do you still love him?" I ask. "My husband."

"I hate him," she says. "But I will always love him."

"And you knew the whole time? That he was—"

"Your husband?" she says, cutting me off.

I nod.

"After our first night together, yes, I found out."

"And you kept going," I say. "You kept seeing him."

"I fell in love," Eve says.

I swallow hard, taking this in.

"Do *you* still love him?" Eve asks me.

"I hate him," I say. "But I will always love him."

And there it is. *The truth.*

We both hate and love the same man. We always will. Fate has, for better or for worse, brought this professor and her student together under the most unlikely and unfortunate of circumstances.

"So what do we do now?" I ask Eve.

"We live our lives," she says. Then her eyes dart to the IV I'm hanging onto. To the tubes stuck in my arms. To the dark circles inhabiting the space beneath my eyes. "Or what's left of them," she adds.

With that, she tears her gaze from me and looks out the window. Tears fill her lashes, and finally spill down her face. "I wish Coralie had just killed me," she says.

I know how she feels. I've wished for death so many times.

Now that I'm actually facing it, though, now that I'm truly unsure if I'll wake up tomorrow morning, I don't know if I wish it were so.

I step forward, place my hand over hers.

"You finally took my advice," I say. "You finally told the truth in your writing."

She looks back to me, the sorrow in her gaze devastating.

"What was it all for?" she asks.

I won't fluff her up by telling her she's going to be a Number One New York Times Bestselling Author. Or by telling her that her writing was powerful and haunting and all the things I've always wished my writing would be. Or that it nearly killed me to read her words.

But there is one thing I must say, if it is the last thing I ever get to say to her.

"It was to show that you are just as much the darkness as you are the light. Your darkness is vicious, but you're one of the only people I've ever known who's had the courage to bring that darkness out into the light and put it on display. And now, you have to find a way to live with it. You have to find a way to move forward. Do you understand?"

She nods. Tears continue their sad trajectory down her pale cheeks.

I imagine she needs a mother's hug after everything she's been through.

But I am no mother. And I will not hug her.

All I can do now, if I don't want to harm her, is walk away.

So, that is what I do. I leave Eve and all her sorrows and tragedies, scars and tears, and I walk away.

76

EVE

The When: Sunday May 21st, 2017
The Where: L'Hôpital Hôtel-Dieu

I'm beginning to wish I was strong enough to leave this damn hospital. Sophia Grayson has no more than stepped out of my hospital room when a police officer walks in. He's accompanied by a nurse who walks up to my bed and asks if I feel up to answering some of his questions.

No.

That is what I want to say. I don't want to talk to this police officer; I want to talk to one person who is on my side, who is my friend, who knows me, who cares about me.

But then I realize that I have no one like that in my life.

I've alienated myself completely. There is no one left to protect me.

And no one left to blame but me.

I nod at the nurse, letting her know that I'll answer this officer's questions.

What choice do I have at this point?

"Bonjour Mademoiselle Winters, I'm Officer Breton.

I'm working on your case and need to ask you a few questions if that's okay with you."

I give him the slightest nod of my chin; I don't feel like talking.

He pulls a notepad and pen out of his breast pocket and walks up to my bedside. He's not wearing the police uniform I would be expecting but rather a crisp black button-down shirt and a pair of dark jeans. And with the gray circles beneath his bloodshot eyes, he looks about as exhausted as I feel.

"First, I'd like to say on behalf of my entire team at La Brigade Criminelle, that we are so happy you're alive and safe. I know it's been quite an ordeal for you, so we'll just cover a few basic questions today about what happened, and we'll do a more detailed round of questions when you're feeling a little better."

I nod again, holding my silence.

"When was the first time you met Coralie Devereaux?"

Clearing my throat, I summon up what little energy is inside of me to answer questions that I have no desire to answer. "The night she came to my apartment and attacked me. The night before my book release."

"So this was on Monday, the 15th of May?"

"Yes."

"Was it Ms. Devereaux who inflicted these wounds upon you? The broken bones, the cuts?"

"I believe so."

"You're not sure?"

"I've been heavily drugged for the past week. So I don't remember much at all about that night. I have a very vague memory of her attacking me. But I can't give any more detail than that."

He nods, jotting down notes in his notepad.

"Did you also see Andrew Grayson that night?"

"Yes, I believe so."

"Before or after Coralie came to your apartment and attacked you?"

"I...I'm not sure."

"Think, Ms. Winters. Did Andrew Grayson come to your apartment? Did he hurt you, too? Did he take you that night?"

"I...I think it was him. Coralie told me it was Drew who had me all along. And I do know that I saw him that night. But I honestly can't remember what happened."

"I see. We'll come back to this once you're feeling a little better. Your memory may start to come back over time."

"I hope it doesn't," I say.

"I understand," he says. "We do have Monsieur Grayson in a 48-hour hold at the moment. If he did this to you, you have my word that we will put him behind bars for a very, very long time."

I nod, trying my best to hold back the tears that so want to fall.

Could it really have been Drew?

I don't want to believe it.

"Can you tell me what happened last night?" the officer asks.

"Coralie came to the place where I was being held hostage, and she untied me from the bed. She said she was going to save me, take me to the hospital. She said Drew would be back soon and that he was going to kill us both. But she was lying—about saving me at least. She was taking me outside the city to kill me."

"Do you know where you were being held? Did you see anything there when she untied you?"

"No. It was nighttime. I was injured and dizzy. I didn't see anything."

"Was it Coralie who shot you in the leg?"

"Yes."

"Do you remember shooting Coralie last night?" he asks.

"Yes, I shot her in self-defense. She was trying to kill me."

"Can you confirm that you shot her twice, once in the stomach and another time in the chest?"

"I...I only remember the one shot. To the stomach."

"Perhaps the shock, your memory loss, all of it, is making you forget?" he says, reaching up to scratch his scruffy beard.

I pause, combing my gaze up and down his rather informal attire.

"Yes, that must be it," I concede.

And then I do something that this kind officer is certainly not expecting in his routine line of questioning—I reach out and grab his right wrist.

"Was it you last night?" I ask. "Who found me?"

He nods, sadness lining his eyes. It isn't the look of a hero.

"Thank you," I say, squeezing his wrist. "Thank you for saving me."

He nods. "I was just doing my job, Mademoiselle."

I let go of his wrist and ask, "Can we continue this another day? I'm not feeling well."

"Of course," he says, tucking his pen back into his front pocket. "I'll leave my card on the table right here. If you remember anything, call me anytime, day or night."

"Thank you," I say again.

As Officer Breton shows himself out of my hospital room, I keep my mouth shut on the things I *do* remember:

38126*

Coralie's words: *The police can't help us, Eve, because Drew is working with them. They've been protecting him all along.*

And the cherry on top of Coralie's blood-filled cake:

I know Kate.

The diamond girl.

77

EVE

The When: Tuesday June 6th, 2017
The Where: Home

My first steps back into my apartment are not easy steps to take, but I am fully aware at how lucky I am to be taking them. How lucky I am to be walking at all.

How lucky I am to be alive.

One of the two officers they have sent to escort me back to my apartment is Officer Jean-Marc Devereaux. I now know him to be one of the lead officers in my case, and more importantly, the older brother of the woman I shot—Coralie Devereaux.

Coincidentally, or perhaps not at all, his father was the lead Brigade Criminelle officer on the case of my missing sister, Kate. He never found her, obviously.

And so, I find it curious that *this* is the officer they have sent to take me home, and even more curious that this man is back on the job so soon after his sister died, but nothing surprises me at this point in my ordeal.

I'm sure Officer Devereaux wants to get a good look at

the woman he was trying to find—the woman who he believes killed his sister.

Maybe he wants to kill me, too. But the presence of the younger officer he has with him—a wide-eyed polite one named Officer Leroux—will surely prevent it from happening today. At least I think so.

Nothing is truly sure at this point, though. *This I know.*

I lean on the crutch the hospital gave me as I limp through my doorway and over my hardwood floors.

They are shiny—too shiny. The officers told me they arranged to have a professional cleaning done. They've done their best to remove the stains, they said.

My blood.

But I'll always be stained. That is the one thing that *is* sure, I realize.

The two officers hover in the doorway as I place my hospital bag filled with medication and doctor's instructions on one of the side tables next to the couch. Then I begin my hobble through my living room, and I take it all in. The magenta pillows, the crystal chandeliers, the gray couch, the white chairs.

The dull brown stains on those chairs, couches, and pillows.

I'll arrange to have the furniture removed today.

Or perhaps, I'll keep it—stains and all. A badge of honor. A tattoo.

A reminder of how much pain I've endured. And how much pain I've caused.

As if I could ever forget.

The charming tree-lined Place Dauphine still sits unharmed, unstained, just beyond my windows.

At least something in Paris hasn't changed.

Glancing back at the officers, I give them a curt nod.

They've taken a few steps inside, moved farther into my space, and I want them to go. "I think I'll be okay from here," I tell them.

Officer Devereaux lifts a brow in my direction. The circles beneath his eyes are epic; I wonder if he's been taking care of Coralie's baby now that she's dead. And now that the baby's father, Drew, has officially been arrested for my kidnapping.

"You're sure?" Officer Devereaux asks me.

"Yes. I'd like to be alone."

"Of course," he says. "You have our number if you need anything."

I nod at them and watch as the younger one, Officer Leroux turns and walks out.

But Devereaux doesn't budge.

"I said I'll be fine," I say, hobbling toward him. *He needs to go.*

"I have no doubt, Mademoiselle Marvel."

His use of my former last name sends a chill down my spine.

"That's not my name anymore," I say firmly.

"I just have one question for you, if you don't mind," he says.

"I do mind, actually. After everything I've been through. After everything your sister did to me, *I do fucking mind.*"

He is silent for a few moments, until finally, his big question:

"Did you kill her that night?"

I am about to say *yes, you saw the reports, I shot her twice—once in the stomach and once in the chest. Yes, I killed your miserable sister.*

But then he takes another step forward, grabs my upper

arm, and looks me hard in the eye. "Did you kill my sister that night, Sara? Tell me the truth."

I don't trust the police right now. Not one bit.

But something about his dark, wounded gaze lets me know that this one might be different. He might not be twisted and sick and full of lies. He may actually just want to know the truth about how his sister died that night.

And so I tell him the truth—or at least what I know of it.

"Your sister was trying to kill me. She shot me in the thigh. I managed to get the gun from her after that, and I shot her in the stomach. That was it. Once. In the stomach. And before I crawled back to her car to try to call for help, she was still breathing."

His pupils widen. "You're sure."

"Yes. I am one hundred percent sure."

His hand lingers on my arm, and our gazes linger in each other's.

Can I trust him?

Can he trust me?

Neither of us is sure, that much is clear. But I've told the man what I know.

"I'm sorry for what she did to you," he says. There is pain swimming in his dark eyes. Pain I can hardly stand to look at. "My sister was unstable for a long time. None of this was your fault."

"Thank you," I say, knowing, though, that so much of this *was* my fault. I became a prostitute to see if I could land myself in the same circles that my sister Kate had landed in on that fateful night when she disappeared twelve years ago. I wanted to find out the truth about what had happened to her. If she'd been killed, I wanted to know. But more importantly, I wanted to know who had done it.

That, and I needed money. Desperately.

Prostitution solved both of those problems.

Then it was me who fell in love with one of my clients—a client who was married to my former professor.

And then, after staying hidden from the world for so long, I wrote a book about it all.

A book of truth masked in lies.

Truth and lies that I will never again be able to hide from.

All the better, I think to myself—*all of that hiding was exhausting.*

Officer Devereaux drops his hand from my arm and nods at me. "You have my card. If you need anything."

"Thank you," I say again.

But just as he turns to leave, his arm brushes over the bag I'd brought home from the hospital and its entire contents spill to the floor.

Given my current physical limitations, Officer Devereaux gets to the spill faster than I can, and he begins scooping up all of the paperwork and medications from the floor, placing them back into the bag.

When he's finished, he hands me the bag. "Sorry about that."

"It's no problem," I say. It's no problem unless he's a sneakier detective than I think he is.

"Are you sure you're okay here alone?" he asks. "We can send someone to help, just for the first few days at least."

I shake my head firmly. "I'll be fine. I've been through worse."

He nods. He knows how true that statement is.

As he turns to leave, I know I should say something along the lines of: *I'm sorry for the loss of your sister. I'm sorry I shot her.*

But I don't. Because I don't want to lie anymore.

Just like Sophia said to me on that lovely day when she visited me in the hospital—I am both the light and the darkness, and I must find a way to move forward with all of it.

And so, my version of moving forward is no more lying. No more pretending to be something I'm not.

I say nothing more to Officer Devereaux, and I lock the door behind him as he leaves.

A breath of relief once he's gone. I'm alone.

And there is work to be done.

With the help of my crutch, I hobble across the room and take my inconspicuous silver and white clock off the wall. I check it over to be sure it hasn't been tampered with or damaged.

Despite the hurricane that swept through this apartment, my clock appears to be intact.

Next I make my way to the kitchen and open the drawer with the tools. Or rather, *the* tool: a single screwdriver.

Finally, I head back to my bedroom closet where I gingerly position myself on the ground and begin removing the shoes from the shoe rack I have bolted to the wall.

Once I've removed all of the shoes, it's time for the screwdriver.

Four screws loosened and removed, and the rack is now off the wall.

Then, a quick push to open the tiny compartment I'd built just after I moved into this apartment. Reaching inside, I smile when I feel the smooth iPhone, right where I left it, and a spare charger.

Looks like *la Brigade Criminelle* could've been a little more thorough in their search through my home.

Thankfully they weren't.

78

OFFICER JEAN-MARC DEVEREAUX

MARDI 6 JUIN 2017
PLACE DAUPHINE ~ PARIS, FRANCE

EVE WINTERS WAS MUCH COLDER in real life than the woman he'd been imagining this past week. The problem was that he'd imagined Eve to be something like Mia, who had been warm and fiery, sexy and sweet.

Even with her crutch and all her bandages, Eve Winters was definitely sexy. But warm and sweet—not so much.

Then again, what had he expected? His own sister had nearly killed Eve—*twice*—and his father had failed to find her younger sister Kate all those years ago, which had ultimately played a massive role in the downward and catastrophic spiral of her entire family. Eve had been through more in her short twenty-nine years on this Earth than most people lived in a lifetime—hell in two or three goddamn lifetimes. Of course the girl was cold.

He hoped, over time, that she would warm up.

But warming her up wasn't his main concern right now. After the death of his little sister and the arrest of Andrew

Grayson, Devereaux had become a full-time father to his sweet niece Adelaide, all while juggling his work at La Crim'.

He'd taken two full weeks off of work after he'd kneeled over his sister's lifeless body in the field that night, and he'd spent nearly all of that time with the baby.

Once again, his sweet little angel had brought him back to life. Now he was back to work on a more part-time basis, though, as Adelaide had to be—and would always be—his number one priority.

But today, while Adelaide was in the care of a trusted nanny that he'd recently hired (following a thorough background check, of course), he had a few important errands to run.

After Eve had closed the door behind him, Devereaux pulled his phone out of his pocket and made a quick note as he made his way down the stairs. He saved the note in his phone, not sure when or how this information would prove to be useful, but something in his gut told him that it would be soon.

Leroux was waiting for him at the bottom of the stairs. "Everything go okay after I left?" he asked.

Devereaux nodded at his younger colleague. "As okay as it could go."

The two men walked back to the office together, and just as they arrived at 36 Quai des Orfèvres, Devereaux nodded at Leroux to go ahead. "I have to get a few things done. I'll see you back here later on."

Leroux didn't ask any questions—the young officer knew better.

Devereaux hopped in his car and stared at the box resting on the passenger's seat.

It was the unopened box of Coralie's belongings that

one of the technicians had handed him earlier this morning. Some odds and ends left over from her car, after they'd combed it for evidence, of course.

He wasn't sure when he'd have the heart to go through it. Maybe later today. Perhaps tomorrow.

Perhaps not at all.

He raced home to his apartment and found that the nanny had taken Adelaide out for a walk, just as he'd asked her to do. Perfect.

Devereaux pulled up the secret email account he'd created just for this purpose and clicked on the one incoming email he'd received only two hours ago.

It had cost him a pretty penny to convince the video editor who Breton had hired to edit Coralie out of the street camera footage to email him the original video from the night of Monday, May 15th, and to agree to keep his mouth shut about the whole thing.

But Devereaux was convinced it would be worth it.

He would either discover that Breton had told the truth and that they'd imprisoned the right man—Andrew Grayson.

Or he would discover that Andrew Grayson hadn't been their man after all.

Devereaux's finger hovered over the mouse.

A deep breath filled his lungs before he pressed it:

Play.

79

EVE

The When: Tuesday June 6th, 2017
The Where: Home

With both my secret iPhone and its charger in my hand, I find my way back to my feet and use my crutch to make it over to a plug on my bedroom wall.

Once the phone is plugged in, I power it on.

There is only one app I care about on this phone: the app that connects to the hidden camera in my silver and white clock.

I'd first bought the secret clock camera right after I'd arrived in Paris and begun my prostitution escapades. I had other clients before Drew who weren't nearly as wealthy as he was and who were much sketchier. After what had happened with Kate when we were young, I knew that mingling in those types of crowds could go south very quickly, so I'd set up the camera and the secret phone just for that reason. In case something ever happened to me in my apartment, it would all be recorded.

Of course I'd hoped that nothing *would* ever happen, but it did.

And now it's time to see the truth.

The *real* truth, the one that isn't mixed up in all the lies I've told or in all the lies everyone else has told.

I open up the hidden camera app and scroll back to the night of Monday, May 15th.

The night I was taken.

And finally, in the quiet of my bedroom, where I sit alone and injured but still so very alive, I press the button I have been dreaming of pushing for the last two excruciating weeks in the hospital:

Play.

80

EVE

The When: The Night of Monday May 15th, 2017
The Where: Place Dauphine

My bags are packed, and in twenty minutes I'll be leaving for Charles de Gaulle Airport. I haven't been back to New York since I moved out of my Greenwich Village apartment a year and a half ago. It was the same apartment where I'd lived alone all through my twenties. I never lived there with a man named Lucas because "Lucas," as I've written him in my "memoir," doesn't truly exist. He's a composite of all the men I've slept with, loved, and then left because I haven't wanted to tell any of them the truth about who I really am.

I suppose I've stayed away from New York for an entire year and a half for that exact reason: to break the ties I had with everyone I knew there and start over in a new city, as a new woman.

But now, the world I have left behind and the new one I've created are going to merge...for better or for worse.

My memoir, *The Mistress of Paris*, releases tomorrow,

and my publisher is flying me to New York to kick off the release with a party at Le Midi, a French bistro near Union Square. All sorts of industry pros will be there, including my agent, Abbey Strumeyer, along with some of her other more notable clients, not the least of which is Sophia Grayson: my former professor and the wife of my married lover and top-paying client.

I don't believe that Sophia is aware that the book I have written is about her husband, and with the way I've written the story—specifically not revealing Drew's identity—I don't believe she will find out.

Still, sharing a cocktail with her over the release of my new book will be anything but comfortable after I have spent almost an entire year buried beneath the sheets with her husband.

My New York City week that follows is packed with interviews and book signings and all sorts of events that never in a million years would I have dreamed I would be doing at this point in my life.

I mean, I was a prostitute for god's sake. I had sex with men for money.

Lots of men. Not just Drew.

Before I met Drew, I had a *Madame*—a female pimp—who took most of my prostitution money, but who set me up with all of my clients. I had a boyfriend named Marcel, too. We did loads of drugs, me and Marcel. He took my money, too—money that was supposed to go to greedy Madame. Soon Madame sent one of her men to beat me up if I didn't produce the money that Marcel had taken for drugs.

I'd gone to the dark side, and it was all an absolute mess.

A mess that led me to Drew.

He was the first client I'd found on my own, without Madame's aid. The first client who paid me exorbitant amounts of money to spend the night with him, and I got to keep every penny.

And he was the first—and only—client with whom I fell in love.

It was a fucked-up, sick kind of love that inspired me to write a novel. A novel that I would later pitch as truth—*as a memoir*—and sell to a major New York publishing house for an insane book advance.

It was Drew's wife, after all, who originally told me I had to start telling the truth in my writing or I would never make it in this business.

She was right, of course.

So, I wrote the truth, and then I stretched it...quite a bit.

My sister "Willow" is based on who I would imagine Kate to be at this age, but really, she's me. It's all me. A one-woman show. Because my real sister, Kate, she's gone. She's been gone for years now. And despite my entry into the world of underground clubs and drugs and prostitution in Paris—all an attempt to find out what happened to my baby sister all those years ago—I never found out what happened to her.

Instead, I've become a published author.

Well, as of tomorrow.

As of tomorrow, I'll no longer be having sex for money. I'll no longer be visiting Drew at our exorbitant penthouse suite at the Ritz. I'll be doing book tours and signings and enjoying fancy lunches and dinners with my publisher and my agent and journalists who want to interview the high-class hooker from Paris who wrote a book about it.

They have no clue that this high-class hooker has a past that is even more fascinating and gruesome than the one I've written about in this book. I'm sure they'd all *love* to have a memoir from the famous living Marvel sister, but I'm just not going to give that to them.

I had to erase that past.

I am no longer Sara Marvel, and I can never be her again.

My father doesn't even know I'm back in Paris. I haven't seen him since the day he was convicted to life in prison for killing my mother.

Or rather, for helping *me* to kill my mother.

Yes, I most certainly had to erase that past.

And create a new future.

A future that is a mixture of truth and lies, sure, but a new future all the same.

I grab my phone to text my driver. It's time to go.

But just before I send the message, there is a loud knock on my door.

I cross the hardwood floors of my magnificent apartment overlooking Place Dauphine. It's the apartment I bought and furnished with the insane amounts of money Drew paid me to be his lover.

And when I glance through the peephole in the door, there he is.

A mess of bloodshot eyes and ruffled hair and a beard that needs to be shaven.

Mr. Andrew Grayson.

Drew. *My Drew.*

I open the door.

He's holding my book—the copy I left for him at his apartment this morning. I didn't think he'd get through it so quickly. Or that he'd find my apartment on Place Dauphine before I left for New York.

I thought I'd have some time to enjoy the release this

week before dealing with the mess he would become when he read what I'd written about him, about us.

Apparently, I was wrong.

He walks inside in silence, and finally, he calls me out on my lies.

"Eve?" he says. "Is that really your name?"

I resist the urge to break his gaze. "Yes," I say. "My name is Eve Winters."

"And Willow, your sister. The *real* Willow. Does she live here?" he asks, shaking his head as if it may explode into a million pieces.

"No, Willow's gone," I say. "She's been gone for a while now."

I think of Kate's face as I say this. The way she looked on that night so long ago when I left her in that sketchy underground club. She was straddling some older Frenchman. Hopped up on ecstasy and cocaine and who knows what else while she let him lick her neck and pull her bra strap down.

I wanted no part of whatever was about to go down in that rank club that night. It terrified me.

But Kate, she wasn't afraid; *she loved it.*

I'd begged her to come with me, but she'd responded by burying her drugged-up head into this man's neck and then peering at me through hazy eyes. Then she winked at me and grinned. It was a sly and devious grin—that was my Kate.

She wasn't going anywhere.

And she never came home.

Twelve years later, I stand here in my apartment gazing deep into Drew's eyes—the eyes I've loved so fiercely for so many months now—and I tell him again, "Willow's gone. And she's never coming back."

Willow, the girl *he* knew, is no longer. Instead, Eve stands before him.

"Goddammit, Willow. Goddammit." Tears are streaming down his face now; I don't think he even notices them.

"You need to go," I say.

He runs a hand through his hair and bites his bottom lip, the way he always does before he strips my clothes off and climbs on top of me.

I shake my head at him. He's an animal.

"Go," I tell him. *"It's over."*

"I fucking loved you. I fucking love you," he says, taking a step toward me.

No. It has to be over.

He extends his hand, waiting for me to take it. I stare down at his open palm for a long while, knowing I need to turn him away. Knowing that the very reason I wrote the memoir was to end this toxic affair.

"Take my fucking hand, Willow," he says through gritted teeth.

"I have to go the airport soon. I don't have much time."

"One last time," he says. "Then I'll be out of your life forever."

When I don't respond, he grabs my hips and shoves me toward the couch.

I know Drew well enough to know that even if I fight back, he won't stop. So I don't fight. I don't tell him to stop.

Because the truth is, I don't want him to.

81

SOPHIA

Tuesday the 6th of June, 2017
Eve's flat ~ Paris

Drinking tea in Eve's flat while I watch a video of my husband shagging her on this very couch is not at all how I imagined my afternoon to be today.

Then again, nothing in my life is how I imagined it to be at this point, so I don't even allow myself to feel the shock that so desperately wants to settle itself into my bones.

After all, it's just two people shagging, and one of those people simply happens to be my husband.

Eve doesn't suggest that we fast forward through this part of the video, and I don't either. After surviving an intense surgery to remove the cancer that had spread to my lungs, followed by my first brutal chemo treatment earlier this week—and all of that while my husband has been arrested for the kidnapping of Eve Winters, and imprisoned as he awaits his trial—I know I can handle a sodding sex scene starring my husband and his prostitute.

I feel a bit like a warrior these days, like I can handle anything.

So when I received Eve's email earlier today telling me that she had something *very important* to show me, something that would prove to be *integral* in Drew's case, I knew I had to come to her flat. I actually wanted to.

I don't want to hide from the truth any longer, and I think that Eve is at the same point in her life.

Plus, Eve and I both still love and hate the same man, and so we are forever connected, whether we like it or not.

In the video, Drew doesn't even have the patience to take Eve's knickers off. He's got her smashed down on this couch and is taking her, rather violently, from behind. The angle of the camera doesn't show me his face, but I imagine it to be red and full of rage and sadness. He'd just found out about her book. That she'd lied to him. That the girl he'd fallen in love with wasn't at all who she said she was.

And he needed to stake his claim over her, one last time.

When he finishes, he stands, puts his pants back on, and lets himself out of her flat without even saying goodbye to her.

A right wanker if I do say so myself.

In the video, Eve has tears running down her face as she tears off her soiled knickers and stuffs them into the couch. She throws on her jeans and shoes and heads for the door where her purse and suitcase are waiting.

Not more than a few seconds pass before a new crazy face appears in her flat:

Coralie Devereaux.

82

EVE

The When: The Night of Monday May 15th, 2017
The Where: Place Dauphine

Just before I leave my apartment, I rest my forehead on the open door, close my eyes, and count my inhales and exhales. My heart is still pounding from my encounter with Drew.

This was never going to be easy.

I knew that, of course.

I continue to count my breaths until I calm down enough to remember that I never messaged my driver to come pick me up. I spin around, searching the living room for my phone, when, all of a sudden, a pair of hands shoves me from behind.

"What the—?"

I regain my balance and turn around to find a voluptuous blond girl with a frantic, crazed look dancing in her eyes.

I recognize her immediately as Coralie, the girl Drew had a baby with last year. I've only just recently found out about Coralie and the baby—it was yet one more wretched twist in my already sordid love story with Drew.

Coralie doesn't greet me with a bonjour or a bonsoir, but instead charges straight for me and shoves me again. I trip over my suitcase and fall onto my back. She slams the door closed behind us and locks it.

What in the—?

I don't have time to ask questions, though, or to figure out what in the hell she is doing here, because she's on top of me pulling my hair, smacking my face, spitting at me, growling, screaming—an absolute rabid animal who has totally and completely lost her shit.

I fight back as best I can, but for her fairly petite size this girl is strong.

With each hit, she screams at me in French. "It's been you all this time! You're the woman he's been seeing. Fucking! Paying! Do you know that he has a baby? With me? Do you know that I am the mother of his fucking child? You dirty bitch! He's supposed to be with *us*. *We* are his family! And YOU. You stole him from me. From his daughter. He thinks he loves you but you're just a dirty *pute*. And you need to go! Disappear! Do you understand? Do you fucking understand me? You need to disappear from Drew's life!"

Even though my nose is bleeding now and my arms are exhausted from trying to hold her off of me, *yes, I fucking understand.*

In a jealous rage, she must've followed Drew to my apartment and was probably listening outside as we had sex.

And now that he's gone, she's come for her revenge.

"Get off of me!" I scream in French. "I don't even know you!"

But this only revs her up more.

Our rumble takes us to the other side of the living room

where a tall glass vase filled with a dozen violet roses sits atop my coffee table. Just as I'm eyeing it and trying to pry her off of me, she sees where my gaze has gone and lunges for the vase.

This gives me a tiny window to try to get to my feet, but she's quicker.

She raises her skinny little arms over her head, and down comes the glass vase I used to think was so beautiful.

Glass and thorns and water crash onto my head. Blood pours over my eyes as I collapse to the ground, my head taking a hit on the sharp corner of the coffee table on my way down. She is on top of me again, glass shards in her hands, pounding me and slashing my skin to shreds.

I try to fight back, but the blood loss, the pain, the shock is all too much.

She's going to kill me.

It's the same thought I had when my mom slashed me with a knife all those years ago. I was strong enough and young enough to fight back then. And I had my dad—my violent, drunk dad—who stepped in and handled it with me.

But now, I have no one to step in.

And nothing to protect me from the folly of a woman scorned.

83

SOPHIA

Tuesday the 6th of June, 2017
Eve's flat ~ Paris

The estrogen-charged battle between Coralie and Eve is absolutely vicious.

Much bloodier than I ever could have imagined.

At the point in the video where Eve stops fighting back, where it is clear she has gone unconscious, Coralie finally ceases her insane attack. She stands from Eve's limp, beaten body and stares at her victim in silence.

There are no tears. There is no remorse on her face.

And then, the maddest French girl there ever was flees the sodding scene, carelessly leaving the front door cracked open behind her.

The very alive Eve who is sitting next to me today, reaches down and fast-forwards the video several minutes until the moment when her door is pushed open again. All that time, she was lying there on the floor, unconscious and bleeding, but breathing all the same.

And now, instead of the help she so desperately needs to walk through that door and save her, a man appears.

A man who is clearly and decidedly *not* my husband.

84

EVE

The When: Tuesday June 6th, 2017
The Where: Home

The end of the video is actually the most disturbing part for me to watch. He's so swift, so practiced, so hauntingly good at what he does. It's sickening.

He walks in, already wearing white booties and latex gloves. There is no hesitation or panic as he sees me lying on the ground unconscious, covered in cuts and scrapes and bruises and blood.

In seconds, he has my cell phone tucked into his back pocket, and he scoops me off the ground and flees my apartment, carrying me like a limp baby.

He closes the door behind him, and that is that.

I wait a moment to let Sophia process what she has just seen, and then I stop the video and look to her.

"Bloody fucking hell," she says, shaking her scarf-wrapped head.

She hasn't lost her hair yet, but I imagine after the chemo this week it is beginning to fall out.

"Well, I understand why you didn't take this to the police immediately," she says. "Am I the only other person who's seen it?"

"Yes. I wanted you to be the first to know what I plan to do with the video. And I wanted your consent before I do it."

"My consent?" Sophia says, furrowing her brows. "What exactly are you planning to do?"

I close the laptop and explain my plan to Sophia. We're in this together now, and I don't want to do one more thing to screw with her life—not without her permission anyway.

85

OFFICER JEAN-MARC DEVEREAUX

MARDI 6 JUIN 2017
RUE VAVIN ~ PARIS, FRANCE

OFFICER JEAN-MARC DEVEREAUX rewound the video over and over again to the same spot to be sure that what he thought he was seeing was real.

And every time he re-watched the clip, the image staring back at him from the screen confirmed his worst fears.

After the tenth time, he made himself stop watching the video. And he sat, in silence, absorbing the truth for the very first time since Eve Winters went missing.

The other puzzle pieces were all clicking into place in that overworked, exhausted brain of his, and he knew at once that he could not sit on this for very long.

But first, Coralie's box of items from her car.

Now, after what he'd seen in the video, it seemed more important to him than ever to go through the last remaining pieces of his sister's life. It wasn't likely there would be anything useful in the box, seeing as how the technicians had already combed all of it for evidence and had decided they were done with it.

But, as Jean-Marc knew all too well, the truth wasn't always as easy to spot as one might think. Sometimes it was hidden, tossed away, discarded even, in a place no one would ever think to look.

He stood and charged toward the box he'd placed on the kitchen table. Opening the lid, he found a random mess of things that Coralie had let build up in her tiny car over time. One of Adelaide's pacifiers, two pens, a half-empty pack of gum, a dirty red scarf, a stained coffee cup, a single cufflink that must've belonged to Julien, and more odds and ends.

Nothing useful.

Nothing useful until he reached the bottom of the box.

There Jean-Marc found an envelope with Coralie's name written across it in handwriting he knew—Julien Breton's handwriting.

He reached into the envelope and pulled out a card.

My Beautiful Coralie,

I have always wanted to give you a home, and I know my apartment is too small for me, you, and Adelaide to live in comfortably for the long term. It was my bachelor pad for so many years while I waited, not so patiently at times, for you to come around and see how much I have always adored you, how good I would be to you, how perfect we would be together.

Now that we are finally together, it is time for us to have a home of our own. That is why I have bought us a new, beautiful three-bedroom apartment. You'll find our move won't be far...it is just upstairs from where we are now. But with more space and a magnificent view. In fact, we're on the top floor, and we even have a loft.

Only the best for my baby and her baby. I love you, my sweet Coralie. I always have, and I always will.

Love,
Julien

P.S. This is your key to our new beautiful apartment, to our new beautiful life together, and more importantly, to my heart. It will always be yours.

The letter pulled at Jean-Marc's heartstrings, for sure. Someone had finally loved Coralie the way she needed to be loved, and she'd thrown it all away by letting her obsession with Andrew Grayson and her jealousy over his love for Eve turn her completely mad.

Hell, Jean-Marc hadn't even supported Coralie's and Julien's union. That was for his own selfish reasons, of course, but he'd never fully understood just how much Julien had truly loved his sister.

He'd never understood the depth of this love until just moments ago when he'd watched a street camera recording that clearly showed Julien Breton—*not* Andrew Grayson—parking his car not far from Eve's apartment at Place Dauphine the night of Monday, May 15th. The video showed Julien running toward her apartment, and then, not long after, returning to his car with a limp body in his arms.

A body which he laid in the back seat of his car before climbing in the driver's seat and speeding away.

It was Eve's body.

Julien loved Coralie so much that he'd participated in her madness, covered it up, and kept Eve locked away and drugged all week until Coralie freed her, drove her out to the countryside, and attempted to murder her.

Jean-Marc slipped his hand into the envelope where Julien's card had been and pulled out the key to the home Julien had bought for Coralie.

In the weeks since Eve had been found and Andrew Grayson had been arrested for her kidnapping, Jean-Marc's team *still* hadn't been able to figure out where Grayson had been keeping Eve. Eve claimed to have no recollection of what she'd seen there, Grayson was still firmly insisting he hadn't taken Eve, and Coralie was dead—leaving Devereaux's team with no clear answer on the matter. They were able to arrest Grayson based on his DNA being a match to the DNA that was all over Eve's apartment, as well as the *edited* street camera footage that showed Andrew Grayson walking toward Eve's apartment that night, as well as the fact that Eve herself had initially told the police that Coralie confirmed it had been Grayson holding Eve hostage all along.

But they still didn't have a confession out of Grayson.

Or the location where he'd been holding Eve hostage.

And they didn't have either of those things because all along, it hadn't been Andrew Grayson who'd kidnapped and drugged Eve.

It was the man who loved Devereaux's sister so much that he would use the new home he'd bought for her to store the beautiful body of the woman Coralie had nearly killed in a fit of jealousy and rage.

Devereaux held up the key to the apartment and knew what he had to do.

Up, up, up to the top floor, just as Julien had instructed in his letter to Coralie, and Devereaux found the apartment on rue de Malte that would've belonged to his sister had she not gone completely mad. Had she not provoked her own tragic death.

Devereaux had done his homework before coming over, texting Leroux to make sure that Breton was at the office. Leroux had said that he was, and hadn't asked any questions.

Devereaux knew the coast was clear, so he turned the heavy key in the lock and opened the door. Inside, he found an apartment in the throes of renovation. There were paint cans and paint brushes strewn about, a chair or two covered with sheets, but nothing else on this floor.

Nothing else except the beeping of an alarm system right next to the front door.

Jean-Marc pulled his cell phone from his pocket and retrieved the note he'd taken just after leaving Eve's apartment.

*38126**

This code had been scribbled on a slip of paper that had fallen out of Eve's hospital bag when he'd escorted her back to her apartment. The minute he'd seen the numbers, his brain knew to memorize them.

If he punched in this code and it worked, the question of where Eve had been held hostage that week would definitively be answered.

Devereaux lifted his forefinger and slowly, carefully punched in the numbers:

3
8
1
2
6
*

86

SOPHIA

Tuesday the 6th of June, 2017
Eve's flat ~ Paris

Eve has explained her plan to me.

We sit in silence for a few moments while she lets me consider her proposal.

It's bold, that's for sure. And while it will save Drew from prison, it will ruin him in a different kind of way.

The kind of way he rather deserves, after everything, I suppose.

I don't overthink it. My gut says yes.

I nod at Eve. "Let's do it."

She doesn't smile, but I can see the satisfaction gleaming in her eyes. Finally, the two of us are on the same page about something.

"When?" she asks.

"There's no time like the present."

To this, my former student actually grins. Her fingers zoom across the keyboard, pulling up her email account. She enters the email addresses of contacts she has scouted out at three of France's major newspapers, along with the email addresses of every single officer at la Brigade Criminelle that she could scrounge up. Then she attaches the video clip she has just shown me.

As she is crafting the email, I tell her, "I want this to come from both of us. Copy me and sign my name at the bottom, along with yours."

Eve lifts her haunted eyes to mine, and in that moment, as our gazes lock, I know we have found a truce.

We will release our darkness, our truth, our demons into the world, *together*.

No more hiding. No more living in fear.

No more pretending to be bloody perfect.

87

OFFICER JEAN-MARC DEVEREAUX

MARDI 6 JUIN 2017
36 QUAI DES ORFÈVRES ~ PARIS, FRANCE

OFFICER JEAN-MARC DEVEREAUX climbed the winding staircase at 36 Quai des Orfèvres knowing that nothing would ever be as it was before. Walking this staircase would never be as thrilling as it once was, smoking his cigarettes and taking a coffee on the rooftops of the building would never again be as relaxing, and hashing out a new case with his team would never again be as exciting.

Granted, in only a few short months, la Crim' would be abandoning their longtime home for their new building across town, but as Jean-Marc reached his floor, he realized that from this moment on, 36 Quai des Orfèvres was no longer a home to him anyway.

He walked slowly toward the room where Breton had called in his team for a meeting on their newest case. Devereaux paused at the door, his palm sweating around the heavy key that had given him an answer he wished he never had to know.

An answer he wished weren't true.

But instead of running from the truth, like everyone in his life had been doing these days, he gritted his teeth and walked straight into it.

Breton sat at the head of the table, surrounded by Tessier, Durand, Martinez, and Leroux.

The four of them had no idea. No idea that the man they'd been trusting to lead them to the truth had been the one deceiving them all along.

Breton nodded at Devereaux as he entered the room. Devereaux made his way around the table, and just as Breton was in the middle of a sentence, Devereaux placed the apartment key on the table in front of his boss.

Breton stopped talking and looked up to Devereaux, clearly annoyed.

"You never told me you bought a place for you, Coralie, and the baby," Devereaux said.

"I didn't think you'd want to know," Breton quipped. "Now have a seat. We're right in the middle of this and you're late."

Devereaux took his phone out of his pocket, pulled up the note he'd taken with the alarm code, and flashed the screen in front of Breton's face.

Breton focused his eyes on the code, then looked up to Devereaux. "What is—?"

"Eve had this alarm code written down on a slip of paper in her hospital bag," Devereaux said.

Breton went silent. The color drained from his face. He knew that Devereaux knew.

The truth.

The others were quiet too. Devereaux could practically hear their wheels turning.

A phone dinged, drawing Devereaux's attention to

Martinez as she checked her screen, but he quickly got back on track.

"You fired the second shot," Devereaux said to Breton. "That night in the field. Eve only remembers firing once, in the stomach. But it was you, the second time, in the chest. You shot my sister in the chest."

"This is insane," Breton snapped. "Eve had been drugged and injured, of course she doesn't remember—"

Devereaux grabbed Breton's collar and pulled him up from the chair. He didn't have time for games anymore. He didn't have time for Breton's lies.

"You took Eve that night," he spat in Breton's face. "You hid her in the apartment you'd just bought upstairs. You drugged her. You lied to all of us. And then you killed my sister." Devereaux pushed his boss up against the wall, slamming his head in the process. "You fucking killed my little sister."

Breton didn't argue this time. Instead a single pathetic tear rolled down his cheek.

"She was like a dying animal," Breton cried out, losing his calm. "You and I both know that. She was destroying everything in her path, including herself. I couldn't stand to see her that way anymore. I had to put her out of her misery."

"No, you had to make sure she was dead so she wouldn't talk. So she wouldn't turn you in for the kidnapping of Eve Winters."

Devereaux's fist found Breton's tear-stained cheek before he even knew what he was doing.

"I loved her," Breton cried after Devereaux's hit had registered. "I fucking loved your sister."

Devereaux knew that in his own sick way, Breton meant

it. He had loved Coralie. But true love doesn't end in murder.

"Devereaux." It was Martinez's gruff female voice, behind him. "You need to see this."

Devereaux paused, looking into Breton's defeated gaze, wishing he could shoot him in the chest. Tear out his fucking heart.

But then he'd be just as bad as both Breton and his sister. And he wouldn't sink that low. He would never.

He didn't let go of Breton as he turned to Martinez. "What is it?"

She held up her phone, and then pressed play on the screen.

It was a video that appeared to have been taken in Eve's apartment, with a timestamp of Monday, May 15th.

"Eve Winters and Sophia Grayson just emailed this video to the press and to practically the entire Brigade Criminelle," Martinez said.

"Turn that fucking video off," Breton snapped.

But Martinez didn't turn it off. And soon all of the officers had pulled out their phones and found that the very same video had been emailed to them, too.

Sounds of Eve Winters moaning beneath a possessive Andrew Grayson filled the office. Next were the sounds of Devereaux's sister Coralie screaming and brutally attacking an unsuspecting Eve.

And finally, the silent, swift kidnapping of Eve's beautiful body, by their gloved and experienced boss, Julien Breton.

"Putain," was heard around the office as all eyes, shocked and disappointed, turned to Breton.

Tears rolled freely down his face now. He looked to Devereaux, once his best friend and colleague, and he said the same words he'd said that night as he'd kneeled over Coralie's lifeless body: *"I'm sorry. I'm so sorry."*

Devereaux knew Breton was sorry. But an apology could never bring his sister back. An apology could never change the fact that the night Coralie called Breton to tell him that she may have just killed Eve Winters, instead of doing what he knew he had to do and calling it in, Breton had kidnapped Eve, tied her to a bed, drugged her, and traumatized her. All while pretending to be on the same team as Devereaux and the other officers who'd worked so hard to find the very girl that Breton had been holding hostage.

Devereaux watched as Tessier stood, cuffed Breton, and led him out of the office for good.

Julien Breton would never again be on their team.

And Andrew Grayson was about to get the best news of his life.

88

SOPHIA

FRIDAY THE 7TH OF JULY, 2017
RUE DE LILLE ~ PARIS

BABY ADELAIDE coos in my weak arms. I rock her and sing to her in the Paris nursery that Coralie and Drew made for their little girl.

But Coralie is gone now.

And for as long as my body will keep going, I get to be this little girl's interim mother.

Drew's footsteps arrive at the top of the stairs.

When I lift my gaze to his, I find his tired eyes beaming down at me. He walks over to us, runs a gentle hand over the scarf that is wrapped around my bald head, draping down over my skinny neck. His lips find my forehead, and then Adelaide's.

He crouches down before us, cuddling us in his arms. Both of us hanging onto this little girl with every ounce of life we have left.

Drew has undoubtedly got more of it left than I do.

In the end, my husband was found innocent of anything to do with Eve's disappearance.

After all of *that*, he walked away with a fine for having hired a prostitute and partial custody of his daughter, to be split with the baby's uncle, Jean-Marc Devereaux.

Following the racy video that Eve and I released to the press and to the entire Brigade Criminelle, Officer Julien Breton was arrested and is currently awaiting trial for Eve's kidnapping *and* for the murder of Coralie Devereaux.

Jean-Marc Devereaux is still hard at work at the Brigade Criminelle and hard at work being a part-time father to baby Adelaide. All while grieving the loss of his sister.

And as for Eve, I haven't spoken to her since the day we released the video to the press. But I did receive this handwritten note from her in the mail recently.

> *Sophia,*
> *Thank you for being brave enough to release the truth with me. I hope to see your memoir on the shelves one day. I'll be the first to buy it.*
> *Eve*

The note sits on Adelaide's dresser, open for Drew to read as he likes. I'm not keeping secrets from him any longer. He knows the whole story now. The Paris affair during my internship at the bank all those years ago. The abortion. How it all went down with my lover—his boss—Dimitri Dumas. How I tailed Drew through Paris dressed as Lucy Taylor, the spy. I've even shown him the wig.

And he's still here.

He's told me all about how he met Coralie, had a brief romance with her before he realized she was emotionally unstable. Then discovered she was pregnant. And just before the baby was born, he met Eve. Hired Eve. Fell in love with Eve.

Lost Eve.

And I'm still here.

We rock Baby Adelaide until she falls asleep in our arms. Together, we stand and carry her downstairs to our bed, where we lie her down between us, kiss her lightly on each cheek, and lie awake, gazing into each other's eyes.

Staring straight into the truth.

Until my dying day, I will never look away.

I will never again shadow my eyes from the stunning magnificence of knowing the full truth of my husband, of showing him mine, and of loving and hating each other—not in spite of the truth, but because of it.

89

EVE

The When: Tuesday July 11th, 2017
The Where: Home

I AM SIPPING a strong French espresso when I hear the knock on the door I've been expecting.

It's Jean-Marc, the striking brother of Coralie Devereaux, standing in my hallway wearing jeans, a black T-shirt, and sneakers.

I asked him to leave the Brigade Criminelle uniform at home for today's house call. I don't want to see him like a police officer—I don't trust the police much anymore, and for good reason.

Jean-Marc doesn't shake my hand or give me the very French *bisous* on the cheeks. Instead, he walks right in and follows me to the kitchen table where we each take a seat.

"I have something I wanted to show you," he says, reaching into his pocket and pulling out a small shiny object. He drops it on the table.

A cufflink.

"This was found in Coralie's car," he says. "After you

mentioned Breton's missing cufflink that day on the phone, I remembered I had seen this in a box of her things."

Wrapping my hand around the clue that gave away my kidnapper's identity long before I'd had a chance to watch the video taken in my apartment, I close my eyes and remember how it felt when this little gem had first dropped into my hand.

It was my first glimmer of hope in the horror movie that had become my life after I was taken.

And then I remember the terror I felt when I'd grabbed Officer Breton's wrist at my hospital bedside and realized he was missing a cufflink. That was the moment I knew that the police officer who was claiming to have saved me was the same man who'd kidnapped me and killed Coralie.

I open my eyes. "This is it," I tell Jean-Marc. "This was how I knew it was him."

"You're a good detective," he says, watching as I release the cufflink and slide a photo across the table for him to see.

"I wish I never had to be, but thank you," I reply before nodding down at the photograph.

"My sister, Kate," I say. "This was a photo of her that I took the day before she went missing. I think she's still alive."

He nods, taking the photo in his hands and studying it.

"Before Coralie passed out, she said my name—my real name—Sara Marvel. And Kate's name too. She said she knew her. And the way she said it made it sound as if Kate could still be alive."

"Did Coralie say anything about where Kate might be?" Jean-Marc asks.

I'm relieved he's not dismissing me immediately, as every other officer I've spoken with in the last month has done.

"That case is closed, Mademoiselle," they always say to me. "We did everything we could to find your sister. We're sorry for your loss."

It's bullshit.

But Jean-Marc, he's different from all the bullshit politics in his organization. That much is clear.

"No, she didn't say where Kate might be, but she did give me Kate's nickname," I say.

"What was it?"

"Coralie called her *The Diamond Girl.*"

Jean-Marc's eyes lift from Kate's photo up to me. Slowly. Surely.

He knows something.

He reaches over and grabs my hand. "I'm going to help you find your sister, Eve. I'll do everything I can."

For the first time since my little sister went missing, I feel a swell of emotion in my heart that I can only label as *hope.*

THE DIAMOND GIRL

My glass swirls with champagne. His hands wrap around the bare skin on my thighs.

He spreads my legs.

I guzzle the fizzy alcohol.

He doesn't spend time fondling my breasts or kissing my neck or doing any of the things I need him to do so that I can be ready for him.

He never does.

Instead the glass of champagne tumbles out of my hands, spilling its last few sips onto the black satin sheets in our dark chamber as he pushes me against the pillows.

The flat-screen television on the wall facing the bed is flashing pictures with no sound.

It's been years since I've watched a TV screen.

My life is a constant interchange of saliva, champagne, jewels, and the spreading of my legs.

It's not a life that includes turning on the mundane news of today.

There is money to be made.

A girl's photograph pops up on the screen just as he enters me.

I focus on the lost look in her eyes, the way her hair falls down over her shoulders, the seductive pose of her legs against the wall.

A headline stretches across the bottom of the screen, beneath her photo, as he hooks his arms beneath my knees and spreads me open even farther.

Author Eve Winters Found Alive

I wonder who this girl is. Something about the way her eyes stare back into mine with such an impenetrable sadness makes me wonder if she wouldn't have rather been found dead.

He pounds every bit of the 57-year-old life force he's got into the space between my thighs, and I give him all the right moans and hip swirls to get him right where I want him.

Powerless to my beauty.

Handing over his fortune.

Lost in the idea of a fantasy; the poor bastard actually thinks this is real.

They don't call me *The Diamond Girl* for nothing.

A NOTE FROM DANIELLE

Thank you so much for reading the first book in my new *City of Darkness* series, *All the Beautiful Bodies*. I hope the story kept you on the edge of your seat, and I am excited to tell you there will be more to come! Stay tuned for the sequel where we will dive into the story on Eve's missing sister.

If you would like to leave an honest review for *All the Beautiful Bodies* on the site where you purchased the book, I would appreciate it so much. Reviews are so incredibly helpful for authors, and I have been touched by the lovely reviews many of you have left for my books over the years.

Under my pen name of *Juliette Sobanet*, I have written several other books based in Paris. Read on for descriptions of all of my novels and to find out how you can receive three of my bestselling books for *free*!

Danielle Porter

YOUR EXCLUSIVE DANIELLE PORTER STARTER LIBRARY

One of my favorite parts about being a writer is building a relationship with my amazing readers! I love hearing from you, and I also love letting you know what's going on in my world. Occasionally I send out brief newsletters with details on my new releases, special offers just for you, and other exciting book news.

If you'd like to be the first to find out about my new releases and receive your *free* Starter Library of books I've written under my pen name *Juliette Sobanet*, I'll send you:

1. A free copy of the award-winning first novel in my *City of Love* series: *Sleeping with Paris.*
2. A free copy of the bestselling novella in my *City of Light* series: *One Night in Paris.*
3. A free copy of the first spicy novella in my *City Girls* series: *Confessions of a City Girl: Los Angeles.*

To receive your free ebooks, simply head over to my

website at *www.juliettesobanet.com* and sign up for my newsletter. I'll be thrilled to send them to you!

ALSO BY DANIELLE PORTER & JULIETTE SOBANET

CITY OF DARKNESS SERIES

All the Beautiful Bodies
City of Darkness Book 1

Take a trip to the dark side of Paris...

After surviving a brutal childhood, Paris-based writer Eve Winters has lived her entire adult life totally under the radar. That all changes one warm spring day when she releases an explicit memoir detailing her dangerous foray into the world of high-end prostitution, and her scandalous affair with a prominent married businessman. The morning of the release, Eve is set to land in New York for her glamorous book launch party...but there's just one problem—she never boarded the plane.

Across the Atlantic, in a Park Avenue penthouse fit for a queen and her millionaire husband...

Acclaimed New York author, writing professor, and socialite Sophia Grayson is all set to attend the book release party of her former student, Eve Winters. *Except*...Eve never shows. When the news travels from Paris that the author has gone missing, Sophia spends the evening reading Eve's shocking memoir. What she discovers in its pages turns her perfect Park Avenue façade upside down and sends her searching for the truth in the one city she'd sworn off forever, the city where she'd locked away her own sordid past and thrown away the key...*Paris*.

Stay tuned for the sequel to *All the Beautiful Bodies*,
coming soon...

CITY OF LIGHT SERIES

One Night in Paris
City of Light Book 1
A Novella

When Manhattan attorney Ella Carlyle gets a call that her beloved grandmother is dying, she rushes to Paris to be by her side, against the wishes of her overbearing boyfriend. Ella would do anything for her grandmother and jumps at the chance to fulfill her dying wish. But things take a mystical turn when Ella is transported to a swinging Parisian jazz club full of alluring strangers...in the year 1927! As the clock runs out on her one night in the City of Light, Ella will attempt to rewrite the past—and perhaps her own destiny as well.

Dancing with Paris
City of Light Book 2

In Paris, a past life promises a second chance at love.

Straitlaced marriage therapist Claudia Davis had a plan—and it definitely did not involve getting pregnant from a one-night stand or falling for a gorgeous French actor. She thinks her life can't possibly get more complicated. But when Claudia takes a tumble in her grandmother's San Diego dance studio, she awakens in 1950s Paris in the body of Ruby Kerrigan, the glamorous star of a risqué cabaret—and the number-one suspect in the gruesome murder of a fellow dancer.

As past lives go, it's a doozy...especially when an encounter with a handsome and mysterious French doctor ignites a fire in Claudia's sinfully beautiful new body.

But time, for all its twists and turns, is not on her side: Claudia has just five days to unmask the true killer, clear Ruby's name, and return to the twenty-first century. To do so, she must make an impossible choice, one that will change the course of *both* of her lives forever.

Midnight Train to Paris
City of Light Book 3

When hard-hitting DC reporter Jillian Chambord learns

that her twin sister, Isla, has been abducted from a luxury train traveling through the Alps, not even the threat of losing her coveted position at *The Washington Daily* can stop her from hopping on the next flight to France. Never mind the fact that Samuel Kelly—the sexy former CIA agent who Jillian has sworn off forever—has been assigned as the lead investigator in the case.

When Jillian and Samuel arrive in the Alps, they soon learn that their midnight train isn't leading them to Isla, but has taken them back in time to 1937, to a night when another young woman was abducted from the same Orient Express train. Given a chance to save both women, Jillian and Samuel are unprepared for what they discover on the train that night, for the sparks that fly between them . . . and for what they'll have to do to keep each other alive.

Midnight Train to Paris is a magical and suspenseful exploration of just how far we will go to save the ones we love.

CITY OF LOVE SERIES

Sleeping with Paris
City of Love Book 1

Charlotte Summers is a sassy, young French teacher two days away from moving to Paris. Love of her life by her side, for those romantic kisses walking along the Seine? Check. Dream of studying at the prestigious Sorbonne University? Admission granted. But when she discovers her fiancé's online dating profile and has a little chat with the busty redhead he's been sleeping with on the side, she gives up on committed relationships and decides to navigate Paris on her own. Flings with no strings in the City of Light —*mais oui!*

Determined to stop other women from finding themselves in her shoes, Charlotte creates an anonymous blog on how to date like a man in the City of Love—that is, how to jump from bed to bed without ever falling in love. But, with a slew of Parisian men beating down her door, a hot new neighbor who feeds her chocolate in bed, and an appearance by her ex-fiancé, she isn't so sure she can keep her promise to remain commitment-free. When Charlotte agrees to write an article for a popular women's magazine about her Parisian dating adventures—or disasters, rather—will she risk losing the one man who's swept her off her feet and her dream job in one fell swoop?

Kissed in Paris
City of Love Book 2

When event planner Chloe Turner wakes up penniless and without a passport in the Plaza Athénée Hotel in Paris, she only has a few fleeting memories of Claude, the suave French man who convinced her to have that extra glass of wine...before taking all of her possessions and slipping out the door. As the overly organized, go-to gal for her drama queen younger sisters, her anxiety-ridden father, and her needy clients, Chloe is normally prepared for every disaster that comes her way. But with her wedding to her straitlaced, lawyer fiancé back in DC only days away and a French con-man on the loose with her engagement ring, this is one catastrophe she never could have planned for.

As Chloe tries to figure out a way home, she runs into an even bigger problem: the police are after her due to suspicious activity now tied to her bank account. Chloe's only hope at retrieving her passport and clearing her name lies in the hands of Julien, a rugged, undercover agent who has secrets of his own.

As Chloe follows this mysterious, and—although she doesn't want to admit it—sexy French man on a wild chase through the sun-kissed countryside of France, she discovers a magical world she never knew existed. And she can't help but wonder if the perfectly ordered life she's built for herself back home really what she wants after all...

HONEYMOON IN PARIS
CITY OF LOVE BOOK 3

The sassy heroine of *Sleeping with Paris* is back! And this time, chocolate-covered French wedding bells are in the air...

It's only been a month since Charlotte Summers reunited with her sexy French boyfriend, Luc Olivier, and he has already made her the proposal of a lifetime: a mad dash to the altar in the fairytale town of Annecy. Without hesitation, Charlotte says *au revoir* to single life and *oui* to a lifetime of chocolate in bed with Luc. She's madly in love, and Luc is clearly *the one*, so what could possibly go wrong?

As it turns out, quite a lot...

On the heels of their drama-filled nuptials in the French Alps, Luc whisks Charlotte away to Paris for a luxurious honeymoon. But just as they are settling into a sheet-ripping, chocolate-induced haze, a surprise appearance by

Luc's drop-dead gorgeous ex-wife brings the festivities to a halt. Luc never told Charlotte that his ex was a famous French actress, *or* that she was still in love with him. Add to that Charlotte's new role as step-mom to Luc's tantrum-throwing daughter, a humiliating debacle in the French tabloids, and the threat of losing her coveted position at the language school—and Charlotte fears she may have tied the French knot a little too quickly.

Determined to keep her independence and her sanity, Charlotte seeks out a position at *Bella* magazine's new France office while working on a sassy guidebook to French marriage. But when Luc's secret past threatens Charlotte's career *and* their future together, Charlotte must take matters into her own hands. Armed with chocolate, French wine, and a few fabulous girlfriends by her side, Charlotte navigates the tricky waters of marriage, secrets, ex-wives, and a demanding career all in a foreign country where she quickly realizes, she never *truly* learned the rules.

A Paris Dream
City of Love Book 4
A Novella

After the loss of her beloved sister and both of her parents, overworked talk show assistant Olivia Banks sets off on a Paris adventure to fulfill the dreams she and her sister once had as little girls. Olivia only has one day to devote to the City of Light before she must return to her demanding job back in Manhattan. But when she steps out of the cab onto the cobblestoned streets of Montmartre and meets a sexy *boulanger* who wants to help her make all of those dreams come true, Olivia realizes that Paris may have more in store for her than she ever could have imagined.

TRUE STORIES IN THE CITY OF LOVE

Meet Me in Paris: A Memoir

What does a romance novelist do when she loses her own happily ever after? Take a lover and travel to Paris, obviously. Or at least this is what Juliette Sobanet did upon making the bold, heart-wrenching decision to divorce the man she had loved since she was a teenager. This is the story of the passionate love affair that ensued during the most devastating year of Sobanet's life and how her star-crossed romance in the City of Light led to her undoing.

Meet Me in Paris is a raw, powerful take on divorce and the daring choices that followed such a monumental loss from the pen of a writer who'd always believed in happy endings...and who ultimately found the courage to write her own.

I Loved You in Paris: A Memoir in Poetry

In this companion poetry book to her sizzling memoir, *Meet Me in Paris,* Juliette Sobanet gives readers a heartbreaking look into the raw emotions of a romance novelist as she loses her own happily ever after. From the impossible pull of forbidden love to the devastating loss of her marriage, and finally, to rebuilding life anew, Sobanet's courageous poems expose the truth behind infidelity and divorce and take readers on a passionate journey of love, loss, and ultimately, hope.

CITY GIRLS NOVELLA SERIES

Confessions of a City Girl: Los Angeles
City Girls Book 1

When talented DC photographer Natasha Taylor meets alluring investor Nicholas Reyes at her first exhibit, a harmless invitation to join him for a weekend in Los Angeles turns into a passionate love affair that awakens Natasha in ways she never could have imagined.

Confessions of a City Girl: San Diego
City Girls Book 2

When overworked CIA agent Liz Valentine sets off for a yoga retreat on the gorgeous beaches of San Diego, the last thing she expects to find is love. But when one oh-so-enlightened yoga instructor catches her eye—and her heart—Liz must decide if the loveless life of a secret agent is truly what she wants after all.

Confessions of a City Girl: Washington D.C.
City Girls Book 3

When recent divorcée and famous romance novelist Violet Bell loses her once lustrous career writing happily-ever-afters, a whirlwind weekend in the Nation's Capital with her closest college friend—a sexy British speechwriter named Aaron Wright—could have her wondering if *Mr. Wright* hasn't been right underneath her nose all along...

Confessions of a City Girl Boxed Set

Read all three *City Girls Novellas* in one sizzling boxed set!

ACKNOWLEDGMENTS

The process of writing this book has been a beautiful and wild ride, and there are many to thank who've supported me along the way.

To my amazing agent Kevan Lyon, thank you for your invaluable feedback—you helped me turn this story into the book I truly wanted to write. Thanks to Jill Marsal for your helpful input, and to my foreign rights agent, Taryn Fagerness, for bringing my books to new landscapes.

To all of my wonderful friends and family who have given me love and support while I took on the very long task of writing this thriller—you've been hearing about it for three years now, and you've believed in me all the way. My gratitude for each of you is immeasurable.

I would especially like to thank: Brooke Lyn Meeler, for our productive countertop brainstorming sessions as well as for helping me and the cats move to France while I was right in the middle of writing this book; Deirdre Witte, for our talks which make me laugh more than anything else in this world, and for your unwavering support in helping me to make my France and writing dreams come true; Patrick

Daly, for being there for me from the very beginning of this novel to the end; Sophie Moss, for your invaluable writing advice and friendship; Dimitri Danon, for your cover art expertise and tutorials, and especially for all the laughs; Mark Davis, for being the best English English language consultant ever (yes I meant to write English English!); Ben Ponte, for helping me to choose the title for this book and for being one of the few who understands true artistic dedication; Robin Reed, for being an absolute gem of a friend, and for sharing our big writing dreams together; Behzad Khorsand, for our awesome talks and your awesome friendship; and Pedro Monteiro, for being a Brazilian angel who has descended from heaven to keep me laughing and eating only the very best food while I write.

To the boys at Bahia and two of my very best friends: Micah Cranman and Carl Israelsson. I wrote most of this book while living with you, and despite the fact that I was plotting murder on the page, those were some of the silliest, happiest, best days of my life. Thank you.

To Deborah Moser, who shares my absolute love for Paris and all things French—your support means everything. And to Kathy Austin, thank you so much for our talks on writing and France—you totally get it.

To Bridget Hutchens, Liz Nicol, Angie Tennis, Kelly Bufton, Amanda Boehmer, James Shea, and Shawn Grant: Your unconditional love, your unending support for my writing, and your phone calls always keep me smiling. Thank you.

To my first critique partners and writing teachers: Karen Johnston, Sharon Wray, and Mary Lenaburg. Most of what I learned about writing, I learned from you. Thank you.

To my mom, thank you for listening to me endlessly as I

hash out my writing and publication ideas over the phone. Thank you for your love, your patience, your guidance, and your encouragement.

To my dad, thank you for telling me all of your silly dad jokes and for reading me your song lyrics. Clearly I'm not the only writer in the family.

To my big beautiful cats, Bella and Charlie, who have carried me through so many major life transitions as I wrote this book and who have loved me unconditionally and taught me so much. Thank you.

My most heartfelt thank you goes out to all of my lovely, loyal readers. Your continued support for my writing amazes me every day, and I am beyond thankful for each and every one of you. I am especially thankful to the readers in my Exclusive Reader Club for your extra support in reading early copies of this book.

Finally, thank you to the city which has inspired this book, and nearly every other story I've written. Paris, you are magnificent.

ABOUT THE AUTHOR

Under her pseudonym of *Juliette Sobanet*, Danielle Porter is the award-winning author of five Paris-based romance and mystery novels, five short stories, a book of poetry, a bestselling memoir, and the screenplay adaptation of her first novel, *Sleeping with Paris*. Under her real name of Danielle Porter, she is the author of a new thriller titled, *All the Beautiful Bodies*. Her books have reached over 500,000 readers worldwide, hitting the Top 100 Bestseller Lists on Amazon US, UK, France, and Germany, becoming bestsellers in Turkey and Italy as well. A French professor and writing coach, Danielle holds a B.A. from Georgetown University and an M.A. from New York University in Paris. Danielle lives between France and the U.S. and is currently at work on her next novel. To receive three of Danielle's books for free, visit her "Juliette Sobanet" website at *www.juliettesobanet.com.* She loves to hear from her readers!

Made in the USA
Middletown, DE
23 July 2020